THE MAGIC BULLET

OTHER BOOKS BY LARRY MILLETT

The Magic Bullet

A LOCKED ROOM MYSTERY

FEATURING SHADWELL RAFFERTY
AND SHERLOCK HOLMES

LARRY MILLETT

A MINNESOTA MYSTERY

University of Minnesota Press
Minneapolis
London

Published by the University of Minnesota Press
111 Third Avenue South, Suite 290
Minneapolis, MN 55401-2520
http://www.upress.umn.edu

Library of Congress Cataloging-in-Publication Data
Millett, Larry.
 The magic bullet : a locked room mystery featuring Shadwell Rafferty and Sherlock Holmes / Larry Millett.
     p. cm.
"A Minnesota mystery."
 ISBN 978-0-8166-7480-0 (alk. paper)
1. Rafferty, Shadwell (Fictitious character)—Fiction. 2. Holmes, Sherlock (Fictitious character)—Fiction. 3. Private investigators—Fiction. 4. British—Minnesota—Fiction. 5. Minnesota—Fiction. I. Title.
PS3563.I42193M34 2011
813'.54—dc22

                            2010044065

Printed in the United States of America on acid-free paper

The University of Minnesota is an equal-opportunity educator and employer.

18 17 16 15 14 13 12 11   10 9 8 7 6 5 4 3 2 1

CONTENTS

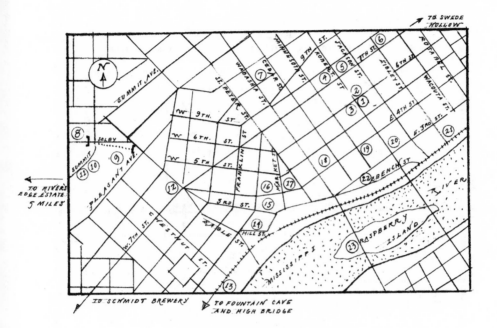

Downtown St. Paul, 1917

1. Dodge Tower
2. Ryan Hotel and Shad's Place
3. Chamber of Commerce Building
4. Golden Rule Department Store
5. Emporium Department Store
6. Klemmer Lock Company
7. Old state capitol
8. St. Paul Cathedral
9. Selby Avenue streetcar tunnel
10. James J. Hill House
11. Louis Hill House
12. Seven Corners
13. Little Italy
14. Police headquarters
15. Public library
16. Rice Park
17. St. Paul Hotel
18. City Hall and County Courthouse
19. Germania Life Building
20. U.S. Hotel
21. Union Depot
22. Abandoned warehouse
23. Minnesota Boat Club

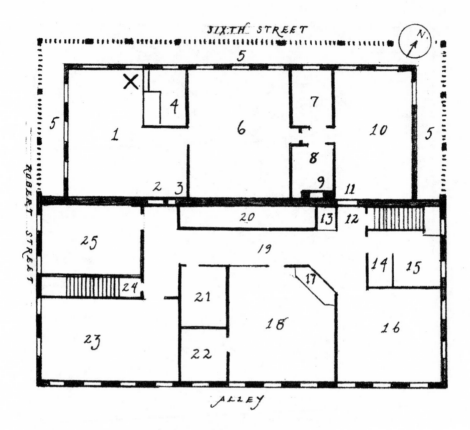

Dodge Tower Penthouse

X Body of Artemus Dodge found here
1. Artemus Dodge's office
2. Security door
3. Pass-through
4. Desk and podium
5. Balcony (barred)
6. Apartment parlor
7. Bathroom
8. Closet
9. Wall safe
10. Bedroom
11. Emergency door
12. Main stairs
13. Penthouse elevator

14. Guard's station
15. Guard's room
16. Office lobby
17. Reception desk
18. Gertrude Schmidt's office
19. Hallway
20. Top of main elevator shafts
    (inaccessible)
21. Men's lavatory
22. Women's lavatory
23. Office of Steven Dodge and
    Alan Dubois
24. Rear staircase
25. J. D. Carr's office

INTRODUCTION

Between the 1880s and his death in 1928, Shadwell Rafferty investigated more than fifty criminal cases, mostly in the Twin Cities of St. Paul and Minneapolis, but also as far away as New York City and Seattle. A barkeep whose downtown St. Paul establishment was long the city's most popular watering hole, Rafferty belonged to that remarkable species of amateur but highly skilled detectives who began their careers during the gaslight era. Like others of his kind, however, Rafferty labored in the giant shadow cast by Sherlock Holmes.

Rafferty and Holmes became good friends and worked closely together on at least four sensational murder cases, several of which Dr. John Watson saw fit to present to the public. Some years ago, I made my own modest addition to this literary legacy with an account of Rafferty and Holmes's investigation into the murderous activities of the so-called Secret Alliance in Minneapolis in 1899.

Despite his relationship with the famed detective, Rafferty remains a rather obscure figure, in part because he lived and worked in a community little known beyond America's borders, whereas Holmes—based in London during the height of the British Empire—was assured a global audience once his achievements began to be publicized. Perhaps more important, Rafferty had no Dr. Watson to chronicle his adventures. Nor did Rafferty produce any full-fledged accounts of his own. He intended to write a memoir but managed to complete only a bare outline before his death at age eighty-three.

The historical record regarding Rafferty is not entirely barren, however. He left behind eight boxes of miscellaneous papers, which eventually found their way into the archives of the Minnesota Historical Society in St. Paul. Like his friend and benefactor railroad baron James J. Hill, Rafferty was a pack rat. His papers therefore include all manner of ephemera—bills and receipts, insurance documents, advertising souvenirs and premiums, postcards, and even a few letters from celebrity visitors to Rafferty's tavern, among whom were Mark Twain in 1895, young Winston Churchill in 1901, and Theodore Roosevelt in 1912 and again in 1917.

Fortunately, the boxes also contain items of great value in tracing Rafferty's career as a detective. Ten bulging scrapbooks, arranged haphazardly, offer a treasure trove of newspaper clippings, letters (including twenty-one from either Holmes or Watson), telegrams, and other documents relating to Rafferty's various investigations. Equally important are three moleskin notebooks in which Rafferty jotted down his observations and thoughts. They begin with an entry from 1884 titled "The Missing Drake Diamonds" and end in 1928 with a brief reference to "The Last Case." The notebook entries, which are succinct and even cryptic at times, cover all fifty-six cases Rafferty investigated during his career.

The entry for the Artemus Dodge case, the extraordinary locked room mystery from 1917 that is the subject of this book, serves as a typical example of Rafferty's diarylike style. The entry begins this way: "Oct. 1, 1917. Asked by Louis Hill to investigate murder of Art. Dodge, financier, in SP [St. Paul]. Strange business. Shot in fortified office atop Dodge Tower, 30 stories up. 'Impossible crime' or so papers said. . . ."

The newspaper clippings in Rafferty's scrapbook provide far more information on the case, which was St. Paul's second sensational murder in 1917 (the first, in April, was the execution-style shooting of Alice McQuillan Dunn at her parents' home). While the Dunn affair has drawn some attention from historians—most notably in Walter N. Trenerry's valuable book *Murder in Minnesota*, published in 1962—the Dodge case has been all but forgotten. Its lack of notoriety is surprising given the brilliant staging of the crime and Rafferty's equally brilliant work in unraveling the mystery.

The story you are about to read is a fictional reconstruction based on the facts of the case as I have been able to establish them through historic research. I began my research by reading St. Paul newswoman Isabel Diamond's book, *Secrets of the Miracle Murder,* which was a best seller when it appeared in 1918 but is now very hard to find. I have given Diamond a role in my tale, based in part on her own account. My other sources include Rafferty's personal papers as described above, newspapers and periodicals (especially the *St. Paul Pioneer Press*), St. Paul Police Department records (among them the case files of Inspector Mordecai Jones, the lead detective in the murder investigation), the Dodge family archives at the New York State Historical Society, and a variety of published works dealing with the World War I period in Minnesota.

I have also dipped into one other important source of information— the recently discovered "Dodge Fragment," a brief but tantalizing manuscript written by Dr. Watson sometime in late 1917. The four-thousand-word "fragment," most of which I have incorporated into this book, was found quite by chance in 2007 in the attic of a London townhouse, and it is being published here for the first time.

The manuscript shows, among other things, that Rafferty was in regular contact with Holmes, first via telegram and later by letter, regarding the Dodge case. Another of its revelations is that Holmes, by a stroke of good fortune, was able to obtain, in London, a floor plan of the office where Artemus Dodge was so ingeniously murdered. Holmes's examination of the plan proved crucial to solving the crime, one that the *Pioneer Press* later described—without exaggeration, I believe—as "the most bizarre and fantastic murder in the history of the Northwest."

Book One

THE MAGIC BULLET

lthough it was unseasonably warm for the first day of October, Artemus Dodge had no use for an open window. There were half a dozen big windows in Dodge's thirtieth-floor office, but he always kept them shut. *Always.* Heaven only knew what a breeze might let in, and Dodge believed a man in his position could never be too careful. His newly completed office and its adjoining apartment occupied the penthouse of Dodge Tower, the tallest skyscraper between Chicago and the West Coast. With its brooding walls of dark gray St. Cloud granite, the tower was Dodge's monument, and he did not intend for it to become his tomb.

As one of the nation's leading financiers, Dodge had made many enemies over the years, and he'd designed his penthouse suite to be airtight and unassailable, a fortress in the sky. The office and apartment, which Dodge had moved into only a month earlier, were set six feet back from the main walls of the tower behind a balcony protected by thick steel bars.

Dodge had insisted on installing the bars to foil any "climbers," as he called them, who might try to scale the skyscraper and break into his inner sanctum, which inevitably became known as "Dodge's Birdcage." Spaced just two inches apart, the bars obstructed a spectacular view, not that Dodge cared. He thought St. Paul a drab city, and he rarely looked out his windows to take in the panorama of the downtown commercial district and the sweeping curve of the Mississippi River as it turned south on its long journey to the Gulf of Mexico.

The tower, far taller than any other building in St. Paul, reflected Dodge's belief that there was safety in altitude. There was safety, too, in the thick layers of steel and concrete that insulated the walls, floor, and ceiling of his office-apartment from the roiling world below. The finest doors, locks, and alarms money could buy provided additional protection.

Despite these precautions, Dodge felt uneasy as he sat back on the tufted French sofa in his office, smoking his first cigar of the day. A potentially devastating financial problem had come up as quickly as a spring thunderstorm. He'd already notified his staff that there would be an important meeting at nine o'clock sharp, and Dodge saw no way to avoid an unpleasant confrontation. The problem was a cancer threatening the very foundations of his business. He knew that the disease would have to be cut out. There would be anger and recriminations, but business was business, and Dodge planned to act decisively when the time came.

Stubbing out his cigar, Dodge got up to draw open the drapes, a morning ritual. He began with the three windows on the west side of the office. Like all of the penthouse windows, they were double-hungs, eight feet high and four feet wide. They looked across Robert Street toward the prominent brow of St. Anthony Hill, where the huge copper-clad dome of Archbishop John Ireland's new cathedral glinted in the morning light. From Dodge's high vantage point, the city looked peaceful enough, but he knew better.

St. Paul was anxious and unsettled, trouble lurking in the air like toxic smoke. Two days earlier Teddy Roosevelt, no friend of men like Dodge, had been in town to help whip up the war fury started by Woodrow Wilson. The president was a damn fool in Dodge's estimation. The nation had no business trying to save Europe from its own stupidity. Still, Dodge was doing his patriotic duty by promoting the sale of war bonds.

The call to arms had aroused the ire of anarchists, syndicalists, labor agitators, and radicals of all stripes. They were on the loose now, largely unmolested by the city's incompetent police. The dark forces, as Dodge called them, had just missed snuffing out his life once before, and he did not wish to give them another chance. Of late, he'd been living like a hermit in his apartment. The isolation didn't bother him. His one true friend and the only voice he needed to hear was the stock ticker chattering a few feet away. Aside from his increasingly tiresome young wife, Amanda, and one other visitor, Dodge had seen only his staff during the past fortnight.

Dodge began opening the drapes on the north side of the office, near his desk. A massive mahogany affair with carved legs, the desk sat atop a low podium that one newspaper had dubbed "the throne of St. Paul's financial king." Dodge didn't mind that characterization. He was in fact the king of his world, and he saw no reason why he shouldn't enjoy the benefits of royalty.

When he drew open the drapes on the window closest to his desk, Dodge was startled by what he saw. Someone had tampered with the window in a most disturbing way. Dodge consulted his pocket watch and saw that it was 8:32 a.m. He stepped up to his desk just as the intercom began to buzz. He bent over and pressed the button to speak.

"You will not believe—" he began.

Just before a bullet tore into his brain, he thought he heard an alarm.

1

"WE WERE DEAD WRONG"

Shadwell Rafferty would always remember October 1, 1917, as the day the magic bullet crashed into his life. Rafferty was no believer in miracles, but he had to admit that the murder of Artemus Dodge was just about the damnedest thing he'd ever seen, a regular Mad Hatter's tea party of a crime. The murder seemed utterly impossible unless the bullet had somehow managed to streak through solid matter like a supersonic ghost before ending the financier's life in a spray of blood and brain matter.

How could it be? Rafferty wondered. How could a bullet, an insensate piece of lead designed to speed toward its target at a thousand feet per second in accord with the fundamental laws of physics, transform itself into a thing of malevolent magic? Rafferty had heard of locked room mysteries, and he remembered how as a young soldier, stuck in the bloody Virginia mud near Fredericksburg, he'd delighted in reading Poe's "Murders in the Rue Morgue." As far as Rafferty could tell, however, no ape had climbed thirty stories to kill Artemus Dodge.

Dodge's murder had come at a terrible time. St. Paul was already on edge, seething with a volatile mix of white-hot patriotism and fierce dissent following the nation's declaration of war against Germany. Even as loyalty day rallies drew huge cheering crowds, militant streetcar workers threatened a crippling strike, and there were wild rumors of radicals plotting unprecedented acts of terrorism. Anarchists had tried to kill Dodge once before, in New York City, and Rafferty knew they would become the prime suspects in his murder. Dodge had chaired the local campaign to sell war bonds, and even though he'd worked entirely behind the scenes, he was strongly identified with the patriotic cause.

Rafferty couldn't help but think how much his old friend Sherlock Holmes would have relished the case. Holmes of course was in England, serving his nation, and with German U-boats prowling the North Atlantic, there was no chance he and Dr. Watson would return to Minnesota anytime soon. "Ah, if you were only here, Mr. Holmes," Rafferty said softly to himself. "What a time we would have with the magic bullet!"

Sprawled across the leather couch in his office, with a glass of Joseph Schmidt's lager to aid his lucubration, Rafferty felt weary, even though it was only five o'clock in the evening. He'd already done his "Christian duty," as he called it, by making a brief meet-and-greet excursion through the popular tavern he owned in downtown St. Paul. Now, as he fought off the urge to sleep, Rafferty let his mind wander back over the events that had begun that morning with a most alarming telephone call.

As befitting his occupation, Rafferty liked to sleep late, and he was deep in slumber when the telephone beside his bed rang at the unholy hour of nine o'clock. He answered the call with a grunt and heard the voice of Louis Hill, son of the fabled Empire Builder, James J. Hill, whose death a year earlier had greatly saddened Rafferty.

"Mr. Rafferty, someone has done it," Hill announced without preamble. "Artemus Dodge has been shot dead in his office."

Before Rafferty could respond, Hill continued: "I know how much my father trusted and respected you, and I am therefore asking you for a favor. The police are investigating the murder, of course, and Inspector Jones in particular is well regarded, but I think he will need help. Can you get over to Mr. Dodge's office at once? Chief Nelligan is already there."

When a Hill talked, Rafferty listened. "I will go," he said, "but how—"

"I know nothing of the details," Hill said impatiently. "Just get over there as quickly as you can and keep me informed. I don't need to tell you that it is a very dark day for St. Paul."

"So it is," Rafferty agreed.

"You have my thanks, Mr. Rafferty, and good luck."

Rafferty didn't know much about the financier or his company, which was known as Dodge & Son, except what he read in the newspapers. With James J. Hill gone, Artemus Dodge was reputed to be the richest man in St. Paul. Rafferty didn't doubt that. He'd watched Dodge Tower rise across the street from his tavern over the past year, and there was nothing in the city of comparable size or splendor. Dodge's only son, Steven, was a partner in the firm and would presumably inherit his father's fortune. The old man had also acquired a young wife in recent years, but Rafferty couldn't remember her name.

According to the newspapers, Dodge was a hardheaded Yankee who'd fought with the celebrated Twentieth Maine Regiment in the War between the States, then settled in New York City, where he piled up a fortune by expert wheeling and dealing in stocks and bonds. He was known as a ruthless short seller, always ready to hole up with the bears on the expectation of bad financial news. Dodge had also been involved with the New York Central and Erie railroads in a series of arcane stock maneuvers that Wall Street insiders, so it was said, still discussed with a mixture of envy and awe. He was, a reporter wrote, "the Great Spider, a weaver of monetary webs so intricate and tangled that few are the men who could ever hope to comprehend them."

Rafferty counted himself among the uncomprehending. Still, he'd watched with interest when Dodge relocated to St. Paul in 1915. The local press claimed that Dodge made the move because of his "close relationship" with James J. Hill, for whom he'd done signal service during the attempt to "corner" Northern Pacific stock in 1901. Whispers on the street, however, hinted at another reason for his move.

Dodge, it was said, had been profoundly shaken by an attempt on his life in 1913. The notorious anarchist Sidney Berthelson had hatched the plot, only to die when the bomb he was carrying exploded prematurely in a stairwell outside Dodge's Wall Street office. After the failed assassination, Dodge became increasingly uncomfortable in Manhattan's dark canyons. His move to St. Paul, at Hill's behest, had stunned the financial world.

Now the old wizard of Wall Street was dead, and Rafferty—for whom high finance was as mysterious as the lost tribes of New Guinea—had been asked to help find the killer. He wasn't sure that he was the right man for the job, but he'd do what he could. After throwing on some mismatched clothes, Rafferty applied a comb to what remained of his hair and to his wiry white beard. He got out his best walking cane—arthritic knees were causing him no end of trouble—and left his suite of rooms in the Ryan Hotel to awaken George Washington Thomas, who lived in the adjoining apartment.

"Come on, Wash," Rafferty shouted when his knocks produced no response. "Tell the lady you're with that you must go. There's been a murder, and you won't believe who it is."

"Give me a second," Thomas yelled through the door. "Who got killed?"

"I'll tell you on the way. Just be quick about it."

At ten minutes past nine o'clock Rafferty and Thomas walked across Sixth Street to Dodge Tower, its tall Gothic entrance presided over by fearsome terra-cotta gargoyles. The sumptuous lobby within was one of St. Paul's wonders, a vast glittering hall set beneath a vaulted ceiling adorned with richly colored mosaics depicting the history of commerce. One of the mosaics showed Dodge himself, hunched over a stock ticker as though worshipping a golden idol.

"I always feel I should take my hat off in here," Rafferty said, gazing up at the ceiling. "'Tis a church devoted to the almighty dollar."

"Well, it won't get Dodge to heaven," Thomas observed.

Rafferty grinned and said, "I'm not sure he'll be goin' there as it is."

A cordon of St. Paul's finest guarded the lobby's elevator bank. Rafferty and Thomas, who were well known to the police, had no trouble getting through. They boarded the financier's private elevator for a ninety-second ride to the penthouse.

"Well, this is fancy," Thomas said, inspecting the cab's quarter-sawn oak panels and brass fittings. "Ever been up to Dodge's office before?"

"For some reason, I've never been invited," Rafferty said. "Can't imagine why. Ah, here we are."

They stepped off the elevator into a well-appointed lobby, which included a reception desk straight ahead and, off to one side, a guard's station with an alarm box mounted behind it. The lobby was decorated in the overwrought style favored by tycoons, corporate lawyers, and crooked aldermen. Rafferty's omnivorous eye took in all the trappings—Louis XIV side chairs, carved walnut paneling, cut-glass chandeliers, floors of swirling Spanish marble. Change the color scheme a bit, he thought, and you'd have a perfectly respectable whorehouse.

Three men and a woman huddled in one corner, talking in low voices. The woman was sobbing softly. The men—two of them quite young, the other perhaps in his fifties—looked grim. One of the younger men wore a flamboyant orange and brown plaid suit; the other was dressed in more conservative navy blue serge. The older man was in crisply tailored pin-stripes. Rafferty assumed from the men's apparel that they were more than mere clerks or factotums. The woman, a silver-haired matron of considerable bulk who wore earrings big enough to hang flowerpots from, was dressed in a starched white cotton blouse tucked into a brown tweed skirt. She was almost surely a secretary.

Rafferty tipped his hat, earning a small nod from the woman, just as Police Chief Michael Nelligan walked into the lobby from a connecting hallway. He was a tall, slender man, and he might have been handsome except for a certain sourness to his features. Around the police department he was known as "the big pickle," and it wasn't a compliment. Nelligan had replaced the legendary John J. O'Conner as chief only a month earlier, and he was eager to make his mark. He had a reputation as a skilled bureaucrat, canny politician, and stern administrator. The chief was also known to be a skirt chaser who pursued and even occasionally hired beautiful women for a night's entertainment. Rafferty knew Nelligan just well enough to dislike him.

Nelligan caught sight of Rafferty and Thomas and came over. He shook Rafferty's hand without much enthusiasm but ignored Thomas, then whispered, "This is a terrible thing, Mr. Rafferty, a terrible thing. Naturally, I hope you can be of some assistance."

"We will do our utmost," Rafferty promised.

Nelligan, who didn't bother to introduce the foursome in the corner, grabbed Rafferty by the wrist and said, "I must caution you not to touch anything. This is an official police investigation, as even Mr. Hill must realize. None of us can afford to make even the slightest error in this matter. Inspector Jones will be here shortly and will, of course, assume command of the investigation. I am sure we can count on your complete cooperation."

"I understand," Rafferty said, removing Nelligan's perspiring hand from his wrist. "Nothing will be disturbed."

The chief offered a wan smile and said, "Then we are all agreed. I look forward to the opportunity of working with you."

Rafferty always enjoyed breathtaking insincerity, and he thought the chief had given a fine demonstration of it. The truth, Rafferty knew, was that Nelligan would be more than pleased to toss him out the nearest window were it not for the influence of Louis Hill.

Mustering his own dishonest smile, Rafferty said: "Likewise, chief. Now, as I'm sure you realize, no one should be allowed to leave the office until a proper search of the premises is undertaken. Inspector Jones will undoubtedly do so once he arrives."

"I would expect nothing less," Nelligan intoned, adding, "Dr. Dahlberg should be here any minute."

Rafferty knew the coroner, whose skills were first-rate. "I'll talk with him if I have a chance. In the meantime, Mr. Thomas and I will go about our business. Is there someone here who can show us the scene of the crime?"

"That would be Peter Kretch, the security guard," Nelligan said, looking around. "He was here just a second—ah, there he is." The chief pointed to a short, chubby man—attired in a maroon uniform adorned with gold epaulets and stripes—who'd just come into the lobby.

Nelligan called the guard over and introduced Rafferty, once again ignoring Thomas, whose black skin seemed to make him all but invisible. Rafferty corrected this oversight, then wrapped an arm around the guard's shoulder and said, "Come along, Mr. Kretch. We have much to talk about."

J. D. Carr, the late Artemus Dodge's chief assistant, watched as Rafferty and Thomas left with Kretch. Why, Carr wondered, had an old saloonkeeper been called in to help investigate the murder of Artemus Dodge? Such a thing would never have been allowed in New York City, where the police were actually professional. Then again, St. Paul was a strange place. Carr, who'd left Manhattan's crowded but anonymous confines to follow

Dodge to St. Paul, found his new city's tribal culture baffling. It was like Boston, he thought, only even more personal.

Nelligan came over to join Carr, who was huddled with the other office employees—Artemus's son, Steven, Alan Dubois, and Gertrude Schmidt. They all took seats at the chief's request. Carr thought Nelligan looked nervous and uncertain as he awaited the arrival of his best detective, Mordecai Jones.

Mrs. Schmidt, the office secretary, immediately began expounding on what a fine and honorable man Artemus Dodge had been. "He always took great care of everyone here. Every Christmas, he would see to it that my husband and I received a turkey. He gave me an antique clock once, very pretty, he'd gotten in Austria. Or was it Switzerland? I still cannot believe he's gone. And to think that I spoke with him just minutes before he . . . before he passed."

"Make sure you tell that to Inspector Jones when he arrives," Nelligan said. "Did you speak with Mr. Dodge in his office?"

"Oh no. Over the intercom, as always. He told me there was to be a special staff meeting at nine o'clock."

"I see. And what time did you speak with him?"

"I believe it was about quarter past eight. Mr. Carr happened to be in my office at the time." She turned to Carr and asked, "Wasn't it about eight fifteen, sir?"

Carr cast a quick glance at the secretary, whom he'd always found a trifle irritating. "Yes, I believe that is correct."

Before Nelligan could ask another question, Mrs. Schmidt fell back into sobs, pausing now and then to reiterate her high regard for Dodge's kindness and generosity.

Carr knew better. He'd spent fifteen well-compensated years working for Dodge and had no illusions about his employer. Dodge was a cold, unendearing man, his heart as empty as a poor widow's purse. He would have led a pinched, bloodless life in some lost corner of New England had it not been for one of nature's inexplicable tricks: he was a genius with money. Carr had seen the old man manipulate it time and again, like a child playing with sand, except that Dodge knew how best to use every last grain to his own advantage.

Carr wouldn't miss the old man, nor would anyone else, as far as he knew, despite Mrs. Schmidt's ridiculous blubbering. But his death meant trouble, a lot of it, and Carr knew he had to be prepared. He'd already instructed young Steven, Artemus's feckless son, to watch himself. Carr had passed on identical advice to Dubois. The two of them were to answer questions but under no circumstances should they volunteer information to the police. If they kept their heads about them, Carr believed, everything would be all right. *If* was the operative word.

Steven Dodge, much more sturdily built than his father but without the old man's steely will, shouldn't be a problem, Carr thought. He was clever enough, and he knew how to be charming, as many women had discovered, usually to their regret. But he hadn't inherited his father's work ethic or his talent for making money, and he'd run into some nasty scrapes as a result. Carr knew all about them—he'd shoveled out the Dodge family stable more than once—and young Steven had been grateful for his help. Carr expected that gratitude to continue.

Alan Dubois was altogether less reliable in Carr's estimation. He was certainly a good worker, and a handsome man to boot—tall and lanky, with a fine thatch of straw-colored hair and wide blue eyes that always seem to regard the world with childlike wonder. Yet he doubted Dubois had much of a backbone. Under pressure, he'd probably snap like a brittle twig. Stick close to me, Carr had advised him, and speak only when you're spoken to. So far the young man had done just that, but he would have to be closely watched.

Carr heard the elevator door open and looked up to see an unexpected—and unwelcome—visitor. Isabel Diamond, whose earlier coverage of Alice McQuillan Dunn's murder had made her the star of the *Pioneer Press* newsroom, stepped out into the lobby and headed straight for Nelligan.

"Miss Diamond, I am most pleased to see you," he said, rising from his chair.

"Sure, Michael, and the pope loves a Protestant," she shot back, not bothering to take the chief's extended hand as she studied the foursome seated around him. "Now, which one of you killed the old buzzard?"

. . . . .

"So, Mr. Kretch, as I understand it you're the fellow charged with securin' these premises," Rafferty said. They'd paused in a hallway that led past the elevator and reception desk to the inner offices. Thomas, who wanted to take notes, searched his pockets for a pencil while Rafferty gave the guard a good looking over. Kretch was no more than thirty but already had the wide, fleshy face of an old man, punctured with close-set light blue eyes. He didn't strike Rafferty as the kind of man who could be trusted, not that most men could.

"Yes, sir, that would be me," Kretch replied with a touch of pride. "You must pardon me for asking, sir, but are you with the police?"

"No, we're assistin' them, just as I expect you'll assist us. 'Tis important we see the evidence clear and unvarnished, with our own eyes, before we see it colored through the eyes of others. You can begin by showin' us the body, Mr. Kretch. While we're headin' in that direction, give us the layout of the place. Wash here will take notes."

"Certainly," Kretch said. "I should tell you that I once worked for the police of this city, as well as for the Pinkertons, so I am familiar with investigative techniques."

"How long were you on the force?"

"Not long. The work didn't agree with me."

Rafferty, who'd been a St. Paul cop once himself, nodded and said, "'Tis not work that would agree with most men. Looks like you've landed nicely on your feet. Guardin' the old man must have paid well."

"Well enough if you don't mind being on call around the clock," Kretch replied.

Once Thomas found his pencil, Kretch led them down the hallway. They passed two closed doors on the left before the hall split to form a T.

Rafferty used his cane to tap Kretch on the shoulder. "Slow down, Mr. Kretch. Tell me about the doors we just went by. Where do they lead?"

"The first goes into the secretary's office. The other door is for the men's lavatory."

"I assume the secretary is the woman we saw in the lobby."

"Yes, sir. Gertrude Schmidt is her full name."

"What about the three fellows in the fancy suits? Who might they be?"

"The husky one in the orange and brown suit would be Mr. Dodge's son, Steven. He's the firm's chief financial officer and also a partner. The tall fellow you saw with him is Alan Dubois, who keeps the books. The older gentleman is J. D. Carr, who is—or I should say, was—Mr. Dodge's second-in-command. They all have offices, if you'd like to see them, sir."

"You can just point them out for now."

"Certainly, sir."

Rafferty was growing exasperated. "Stop calling me 'sir.' I am a saloon-keeper, Mr. Kretch, not a general in the Army of the Potomac."

"My apologies. I didn't mean to offend," Kretch said. The guard's obsequious manner irritated Rafferty, who knew that politeness was often aggression in disguise.

At the split in the hallway, Kretch directed their attention to two doors along the left-hand corridor. One, he told them, provided access to a rear staircase. The other, at the end of the corridor, led to an office shared by Steven Dodge and Alan Dubois. Turning back around, Kretch pointed out the door to J. D. Carr's office, just to their right.

Rafferty said, "So where exactly is the old man's—"

He had his answer before he could finish the question. Glancing down the corridor to his right, Rafferty saw an open doorway leading into a large office, where a body lay beside a desk. All Rafferty could see were the dead man's legs and part of the torso.

"That's just as we found him," Kretch said. "Right in his office. The door was locked and barred as tight as could be, and yet there he was, lying dead on the floor. An awful, awful thing. I just wish we'd been quicker about coming to his aid, but with alarms going off so much of late we just assumed it wasn't anything serious. We were dead wrong."

2

"MAY GOD HAVE
MERCY ON OUR POOR SOULS"

"What do you mean about alarms goin' off all the time?" Rafferty asked, looking into Kretch's bland eyes. "Don't tell me somebody's been tryin' to break into Mr. Dodge's fortress?"

"No, it's just that we've had several false alarms recently. Some sort of a problem with the rear stairway door. The alarm goes off even though the door hasn't been opened."

Rafferty rubbed his chin and said, "I'm always interested in things that don't work as they should, especially if there's murder in the vicinity. We'll take a look at that wayward door in due time. First, be so kind as to show me that pistol you're carryin' under your jacket."

"I didn't know it was that obvious," Kretch said, reaching under his left arm and extracting a revolver from its holster.

Rafferty examined the fully loaded .44 caliber Colt and sniffed its four-inch barrel. The gun did not appear to have been fired recently. He handed the weapon back to Kretch and asked, "Any of the other staff carry a gun?"

"Not that I know of."

A few steps down the hallway brought Rafferty and Thomas to Dodge's private office, which was protected by a shiny steel door worthy of a bank vault. The door was swung open into the office.

Kretch, who trailed behind, said, "We call this security door number one. Cost ten thousand dollars. It's plated with a new kind of steel. Stainless, I think they call it. As I told you, it was locked when we found Mr. Dodge. I opened it afterwards for the police."

"Very nice," said Thomas, who'd once apprenticed as a locksmith and knew fine workmanship when he saw it. "Looks like a custom job all the way."

"It's fancy all right," Rafferty agreed. "Too bad it couldn't keep Mr. Dodge from bein' shot. Mr. Kretch, why don't you stay right here. I'll let you know if we need you."

Rafferty and Thomas went into the office, where Artemus Dodge lay facedown on the floor between his desk and one of the office's windows. The dark mahogany desk and matching swivel chair sat atop a podium, about a foot high, that took up one corner of the office. A telephone, an intercom, and a lamp were the only items on the desk.

"Well, Mr. Dodge didn't suffer," Rafferty said, getting down with some effort on one knee to inspect the body. "He must have died almost instantly and not that long ago. There's a little lividity but no rigor. He can't have been dead for more than a few hours."

"All right, do your sleuthing," Rafferty told Thomas, whose talents included a keen eye for small but telling details. Rafferty often said his long-time partner was the "observingest" man he knew.

Before going through Dodge's pockets, Rafferty made a visual sweep of the office, which was a good twenty-five feet square and conveyed an aura of baronial wealth. Its décor included richly paneled walls of Honduran mahogany, a gilded and coffered plaster ceiling, and an oriental rug that spilled across the darkly stained hardwood floor in an arabesque of colors and patterns. The old man had spared no expense in creating his refuge from the world. Rafferty also took note of three tall double-hung windows along the office's west wall and another three on the north side near Dodge's body. They were all shut, but their damask drapes had been drawn open, flooding the office with light.

At the center of the office, mounted on a pedestal beneath a lead crystal chandelier, was a stock ticker. It was as silent as its master. What sound there was came from the ticking of a Chippendale-style grandfather's clock in the office's far corner. A tufted French sofa, a high-back chair, and a japanned table occupied the wall next to the security door. Atop the table was a porcelain tea set, with one cup set out. A glass ashtray with a crushed cigar butt inside rested on one arm of the sofa. Beside it was an unsmoked cigar, identified by its band as a Ramon Allones robusto. The cigar butt had left its odorous residue in the room, but Rafferty didn't smell even the merest whiff of gunpowder.

The office's one truly personal touch was an oil painting hung between the windows closest to Dodge's desk. It depicted a strikingly beautiful young woman, seated in full equine regalia atop a roan stallion. The look in her blue eyes was most fetching.

Rafferty turned his attention back to the corpse. Dodge was dressed in a dark gray suit, a starched white shirt with French cuffs, a patterned silk tie, black leather oxfords, and black socks. A projectile had punched a sizable hole in the back of his head, just above the neck. Bloodstains soaked his coat and flowed into a puddle that matched the crimson tones of the oriental rug. Rafferty turned Dodge's head to look for an exit wound but couldn't find one. The bullet must still be in the old man's brain. Over the years, Rafferty had seen more bullet wounds than he cared to remember, from the gaping hole bored out by a minié ball to the crisp little incision carved out by a .22. The wound in Dodge's head looked to be large caliber, possibly from a .45.

No weapon lay beside the dead financier. Rafferty wasn't surprised, since the wound didn't look self-inflicted. Suicides rarely shot themselves in the back of the head. It was simpler to put a bullet through the temple or swallow the gun barrel and dine on a last meal of hot lead.

Rafferty went through Dodge's pockets. He found a wallet with $180 in cash, a Mont Blanc fountain pen, a handkerchief complete with nose contents, a bejeweled Cartier watch, and a $200 receipt for the purchase of "1 gown, silk," from Collette's French Fashions at 445 State Street in Chicago. Mindful of the police investigation to come, Rafferty put back everything he'd found.

Grunting like an arthritic old dog, Rafferty got to his feet and went over to Kretch, who was hovering by the door. "I know Mr. Dodge is married, but is it possible he's been entertainin' a lady on the side?"

"I doubt it. His wife is young and quite beautiful, so I don't see—"

"Why he'd look elsewhere for his pleasure," Rafferty said with a skeptical nod. "Is she the lady ridin' the stallion in that portrait on the wall?"

"Yes, Mr. Dodge had that painting made a few months ago."

"I can see how she'd occupy a man's thoughts. When did Mr. Dodge take his young bride?"

"Two years ago. Don't you remember the big wedding at the Palmer House in Chicago? It was in all the newspapers."

"So it was. Trouble is, I've forgotten the lucky bride's name."

"Amanda, sir. Amanda Shay. Mr. Dodge met her not long after his first wife died."

"'Tis touchin' how an old man can reach into a woman's heart by way of his pocketbook," Rafferty said, looking down at Dodge's wizened features. "Has the widow been informed of her husband's death?"

"Not yet. As I understand it, there's been some trouble locating her."

Probably taking her exercise with the chauffeur, Rafferty thought. He said, "Then I guess we'll just have to wait a bit to talk to her, assumin' she's not overcome with grief."

Thomas, who was rummaging through Dodge's desk, called Rafferty over to look at a pattern of tiny red stains around the intercom. "It's the kind of blood spray you get from a bullet wound," he said. "Looks like the old man was standing by his desk when he got shot. Could be he was talking on the intercom to somebody."

"Can you tell where the bullet came from?"

"Afraid not. Usually, blood fans out in one direction from a wound if the bullet remains in the body, but it's all over the place here. I've never seen a spray pattern like it. Very strange."

"No stranger than everything else about this business," Rafferty said. "What about the desk? Anything of note in the drawers?"

"No, but I found something peculiar underneath the desk. It's a piece of wood. Looks like part of a one-by-two. One end's jagged, like it was snapped off."

"I'd break a bone tryin' to get down there," Rafferty said. "Show it to me, Wash, but don't get your fingerprints on it. We don't want to be disturbin' evidence."

Thomas got down on his hands and knees and used a pencil to coax out the wood fragment, which was about three inches long. Rafferty summoned Kretch again and asked, "Any idea where this might have come from?"

"I've never seen it before," Kretch said.

"It's not the only odd thing I found," Thomas said. "Look at the window behind us."

Rafferty glanced over at the window and said, "Well, isn't that curious. Both the lower sash cords are broken."

Thomas said, "I'm not sure 'broken' is the right word. Sash cords usually fray before they break, but these look almost brand-new. I'm thinking somebody cut the cords with a knife. There's something else you should know. This window is unlocked, even though it's closed."

"Wash, you are a regular font of intriguin' information. What about the other windows?"

"They're locked down tight. No bullet holes in them either."

Rafferty scratched the back of his head and said, "So why would anybody bother to unlock this window and cut the cords? It wouldn't help him escape. Those bars out on the terrace look sturdy as can be, and they're too close together for even a fellow as skinny as you, Wash, to slip through. There's also the fact that we're three hundred feet above the street. Maybe we should be lookin' for a mountain climber."

Thomas said, "Well, I don't see how a man could have made it up here on ropes. And even if he did, how'd he get through those bars? There's another problem. The windows all face right out toward Robert and Sixth streets. People would have noticed a fellow up here dangling from a rope. It all seems farfetched."

Rafferty began to feel as if he'd walked into a Chinese puzzle box or some magic cabinet out of the *Arabian Nights*. He said, "The broken sash cords can't be an accident. Somebody cut 'em for a reason. Open the window, will you, and see what happens."

Thomas lifted the lower sash and then let go. The window slammed shut. Rafferty said, "I'm beginnin' to get a crazy idea, Wash."

"Wouldn't be the first time. You can tell me about it later. I want to have a look at the security door."

After his partner drifted away, Rafferty asked Kretch if he knew about the broken sash cords. Kretch shook his head. "Mr. Dodge never mentioned any problem with the window to me. I checked all the windows here and in Mr. Dodge's apartment last Friday night as part of my regular weekly inspection. The cords were fine then."

Rafferty looked at the bars protecting the terrace and asked, "Is it possible the killer came down from the roof on ropes or climbed up from the floor below?"

"I don't see how," Kretch replied matter-of-factly. "There's only one door, from the main staircase, that leads out to the roof, and it has an alarm. As for the office directly below us, it's occupied by a law firm that does much of its work for Mr. Dodge. The lawyers would have noticed anybody trying to climb up here."

"And bein' lawyers, they'd have found a way to charge the fellow for the time they spent lookin' at him," Rafferty said. "By the way, is there a door that opens out to the terrace?"

The idea seemed to appall Kretch. "Absolutely not. The terrace— Mr. Dodge, I should tell you, always called it a loggia—was designed to be inaccessible. It was built strictly as a protective measure and not just because of the bars. It also hides his office and apartment windows from the street because they're set back from the main walls of the building. Mr. Dodge was always worried somebody might take a potshot at him."

"'Twould seem he didn't worry enough," Rafferty observed, turning away from the window. "All right, Mr. Kretch, come along. Let's have a look at the security door."

Thomas was examining the door with his practiced eye, pausing now and then to whistle or mutter something to himself.

"What do you think?" Rafferty asked his partner.

"Well, the door is a Mosler, and it's a real beauty. I can see why it cost the old man ten grand. It's got six-inch-thick steel, a combination lock, a peephole with a wide-angle lens, built-in alarms, timers, you name it. There's also a heavy bar here on the inside for extra security. Doesn't look like anybody tampered with it. No scratches or tool marks. It would take some serious drilling or explosives to open it."

Rafferty pointed to what looked like a small safe built into the wall next to the door. It was about eighteen inches wide, six inches high, and had a combination lock. "What's that?" he asked Kretch.

"It's a pass-through from the hallway. Mr. Dodge used it for documents and the like."

"Ah, I see. Could it have been left open somehow to give a clear shot into the office?"

"Not a chance. There's an interlock system, and the pass-through door can't be opened from this side unless it's locked out in the hallway. Only Mr. Dodge himself knew the combination to the inside door."

Rafferty thought for a minute and said, "All right, let's go back to the big door here. Did anyone in the office other than Mr. Dodge himself know the combination?"

"Just Mr. Carr," Kretch said.

"So you're tellin' me that when Mr. Dodge was workin' in his office, Mr. Carr could come right in through the security door if he wanted to. Is that right?"

"Oh, no. The bar automatically locks into place when the door is closed from the inside. It would have been impossible for Mr. Carr or anyone else to sneak into the office through this door while Mr. Dodge was in here. Also, you should know that whenever the door is opened, a buzzer sounds and a light illuminates at my station."

"Did either the buzzer or light go on this morning before Mr. Dodge's death?"

"No."

Rafferty said, "You seem to be pilin' on the impossibilities, Mr. Kretch. Answer this for me if you would: how in blazes did you get into this fortress of an office and find the body? Am I to assume you're able to float through solid walls like a spirit?"

"Wouldn't that be nice," Kretch said, "but there's no mystery about how we got in. You see, there's another entrance to Mr. Dodge's office and apartment, located off the lobby. We call it door number two, and it's for emergencies only. It also sets off an alarm when it's opened."

Thoughts of doors, locks, buzzers, and alarms began to tumble around Rafferty's brain like a crowd of rowdy drunks. He sighed and said, "We'll look at that emergency door in a minute. First, tell me about the windows here. Were they shut when you found Mr. Dodge's body?"

"Yes, all of them were closed from what I could see."

"What about the drapes?"

"They were open. Mr. Dodge liked to have light in the morning."

Thomas, who'd gone off to continue nosing around the office, called Rafferty over to look at a small hole, probably from a nail, that he'd found in the paneling behind Mrs. Dodge's portrait. The hole was about six inches below the pair of hooks from which the painting hung.

Rafferty wondered if the picture had been moved recently for some reason. He held up the painting and tried to position it as though it was hanging from a nail in the hole.

"How does it look?" he asked.

Thomas stepped back and said, "Too low. Nobody would have hung it there."

"Well, then, I guess we've got another mystery. Maybe Mr. Kretch can enlighten us."

But the guard professed to know nothing about the hole, so Rafferty jumped to another topic. "Did Mr. Dodge smoke cigars?"

Kretch nodded. "He liked the presidentes made by Hoyo de Monterrey in Cuba. It was the only kind I ever saw him with."

"There was another brand of cigar—a Ramon Allones—beside the ashtray on the sofa. Any idea where it came from?"

"I'm afraid not."

Rafferty dismissed Kretch for the time being and said to Thomas, "Let's plow through the rest of this place as quick as we can before Jones the Magnificent sticks his nose in. I'll take the apartment, and you keep lookin' in here."

The apartment consisted of a spacious parlor and a bedroom. A short hall with a bathroom on one side and a walk-in closet on the other connected the rooms. In the bedroom Rafferty found the emergency door mentioned by Kretch. It was made of reinforced steel and had been swung open toward the inside, much like the one in Dodge's office. A wooden panel blocked the doorway. Beyond it, Rafferty heard voices from what he presumed to be the lobby. Rafferty found nothing else of interest in the apartment. All of the windows were closed and locked, there were no bullet holes in the glass, and there were no signs of a disturbance.

Another dead end, Rafferty thought as he went back into the office, where Thomas was staring out the window next to Dodge's desk. The closely spaced bars of the "birdcage" restricted the view, but it was still impressive. A mile or so to the north Rafferty saw the gleaming marble dome of the State Capitol, which rose out of the city's tired old dirt like a fresh white flower. Its far less splendid predecessor, known simply as the old capitol, also poked above downtown's aging jumble of brick buildings.

"This whole thing doesn't make sense," Rafferty said. "It doesn't look like anybody could have gotten in here, shot Mr. Dodge, and then escaped without creatin' a mighty ruckus. Trouble is, I don't see how a shot from outside could have killed him either."

"It's crazy all right," Thomas agreed.

"I'm not sure we know the half of it yet. 'Tis time for the rest of the story." Rafferty motioned Kretch to join them by the window and said, "Now then, Mr. Kretch, be so kind as to tell us everything that happened this morning."

Kretch turned out to be an efficient witness. He reported that the day had begun normally enough, with the office staff arriving at their usual times. At about quarter past eight, Dodge contacted his secretary, Mrs. Schmidt, on the intercom and said there would be a staff meeting at nine o'clock to discuss an urgent matter.

"What was so urgent?" Rafferty asked.

"I have no idea. Mrs. Schmidt told me she didn't either."

"All right. Did Mr. Dodge talk to anyone else in the office this morning?"

"Not that I'm aware of."

"By the way, has Mr. Dodge been staying here at his apartment a good deal of late?"

"Every day for the past two weeks. Normally he stays at his mansion—you know, the big one out along the river. But ever since all the streetcar agitation started, he kept to his apartment. He was afraid there would be trouble."

"Well, he was right about that. Now then, as far as you or anybody else in this office knew, Mr. Dodge was locked up all by himself this mornin' safe and sound, is that correct?"

"Yes. Everything appeared to be just fine."

"When did the trouble start?"

"At precisely eight thirty-two. That's when the rear staircase door alarm began ringing. As I mentioned, we'd been having false alarms of late, so nobody got too excited."

A tall man with short gray hair and a bristling mustache came into the office. He carried a black medical bag in one hand.

"Why, Shad, fancy meeting you here," said Ramsey County Coroner James Dahlberg. "How'd you get involved in this mess?"

"'Tis a long story, Jim, but I can tell you that you're in for a time of it. Mr. Dodge took a bullet to the brain. The trick is how it got there."

"So I'm told," Dahlberg said. "We'll talk later."

Rafferty said to Kretch, "Let's move out into the hallway so the coroner can go about his business."

They walked out to the hall and down to the rear staircase door. Thomas looked it over while Kretch described the events leading to the discovery of Dodge's body.

"As I said, when the alarm went off, no one was overly concerned. Even so, I followed procedures. I locked the main stairway door off the lobby and the elevator door, precisely as specified in the emergency manual prepared by Mr. Dodge himself. After that—"

"Wait a minute, I'm curious about the elevator," Rafferty said. "Who has access to it?"

"You need a key to operate it. All the office staff have one. There's also one kept at the guard desk downstairs."

"Very well. Where were you when the alarm sounded, Mr. Kretch?"

"I'd gone into my room—I have a small sleeping area behind the guard station—to fetch a book. I often read during the day, since there's little else to do. Once the alarm rang, I came down here to check the door. It was closed. By that time, everybody had come out of their offices to see what the fuss was about."

"Tell me who you saw and where they were. Be as precise as you can. Where *exactly* was everyone?"

Kretch rubbed his fleshy chin and said, "I'll do the best I can. I think Mr. Dubois was standing in the hall near the door to Mr. Dodge's office and talking to Mr. Carr. Young Steven, as I recall, was just stepping out of his office, which is right next to the stairway here. I'm not sure about Mrs. Schmidt. She may have stayed in her office for a while."

"What did you do next?"

"I pushed open the door and looked down the stairs but saw no one. I asked Mr. Carr and the others if they'd seen anything suspicious, and they said they hadn't."

"And all the while Mr. Dodge was still in his office?"

"Yes. That was to be expected. His office was where he felt safest."

"A delusion on his part, 'twould seem. Go on."

"I locked the stairway door from the hallway side, as per the emergency plan. Then I went back to turn off and reset the alarm."

"Did you smell anything unusual, Mr. Kretch, or see any smoke?"

"No. I thought of that once I saw that Mr. Dodge had been shot. Odd, isn't it?"

"Odd as can be. Now, just how was Mr. Dodge's body discovered?"

Kretch's answer served only to deepen the mystery. After the alarm rang, he said, Mrs. Schmidt tried to reach the financier via intercom. Uncharacteristically, there was no answer. Next, she dialed the number of Dodge's desk phone as well as the private line in his apartment. Again, no one answered.

"She felt something was wrong," Kretch said. "I did too, so I alerted the others. Steven Dodge and Mr. Dubois immediately pounded on Mr. Dodge's office door and shouted his name, to no avail. Meanwhile, Mr. Carr went into his office and also tried to contact Mr. Dodge, again to no effect. Finally, Mr. Carr decided to use the emergency entrance into the apartment."

"Ah, that would be door number two. I saw it in the bedroom. It connects to the lobby, does it not?"

"Yes, but you can't see it from there because it's disguised by a panel."

"Who besides Mr. Dodge had the combination?"

"Just Mr. Carr and I."

"Aside from the two security doors, are there any other entrances to Mr. Dodge's inner sanctum?"

"No. As I told you, his entire suite of rooms is built like a vault. It's designed to be utterly impregnable. The walls, the ceilings, and the floors are all reinforced. The architects had to make special provisions with the structure just to handle all the extra weight."

By now, Rafferty was beginning to think like Artemus Dodge when it came to security. He said, "I'm guessin' that this hidden door into Mr. Dodge's bedroom has some trick to it. Am I right?"

"You are. The door of course triggers an alarm if it's opened, but it has another, more unusual feature. Once it's opened, it can't be fully closed again except with the assistance of a master locksmith. Even then it's quite a job. Mr. Dodge trusted no one—not me and not even Mr. Carr. If either of us tried to enter his apartment for some improper purpose, we'd leave behind the open door as evidence. When Mr. Carr decided to use the emergency entrance this morning, I and everyone else here can assure you that it was locked tight, as it has been ever since Mr. Dodge moved in."

Rafferty glanced at Thomas, who responded with a subtle nod and headed back toward the office.

"Now, Mr. Kretch, I take it everyone else in the office was gathered around the door when Mr. Carr opened it."

"Yes. We all went inside and found Mr. Dodge's body."

Rafferty had an idea. He said, "So I take it the lot of you rushed right into the old man's office without pausin' to look through the apartment first. Is that right?"

"I know what you're thinking," Kretch said, his fleshy lips curving into a smug smile, "but you're quite wrong. Mr. Carr and I checked very thoroughly to see if anyone might be hiding inside the apartment, as the security plan requires. We found no one. You should also know that the stairway, lobby, and elevator doors were all locked by the time we reached Mr. Dodge. That's how the security system works after an alarm sounds. It requires a set of keys—I have one, as does Mr. Carr—to reopen everything. There's also security downstairs in the main lobby. Anyone who enters this building day or night has to sign in with a guard stationed there."

"You are a paragon, Mr. Kretch, an absolute paragon," Rafferty said. "'Tis apparent nothing escapes your eagle eye. After searchin' the apartment, I assume you and the others went into Mr. Dodge's office."

"Yes. We found him on the floor just as you saw him."

"What time was that?"

"I looked at my watch. It was exactly eight thirty-nine."

"Did anyone touch the body?"

"I think Mr. Carr knelt down to search for a pulse. Sadly, he couldn't find one. It was quite clear that Mr. Dodge was gone."

"What happened next?"

"Mr. Carr instructed me to use the phone on Mr. Dodge's desk to call the police. They arrived within five minutes or so."

Rafferty didn't doubt this estimate. St. Paul's coppers could be downright lethargic at times, but not when a rich man needed protection.

"Did anyone besides you touch or move anything on Mr. Dodge's desk?"

"Not that I'm aware of. As you can imagine, we were all in a state of shock."

"Did everyone stay in the office while waitin' for the coppers to arrive?"

Kretch hesitated. "I think so, but I couldn't swear to it. It's possible someone might have left briefly for one reason or another."

Thomas returned from the apartment and caught Rafferty's eye. "What's the verdict, Wash?"

"Mr. Kretch is right. That door in the old man's bedroom can't be closed without a lot of trouble. There's a channel beneath it with some kind of a ratchet that engages once the door is opened. The whole mechanism will have to be disassembled to shut the door again."

Rafferty said, "Mr. Dodge seems to have thought of everything except how to keep himself from gettin' shot. 'Twas a regrettable oversight on his part. Whoever killed him must have done a lot of plottin' and schemin' to prepare for what happened today. Tell me, Mr. Kretch, was anyone besides Mr. Dodge himself in his office over the weekend?"

"The entire staff works on Saturday mornings, and Mr. Dodge often has them in for conferences and the like. I'd guess all of us were in his office that day at one time or another. You'll have to ask the others to be sure, however."

"Any other visitors over the weekend?"

"Mrs. Dodge was here last night. She always comes in on Sunday evenings if Mr. Dodge is staying over in the apartment. She got here at about six and stayed for two hours, as I recall."

"Is that how long she normally stays?"

Kretch thought for a moment. "No, her visits are generally much shorter."

"Any idea why she stayed so long last night?"

"She didn't say, and I didn't ask."

"Ah, your discretion is commendable," Rafferty said. "Was she Mr. Dodge's last visitor yesterday?"

"Oh no. That would be Mr. Hill. He came by later in the night, at about ten o'clock."

"Louis Hill?"

"Of course," Kretch said. "Who else would it be?"

Rafferty didn't know Louis Hill particularly well, and his early morning phone call had come as a surprise. Far more surprising was the news that Hill might have been the last person to see Artemus Dodge alive.

"Mr. Kretch, you are full of revelations. Was it a usual thing for Mr. Hill to visit Mr. Dodge's office on a Sunday night?"

"No. It was the first time I know of. But Mr. Hill had met here with Mr. Dodge quite a few times. They have joint business interests, as I understand it. In any event, Mr. Dodge called me over the intercom just after nine and informed me that Mr. Hill would be coming up."

"Did he say why Mr. Hill would be visiting?"

Kretch let out a snort suggesting that the question was absurd. "Mr. Dodge does not share that sort of information with me. As I said, Mr. Hill appeared at ten o'clock. I announced his arrival, and he went to Mr. Dodge's office. Mr. Dodge, I presume, opened the door and let him in, since the signal light and buzzer at my station went on. Mr. Hill returned to the guard station at approximately half past eleven, said goodnight, and left. That is all I can tell you."

Thomas, who'd been taking notes as Kretch spoke, said, "Maybe we should take a look at the other offices, Shad, while we still have a chance."

"Good idea," Rafferty said. "'Tis a wonder Inspector Jones isn't here already. Lead the way, Mr. Kretch."

Their first stop was J. D. Carr's office. It was smaller than Artemus Dodge's but well furnished with a rolltop desk, two side chairs, and several bookcases. A brooding seascape, painted in oil, adorned the wall behind Carr's immaculately clean desk. Nothing in the office seemed out of place or unusual. Two windows behind Carr's desk were cracked open, and Rafferty went over to take a look. The windows faced west, across Robert Street, but had no bars like those guarding Dodge's office.

The office occupied by Steven Dodge and Alan Dubois was larger than Carr's but not nearly as orderly. Each man had a desk strewn with papers, ledger books, pencils, erasers, and other paraphernalia. Scattered here and there were travel souvenirs: German beer steins, a pewter replica of Westminster Abbey, a Spanish sombrero, and a framed panoramic photograph of Vienna. A telescope mounted on a tripod stood in one corner. Cigar butts littered glass ashtrays on both men's desks. The office was well lighted by two tall windows facing west and four smaller ones overlooking an alley to the south. Two of the alley windows were open and admitted a pleasant breeze.

Rafferty and Thomas completed their tour by inspecting the men's lavatory and Mrs. Schmidt's office, which also had a small bathroom attached. They found nothing out of the ordinary. As they left the secretary's office, a familiar voice boomed out from the lobby.

"Sounds like Jones the Magnificent has arrived," Thomas said.

"And may God have mercy on our poor souls," Rafferty replied before going out to talk with the man who regarded himself, quite irrationally in Rafferty's view, as the greatest detective in the Northwest.

3

"I NEED YOU NOW MORE THAN EVER"

Inspector Mordecai Jones of the St. Paul Police Department was in a foul mood by the time he arrived at Dodge Tower. A streetcar derailment at the top of the Selby Avenue tunnel had snarled traffic in front of his apartment, delaying the patrol car dispatched to pick him up. Another tangle at Seven Corners had slowed him even more, forcing Jones to walk the last few blocks to the tower. As he neared the skyscraper, his mind clicked back to the tour he'd taken of Dodge's fortified office only a month earlier. The financier had been so proud of his steel-lined aerie that he'd shown it to Jones after reading about the inspector's work in the Alice McQuillan Dunn murder case.

"I wager you'll find no flaw in my arrangements," Dodge had told him, and the old man was right. The numerous security features were beyond reproach, the best Jones had ever seen. Obviously, something had gone terribly wrong.

When Jones finally reached the tower's lobby at half past nine, he found it teeming with police, office workers, and reporters. Ignoring a small herd of press people who rushed over for a comment, Jones headed straight for the elevators, where he found his assistant, Sergeant Francis Carroll.

"What have we got?" he asked as they boarded the private car to Dodge's penthouse.

"Oh, you're not going to believe this one," Carroll said. "It's the strangest thing you ever heard of."

"How so? All I know is that someone shot the old man."

"I don't think I could explain it, sir. You'll just have to see for yourself. By the way, you should know the chief's not happy. He's been wondering why it took you so long to get here."

Wonderful, Jones thought, just wonderful. All he needed was Nelligan breathing down his neck. "How long has his eminence been on the scene?"

"Not sure, sir, but he was already up in Dodge's office when I got here. How do you suppose he made it so fast?"

"Fairy wings, I'm sure," Jones said, although the presence of St. Paul's newly appointed police chief was no joking matter. The chief fancied himself quite the detective, and he'd be a pain in the rear.

Jones himself was regarded as a pain by many of his colleagues. He was supremely self-confident, intolerant of fools, and often abrasive in his dealings with others. Older officers considered him supercilious and disrespectful, an ambitious climber who clearly aimed to be chief of police someday. Even Carroll found the inspector to be overweening at times and in private conversations referred to him as "the Almighty Jones."

Still, there was no denying Jones's talent, and he was already said to be the most brilliant detective in the department's history. A few months earlier, his expert sleuthing had led to the arrest and conviction of Frank Dunn as the mastermind behind the cold-blooded execution of his estranged young wife, thereby solving what many at the time regarded as St. Paul's greatest murder case.

Jones's work in the Dunn case had earned him a promotion to inspector of detectives—the youngest in the department's history. Now, the Dunn affair was all but forgotten, and Jones knew that if he couldn't solve Dodge's murder, his reputation, which he had taken great pains to cultivate, would quickly lose its luster.

The pressure was especially intense because of the immediate suspicion that radicals had conspired to commit the crime. As Jones and everyone else knew, Artemus Dodge had been the target of Sidney Berthelson's bomb four years earlier, and it was easy to conclude that radicals had finally managed to kill the financier, especially since he'd taken on the task of promoting war bonds.

Jones and Carroll encountered a busy scene on the thirtieth floor. A bevy of uniformed officers stood around the office lobby, while off in one corner a half dozen or so civilians were gathered in a loose circle. One of them, a woman whose voice rang through the room like a fire bell, appeared to be doing all the talking. Jones recognized her immediately. It was Isabel Diamond, ace reporter for the *Pioneer Press*.

"Who let you in here?" Jones growled. "Get out, now!"

"Why my dear Mordecai, how nice to see you again," Diamond replied. She was, Jones knew, not only St. Paul's most beautiful reporter but also the most devious. She'd given him fits during the Dunn investigation, scheming her way to one scoop after another. Just last week, she'd created a new uproar by exposing a city commissioner's dalliance with a sixteen-year-old girl. Not a few of the city's great men quaked at the thought of crossing her. Jones entertained no such fears.

"Out," he repeated, grabbing a uniformed officer by the arm and pushing him toward Diamond. "I want her gone this instant."

"Ah now, is that any way to treat a lady?" said a tall, portly man with a wiry white beard who appeared at one end of the lobby. An equally tall but far more slender black man was with him, as was a younger man wearing a guard's uniform. The bearded man, whose broad Irish face was furrowed with age and marked by a scar on his forehead, had the gaudy appearance of a carnival pitchman. He wore a green jacket over a yellow shirt and gold-striped maroon pants that looked to have once done duty in a marching band. Adding to his colorful repertoire was a bright red walking cane with a polished brass handle. Dear God, Jones thought, what have I done to deserve this?

"Rafferty," he said, spitting out the word as though he'd just seen a rat creeping out of the woodwork. "What idiot let you in here?"

"That would be me," said Nelligan, who to Jones's chagrin turned out to be among those gathered in the corner. "Both Miss Diamond and Mr. Rafferty are here with my permission."

"My apologies, sir," Jones said, "but as a matter of department policy—"

"I make the policy," Nelligan said in his usual supercilious way, "and you would do well to remember that. As I said, Miss Diamond and Mr. Rafferty may stay. In fact, I expect you to cooperate fully with Mr. Rafferty, who has been retained as a consultant in this most unfortunate matter. Now, why don't you get on with your work, Inspector. Given your late arrival, which is most disappointing, I'm sure you have plenty of catching up to do. You will find that there are many curious aspects to this case. Mr. Kretch"—Nelligan gestured toward the guard—"can provide all the essential details."

"Of course," Jones murmured, stifling the urge—he'd had it several times before—to plant his fist right on Nelligan's pointy nose. The chief's long, sour face was a pickle with eyes, and Jones hated pickles. Turning to the guard, Jones said, "All right, Mr. Kretch, I guess you're my first catch of the day. Let's have a look at the corpse."

When the whole fantastic case had finally been untangled, Rafferty would look back to his first few hours at Dodge Tower and recall what Sherlock Holmes once told him: "The crime scene itself is always the greatest teacher. Learn to read it, fluently and thoroughly, and even the most baffling of mysteries will become as clear to you as the light of the sun." As usual, Holmes turned out to be right, although for a time the sun had been hidden, from Rafferty and everyone else, by clouds of confusion and doubt.

In hopes of finding some daylight, Rafferty had offered to begin interviewing Dodge's employees while Jones examined the crime scene. The chief, however, wouldn't hear of it. Jones would be in charge of the interrogations. Faced with an idle hour or two, Rafferty concocted a little fib, announcing that he and Thomas would go down to the lobby to check the security arrangements there. Nelligan said that sounded like a fine idea.

After a cursory inspection of the lobby's guard station, Rafferty and Thomas boarded one of the elevators serving the lower twenty-nine floors of Dodge Tower. The operator, a thin young man whose gunmetal gray uniform appeared to be two sizes too large, was eager to talk.

"Morning, gentlemen," he said. "Lots of excitement here today. You heard the news?"

"We've heard," Rafferty said. "Take us to the twenty-ninth floor, if you would, son."

"I'm not sure anybody's up there, sir. I took Mr. Butler and his two assistants down just a few minutes ago. He's Mr. Dodge's lawyer, you know."

Rafferty hadn't known. Now he did. "Yes, we were just going to see him on a business matter. Well, take us up anyway. Perhaps his secretary is still in."

The penultimate floor of Dodge Tower, like all of those below it except for the ground floor, was laid out with a central corridor providing access to offices on both sides. Narrow cross halls led to the stairways at either end of the building. There was only one numbered door—2900—on the north side of the corridor, and a stenciled sign identified it as the offices of Butler & Quinn, attorneys at law. The firm appeared to occupy the entire north half of the floor, putting it directly below Dodge's fortified office and apartment. Rafferty tried the door, but it was locked, and no one responded to his knocks.

"I could pick the lock," Thomas volunteered, kneeling down to study it. "Doesn't look like anything difficult."

Rafferty considered the idea. "No, if one of the lawyers comes back, we'll have some explainin' to do. Let's have a look at that stairway."

The stairway at the west end of the building was the same one that led up to the hallway near Dodge's office. It was protected by a steel door and wired with an alarm identical to the one on the floor above. A sign warned that opening the door would set off the alarm. Rafferty wanted to test the door but not if it meant setting off an unholy clamor.

"Make a note, Wash. Every door and alarm on this staircase, top to bottom, needs to be checked."

"Got it. You think somebody might have fooled with the alarm and gotten in here?"

"Could be. Let's check these other doors."

The south side of the corridor offered five office doors, bearing odd numbers from 2901 to 2909, plus a lavatory. None of the doors had signs to indicate tenants. Rafferty tried the door to 2901, the nearest to the staircase, but it was locked. So were the other four office doors.

"Time for some burglin', Wash," Rafferty announced. "See if you can open 2901 here."

For years, Rafferty had done all of his own lock picking, but his eyesight wasn't what it used to be. Better to let Thomas do it. Rafferty got out his lock-picking set, which along with a derringer and a multibladed pocket knife accompanied him everywhere, and gave it to Thomas. The lock proved difficult, but after a minute of delicate work, Thomas sprung it open.

The office was empty and gave no sign of ever having been used. Cobwebs dangled in the corners and formed filigrees around a central light fixture. The terrazzo floor appeared pristine, as did the unpainted plaster walls. Rafferty inspected the windows, which were all closed. Three faced west over Robert Street. They were locked, and Rafferty found heavy films of dust on their ledges and between the upper and lower sashes. The windows clearly had not been opened in a long time.

Another three windows, smaller than the others, faced south onto a narrow alley. They were locked as well. Curiously, the window farthest back from the street had only a scattering of dust on its ledge and atop its lower sash. This suggested it had recently been opened, or at least dusted. There was also a small crack in the upper pane.

Rafferty showed Thomas the window and said, "This one's different from the others. Could be somebody opened it just to get cross-ventilation out in the hallway. Maybe that's how it got cracked. Or maybe it's connected in some way to all that trickery upstairs."

Thomas suggested that they look into the other four offices as well. All of them proved to be empty, their locked windows thickly coated with dust.

"Well, it was worth a look," Rafferty said as they waited for an elevator. "We at least know something Jones doesn't."

When Rafferty and Thomas returned to the penthouse, Jones was still examining the crime scene, and there was little to do except await his return. Nelligan and the office employees remained huddled in the lobby. A sharp glance from the chief indicated that Rafferty would not be welcome to join the conversation.

"I guess it's heel-coolin' time," Rafferty said just as he spotted Isabel Diamond coming down the hallway. Rafferty knew every journalist in St. Paul, but he'd had only a few dealings with Diamond. By reputation, she was smart, nosy, and unscrupulous—ideal qualities, Rafferty thought, for a news reporter. She wore a navy blue pleated skirt that ended well above the ankle, a matching flared jacket over an embroidered white blouse, and a felt fedora. She was indeed a striking woman. Her large hazel eyes were remarkable, and Rafferty could see why half the men in St. Paul were infatuated with her.

Not one for small talk, she introduced herself with a question: "So what do you think of this business, Mr. Rafferty? Amazing, don't you think?"

"Ah, you are the wordsmith, Miss Diamond. I would not presume to add any poor commentary of my own to the tale."

"In other words, you aren't talking. By the way, who's this colored fellow?" she asked, turning her searchlight eyes on Thomas. "Friend of yours?"

"He is, and he's perfectly capable of speaking for himself."

Thomas introduced himself, and Diamond said, "Since Mr. Rafferty here won't talk, how about you? What have you got to say?"

"Nothing," Thomas replied.

"Well, isn't that sweet. I've come across a pair of clams. All right, but don't think you'll be rid of me so easily. I know what you're up to, Mr. Rafferty, and you'll find in the end that it's better to work with me than against me."

"I'll keep that in mind," Rafferty said, smiling. "Have a pleasant day, Miss Diamond."

Dr. Dahlberg's appearance in the lobby abruptly ended her inquisition. "Doc, what did you find out?" she asked, rushing up to him.

The coroner ignored her question and went over to Nelligan and the group in the corner. Rafferty and Thomas followed.

"It's all right," the chief said. "We have no secrets from the press. What can you tell us, doctor?"

"Not much beyond the obvious. Death looks to have been from a bullet wound to the head. The slug's still in there. I'll remove it when we perform the autopsy. I found no evidence that the shot was fired at close range, and since there was no gun by the body, I don't see how it could have been suicide. The best I can tell you now is that it was homicide by a person or persons unknown."

"So you're sayin' there was no stipplin' or powder burns or the like around the wound," Rafferty noted.

"That's right. But we'll make a more thorough examination at the morgue. Inspector Jones said it's all right to remove the body."

"Yes, by all means," Nelligan said. "Do what you must."

"Hold it," Diamond said. "I still need to know—"

Nelligan shook his head. "Not now, Miss Diamond. We must let the doctor perform his duties. I am sure you'll have an opportunity to talk to him later."

"Count on it," she said.

Jones and Carroll returned to the lobby after Dr. Dahlberg and two assistants wheeled out Dodge's body. The sight of the white-sheeted corpse was too much for Mrs. Schmidt, who broke out in tears. None of the other office staff was so moved, a fact Rafferty noted with interest.

"We need to talk, sir," Jones told Nelligan. "Somewhere private would be best."

"Feel free to use my office," J. D. Carr said.

Nelligan nodded, adding: "Mr. Rafferty can join us."

"I'll come along, too," Diamond said.

"I think it would be a grave mistake to admit Miss Diamond to our meeting," Jones responded. "It could greatly compromise my investigation."

Over Diamond's protests, Nelligan agreed. The chief wasn't anxious to admit Thomas to the meeting either, but Rafferty insisted, and so it was that five men in all gathered in Carr's office. Nelligan sat at Carr's desk while Rafferty and Jones claimed side chairs. Thomas and Carroll were left to stand.

"Well, gentlemen, how does it look?" Nelligan asked.

Like a labyrinth obscured by fog in a house of mirrors with all the lights turned off, Rafferty thought. Jones, however, was the first to reply. He described what he'd found in Dodge's office and apartment. His account offered no surprises from Rafferty's point of view.

"It is a novel case, sir, very novel," Jones said, "but nothing that cannot be solved. Simply because a thing looks impossible does not make it so. There is no need here for men who explain miracles."

Rafferty said, "What Inspector Jones says is true enough, though I'd point out that some things look more impossible than others. This murder may be no miracle, but it's still an extraordinary crime, calculated down to the last detail, and we'll not have an easy time figurin' out how the deed was done."

Jones, who could barely see fit to acknowledge Rafferty's presence, brushed aside such doubts. "There is, I am sure, a simple explanation to how Mr. Dodge was killed, but I need more facts. Therefore, I propose to interview at once everyone who was here at the time of the murder."

"That makes sense," Nelligan agreed. "Quick action is essential. And if you can bring this case to a successful conclusion in short order, Inspector, I have no doubt that the people of St. Paul, including the mayor and leaders of the business community, will be most pleased. Don't you agree, Mr. Rafferty?"

Rafferty grinned and said, "Why, the inspector will be the toast of the town, I'm sure, and will have flower petals strewn before him like a god. 'Twouldn't even be surprisin' if he's made chief of police"—Rafferty paused for dramatic effect—"someday. If you don't mind, I'd like to join in on the interviews. No sense doin' everything twice."

Jones started to protest, but Nelligan cut him off. "I agree. How do you wish to conduct the interviews?"

"One person at a time," Jones said. "We can talk to them right here, starting with Mr. Carr. However, I must remind Mr. Rafferty that I will be in charge of the interviews. Am I correct in saying so, Chief?"

"Yes, of course. This is your case, Inspector. Mr. Rafferty is, as I have mentioned, a consultant. Are you clear on that point, Mr. Rafferty?"

"Don't worry, Chief, I'll be quiet as a church mouse on Christmas Eve."

"Good," Nelligan said, turning toward Carroll. "Please tell Mr. Carr to come in."

The sergeant nodded, but before he could go, Jones grabbed him by the arm and said, "Once you've fetched Mr. Carr, get as many men as you can together and undertake a top-to-bottom canvass and search of this building. Start at the roof and work your way down. Find out if anyone on the floors below saw anything suspicious or unusual today. Check all the stairway doors to see if the alarms are working. Search around the perimeter of the building as well. Oh, and make sure you leave behind an officer to watch over Mr. Dodge's employees. I don't want them wandering about until we've questioned them and searched their offices."

"Yes, sir. As to the search, is there anything in particular we should be looking for?"

"A gun, obviously, or anything else that seems suspicious or out of place. Also have your men open and look out of every single window. If some kind of human fly was climbing the outside walls, he might have left ropes or other evidence behind. Another thing: find the architects who designed this building. We'll need a complete set of plans. Also get someone from the architect's office over here. I want to be certain Mr. Dodge's office is as solidly constructed as it's said to be. We'll also need an alarm specialist to make sure the system here hasn't been tampered with."

"Right away, sir," Carroll said.

Rafferty said, "I'll save you some trouble, sergeant. Reed and Stem were the architects of this building. Allen Stem is the man you'll want to talk to."

"Thank you," Carroll said and then went off to get J. D. Carr.

Rafferty asked Nelligan, "Any word yet of Mrs. Dodge?"

"Yes. She was attending a social event at White Bear Lake this morning. I'm told she's on her way. I'm frankly surprised she's not here by now. Her husband's death must be quite a shock."

She'll survive it, Rafferty thought, and she'll certainly prosper. He could hardly wait to meet her.

Out in the lobby, Steven Dodge separated himself from his coworkers and went over to speak with Isabel Diamond, who was attempting to pry information from Peter Kretch. "May I speak privately with you for a moment?"

he asked. "I'm sure Mr. Kretch won't mind. It concerns my father. I want to be certain that you know the whole story about what a fine man he was."

Diamond looked at Dodge with apparent skepticism but followed him down the hall past the secretary's office. When they were out of everyone else's hearing range, Dodge said: "My place, after work tonight. I need you now more than ever, Isabel."

"Yes," she said, touching his hand, "I know. I'll stop by, I promise."

4

"WAIT UNTIL THE INSPECTOR HEARS ABOUT THIS"

Just as J. D. Carr was about to go in for his interview, Amanda Dodge stepped from the elevator in a swirl of silk and perfume. "I should like to see the chief of police," she announced to no one in particular. "Immediately."

"Why, if it isn't the grieving widow," said Diamond, who'd been roaming the lobby like a caged tiger. "How about a statement for the press? The tragedy of it all, et cetera, et cetera."

"I have nothing to say except that I am a woman in mourning."

"Come on, don't give me that," Diamond said. "You've been waiting for this day ever since you married the geezer. Did you kill him for his money, Amanda?"

"How dare you suggest such a thing!"

A policeman intervened, telling Diamond to "get lost," while another officer went to Carr's office to inform Nelligan that the widow had arrived.

The chief greeted this news with enthusiasm. "I'll go get her," he volunteered, springing from his chair. "We will talk to her here before we interrogate the employees."

Nelligan returned momentarily with Amanda at his side. Jones stood up and offered her his chair, which she accepted with a slight smile. Turning her head slowly to inspect the five men before her, she said in a smoky contralto, "How could this have happened? How could my dear, sweet Artemus be gone?"

· · · · ·

"We will do all in our power to bring your husband's murderer to justice," Nelligan said, looking into Amanda's eyes. "Let me begin by saying that we are all terribly sorry for your loss."

"Thank you," she murmured, managing to squeeze out a teardrop. "It is indeed an awful thing."

Nelligan introduced the others in the room as she took a handkerchief from her purse and dabbed her eyes. Rafferty looked for more tears but didn't see any. Amanda, he could tell, was a woman very much in control of herself. Rafferty knew what it was like to lose a spouse—he thought every day of his wife, Mary, gone for many years—and it was a wound that never healed. Amanda Dodge did not look wounded, and he wondered if she was a red widow, drenched in her husband's blood.

Although he'd seen newspaper photographs of Amanda, Rafferty had never met her. It required only a cursory look at the newly minted widow to see why old Artemus Dodge had been so smitten. Tall and full-figured, she wore a tight-waisted black dress cut just low enough at the neckline to be tantalizing, a cloche hat, and long black gloves. Her fine oval face, punctuated by alert blue eyes that suggested a volatile mix of innocence and guile, displayed none of the sags and warps of age. Nor could Rafferty see any gray streaks in her reddish blond hair, which was pinned up except for a few wavy locks that tumbled down to her shoulders. She was a beauty, all right, and every old man's secret dream of lost youth.

"If I am late, I apologize," she announced, "but I had to return home to put on a mourning dress out of respect for my dear, dear Artemus."

Mourning, however, wasn't what Amanda's tight-fitting dress brought to mind, and Rafferty felt the electric charge that only a beautiful woman can set off in a roomful of men.

"May I see Artemus?" she asked. "I do hope he didn't suffer."

Nelligan said, "I'm afraid your husband's body has already been taken to the morgue. I will send an officer with you to make the formal identification once we're finished here. In the meantime, be assured that there is no reason to believe Mr. Dodge suffered in any way. Death appears to have been instantaneous."

"Well, there is at least some consolation in that." She dabbed at her eyes one more time, straining to find a tear, then said in a firm voice, "Tell me exactly what happened and what is being done to find whoever killed my beloved husband."

Nelligan provided a brief account of the day's events. Amanda listened intently, broke in now and then to ask what Rafferty thought were canny questions, and appeared to be utterly composed. After a time, Jones—who was eager to interrogate the widow—turned the conversation toward her movements in the days before the murder.

"Surely, you cannot think that I had anything to do with Artemus's death," she protested.

"Of course not," Nelligan assured her. "It is a matter of routine. The more closely Inspector Jones can trace your husband's activities and those of the people around him in the days before his murder, the better off we will be in finding the killer's identity. It is as simple as that."

"I understand," she said, keeping her eyes on Nelligan. "Naturally, I will help you in any way I can."

Amanda then confirmed that she'd last seen her husband the day before in his apartment, describing their conversation as "the usual sort between a man and his wife." Rafferty wondered if the visit had also been conjugal, assuming the old man was up to it, but he couldn't think of any polite way to ask the question.

Jones inquired as to Artemus Dodge's mood during her visit. "Was he nervous or upset in any way? Did anything seem to be bothering him?"

She said he'd appeared "a little bit worried" about "some business matter"—she professed not to know what it was—but that he had otherwise been in "reasonably good spirits." She added, "Artemus, as you may know, was never a jolly sort of man. I would describe him more as the stoical type. Even as his wife, it was not always easy for me to know what might be on his mind. He preferred silence to talk whenever possible."

"That must have been difficult for you," Rafferty said, earning a malevolent stare from Jones for butting in.

"A woman learns to accommodate herself to her husband. I was perfectly content to accept his silences."

As she spoke, Rafferty tried to read her face but found it barren of clues. If the lady was a liar, she was a very good one, and there'd be no budging her from her story, and no living witness to contradict her.

Jones's questioning soon turned to how Amanda Dodge had spent the morning. She said she rose early, dressed, ate, and read the morning newspapers. At half past seven she left River's Edge, the Dodge estate, in her chauffeur-driven Cadillac. The drive to the White Bear Yacht Club, about fifteen miles north of St. Paul, took almost an hour. She was still at the club when she received news of her husband's death. After "recovering from the shock," as she put it, she went back to the estate to don her mourning clothes and was then driven to Dodge Tower. Her chauffeur would confirm her story, as would "any number of ladies" at the yacht club.

As to who might have killed her husband, she said, "Artemus had enemies, of course—all men of great wealth do—but I cannot believe any of his business competitors would be behind such a crime. It must be the radicals."

She mentioned threatening letters sent to her husband but claimed that "he didn't take them all that seriously. Artemus received letters of that nature so often that he generally ignored them."

"And yet he began living round the clock in his apartment here, did he not?" Jones asked. "I am informed that he did not leave at any time during the past two weeks out of concern for his safety."

"It's true he stayed here in recent weeks, but I believe it was the unrest caused by the transit situation that caused him to take precautions. Sidney Berthelson was affiliated with some of the streetcar unions in New York, or so I have been told. Naturally, Artemus did not wish to be an easy target again."

The dead terrorist's supposed connection to transit unions was news to Rafferty and apparently to Jones as well, who asked Amanda whether any local carmen were of particular concern to her husband.

"I cannot 'name names' if that is what you mean, Inspector. But I do know that Artemus worked very closely with Mr. McGruder at the safety commission to keep a watch on all the local troublemakers. Artemus told me once that he would 'put nothing' past some of the agitators who are active now in this city."

Rafferty was itching to ask her about the terms of her husband's will, but he held his tongue. It would be better to get the information from Dodge's lawyer on the floor below. He would be able to tell Rafferty about Amanda's background and how she'd wormed her way into the financier's life.

Jones asked more questions about the "radical element," but Amanda could offer no specifics. When Jones paused to glance at his notebook, Rafferty horned in with a question out of the blue. "Your husband's death must have come as a particular shock because of the special event you had planned together. Can you tell us what it was?"

Rafferty received another unpleasant look from Jones, who said to Nelligan, "I must insist that Mr. Rafferty refrain from interrupting me. It is very important—"

"He can ask a question if he wants," the chief said. "Besides, I'm curious about this 'special event' Mr. Rafferty spoke of."

"As am I," Amanda said, staring coolly at Rafferty. "What are you referring to?"

"I was hopin' you'd tell me, Mrs. Dodge. I thought with that expensive item you got from Collette's in Chicago, you must have a big ball or party in the works."

She continued to stare at Rafferty as though appraising a large and irritating pebble she'd found in her shoe, and said, "I really have no idea what you mean."

"What I mean is that a receipt was found in your husband's pants pocket for a dress, and a very nice one at that. It was made for you in Chicago at a cost of two hundred dollars, if I recall correctly."

Amanda smiled, her features perfectly composed, and said, "Oh, of course, I nearly forgot. Artemus liked to buy little gifts for me whenever he could. He was so sweet and kind that way. But the dress wasn't for any particular occasion."

"Ah, then I was mistaken," Rafferty said, thinking a woman like Amanda Dodge might forget many things, but a $200 dress wasn't among them.

After a few more perfunctory questions, the interview ended, and Nelligan leaped from his chair to escort Amanda from the room. "Let me thank you for your help," he oozed. "We know what you must be going through."

"It is, as I said, a terrible, terrible shock. Artemus was my world. I don't know what I'll do without him."

"Well, at least you won't be poor," Rafferty remarked, hoping to put a dent in her well-armored self-assurance. "'Tis said money is grief's surest anodyne."

She took the chief's arm, smiled at Rafferty, and said, "I care nothing about the money. I would throw it into the river in a moment if I could have my dear Artemus back. You know where to find me if you have additional questions. I shall be following your work very closely. I expect my husband's killer to be brought to justice."

"He will be," Nelligan promised.

When the chief returned, he said, "I doubt that Mrs. Dodge could have anything to do with her husband's death. She seems like a very fine woman."

"Ah, but don't forget she's also a very rich one now," Rafferty noted. "I'm predictin' her grief, such as it is, will be short-lived."

"You're a cynic, Mr. Rafferty," Nelligan said. "I don't particularly like cynics. Let's take a short break and then see what Mr. Carr can tell us."

Waiting for the elevator to take her back downstairs, Amanda Dodge noticed that the policemen on duty in the lobby seemed transfixed by her presence. She was used to men staring at her and ignored them. She could not, however, ignore J. D. Carr, who came up beside her and said in a voice loud enough for the policemen to hear, "I just want to extend my deepest condolences, Mrs. Dodge. What a tragic loss you and all of us have suffered."

"Thank you," she said for the benefit of the bystanders. "It will take a long time to recover from this."

Carr abruptly lowered his voice and said, "But I'm sure you'll manage, won't you? Steven will, too, I imagine."

She shot a venomous look at Carr. "Don't be an ass," she whispered.

The elevator arrived, and the door slid open. Carr said, "Just remember, dear Amanda, I know everything."

"Not everything," she said as she pressed the button for the ground floor. "We'll talk later."

"I shall look forward to it," Carr replied.

"How's Mrs. Dodge doing?" Alan Dubois asked when Carr rejoined the group in the lobby.

"She'll be fine," Carr said, "and so will we."

Peter Kretch observed the muted conversation between Amanda Dodge and Carr with great interest. Amanda had fascinated him from the first time he saw her, although she had hardly deigned to notice him. Her quick march into Artemus Dodge's life had been a sight to behold, and not even Carr, using all of his wiles, had been able to stop her. Instead, she'd sped right around his roadblocks and insinuated herself into the old man's graces, not to mention his pocketbook.

Kretch had taken it upon himself to explore Amanda's personal history, which could most charitably be described as checkered. Others might say it was downright scandalous. Born into a large and impoverished Irish family in the so-called Connemara Patch in Swede Hollow just east of downtown, she'd clawed her way out of that hole through sheer force of will, leveraged by the gift of great physical beauty. Not long after her sixteenth birthday, she'd left for a new life in Chicago, and Kretch was pretty sure that her work experience had included a stint in the Everleigh Sisters' famous brothel. Then, at age twenty, she'd married a well-to-do businessman from Peoria who was thirty-five years her senior. Within a year, however, he'd died under mysterious circumstances in a fire at their home, leaving the widow with an estate that, no doubt to her surprise, turned out to possess more debts than assets.

After that, she'd gone back to her maiden name of Amanda Shay and disappeared for a few years, possibly somewhere out west. She'd reemerged in St. Paul in 1915 like a bright spring flower, glittering in gold and diamonds and expensive gowns, and before long Artemus Dodge had found the fragrance irresistible.

Now she stood to become one of the richest women in the Northwest, provided certain aspects of her life didn't come back to haunt her. Kretch knew all about her most recent affair, and if word of it got out, it would indeed be shocking to one and all in a conservative community like St.

Paul. Kretch wondered what she might pay to preserve her reputation and perhaps avoid a long and costly battle in probate court over her late husband's estate. It was a question he intended to ask her soon.

Although Kretch found Carr and the other members of the office staff to be pale mannequins compared to the full-blooded Amanda, they were not without interest. An office, especially one with a small number of people in proximity, was not conducive to keeping secrets, and Kretch had learned his share. When he'd started working for Artemus Dodge, he'd immediately felt a deep current of tension running through the office, but he couldn't put his finger on the source.

The sly and secretive J. D. Carr was certainly part of the problem—maybe even *the* problem. Carr was the kind of man who, at the billiards table, would bank every shot, always avoiding the straight path in favor of the crooked. In time Kretch had learned to read Carr, even to anticipate the caroms by which his schemes moved toward their desired ends. He'd also learned much about the other members of the office staff by the simple expedient of reading their personal papers late at night, when he had the office to himself while the old man slept in his steel-lined coffin of an apartment.

Kretch figured that if his after-hours snooping was ever discovered, he could justify it as a required part of his job, which was to protect Dodge and his office staff. The more he knew about the staff, or so he could argue, the better able he'd be to keep them out of harm's way. Not all the secrets he'd found out were of the savory variety. Steven Dodge had a taste for pornographic photographs and whorehouses. Alan Dubois occasionally used cocaine. Gertrude Schmidt had financial troubles brought on by bad investments. Kretch's most intriguing discovery was that someone in the office—probably Carr—had a fascination with so-called locked room mysteries.

A few months earlier, during one of his nocturnal excursions, Kretch had been trolling through the books in Carr's office when he came upon a leather-bound, gold-embossed volume titled *Collected Papers of the Solvers' Club, 1915–16*. Kretch had never heard of the club, but the name intrigued him. Paging through the thick volume, his attention had been drawn to two items. One was a paper on "Chemical Tests for Detecting the Presence of

Human Blood" authored by none other than Sherlock Holmes. Even more intriguing was an essay written by a certain Dr. Gideon Fell that described the various kinds of locked room mysteries and how to solve them. Kretch had spent the better part of two hours reading the long article, which was both fascinating and instructive. So instructive, in fact, that he'd quietly mentioned it to someone else in the office.

Interviewing Artemus Dodge's office staff consumed most of the afternoon. Jones asked the bulk of the questions. Rafferty, one hand resting on the knob of his cane, sat mostly in silence, rousing himself only rarely to seek a point of clarification. Thomas took copious notes, which Rafferty intended to review at the end of the day.

The employees' statements were entirely consistent with one another, providing an interlocked mutual alibi for the time of the murder. No one knew of any threats against Dodge other than the anonymous letters he'd received for years, nor were there any revelations regarding Dodge's business, which Carr described as "rock solid." Still, Rafferty found it odd that not one of the employees professed to know anything about the special meeting Dodge had announced shortly before his murder. With the notable exception of Gertrude Schmidt, the office staff was circumspect when it came to Amanda Dodge, offering gracious platitudes of dubious sincerity. Even so, Steven Dodge did admit to being "a bit shocked" when his father married a woman so young. As for the old man's will, Carr and Steven Dodge said it was their understanding that the business and all of its assets would go to Steven, while Amanda would receive the couple's mansion and a "sizable cash settlement."

As the interviews droned on, Rafferty found himself focusing on the great unanswered question at the heart of the case: Where had the bullet that killed Artemus Dodge come from? No matter how he looked at it, Rafferty couldn't see how the bullet could have been fired from inside Dodge's fortified office. There appeared to be no way that a killer could have shot Dodge and then escaped without being noticed, unless every single member of the office staff was lying.

Rafferty had entertained the possibility of a conspiracy involving all five employees, but it seemed farfetched. The problem was motive. What could have led five people, one of them the victim's own son, to slay a man who was the source of their livelihood? Rafferty could understand how one or two employees, for reasons not yet known, might want to kill the old man. But could all of them be tied together in a murderous plot? The idea didn't make sense.

Sherlock Holmes had once famously remarked that "when you have eliminated the impossible, whatever remains, however improbable, must be the truth." If a shot from inside the office was impossible, as all the evidence indicated, then Rafferty had no choice but to assume that the fatal bullet came from somewhere else in the penthouse or, more likely, from outside Dodge Tower, presumably from a sniper's nest some distance away.

The fact that the sash cords on the only unlocked window in Dodge office had been severed only served to bolster Rafferty's conclusion. Someone had cut the cords as part of the scheme to murder Dodge, yet the window was shut, and there were no bullet holes in the glass when the old man's body was found. So what had cutting the cords accomplished? The answer, Rafferty believed, would prove crucial to solving Dodge's murder.

After Peter Kretch, the last of the employees to be questioned, had finished his statement, Rafferty rose from his chair and announced that he and Thomas would return to their tavern "to attend to business." Jones and Nelligan offered no objections.

"Those two are glad to be rid of us," Thomas remarked as he and Rafferty rode the elevator down to the main lobby.

"And we of them. Now that we have our freedom, 'tis time to get moving."

Outside, Rafferty and Thomas found that the wind was strong and gusty, as it had been all day, whipping sand and debris into dust devils. The crowds that had gathered around Dodge Tower earlier in the day were gone, and only a few diehards remained to stare dumbly through the lobby windows or chat up the solitary policeman on duty by the front doors. A newsboy peddling the *St. Paul Dispatch* was also on hand. "Artemus Dodge killed, murder of the century!" he shouted. "Radicals suspected!"

"Sounds like the police already have a theory," Thomas said, fishing a nickel from his pocket to buy a paper.

"Or the newspapers do," Rafferty said as he glanced at the front-page headline, which asked: "DID ANARCHISTS STRIKE DOWN ART. DODGE?"

Thomas said, "I take it we'll be heading north, looking for a high place."

"We will," Rafferty acknowledged. "First I'd like to have a little chat with Louis Hill. In the meantime, why don't you take a little walk around the tower here?"

Thomas knew what Rafferty was looking for. "Doubt it will do any good. Jones already sent out some of his men to look around."

"I know, but maybe we'll get lucky."

Thomas nodded. "Now tell me something, Shad. Do you think anarchists or people of their sort killed the old man?"

"Who can say? For all we know there could be a nest of them in town right now. Or all this talk of saboteurs and whatnot could be nothing more than a way of scarin' people. These are strange times, Wash, strange times. 'Tis hard to know who to believe."

The gun, resembling a small-caliber automatic pistol, lay next to a trash can in the alley beside Dodge Tower. A young policeman spotted it and immediately sent for Sergeant Carroll, who arrived within minutes.

"Well, isn't this odd," Carroll said, bending down to take a closer look at the nickel-plated weapon.

"At first I thought it was the real thing," the policeman said.

"I'd say it's a Daisy No. 8," Carroll said. "Bought one for my son this summer. I wonder what that red stain around the muzzle is."

"Looks like blood, sir."

Carroll stood up and shook his head. "A squirt gun with blood on it. Wait until the inspector hears about this."

5

"THIS WILL SAVE ME A LOT OF TROUBLE"

"What are you doing about this brazen act of terrorism?" John McGruder demanded. His sharp gray eyes dug into Michael Nelligan like claws.

"We are doing all we can," the chief replied, trying to maintain his composure in the face of McGruder's withering stare.

They were sitting in McGruder's drab office in the old state capitol, where Nelligan had been summoned late in the afternoon. The chief knew he would be in for a hard time. McGruder was a cold and remorseless man who wore his righteousness like armor, and as chairman of the newly created Minnesota Public Safety Commission he wielded extraordinary power.

Nelligan tried to sound reassuring, though he doubted it would do much good. "We have men spread out across the city, and of course Inspector Jones is an excellent investigator. Whoever murdered Mr. Dodge will pay for his crime."

"Don't waste my time," McGruder said. "Give me the specifics. Who do you have in custody? What have you asked them? What have they told you?"

"I do not have specifics at the moment. You must realize, Mr. McGruder, that this is a large and complex investigation that has only just started."

"What I realize is that you do not seem to be in charge of your own department. How else to explain your ignorance as to the current circumstances of the investigation? By now you should have rounded up every radical, syndicalist, and shirker in this city and sweated the whole dirty lot of them. A little persuasive work with the rubber hose would get them talking. Instead, from what I gather, you've wasted the day interviewing Mr. Dodge's staff."

"I would not consider it a waste of time to interview the witnesses to a murder."

"Witnesses who saw nothing, if the newspapers are to be believed," McGruder retorted. "Is there no one in this city who knows how to run a murder investigation?"

Nelligan was not used to being spoken to with such contempt, but he had little choice except to take the abuse. McGruder—a stocky man in his midfifties with a blunt balding head and eyes as hard as diamond cutters—could have Nelligan fired in an instant, and both men knew it. Only a few months earlier McGruder had been an obscure if well-remunerated corporate lawyer in Minneapolis. Now, he was the most feared man in Minnesota.

McGruder had made his fortune defending railroads against lawsuits brought by injured workers. He'd earned a reputation as a fierce advocate in the courtroom. After hours of cross-examination, one shaken witness had remarked that it was "like being shaved by a blind barber. You know there will be blood. All you can do is pray that it won't be enough to kill you."

Above all, McGruder was a patriot. When the Spanish-American War had broken out, he'd joined the army at the age of thirty-five in hopes of marching off to battle. Instead, he'd ended up shuffling papers at a desolate base in the Carolinas, earning good-conduct medals but no glory.

Then came the Great War, and with it the chance of a lifetime. The safety commission, created by the state legislature after the declaration of war, was a legal anomaly endowed with "teeth eighteen inches long," as McGruder liked to say. It could seize property, issue subpoenas, investigate or spy on whomever it pleased, and shut down taverns or other businesses thought to undermine the war effort. It also had the power to remove public officials from office on the merest suspicion of disloyalty. There was no check on the commission's powers. It reported only to itself.

McGruder relished his power and didn't hesitate to apply the screws to Nelligan. "I need not remind you that it would be easy enough to suggest to the mayor that you are wanting in the performance of your duty. Such a complaint would not advance your career. Are you in agreement, chief?"

Nelligan swallowed his pride and nodded.

"Good. I think the solution is for me to take over this investigation and for you to follow my lead. Send Inspector Jones up to see me tomorrow. I will show him how to solve Mr. Dodge's murder. I will also assign some of my men to help him."

Nelligan waited for the next shoe to drop, but McGruder simply stared at papers on his desk. When he finally looked up, he said, "That will be all. I will be in touch if I need anything else from you."

After Nelligan left, McGruder wondered if the chief would have to be replaced. He was weak and did not understand what it took to win a war. There had to be unwavering devotion, iron discipline, and 100 percent patriotism. Dissent was treason and should be treated as such. McGruder knew all about the bombing four years earlier that had nearly killed Artemus Dodge. He was sure the radicals had struck again and finally killed the financier. McGruder intended to hunt down each and every one of them and expunge them from the face of the earth. As traitors, they deserved nothing less.

At quarter to four, Shadwell Rafferty rang the front doorbell of Louis and Maud Hill's home on Summit Avenue. Rafferty, who'd telephoned Hill in advance, had never been in the house, even though it stood next door to James J. Hill's mansion. That rock-bound edifice held many memories for Rafferty, going back to the ice palace murders of 1896, when he'd first met Sherlock Holmes. Rafferty and the elder Hill had become friends, and he'd spent many hours at the mansion, smoking cigars in the library and listening to the great man expound. He still found it hard to believe that the Empire Builder was gone, killed by of all absurd things an infected hemorrhoid.

Louis Hill, James J.'s second son and his business successor, was something of a mystery to Rafferty. He'd met him at a few civic events but didn't know him well. Louis's red brick Georgian house, greatly enlarged by a recent front addition, was quite a contrast to the old man's hulking sand-stone pile. With its Ionic portico and carefully disciplined windows, it suggested the refined elegance of second-generation wealth.

The servant ushered Rafferty down a hallway of baronial proportions, past a grand staircase, and into a solarium that afforded a panoramic view of the Mississippi River valley and the spindly iron maze of the High Bridge climbing toward the bluffs of Cherokee Heights. Rafferty took a seat on a plush gold sofa with armrests of curling white wood—some sort of French antique, he guessed—and waited for several minutes until Louis Hill appeared from a side door and came over to greet him. Hill was a compact man in his forties, taller than his father but not nearly as husky, with a trim red beard well streaked with gray and lively eyes behind pince-nez glasses. He was wearing a red silk robe, slippers, and a welcoming smile.

"Mr. Rafferty, how good to see you," he said, as though they were old friends. Rafferty rose and shook his hand. It was a good solid handshake, but nothing like the iron vise of his father's grip. James J. had been a massive boulder of a man, hard and flinty. Louis was made of less adamantine material. Around St. Paul he was known as a bon vivant and promoter. He'd led the Great Northern Railway before resigning to devote his energies to the development of Glacier National Park, on the railroad's main line. He'd also revived the St. Paul Winter Carnival in 1916. Much more so than his father, he was a man who enjoyed a good party.

"'Tis a pleasure to see you as well," Rafferty said, "despite the unfortunate circumstances that bring us together."

"Well, I will help in any way I can. First, I suggest we have a drink. Would a Scotch and soda do?"

"Very nicely. At my age a man should never miss the opportunity to enjoy fine Scotch. I will gladly consume your liquor, Mr. Hill."

"Splendid," Hill said, then called out to the servant, "Two of the usual, John."

Once the drinks arrived, Hill said, "I understand you are interested in my meeting last night with Mr. Dodge."

"I am. 'Twould be most helpful if you could tell me all that you recall about it."

Hill took a swallow of Scotch and said, "It began as a perfectly normal business conversation. Mr. Dodge, as you know, was a great friend of my father's, and I have endeavored to maintain close ties with him given our mutual business interests. We talked many times over the past year or so."

"Were you surprised that he asked to see you last night?"

"Yes. It was not his normal practice to see visitors on a Sunday. At first, I couldn't understand why he'd asked me to come over, since there was nothing urgent about his manner. Then, after we'd had a drink in his apartment, he dropped the bombshell, as it were."

Hill paused, as though waiting for Rafferty to interrupt. Rafferty finally obliged him. "I'm all ears," he said.

"I am sure you are, but I must warn you that what I am about to say has to remain in the strictest confidence, at least for the time being."

"You may rely upon my complete discretion, Mr. Hill."

"Very well. The revelation Mr. Dodge made concerned his wife. He told me—and you will appreciate now why your discretion is essential—that she was having an affair with a younger man. As a result, he intended to divorce her and, if possible, write her completely out of his will. He was very worried about the publicity a divorce might generate, and so he was considering whether to 'buy her off,' as he put it, to avoid public embarrassment."

"Did Mr. Dodge say how he'd come to suspect his wife?"

"No, nor did he identify his wife's supposed lover."

"It sounds like Mr. Dodge was certain about Amanda's infidelity."

"He was. Most of our subsequent conversation concerned how he might best go about removing her from his life. I could tell he was angry, even though he did his best to maintain his usual stoicism. I gave him the name of a lawyer who specializes in divorce matters, and I also offered advice on how to deal with the press. He seemed very grateful for my assistance."

"I'm sure he was. Was there anything else the two of you talked about?"

"Mr. Dodge made an interesting statement as I was leaving. He said he would soon have to deal with another matter that also involved 'great treachery,' as he put it. Naturally, I asked him about it, but he refused to offer any details. All he would say is that he intended to resolve the matter shortly, with 'profound consequences,' to use his own words."

"Do you have any idea at all what he might have been talkin' about?"

"Not specifically, but it must have had something to do with money. Mr. Dodge could be a puzzling man. He thought little of talking with perfect candor about his intimate relationship with his wife, but once the subject turned to money, which was truly dear to his heart, he was rarely, if ever, forthcoming."

Although Rafferty was working for Hill, he was not the sort to be obsequious, and he posed a blunt question: "I'm curious why you didn't tell me when you called this mornin' about your meetin' last night with Mr. Dodge. 'Tis information that would have been useful this afternoon when the coppers and I interviewed Mrs. Dodge."

Hill shot an irritated glance at Rafferty while he fiddled with his glasses—a nervous trait Rafferty had already noticed. "I did not think it had anything to do with the murder. Besides, I am not in the business of peddling gossip."

"Have you mentioned any of this to the police?"

"No, and I do not intend to unless my hand is forced. The police are in bed with the newspapers, and there would be unpleasant publicity if word got out that Mrs. Dodge had been having an affair. I am sure you understand my concerns. As I said, I am counting on your discretion, just as my father did so many times."

Rafferty wasn't surprised that Hill had been reluctant to bring up Amanda's affair. The rich were like any clan, and they protected one another when they could.

Hill now switched the subject, asking Rafferty if he was aware of Dodge's increasing fear that "radical elements" were once again plotting to kill him.

"I am. Did Mr. Dodge seem upset when you talked to him last night?"

"Very much so. As you probably know, he had been staying in his apartment precisely because he feared another assassination attempt. It would seem his fears were all too justified."

"Did Mr. Dodge mention any specific threat that he was especially worried about?"

"No, but I should think that Mr. McGruder at the safety commission would be able to identify the most likely culprits. Have you talked to him?"

"Not yet," Rafferty said. Truth was, Rafferty wanted no part of the commission. McGruder and his loyalists, all of the "dry" persuasion, had already shut down several saloons in the name of patriotism. It was dangerous nonsense, to Rafferty's way of thinking.

Keeping such heretical thoughts to himself, Rafferty said, "I have but one more question. Was there anyone else in Mr. Dodge's office or apartment when you visited with him last night? Think hard upon it if you would. Even if someone was admitted for only a moment—Mr. Kretch, the guard, say, or even Mrs. Dodge—please tell me."

"There was no one else," Hill said without hesitation. "That fellow Kretch was on duty, of course, but he merely directed me down the corridor to Mr. Dodge's office. Mr. Dodge himself let me in and later saw me out. He was perfectly fine when I left. Now, please tell me what you are doing, Mr. Rafferty, to catch the person or persons responsible for this crime."

Rafferty described in some detail what he—and the police—had found so far.

"Do you think an arrest will be made soon?"

"I must tell you in all honesty, Mr. Hill, that I don't know. For one thing, 'tis not yet apparent how the murder was done."

"Well, I will not deter you from your work," Hill said, rising from his chair. "Keep me informed of your progress. I do not have to remind you how important this case is. The sooner someone is behind bars and made an example of, the better. Good evening, Mr. Rafferty."

"You'll never guess what the coppers found in the alley behind Dodge Tower," Thomas said when Rafferty returned to the saloon.

"I'm thinkin' it wasn't a signed confession."

"We should be so lucky. They found a water pistol, Shad, with what looked to be blood on it."

"A bloody squirt gun? Well now, that's a queer item. What do the coppers make of it?"

"I'm not sure. The one I talked to said they'll run some tests to see if it's blood."

"Did the coppers find anything else?"

"Not that I know of. They didn't want me nosing around, so I didn't get much of a chance to look for the other part of that one-by-two we found under the old man's desk. It's possible the coppers might have it, but I don't think so."

"If Jones's men did manage to find it, you can bet we'd be the last to know," Rafferty said. "Any news from Chicago?"

"There is. I called Collette's French Fashions and talked to the proprietress, whose name is actually Marie. Don't know what happened to Collette. I had to do a little fancy footwork to get her to come around, but she finally told me who paid for that two-hundred-dollar dress for Mrs. Dodge."

"I'm guessin' by the ridiculous grin on your face that it wasn't Mr. Dodge himself."

"Nope, it was none other than Alan Dubois."

"Ah, now that's interestin'," Rafferty said, then told Thomas about Amanda Dodge's supposed affair with a younger man.

"Ain't that something. Do you suppose the old bird was killed for love?"

"Maybe. We'll have to have another chat with Mr. Dubois. In the meantime, have you managed to get notes together from the interviews?"

"They're all ready. Had to do them up fast and dirty, but I figured you'd want to see them right away."

"Ah, Wash, I don't know what I'd do without you." Rafferty took the notes, paused to draw a glass of red lager from a special batch concocted at Yeorg's Brewery, then retired to his office. He sprawled out on his plush sofa, one leg elevated, the other resting on the Persian carpet he'd received as a gift from James J. Hill. The house pianist had begun to practice, and a ragtime tune filtered in from the bar, its syncopated rhythms so hypnotic that Rafferty had to make an effort to concentrate as he read the notes. Written in his partner's usual crabbed hand, the notes included a brief summary of each employee's appearance, demeanor, and testimony during the afternoon of interrogation. The first concerned Carr:

J. D. (John David) Carr. Age 59. Born Canton, Ohio. Graduated Harvard. Unmarried. Possibly type of man not interested in women. Short, thin build, elongated face, prominent nose, close-set blue eyes, gray hair thinning at top. Precisely cut black and white pinstripe suit, custom made. White shirt, black bow tie, perfectly polished Oxfords. Speaks in clipped, precise manner.

Employed by Art. Dodge since 1902. Personal assistant since 1907. "Jack-of-all-trades." Handles correspondence, schedules appointments, meets with public officials, responds to press inquiries, etc. Believes murder committed by radicals but can't say how. Knows of no financial problems with Dodge's business. Says Dodge appeared to be "happily married" to new wife. Doesn't know why Dodge planned special meeting at 9:00 a.m.

Last saw Dodge late Saturday a.m. in office. Discussed "certain correspondence of a routine nature." Recalls that drapes were closed on window closest to Dodge's desk (the one with broken sash cords). Dodge acted normally but seemed "upset" about something. Couldn't say what it was.

In office this a.m. when stairway alarm went off. Came out into hallway. Saw Dubois. Asked what had happened. Dubois said he'd just heard alarm himself. Steven Dodge then came out of his office. Kretch arrived seconds later and checked stairway door. Found no one. Events then occurred as described by Kretch, leading to discovery of Dodge's body. Positive security door barred from inside when he and others found body. Maintained vigil until police arrived. Does not recall seeing anyone leaving Dodge's office during that time but admits situation "chaotic."

Impressions: fastidious, smart, secretive. A politician. Probably knows more than he's telling but will be tough to cross up. Has an answer for everything.

Rafferty thought Thomas's impressions were exactly right. Carr had responded coolly and capably to all of Jones's questions. He was very much in control of himself and could not be rattled. As far as Rafferty could tell, Carr had no motive for killing his employer. On the other hand, Carr struck Rafferty as the kind of man who could plot out an elaborate murder scheme. Rafferty turned to Thomas's next report:

Steven Dodge. Age 35. Only child of Art. Dodge and first wife. Born New York City. Graduated Yale. Medium height, muscular build, broad shoulders. Orange and brown plaid suit, ruffled shirt, pale yellow vest and matching handkerchief in breast pocket. Thick, curly black hair, slightly crooked nose probably broken at least once, fleshy lips, deep-set brown eyes. Handsome, athletic, likely a ladies' man. Melodious baritone voice. Heavy smoker, mostly cigars. Claims he is thinking about enlisting in military to go overseas but is probably too old.

Went to work for father in 1914 after "knocking about" for a decade or so following college. Lived in Germany for a time and also in France. Fluent in German, knows a "good bit" of French. Briefly wed after "a stupid fling" in Paris but marriage later annulled. Serves as chief finance officer for father and says business is "in excellent shape." Convinced that "agitators" murdered his father. Admits not being especially "close" to father but says he has come to have "great respect" for him. People who murdered him "should be hanged." Says he doesn't know Amanda Dodge very well but that he had "no problems with her."

Last saw his father just after noon Saturday in his office when they "went over accounts." Noticed nothing unusual. Says drapes were closed. Doesn't know why special meeting scheduled at 9 a.m. today but assumes it concerned some new "business arrangement."

When alarm rang this a.m., went out into hallway but in no particular hurry because of earlier false alarms. Dubois had gone to use lavatory and saw him in hallway as well as J. D. Carr. Kretch arrived soon thereafter. When Mrs. Schmidt unable to reach Art.

Dodge, pounded on security door with Dubois but got no answer. Then followed Kretch and Carr to discover body, etc. Stayed with others in office while awaiting police. Checked to see if security door to office had been tampered with and found that it was "closed tight." Kretch verified this. Stayed in office until Nelligan and two police officers arrived.

Impressions: reasonably intelligent but lazy. A playboy and a dandy. Likes spending money more than making it. Probably dissolute when it comes to women. Rattled dice in pocket during interview and undoubtedly frequents local gaming halls.

Once again, Rafferty found it hard to argue with Thomas's assessment. Steven Dodge was definitely a shifty character, spoiled by money and good looks. But a killer? It didn't seem likely. The next interview had been with Dubois:

Alan Dubois. Age 34. Born Philadelphia. Educated at Yale, where he and Steven Dodge were roommates. Unmarried but says he's seeing a woman. Tall, gangly, narrow face with bony cheeks, pale blue eyes, pencil lips, freckles, and straw blond hair combed to one side. High, reedy voice. Blue serge suit, white shirt, and red striped tie. Polished black loafers. Overall appearance very neat.

Hired by Art. Dodge as clerk and bookkeeper in 1914 on recommendation of Steven, with whom he remains a "good friend." Enjoys work and says Art. Dodge a "stern boss" but fair. Has "not a clue" as to who might have committed murder. Also professes no knowledge as to purpose of scheduled 9 a.m. meeting.

Worked on Saturday a.m. and saw Art. Dodge briefly in his office to discuss an accounting matter. Can't remember if drapes open or closed, but didn't notice broken sash cords. Office activities that day "completely routine."

Arrived at work today at usual time of 7 a.m. Was leaving lavatory when alarm sounded but did not see anyone by stairway door. Confirmed that Carr and Steven Dodge quickly came out of offices after hearing alarm. Also confirmed that he and Steven tried to get

old man's attention by banging on security door. Followed everyone
else into Art. Dodge's office, etc. Agrees that office door was barred
on inside. Says no one could have been hiding in office or apartment because Kretch made sure to check. Waited with others for
police. Says Mrs. Schmidt may have left briefly for some reason.

Impressions: intelligent, mild-mannered, calm, polite. Probably not the kind of man to take risks.

Rafferty wasn't sure he agreed entirely with Thomas when it came
to Dubois's character. There was a certain confidence in the clerk's manner that indicated he might have a stronger backbone than his appearance
suggested. Still, why would he want to kill Artemus Dodge? With a sigh,
Rafferty turned to Thomas's report on Schmidt:

Gertrude Schmidt. Age "none of your business, sir," but looks to
be about 60. Born in Austria, immigrated to U.S. with parents at
age of 10. Raised on farm in Stearns County, Minn. High school
education. Moved to St. Paul, married railroad worker, who died
in 1908. Trained as stenographer to support herself and two children, now grown. Heavyset, ample bosom, fleshy face with double chin, small black eyes, coarse gray-black hair pulled back in
bun. Plain white blouse, brown tweed skirt, small gold pendant.
Still speaks with slight German accent.

Met Carr at meeting of St. Paul Temperance League. Connection led to her hiring as Art. Dodge's secretary. Believes Dodge a
"prince among men" who was always good to her, but says Steven Dodge "not half the man his father was." Considers Amanda
Dodge "a gold digger" and "wouldn't put anything past her."
Thinks Dubois is "weak but decent." Isn't so sure about Kretch,
who she says is "a hard man to get to know." Thinks meeting at
9 a.m. was to discuss "some kind of a problem" but can't—or
won't—be more specific.

Last saw Dodge at 11 a.m. Saturday when she came into his
office and he dictated two letters of "a business nature." Says one

involved the terms of a loan with the First National Bank. The other concerned "a partnership matter of some kind." Says drapes were closed.

This a.m. she talked with Dodge over intercom regarding 9 a.m. meeting. Then did "usual work" until alarm sounded. Rest of her account squares with what others said. Acknowledges leaving Art. Dodge's office moments after body found to "use the powder room" in her office.

Impressions: nobody's fool, outspoken, tough, a sharp observer.

That she was, Rafferty agreed. He could see no earthly reason why she might have wanted Artemus Dodge dead, but until he knew more, everyone in the office would continue to be a suspect. Thomas's next subject was Kretch:

Peter Kretch. Age 29. Unmarried. Pudgy, reddish blond hair, watery blue eyes, boyish looking. Uniform crisply starched, shoes well polished. Born in St. Paul. Graduated Central High School. Worked odd jobs before joining St. Paul Police in 1912 as patrolman. Didn't like the work and quit after six months. Hired by Pinkertons and worked undercover in western mines for two years. Quit—"I didn't like being a spy"—and returned to St. Paul. Met Steven Dodge at a tavern (but not ours, Shad!) and learned his father was looking for a security man. Interviewed and was hired. Started a few months before Dodge Tower opened and helped design alarm system. Says work "can be boring" but still best job he's had. Wishes he could have done more to save Dodge's life.

Says he last saw Dodge about noon on Saturday in his office to discuss "minor security matters" such as false alarms from stairway door. Claims he's "pretty sure" drapes were closed. Had nothing bad to say about Art. Dodge, his wife, or fellow employees.

Impressions: no genius but canny and observant. Tends to tell people what they want to hear. A follower and not a leader.

Those comments were right on the nose, Rafferty thought. Yet he wondered how an apparently weak character like Kretch could have survived in police work or as an undercover investigator, which demanded steely nerves if nothing else.

Amanda Dodge also came in for scrutiny, and Thomas concluded his notes by describing her as "smart, tough-minded, and willful. A woman not to be underestimated." It was hard to disagree with that assessment, but could the widow really be a murderer? Rafferty wasn't ready to rule out the possibility.

Thomas's notes didn't fully reflect how intensely Rafferty had questioned each employee about the drapes on the window with the severed sash cords. Except for Dubois, who couldn't remember one way or the other, they'd all said the drapes had been closed on Saturday. For his part, Jones had been mystified by Rafferty's interest in "this silly business of the drapes," as he called it. Rafferty thought otherwise but hadn't bothered to argue the point with the inspector.

Overall, the interviews had shed little light on the murder. There simply was no smoking gun. Rafferty chuckled to himself because the metaphor was all too apt. Not only was there no gun, there was no smoke, since none of the employees had heard a shot or smelled gunpowder.

Rafferty put down the notes and dug out his watch. It was already past five o'clock, and there was still much work to do. He stretched his legs, took a deep breath, and drank the last of his beer. His stomach was sending out noisy distress signals. It was time for supper.

Inspector Mordecai Jones, lost in thought, chewed on a stale baloney sandwich in his office deep within the dingy bowels of police headquarters on Hill Street. It was still unseasonably warm, and he'd loosened his collar and bow tie before sitting down at his desk. He was tired but knew he couldn't rest, not with a hornet's nest of questions buzzing in his head. He got out a pad and pencil and began jotting down notes.

The morning had been all mystery, the crime scene a magician's cabinet full of secrets and deceptions. As far as Jones was concerned, the afternoon hadn't turned out much better. The water pistol, which had already been sent to the police laboratory for testing, was simply baffling. Its presence near the murder scene couldn't be a coincidence, especially if there was blood on it. But what purpose had the squirt gun served, and why had it been discarded in a place where it could be so easily found? Jones had no answers.

A floor-by-floor search of Dodge Tower, meanwhile, had produced only a few possible clues. An unlocked window found in a vacant office on the twenty-ninth floor seemed vaguely suspicious, but Jones was more interested in a plumber from McQuillan Brothers, a well-known local firm, who'd been seen on the same floor not long before the murder. Sergeant Carroll was trying to track the man down.

Jones's men had also searched the penthouse, even requiring Dodge's employees to empty their pockets and submit to a pat down. The employees—especially Carr—had complained bitterly, but Jones didn't care. No one was exempt from suspicion. Later, a locksmith had been called in to examine the security doors and open the small private safe in Dodge's apartment. The doors proved to be in perfect working order, with no sign of tampering, while the safe yielded nothing of value.

The interrogation of Dodge's employees had been the biggest disappointment of all. Jones had hoped to scare up an incriminating statement or two, but everybody's story was perfectly consistent. For the moment, he didn't consider any of them to be prime suspects, but they weren't in the clear, either.

Amanda Dodge might be another story altogether. Jones was a confirmed bachelor, but he'd grown up with three sisters, and he knew that she had been lying when she claimed to have forgotten about the dress from Collette's. The fact that Dodge had the receipt in his pocket indicated its importance. Jones suspected that Dodge had either bought the dress for someone other than his wife or that he'd found the receipt and concluded that another man had bought it for Amanda. A young woman married to an old coot like Dodge might just take her pleasure in a more virile man's bed, Jones thought, and if she'd done so, she might have a motive for murder. The question was how she could have pulled it off.

Jones had one other lead to pursue. Kretch had told him about Louis Hill's visit with Dodge. What was so important that the two of them had felt the need to talk on a Sunday night? Jones picked up his telephone and asked the operator for Hill's residence. The servant who answered reported that Hill was "unavailable" but took a message. Jones would just have to wait for Hill to call him back.

When Artemus Dodge's employees were allowed to leave at five o'clock, J. D. Carr lingered by the elevator until he saw Gertrude Schmidt emerge from her office with her coat and purse.

"What a horrible day this has been for all of us," he said.

"Yes," she said, fighting back a tear. "I still cannot believe what happened."

"Nor can I. But we will all get through it somehow. By the way, I believe you mentioned to me earlier that Mr. Dodge had dictated two letters to you on Saturday morning. Do you recall if one of them by chance concerned the Blue Sky Partnership?"

"Yes, it did."

"May I ask to whom was the letter addressed?"

"It was to Mr. Butler, the lawyer."

"Then it must be the letter I had in mind. Do you remember any of the specifics? I only ask because an issue has come up involving the partnership, and I want to be sure I'm aware of Mr. Dodge's final intentions in the matter."

"Well, it was a long letter," Mrs. Schmidt said, "and there were a great many financial calculations. The gist of it was that Mr. Dodge wanted to know the best way to dissolve the partnership and liquidate its assets. He also made mention of an audit, which I believe Mr. Butler was already aware of."

It was just as Carr feared. He'd known from the start that the partnership was a huge mistake. "Has the letter been delivered yet?"

"No. It's on my desk. I was going to send it out this morning, but in all the, well, you know, excitement—"

"You didn't get around to it. Perfectly understandable. I'm thinking it might be best to give me the letter so as to avoid any undue complications when it comes to handling Mr. Dodge's estate."

Mrs. Schmidt found the request curious, but Carr was in charge of the office, so she went back for the letter. When she returned with it, Carr was holding the elevator door open for her. "Thank you so much," he said with an uncharacteristically warm smile. "This will save me a lot of trouble."

When they reached the main-floor lobby, Mrs. Schmidt stepped off the elevator, but Carr remained behind. "I just realized that I forgot an important paper," he explained. "Go ahead without me. I will see you in the morning as usual."

"Of course, sir," she said, wondering how Carr, a meticulous man who never forgot anything, had somehow left an "important paper" behind.

6

"I AM THINKING HE IS UP TO NO GOOD"

The Ryan Hotel's dining room was a Gothic fantasy with knobby cast-iron columns and pointed-arch windows overlooking a grassy courtyard. Like the hotel itself, the dining room had seen its best years, but the kitchen still put out a "fine spread," according to Rafferty. Over a meal of roast beef, mashed potatoes, and larded peas, Rafferty and Thomas discussed the day's events and read the newspapers.

"I'm still mighty curious about that water pistol," Rafferty said. "An idea has popped into my head, though it may be a foolish one."

"Care to tell me about it?"

"Not yet. I want to know about that supposed blood first. For the moment, the squirt gun is just another mystery to ponder. Now, let's see what our friends in the press have to say."

All three St. Paul dailies had published special editions by late afternoon, but it was the *Pioneer Press's* banner headline—"MIRACLE MURDER IN ST. PAUL"—that best captured initial reaction to the crime.

Rafferty, to his chagrin, found that he was mentioned in every story. He received especially heavy play in Isabel Diamond's account for the *Pioneer Press*. She described him as "one of the city's old-time detectives who is reputed to be a friend of Sherlock Holmes. Mr. Rafferty is best known, however, as a saloonkeeper. It is not clear as to how he became involved in the case or what his exact role will be, although it appears he has been engaged to help lead the overall police investigation."

"We are in for it now," Rafferty said, shaking his head. "Inspector Jones will be delighted to read that I'm supposedly leadin' his investigation."

Diamond's story was far more detailed than those of her competitors, causing Rafferty to remark that "she must have a friend in the police department."

Thomas said, "She's a clever woman all right. I noticed that she views you as 'old-time,' Shad, and I don't think it was a compliment."

"I do believe you're right. 'Tis apparent I've become a has-been in the eyes of the younger set."

Although he didn't enjoy being called "old-time," Rafferty had to admit that the appellation was in many ways all too accurate. At seventy-two, he was still strong and fearless, as he'd always been, but his knees were troublesome, his hands arthritic, his stomach far too substantial, and his memory not quite the wonder it once had been.

Age had changed him in other ways as well. In his youth, he'd felt the roar of patriotism in his blood, and at seventeen he'd signed on with the First Minnesota Volunteers to fight the Rebs in Virginia. Now, in the Great War overseas, all he saw was slaughter and heartache as vast armies dined on the tender flesh of the young. Nor was he roused by the home front's seething patriotism. Loyalty, as defined by the likes of John McGruder, now trumped everything else, and Rafferty worried about what might happen if it turned out that radicals had murdered Artemus Dodge. Mob violence, even a lynching, was possible.

"I'm fearful," Rafferty said as he put down the last of the newspapers. "'Tis all talk now of 'radicals' and 'syndicalists' and 'anarchists.' If such people can be tied to Mr. Dodge's murder, who can say what people might do? The public's blood is up."

Thomas said, "I know how you feel, but maybe radicals did assassinate the old man. Don't forget, they tried once before."

"Oh, I'm not forgettin' that. I'm just sayin' this poor old town could be on the verge of blowin' up. War turns people inside out, Wash, and you see the animal beneath the skin."

When they'd finished eating, Rafferty lit a cigar and said, "I fear we have no time for dessert. 'Twill be dark soon, and we need to be on the move. Do me a favor, Wash. Go up to your apartment and get your binoculars and a couple of flashlights. I'll meet you outside at the cab stand."

The initial forensics reports arrived on Jones's desk late in the afternoon. Dr. Dahlberg's autopsy confirmed the obvious—Artemus Dodge had been killed by a bullet to the brain—but there was no evidence of gunshot residue around the wound, which meant the shot hadn't come from close range. No surprise there, Jones thought. The fatal bullet, about .50 caliber in size, wasn't of much help either. It had been so badly mangled in its collision with Dodge's skull that the police department's firearms examiner said it couldn't be traced to a specific weapon. Still, the slug's size suggested that it had been fired from an old rifle or handgun, since newer weapons tended to use smaller caliber ammunition.

The bullet now lay on a bed of cotton in a small wooden box atop Jones's desk, and the mere sight of it made him miserable. Jones had tried mightily to make sense of the bullet, to weave it into a plausible account of the crime. He'd gotten nowhere. The bullet defied all explanation. With an uncharacteristic sigh, he tugged at one end of his long mustache—its languid droop seemed to mimic his own flagging spirits—and took out his watch. It was only half past six, but it seemed much later. At age thirty-six Jones was a still a young man, but he could feel his energy flagging. There was nothing like doubt to tire a man.

Jones had solved other knotty cases during his tenure in St. Paul, and he'd decorated his office with a collection of "toys," as he called the tools of homicidal mayhem. Knives, brass knuckles, saps, garrotes, and even the bottle of Paris Green used by Mrs. Tilly to poison her dumb ox of a husband on the West Side had found a place in Jones's little museum of crime. There were also pistols of every make and model, most notably the .44 caliber Colt revolver used by young Joe Redenbaugh of Kansas City to blow out the brains of poor Alice McQuillan Dunn back in April.

For special visitors, particularly the city's merchant elite, with whom it always paid to maintain good relations, Jones liked to trot out his grimmest prize—a gallon-sized jug said to contain all that remained of Sidney

Berthelson, the anarchist who'd accidentally blown himself up in 1913. Jones's father, Ezekiel, had led the investigation for the New York City police and passed on the grisly souvenirs just before his own death. Yet not even Berthelson in a bottle could compare in notoriety with the bullet that had brought down Artemus Dodge. In the hours since the murder, Jones had done everything a good detective should do, but he still couldn't explain how Dodge had been shot.

Rafferty's appearance on the scene hadn't helped matters. The old man was nothing but a common saloonkeeper, an occupation that Jones, who did not drink or smoke, despised. Why he'd been allowed to stick his fat Irish nose into the investigation was beyond Jones's ken. Rafferty had already made a nuisance of himself, shambling around and posing questions in that ridiculous brogue of his.

Still, Rafferty was reputed to be a clever man. Old-timers in the police department never tired of reminiscing about Rafferty's role in the ice palace affair, in which Sherlock Holmes himself had appeared in St. Paul. Jones, who'd only been in St. Paul for eight years, assumed such stories were the usual mix of exaggeration and lies, and he saw no reason to think Rafferty was anything other than the buffoon he appeared to be. But he'd turned out to be a troublesome buffoon, with friends in high places, and already Jones felt that he was at times being asked to play second fiddle to the fat old fool.

Jones did not find a secondary role appealing. Around police headquarters, he was known as the "red bulldog" because of his husky build, his tenacity, and his thick head of red hair. Bulldogs yielded to no one, and Jones would take on Rafferty when the time was right.

For the moment, Rafferty would have to wait. The magic bullet, resting on its soft white bed like some perverse piece of jewelry, demanded Jones's attention. He picked up the slug and examined it under the bright light of his desk lamp. He rolled it between his thumb and forefinger, felt the slight press of its weight against his flesh.

"Speak to me," he said softly. "Tell me your secret."

The bullet maintained its Delphic silence. Jones could almost feel it mocking him. Go ahead, it seemed to say, explain how I killed the great Artemus Dodge. Go right ahead. I'm listening. Jones returned the bullet to its box and decided to get some fresh air. He went down a short corridor to the station's lobby. Jones nodded to the sergeant on duty and headed for the front entrance. To either side were a pair of double-hung windows that had been propped open to let in the breeze. Jones glanced at the windows, then came to a dead stop as though he'd run into an invisible wall.

"Are you all right, Inspector?" the desk sergeant asked.

Jones said, "Better than I have been in quite some time. Is Sergeant Carroll still here?"

"He left not more than a minute ago, sir."

"I'll catch him," Jones said, and raced out the door.

Downtown St. Paul's riverfront was a bleak maze of railroad tracks, dirt roads, junk heaps, whorehouses, and shanties strung along a narrow flood-plain beneath steep sandstone bluffs. At Chestnut Street, where there had once been a busy steamboat landing, the Mississippi's banks were par-ticularly unpleasant, littered with mounds of offal and debris. The river itself was an open drain for the city's vast effluvia, and in the low water of autumn it stank of waste and decay.

Standing atop the riverbank, Harlow Secrest wondered why his infor-mant had chosen such a desolate place to meet. Maybe, being something of a blue blood, the young man found it thrilling to go over to the other side of the tracks and mix with the lower classes. Maybe it was all romance and games to him. Secrest knew better. There was no romance—not even a faint shadow of it—in his line of work.

Known to his bosses at the public safety commission as Operative No. 12, Secrest had been assigned the task of infiltrating and spying on radical groups thought to pose a threat to the republic. The commission's defi-nition of "radical" was broad. It included not only the usual assortment of anarchists, syndicalists, and trade union rabble rousers, but also farm-ers who belonged to the Nonpartisan League and German Americans sus-pected of disloyalty.

Secrest's informant had promised "startling news." If so, it wouldn't be the first time. The man had delivered any number of good tips to Secrest in recent weeks. Unfortunately, he rarely showed up on time, and Secrest wasn't surprised as the minutes ticked away well past six o'clock. Dusk was settling in, and Secrest watched as the lights of the High Bridge came glowing to life like a necklace strung across the river. A block or so downriver lamps burned in the second-floor windows of Nina Clifford's brothel. Perhaps some fellows there were having a good time, even though it wasn't nearly the place it had been in the rambunctious days of old.

Secrest lit a cigar, and in the flare of his match he saw a rat scurrying from a large pile of garbage. He gave the beast a mock salute as it darted off into the darkness. Professional courtesy, he thought bitterly, one rat acknowledging another. Secrest hated what he did—he was a spy, pure and simple, a professional liar and insinuator—and he'd sent his share of men to the gallows or a life at hard labor. But the money was too good to pass up, and a man had to live as best he could. A clean conscience wouldn't fill your stomach or put a roof over your head.

Behind him, a Milwaukee Road freight train, its brakes squealing, crept down the steep grade of the Short Line hill. The racket got on Secrest's nerves. He turned around for a look and saw a figure walking toward him out of the gloom.

"Good evening," the man said in a familiar voice.

"Christ, you surprised me. Are you part Indian or something, sneaking up that way?"

"No, I just believe in being careful."

"Well next time, don't come up on a fellow like that. I got your message. You said you had some 'startling news.' Let's hear it."

"Patience," the man counseled in his usual condescending manner. He was tall, well over six feet, and literally looked down on Secrest, who knew the man's type all too well. God's gift to the world, this one thought he was, and smarter than everybody else just because he was lucky enough to have been born rich.

"I don't have much time for patience right now," Secrest said.

"Well then, I guess we'd best get to it. I have been in contact with my sources, and they all confirm that a fellow going by the name of Walter Battle has recently arrived in St. Paul. The name is an alias, of course, but I'm informed that he is a most dangerous character."

"An anarchist?"

"Perhaps. My sources have been rather tight-lipped, except in one particular. They tell me Mr. Battle, whoever he may be, was responsible for the murder of Artemus Dodge."

Secrest let out a soft whistle. "Are your sources reliable?"

"Of course."

Secrest was intrigued but skeptical. He'd read all the newspaper accounts of the crime and what a great mystery it was. "How did he manage to pull it off?"

"I have no idea, but I think you'd agree that the murder was brilliantly planned. If this mysterious Mr. Battle was behind it, he must be quite a genius."

"I suppose so. Is he still in St. Paul?"

"Probably. My sources think he may planning another act of terrorism in connection with the impending streetcar strike. In fact, if I'm not mistaken, there will be a secret union meeting this very night at Dietsch's Hall regarding the strike. Are you aware of it?"

"I am," Secrest said. "I intend to be there. It starts at ten o'clock."

"Good. I suggest you keep your eyes open. Perhaps Mr. Battle will put in an appearance, and you'll have a chance to become a hero."

"Heroes usually end up dead."

"Freedom always has a price, doesn't it?" the man said. "One more thing. Don't talk to the police—at least not yet—about what I've just told you. There are traitors in their ranks. Put your trust only in Mr. McGruder at the safety commission. I'll be in touch when I have more to report. Good luck to you. Oh, and have a cigar. I just got in a new supply. They're really quite excellent."

"Thanks," Secrest said. He watched the tall man make his way across the tracks and up the hill on Chestnut. Alan Dubois was an exceptional source of information, Secrest had to admit. Too bad he could be such an arrogant ass.

Secrest headed toward the nearest streetlight to check his pocket watch and take a better look at the cigar Dubois had given him. It turned out to be a Ramon Allones robusto from Cuba, and it was a far more expensive brand than Secrest was used to smoking. Maybe Dubois wasn't such an ass after all.

. . . . .

Isabel Diamond arrived at Steven Dodge's townhouse, a rambling brick Victorian a block off Summit Avenue, well after dark.

"My love, it's so good to see you," he said, kissing her on the cheek as she stepped inside. "You look beautiful, as always. Something to drink?"

"Not now. I still have another story to write tonight."

Dodge followed her into the front parlor, where she sat down on a red velvet love seat that clashed violently with an Aubusson rug he'd recently purchased in France. The love seat was one of many mismatched pieces of furniture in the townhouse, which spread over three floors and twelve rooms. Dodge had no taste in furniture, clothes, art, or anything else as far as Diamond could tell, and his house had the feel of a giant boy's playroom, full of toys, chaos, and cats. At least six felines roamed the house, but Diamond knew the names of only two—Morpheus and Hades. Morpheus, as befitting his name, dozed on the love seat's armrest like a sleeping sphinx. Hades was presumably in the nether regions of the house hunting mice.

Dodge mixed himself a whisky and soda, then sat beside her, wrapping an arm around her shoulders. One of the cats jumped up to sit in his lap. "What a busy day you've had! I suppose you'll be all over the front page of the *Pioneer Press* in the morning. That must be very exciting for you."

"I'm past that. Besides, my dear, let's talk about you. My day has been nothing compared to yours. Seeing your father dead—why, I can't imagine what you must have felt."

"Yes, it was an awful thing. I'm still in shock, if you want to know the truth. But I'll get over it. I have to. Father always taught me to be brave."

What a crock, Diamond thought. As a newspaper reporter, she was a connoisseur of insincerity in its many guises, and she saw no evidence of mourning in Steven's wide brown eyes. Then again, why should there be? She'd spent enough time with him to know that he'd always been on distant terms with his father.

"Well, it's quite a mystery, if nothing else," she said. "How do you suppose the murder was accomplished?"

Dodge took a gulp from his drink and said, "Can you keep a secret, Isabel? I mean, really and truly?"

"Of course."

"Well, not ten minutes ago I got a call from Chief Nelligan. He says the police have all but ruled out the possibility that Father was shot from inside his office. There had to be an assassin somewhere outside the building."

Diamond's heart began to race. "Really? I just wonder how that could be. Tell me more, my love."

"I shouldn't," he said, sliding his left hand down toward her breasts. She gently pushed it away, feeling the urgent warmth of his body next to hers. They'd been seeing each other for several months, and he'd done his utmost to bed her. She'd resisted, not because of any great moral scruples—she'd surrendered her virginity, quite happily, long ago—but because she knew that once Dodge managed to have sex with her, he'd dump her and move on to the next conquest. She wasn't ready for that to happen while there was still useful information to be had.

Still holding his wayward hand, she turned and kissed him with just enough passion to keep him interested. "You know you can always talk to me. Now, what exactly did the chief say about your poor father's murder?"

With her children on their own and her husband long dead, Gertrude Schmidt was content to live by herself in a small apartment on the Grand Avenue trolley line. She'd made a cozy nest of it, filling the parlor with examples of her embroidery and quilt work, along with shelves full of Hummel figurines bought years ago on a trip to Germany arranged through her friends at the Volkfest House on Summit Avenue. She was proud of her German Austrian heritage, but now it caused her much anxiety.

"I suppose you and your kind will be supporting the Huns," one of her neighbors had said to her after the declaration of war against Germany. "I know how you people stick together." Other residents of her building had stopped greeting her in the hallway, even after she'd said "hello," and she could see the suspicion in their eyes.

Then, in September, a man who identified himself as an agent of the safety commission had come to her door, demanding to know about "unpatriotic statements" she'd supposedly made. Another neighbor, it turned out, had "reported" her for saying the war was "a bad idea" and that America had no "business in it." She'd not denied those sentiments and finally told the agent, in the strongest terms, to leave her alone.

Her one true friend in recent months had been J. D. Carr. He'd told her not to worry about the "fools" at the safety commission, promising Artemus Dodge would "put a stop to it" if they caused her any more trouble. She admired Carr for both his courage and kindness, even if he was *schwul,* as they said in the old country.

Still, she was surprised when he appeared at her door just after supper. "I am very sorry to bother you," he said, removing his badly outdated bowler hat, "but there is a matter of some urgency I must discuss with you. Since I happened to be in the vicinity, I thought I would drop by. May I come in?"

"Of course," she said, directing him to a couch in her parlor. "Please have a seat. Would you like some tea or coffee?"

"No, but thank you."

He seemed nervous, tapping his fingers on the couch's armrest. Normally, he was a model of calm, a man whom everyone in the office relied upon to resolve the delicate problems that often arose from Artemus Dodge's financial dealings. Mrs. Schmidt called him the "whisperer," since he always seemed to be in a hushed conversation with someone or other.

"I have been thinking about our talk in the elevator," he began, "and I have a favor I must ask of you."

"You have been very good to me, sir, and you know I will help you in any way I can."

"I appreciate that, Mrs. Schmidt. The favor I ask is that you make no mention to anyone of the letter you gave me as we were waiting for the elevator."

The request did not come as a complete surprise. It was clear that the letter must have contained incriminating information of some sort. She asked, "Is there more you wish to tell me about this letter? If something illegal was going on—"

"Oh no, not at all," Carr insisted. "For reasons that I cannot reveal at the moment, the police must not know of the Blue Sky Partnership. My motives are entirely honorable. I am concerned about potential embarrassment to Mr. Dodge and his family, and I can assure you that partnership has nothing whatsoever to do with his murder. The police and that man Rafferty may interview us again. All I ask is that you refrain from mentioning the letter or that you turned it over to me. Can I count upon you to do that?"

"Of course. I would not want to harm Mr. Dodge's good name or that of his family."

"Excellent," Carr said, standing up. "I knew you would understand. Thank you so much. Again, my apologies for disturbing you at home. I will see you in the morning."

After Carr left, Mrs. Schmidt gave a good deal of thought to what he'd said. She also found herself still wondering why he'd suddenly gone back up to the penthouse in Dodge Tower after she'd turned over the letter. Was it possible he'd returned to steal the copy of the letter from her files? She'd find out in the morning.

"I am thinking he is up to no good," she said to herself as she went to get her purse from the kitchen. Carr was very smart, but he could not have known that she always kept her stenographic notebook in her purse. If both copies of the letter were in Carr's hands, she could always make another from her shorthand notes. Then, if need be, she'd take steps to protect her own interests.

7

"THESE MEN HAVE BUSINESS WITH ME"

"'Tis time to do some lookin' and figurin'," Shadwell Rafferty said. He and Wash Thomas had finished their dinner and stood on Sixth Street in front of the Ryan, gazing up at Dodge Tower. The building's pyramidal roof, sheathed in copper, glowed in the last rays of the setting sun like the burning end of a giant cigar.

"If the bullet came from outside Dodge's office, it must have been fired from north of here, and probably from a high elevation," Thomas suggested.

"Just what I'm thinkin'," Rafferty said. Using Thomas's binoculars, he scanned the tower's upper floors, including the "birdcage." He couldn't see the penthouse windows because of their setback. A shot from the street at Dodge's office was out of the question.

A row of taxis idled around the corner on Robert Street. Rafferty and Thomas got into the first one in line, a bright yellow Model T. "We'll be goin' to Merriam's Lookout," Rafferty told the driver, a large man with a stubby head and rolls of fat ringing his neck like a collar of sausages.

The driver eased his cab into gear and said, "You gentlemen must be sightseers."

"So we are, and we're on a tight schedule," Rafferty said. "Now step on it if you would."

Merriam's Lookout, which commanded a panoramic view of downtown St. Paul, was a cul-de-sac set behind a circling granite wall on a broad hill just above the new Minnesota State Capitol. The lookout took its name from a prominent father and son who'd built mansions nearby in the 1880s when St. Paul was still a city of fresh dreams. Some of the big houses that once crowned the hill were already gone. Others had faded into shabby gentility, their wealthy owners replaced by a much lower class of roomers. The lookout itself had gone to weeds.

Rafferty instructed the cabbie to stop by a rusty iron railing atop the wall. "We'll take in the view here. Kindly wait for us."

"It's your dime," the cabbie said.

Rafferty and Thomas stepped out into a strong southerly wind that slapped at their faces as they took in the modest splendors of St. Paul's skyline. The day had turned to purple twilight, and darkness wouldn't be far behind. Dodge Tower dominated the scene, its gray granite walls giving way to shadows in the dying light. Although it wouldn't have cut much of a figure amid the behemoths of New York or Chicago, the tower was impressive against the backdrop of its more modest neighbors.

"What do you think?" Rafferty asked after he and Thomas took turns looking through binoculars to scout out a possible sniper's nest.

"Well, the first thing I'd say is that it's too far from here for a good shot at Dodge's office."

Rafferty nodded. "You'd have to be Annie Oakley on her best day. A round from a scoped Springfield, say, would get there all right, but puttin' it into the old man's head with the wind blowin' like it is . . . well, you'd need more luck than most of us have in a lifetime."

Thomas scanned the skyline again, concentrating on what lay north of Dodge Tower. One building stood out, its central tower rising to a dome and cupola.

"The old capitol," Thomas said. "That would have to be the spot."

Rafferty said, "My thoughts exactly. From what I know, it's mostly vacant now, and the lookout in the tower is closed. But if I were goin' to take a potshot at Artemus Dodge, that's where I'd go."

Artemus Dodge's twenty-two-room mansion, known as River's Edge, stood amid forty acres of hilly, wooded land overlooking the Mississippi in the southwest corner of St. Paul. It was by far the city's largest estate, and the newspapers, which had devoted numerous stories to its creation, liked to call it "Xanadu by the Mississippi."

Despite the millions he'd spent on it, Dodge's dreamland suffered from a defect that became glaringly apparent once he and Amanda moved into the mansion. Although the grounds were fenced, intruders—mostly boys in search of mischief—regularly found their way into the woods, and not even a full-time security guard could keep them out. And if boys could wander the estate, Dodge knew, so could men with more sinister intentions. He'd considered chopping down his private forest and turning the grounds into a transparent prairie, but he couldn't do it. He was a New Englander, and he loved his trees. But the growing unrest in St. Paul had finally convinced him to take refuge in his downtown fortress while Amanda and five servants tended to the estate.

Insulated from the clamor of the city behind its curtain of trees, the mansion could be eerily silent, especially at night, and at times Amanda Dodge felt more like a prisoner than the matron of a grand estate. She found the house dark and gloomy and would have preferred to live on Summit Avenue, where the city's elite concentrated like gold nuggets in a pan and where grand balls and parties were a way of life.

After talking with the police and that curious man Rafferty at Dodge Tower, Amanda had returned to River's Edge and dismissed the servants for the rest of the evening. She needed privacy and time to think. She also wanted to take one more look at the contents of the safe Artemus had built into a basement wall. He'd only reluctantly given her the combination—a sure sign, she thought bitterly, that she'd never earned his full measure of trust.

Amanda had made a habit of opening the safe every few weeks to see what her notoriously secretive husband was up to. She'd found money, family jewels, stock certificates, and other small treasures but nothing of great significance. Now, with Artemus dead and a huge inheritance awaiting her, she didn't want any last-minute surprises.

She retrieved a flashlight from the butler's pantry and went down to the basement. When she opened the safe and peered inside, her heart skipped a beat. A folder she'd never seen before lay in one of the safe's small compartments. Had Artemus discovered her little indiscretion and tried to write her out of his will?

Once she paged through the papers inside the folder, she felt relieved. They had nothing to do with her. Instead, the documents—ledger sheets, receipts, earnings reports, and a long letter written by Artemus—concerned a business enterprise called the Blue Sky Partnership. Amanda had no expertise in either finance or the law, but when she read the letter, she grasped its significance at once. There had been fraud within the company of Dodge & Son.

Amanda went back upstairs to the mansion's walnut-paneled library to smoke a cigarette (Artemus, she thought gleefully, would have been shocked) and think. The onerous duties of being a rich man's widow would fall upon her shortly. She wasn't looking forward to the funeral or the hours spent with lawyers and accountants discussing stocks and bonds and debt obligations and all the other details of her late husband's business enterprises. How much easier it would be, she thought, if they would just give her the money so that she could enjoy the rest of her life spending it.

As she stubbed out her cigarette, the telephone rang. She thought it might be the police, but when she answered, the voice on the other end of the line was familiar.

"I trust you are doing well during this tragic time," Peter Kretch said with his customary unction.

"As well as can be expected. What is it you want, Mr. Kretch?"

"A meeting. Let us say in fifteen minutes, by the front gates of the estate. I have something to show you."

"I don't understand—"

Kretch didn't let her finish. "It's a photograph, my dear Amanda, showing you with a certain gentleman who is not your husband. In fact, I have in my possession several pictures that the police would be most interested to see, since they suggest a motive for murder."

Amanda knew what would come next. "You'll want money, I suppose."

"I always said you were a clever woman. We'll discuss the terms when we meet. Oh, and make sure you come alone. If anything happens to me, the photos go to the police. See you soon."

Amanda hung up, feeling queasy. She took a deep breath, trying to calm herself, then went up to the master bedroom. Artemus had always kept a loaded pistol in the nightstand. If that blackmailing bastard Kretch wanted trouble, she'd be ready for him.

Darkness had settled in by the time the cabbie let Rafferty and Thomas off in front of the old state capitol, a red brick relic at Tenth and Wabasha streets. It had been built quickly and none too well in the early 1880s after the first capitol burned in a fast-spreading fire that sent lawmakers scurrying for their lives. The building had never been loved—one newspaper dubbed it "a useless, miserable and rotten pile"—and it had been used mainly for storage after the new capitol opened in 1905.

Rafferty and Thomas mounted a stone staircase leading up to the main doors, then entered a gloomy, echoing vestibule with gray marble walls and crumbling plaster ceilings. An elderly guard in a faded blue uniform sat behind a makeshift table. He didn't look happy to see them.

"Building is closed," he said.

"Ah, but you're here," Rafferty replied amiably. "So I'm thinkin' it must be open."

"I don't like smart alecks," said the guard, who had the small alert face and dark little eyes of a carnivorous bird. "You can go out the same way you came in."

Rafferty noticed a small hand-printed sign next to the guard's desk. It said, "Minnesota Public Safety Commission, Room 300." Rafferty had forgotten that the commission maintained its offices in the building. It was strange that the commission had moved into such a musty old place when far nicer quarters were available in the new state capitol. Perhaps it was a matter of security, since it looked as though the commission was the building's only tenant.

"We are here to report some suspicious activities," Rafferty announced.

"Not without an appointment, you're not. Now I'm telling you for the last time, leave."

Rafferty was seized by an urge to throttle the obnoxious fellow but thought the better of it when a much younger guard, armed with a carbine, came marching up to the desk.

"Escort these men out," the older guard said.

"No need," Rafferty said. "We'll be leavin'. Your warmth and hospitality have been much appreciated."

"Now what?" Thomas asked as they stood out on the front steps.

"We've got to find somebody to let us in. We need a telephone."

"Every bar on St. Peter Street has one."

"Then St. Peter it is," Rafferty said. "Maybe the gates to heaven will open for us there."

Amanda Dodge, a pistol in the pocket of her black raincoat, walked down the long curving driveway of River's Edge toward Mississippi River Boulevard. The night was warm and windy, with a sliver of a moon drifting fitfully above low scudding clouds. She crossed the estate's gurgling brook on a small stone bridge and came up to the front gates, which were nearly twenty feet high. A pair of lamps mounted on the gateposts sent out small circles of light as Peter Kretch strode up. He peered through the bars of the gates as though interviewing a prisoner.

"You're right on time, Amanda," he said. "Your late, lamented husband used to tell me that timeliness was godliness, or words to that effect."

Amanda was in no mood for idle conversation. "Show me the photograph," she said, "or leave."

"As you wish," Kretch said, making a small bow. He produced a four-by-five-inch photograph from his coat pocket and handed it to her through the bars.

As she studied the photograph, Amanda wondered why Artemus had hired such a greasy and obnoxious man. Maybe he'd been blackmailed too over some peccadillo. The photograph was just what Amanda feared it would be. Kretch had probably taken it himself at her paramour's apartment. The angle suggested that he'd been hiding outside a bedroom window. The thought of him peeping at her was revolting, and she considered shooting him dead on the spot. But she knew he'd have copies of the photograph, and probably other pictures as well. A scandal would be extremely inconvenient for her at the moment.

"What do you want?" she asked.

Kretch's toothy grin was a rictus of greed. "Fortunately for you, I am not an avaricious man, Mrs. Dodge. But I have needs. A payment of five thousand dollars would cause this photograph to vanish forever."

"And what of the other pictures you undoubtedly have?"

"Well now, those would constitute separate matters. But why get ahead of ourselves? I'll need the money in cash, and no later than tomorrow. I'll call you in the morning to make arrangements."

"I'm sure you will. Now, do me the favor of leaving at once."

"Certainly, and let me say it has been a pleasure doing business with you."

Walking back to the house, Amanda had an idea. There just might be a way, she thought, to give Peter Kretch exactly what he deserved.

Billy Banion needed a smoke, and he knew just where he could feed his addiction without getting into trouble. As one of the National Guardsmen assigned to protect McGruder and his fellow public safety commissioners, he regularly patrolled the old capitol. It was dull and lonely work—the commission was the building's only tenant—and Banion looked forward to taking cigarette breaks. He had to be careful because McGruder despised the smell of tobacco. Banion had discovered that the building's tower, reached through a door off the rotunda, was a safe place to smoke. Even McGruder's big nose didn't reach that far.

Most of the other guards never bothered to check inside the tower, so Banion had little fear of being caught with an illicit cigarette. Shortly after five o'clock he stopped at the tower door, which was always locked. Out of habit, he tried the knob before getting out his key. To his surprise, the door was unlocked. Banion inspected the door but saw no sign of damage, and when he tried his key, the lock worked perfectly. He stepped inside, turned on a light, and peered up the winding staircase. No one was in sight. He called out but heard only his echo.

By rights, Banion knew, he should go up to the lookout to see if anyone was hiding there. But climbing 250 or so steps to a platform greased
with pigeon droppings didn't appeal to him. So he lit a cigarette and continued to listen. All was quiet. He assumed one of the other guards had left
the tower door open. Not all of them were as responsible as he was. Banion crushed out his smoke, went back out into the rotunda, and locked the
door. He'd make a note of the unlocked door on his daily log.

Alan Dubois, alone in his small apartment on Holly Avenue, was worried.
His secret life as a double—or was it triple?—agent provided the excitement he craved, but his situation was becoming untenable. The whole
sorry business of the Blue Sky Partnership could blow up at any moment,
and if it did, how could Dubois explain his own profiteering? For that matter how could he explain his whole life—the false facade of command-
ing confidence, the depraved impulses he couldn't control, the lies he told
every day?

Dubois had been drawn to the revolutionary underground by roman-
tic notions of adventure, honor, and justice for the downtrodden masses.
But the more radicals he met, the less appealing he found them. They
argued over petty doctrinal differences, had the sexual fidelity of alley cats,
and rarely bathed, while the worst of them were ruthless killers without a
dream.

Dubois was different. He needed the dream and would wither away
and die without it. Now he was having second thoughts about every aspect
of his life in the shadows. Maybe he wasn't doing the right thing after all.
Maybe he was just a pawn for people who cared nothing about him or the
cause to which he'd devoted himself.

And what if his other big secret came out? There were places for a man
of his kind in St. Paul, and they were usually very discreet. He was at the
moment well below suspicion but even the merest wisp of a rumor could
ruin him.

Dubois began to think that he'd have to leave St. Paul for good. A fresh
start somewhere else might give him a chance to sort out all of his agonizing doubts. There was only one person in the world he could talk to, one

person who understood his wounded heart. He picked up the phone and asked the operator to connect him to the residence of J. D. Carr.

"I need help," he said when he heard Carr's voice. "I need help more than I've ever needed it before."

Sergeant Francis Carroll, tired from his long day's work, was ready to head home when Jones rudely interrupted his plans. Only later would the sergeant learn that the sight of an open window at the police station had suddenly inspired his boss. Carroll was a half block away from the police station when Jones came rushing out like a man on fire, a flashlight in his hand.

"Come along, Fran," he shouted. "By God, I think I've figured this thing out!"

It was past seven, and Carroll was looking forward to a night with his family, but he knew that once Jones had an idea, there was no stopping him. Jones was the kind of man who couldn't let anything go. If there was a lead to be pursued, no matter how vague or tenuous, Jones would go after it immediately, and the hour didn't matter.

The red bulldog had not acquired his tenacious reputation for nothing. Some of his colleagues, in fact, regarded him as downright obsessive. But that was how crimes got solved, Carroll thought, by digging and digging and digging and never giving up. And God knew, the murder of Artemus Dodge would be a test even for a man of Jones's fierce determination.

Once Carroll had fetched his own flashlight, they walked up Wabasha Street, which was fairly quiet except in the theater district at Seventh, where the chaser lights of the Alhambra, Blue Horse, Gem, and Majestic, among others, lit up the night, attracting animated clusters of young people. Jones, who'd been moving at his usual breakneck pace, kept going up to Exchange Street, where he stopped and wheeled around. The office lights of downtown buildings still burned through the darkness, the highest of all illuminating Dodge Tower.

"He had to be here," Jones said, turning his head and, with a dramatic flourish, extending his left arm toward the old capitol. "I have been thinking about this, and I have no doubt."

Carroll was confused. "Who had to be here, sir?"

"The shooter, sergeant, the shooter. Let's go inside."

"But I don't see how," Carroll said, thinking of the scene in Dodge's office—the windows all closed and not a bullet hole to be found anywhere.

"You will. Trust me."

Jones bounded up the front steps and tried the glass doors. They were locked, but there was a light in the lobby, and Jones pounded away like an angry child until an old man in a guard's uniform appeared. Jones waved his badge through the glass. With a nod, the guard let them in.

"You should have used the intercom," said the guard, pointing to a small button and speaker next to the doors. "No need for all of that pounding. Besides, the building is closed."

Jones didn't care about the security arrangements. "We need to go up into the tower right now. It is a matter of urgent police business."

The guard scratched his stubbly chin and said, "Well, I don't know anything about it. You'll have to talk with Mr. McGruder. Wait here and I'll call him."

"We'll wait inside," Jones said, slipping his foot inside the door before the guard could close it.

The guard grumbled and said, "All right, but don't the two of you leave my sight until I've talked to Mr. McGruder."

Jones said, "Just be quick about it. We have no time to waste."

"Nobody in this old world has time to waste," the guard muttered before speaking into the intercom on his desk. "Mr. McGruder, there's an Inspector Jones of the St. Paul Police here. He wants to go up into the tower for some reason."

The reply came immediately: "Is that so? Well, send him up to my office."

"Very good, sir."

A voice boomed out behind them. "Wait a minute," said Rafferty, approaching from the vestibule, Thomas at his side. "The door was open, so we let ourselves in."

"You again!" the guard said. "I thought I was rid of you."

"I'm not easily gotten rid of. 'Tis one of my most charmin' traits. By the way, I talked to Mr. McGruder a few minutes ago on the telephone. Tell him Shadwell Rafferty and George Washington Thomas await the pleasure of his company."

Jones, whose temper was on the verge of a Vesuvian eruption, glared at Rafferty and said, "What in blazes are you doing here?"

"Same thing as you and Sergeant Carroll are. I'm lookin' for evidence of murder." This statement was true. What Rafferty said next was not. "In fact, I was intendin' to call you once I had a chance. Cooperation is my motto. Yours too, I'm sure."

Jones said, "Well, it's a good thing I wasn't sitting around waiting for your call, or I might have missed this golden opportunity to be with you."

The guard, whose crankiness gave way to confusion, said, "I don't know what the two of you are jawing about, but until—"

"It's all right," said John McGruder, as he strode down the hallway from the rotunda. "These men have business with me. We can talk in my office."

8

"THIS IS A RUM CASE ALL AROUND"

The safety commission's office occupied a suite of nondescript rooms with cracked plaster walls, battered oak wainscoting, and furniture that looked as though it had been salvaged from one of the cheap hotels on St. Peter Street. Posters extolling the virtue of buying war bonds along with photographs of President Wilson and Minnesota Governor J. A. A. Burnquist provided the only decoration.

McGruder had chosen to locate the commission's offices on the third floor for reasons of security. Buried deep in the innards of the old building, the offices were hard to find and easy to defend. McGruder's private office was as drab and barren as all the others.

"So, I am to understand that you, Mr. Rafferty, are of the opinion that Artemus Dodge may have been killed by a sniper firing from this very building," McGruder said. "Is that what you also believe, Inspector?"

Unhappy to hear that Rafferty was one step ahead of him, Jones's only response was a nod.

McGruder said, "Well, I must say it sounds incredible. This building is quite secure. As you have discovered, guards are stationed here around the clock."

"Yes, we've enjoyed meetin' that friendly old fellow at the front desk," Rafferty said. "The truth is, there are ways around most every security system, which is why we must have a look at the tower. You see—"

"I agree," said Jones, elbowing into the conversation. "I have made a close study of the evidence, and the tower is the one place in all of downtown where a sniper could have gotten an almost straight-on, unobstructed shot at Mr. Dodge's office."

"And yet, if I read the newspapers correctly, Inspector, the windows in Mr. Dodge's office were all closed, and none of them had been pierced by a bullet," McGruder noted. "How do you explain that?"

"I have a theory that might account for those circumstances."

"What might that theory be?"

"I would prefer not to go into that at the moment. First, I want to see what evidence there may be in the tower."

"I doubt you'll find anything up there except pigeon crap."

"Perhaps. In any case, there is no need for you or Mr. Rafferty to come along. Sergeant Carroll and I can handle the job."

"Nonsense. We'll all go," McGruder said.

Out in the hallway, McGruder instructed Billy Banion, the closest National Guardsman at hand, to follow them. The door to the tower was just off a third-floor gallery that circled the old capitol's rotunda. Rafferty had been in the building many times to lobby the legislature as a sworn enemy of the "drys." Then it had been alive with the sweaty business of politics. Now the rotunda was dim and empty.

When they reached the tower door, McGruder ordered Banion to open it with his passkey. The guard hesitated, then said in a halting voice, "I think you should know, sir, that I found the door open earlier today."

"Open?" McGruder repeated in disbelief. "How did that happen and why was I not informed?"

"Well, sir, as I said—"

Rafferty stepped in to rescue the guard from a tongue lashing. "Now, son, don't be alarmed. We're not blamin' you for anything. Isn't that right, Mr. McGruder?"

"It is not a matter of blame. It is a matter of responsibility. This door is supposed to be checked every day."

"And perhaps someone failed to do so, but right now we need to hear what this strappin' young fellow has to say. Go ahead, son."

Banion told of discovering the unlocked door after coming on duty late in the afternoon. He said he'd checked inside the tower and found nothing amiss.

"Did you go up into the tower?" Jones asked.

"No, but I intended to make a note in my report about the open door."

"Wonderful," McGruder said, "just wonderful. And you've been smoking, haven't you. I can smell the stench of it."

"Yes, sir, I had a smoke when I went into the tower. I'm sorry, sir."

"It is a disgusting habit. Get out of my sight. Go on, get out!"

Banion slunk away, and McGruder said, "All right, let's do what that good-for-nothing guardsman should have done. I warn you, it's a rotten, filthy mess up there."

The old capitol's tower, like the rest of the building, had been put up in a hurry. By the early 1900s the tower had begun to settle and tilt, causing bricks to crack, floors to sag, and bolts to loosen. Its open-air lookout had then been closed as a safety precaution, and pigeons became its only regular visitors. As Rafferty labored up the tower's narrow iron staircase behind McGruder and the others, he found himself wishing that the builders had done a better job. The staircase, which hugged the tower's brick walls, rattled and shook under their footsteps, and it did not require a vivid imagination to think that they all might be sent plunging to their deaths at any moment.

McGruder switched on a series of lights along the way, but they provided minimal illumination. Rafferty had climbed up to the lookout years before. He'd thought nothing of it then. Now it was a struggle, and he lagged well behind the others. By the time Rafferty reached the lookout, he was sweating profusely and breathing hard. McGruder had found the stairs a challenge as well, but Jones, Carroll, and Thomas were barely winded. Their arrival had caused the pigeons to make a noisy exit, wings beating as they scattered into the darkness.

Wiping sweat from his brow, Rafferty said, "Well, I hope I'll not have to make this climb again, especially in view of what the pigeons have left for us as a reward." The "reward" was a film of whitish brown scum that covered the lookout's floor and stained its walls and parapets. Even in the cool evening air, the stench was terrific, and Rafferty fought an urge to gag.

Situated beneath the tower's dome, the lookout was thirty feet square with arched openings on all four sides. Jones took a flashlight from his coat pocket and aimed its beam toward the south side of the lookout. Footprints were visible in the pigeon droppings. "Is this area regularly patrolled?" he asked McGruder.

"No, but I'm sure some of the guards come up here every so often, probably to smoke."

Jones nodded and said, "We must search every inch of this platform. It will not be a pleasant job, but it must be done."

"That's putting it mildly," Thomas said, staring down at the pigeon goop that had already besmirched his new shoes.

"If we're to be minin' guano, shovels would be helpful," Rafferty said. "Perhaps we should come back in the mornin', better equipped."

Jones would have none of it. "No, we are here, and we must do our duty. Sergeant Carroll, why don't you start over by the south window there."

"Yes, sir," Carroll said, wondering if the inspector expected him to get down on his hands and knees and rummage through the filth.

Rafferty came to the sergeant's aid. "Here, use this," he said, handing over his cane. "It'll make do as a shovel."

"Thanks," Carroll said as he followed Jones to the south side of the lookout, which offered a view toward Dodge Tower through a trio of arches. Rafferty, Thomas, and McGruder trailed behind, none of them eager to muck about in the pigeon droppings.

Peering through the arches, Rafferty had no trouble spotting the tower's distinctive silhouette five blocks away. He got out Thomas's binoculars and focused on the penthouse. Lights still glowed in Dodge's office, but the drapes were closed. Rafferty wondered who'd done that. Kretch probably.

"Take a look for yourself," Rafferty said, handing Thomas the binoculars. "There'd be a shot from here to Dodge's office all right, but you'd have to be a fabulous marksman to slip a bullet between those bars guardin' the window and hit the old man, especially with the wind swirlin' and blowin' like it is today. Even with a second bullet or a third bullet or a dozen of 'em you'd have no guarantee of killin' him."

"Not a shot I'd feel confident about," Thomas agreed, "but possible, I suppose."

"Of course it's possible," said Jones. "It has to be possible because there is no other explanation for what happened."

"Maybe," Rafferty began, "but—"

"Got something," Carroll announced. The sergeant gingerly picked up a small round object with the aid of a handkerchief. He cleaned it off and said, "Well, I'll be damned. It's a streetcar button!"

Everyone knew what he meant. A "button war," as the newspapers called it, had been raging for the past month. The Twin City Rapid Transit Company, hoping to establish an in-house employees' union it could control, had issued blue buttons to be worn on the caps of motormen and conductors. The International Amalgamated Association of Street and Electric Railway Employees of America, which was fighting to organize the same group of men, had responded by issuing yellow buttons of its own. With a strike looming, the buttons had become such fiercely disputed emblems that fistfights sometimes broke out between their wearers. The button found by Carroll was of the yellow, union variety.

"A curious thing to find up here," Jones remarked.

"Not to my way of thinking, it isn't," McGruder said. "Does anyone doubt that the unionists and their allies killed Artemus Dodge?"

"A single button isn't what I'd call conclusive proof," said Rafferty.

"Nonsense," McGruder shot back. "This is evidence of a murderous conspiracy if I ever saw it."

"Do you have any suspects in mind?" Jones asked. "There are plenty of candidates, after all."

"No, I have no one in mind. I am merely stating the obvious, which is that the murder of Artemus Dodge could not have been the work of some common scoundrel. It was a crime that required much planning and sophistication."

"Sounds like you're lookin' for Professor Moriarty," Rafferty said, "except last I heard he was somewhere at the bottom of the Reichenbach gorge."

"Do you find all of this amusing, Mr. Rafferty?" McGruder asked, the lines on his forehead tightening like stretched wire. "Because if you do—"

"'Tis you who amuses me," Rafferty responded. "You've got radicals on the mind, from what I can tell, and you're startin' to see 'em every-where. Had an aunt like that, only she saw leprechauns."

"How dare you," McGruder said. His cheeks reddened. "I will see to it—"

"I think it's time we all calmed down," Jones interrupted in his com-manding basso. "Petty arguments will do us no good. But I must tell you, Mr. McGruder, that I sincerely hope the commission is not withhold-ing information that might be of use to my investigation, especially if it involves a key suspect."

"That is a most improper suggestion," McGruder said, still hot. "If there is any problem that should concern you, Inspector, it is the leaks for which your department has become notorious."

Jones glared at McGruder and said, "There has never been a proven instance of any improprieties when it comes to our dealings with the com-mission. We do not 'leak' information to radicals or others of their type, and never have. On the other hand, the commission's refusal to share infor-mation has been a constant problem, as you well know, sir."

"I do *not* know that," McGruder retorted. "And you would be well advised, Inspector, to watch your tone of voice with me. I am not a man to be trifled with. I will talk to the chief of police about your insinuations."

"And he will back me up."

"We will see about that."

Rafferty was about to intervene in the unlikely role of peacemaker when Carroll, who had been assiduously sifting through the pigeon detri-tus, spoke up: "Oh, my God, have a look at this."

Carroll was down on his haunches, the beam of his flashlight directed toward a spot on the floor. Jones and McGruder abandoned their argument and went over to Carroll. Rafferty and Thomas followed suit. All four men stared over the sergeant's broad shoulders as he lifted a shell casing out of the muck.

"Looks like it could be from a .50 caliber rifle," Rafferty said.

Carroll handed the casing to Jones, who for the first time all day man-aged a smile. "So much for the magic bullet," he said, and put it in his pocket.

. . . . .

"I am not sure leaving St. Paul would be the right thing to do," J. D. Carr told Alan Dubois. "The police would surely become suspicious."

Dubois had come over to Carr's apartment just before midnight to commiserate about his problems, although there was only so much he could tell his mentor. "Why would the police become suspicious of me?" he asked.

"Come now, Alan, you must know that the police will thoroughly investigate you as well as everyone else in the office. It's routine procedure. There's something else you should know. I didn't want to tell you over the phone, but I'm told that a receipt for a dress costing two hundred dollars was found in Mr. Dodge's pants pocket. The dress was purchased at a shop in Chicago named Collette's. Does that ring a bell with you?"

Dubois pounded his fist on the arm of his chair. "Damn it, I was just trying to help—"

Carr cut him short. "I know, I know. But once the police tie you to that dress, as they surely will, all manner of new suspicions will blossom. Fortunately, I think there's a ready explanation you can offer the police. Simply tell them you happened to be in Chicago on a business matter when Mr. Dodge asked you to pick up the dress and bring it back with you to St. Paul so that he wouldn't have to hazard shipping it in the usual way. The police may or may not believe your explanation, but there will be no one to contradict you, as far as I can tell."

"You're right," Dubois said, "just as you always are."

"I try," Carr said with a smile. "Now, how about another drink?"

"No, I have too much to do. I'll see you in the morning."

After Dubois left, Carr mixed a bourbon and water—he was officially "dry" but saw no harm in an occasional private libation—and stepped out onto a small balcony off his living room. His apartment occupied the upper floor of one of Summit Avenue's oldest mansions, built for a real estate broker who'd piled up a fortune in the 1880s only to lose it all in the market crash of 1893. For Carr, who liked to take a long view of things, the house served as a constant reminder that greed, like sex and food, was best taken in moderation. Old Artemus, for all his faults, had absorbed that lesson early in life. He loved money with an almost absurd passion, but somewhere in the back of his scheming brain a small alarm had always sounded when an excess of greed threatened to be his undoing.

Carr wondered whether Dubois, held in thrall by his own strange set of passions, possessed a similar warning device. If he didn't, he might soon find himself in very deep trouble.

Rafferty and Thomas left the old capitol well before eight, while Jones stayed behind to search the entire building in hope of finding more clues. The task of hunting for additional shell casings in the dirty white carpet of pigeon droppings had fallen to Sergeant Carroll, who was soon joined by Banion, the guard who'd been caught sneaking smokes. Neither search, Rafferty learned later from one of his police sources, produced any useful evidence.

Back in his office, Rafferty rubbed his aching knees with liniment while the day's events frolicked in his head. He wasn't sure the discovery of the bullet casing had solved anything, even if Jones thought otherwise. There was also the question of how even the most skilled marksman could have killed Dodge with a single shot from so great a distance. An even bigger conundrum was how the bullet could have passed through window glass without leaving a hole. Rafferty had a simple explanation for this seeming feat of magic, and he assumed Jones did, too. But was it a good explanation? Rafferty had his doubts.

The walls separating Rafferty's office from the tavern weren't thick, and he could hear boisterous voices, the occasional clinking of glasses, and syncopated bursts of music from the nimble fingers of Declan Muldowney, the bar's longtime piano player. Rafferty took solace in these convivial sounds. He was an old man, and old men do not like to feel alone.

It was eleven o'clock by the time he began composing a telegram to Sherlock Holmes. The day had been so full of incident that Rafferty scarcely knew where to begin. What he did know was that the message had to be concise. The transatlantic cables were largely given over to official government traffic between the United States and Great Britain, and it had become monstrously expensive to send a private message. Even so,

Rafferty thought it worth the price. If anyone could point the way to a solution to Dodge's murder, it would be Holmes. Rafferty was also relying on London's newspapers to provide accounts of the crime. Dodge was well known in international financial circles, and his murder would certainly be of interest to Fleet Street.

Rafferty was counting on one other potential bit of good fortune. He'd learned from Allen Stem, Dodge Tower's architect, that a prominent English safe company, Chubb, had bid on the security doors in the penthouse. Chubb had requested, and received, a set of plans from Stem. If those plans were still in London, Holmes should be able to take a look at them.

After several false starts, Rafferty finally settled on his message: "DODGE CASE. IDEAS? SHOT FROM INSIDE OR OUT? CHUBB HAS FLOOR PLAN. ADVISE ASAP. RAFFERTY."

Thomas came in to look over the message. He said, "By God, Shad, you've not wasted a word. You've been accused of many things over the years, but never of being concise."

Rafferty produced a great roar of laughter. "At ten dollars a word, I cannot afford to be otherwise. Now, would you take it over to Western Union? I'm hopin' Mr. Holmes can be of help to us. This is a rum case all around, and I'm thinkin' we'll be in for many more surprises before it's done."

9

"I WISH YOU GOOD LUCK"

The man going by the name of Walter Battle sat at a rear table in the Busy Bee Café on Wabasha Street, looking like any other eager young drummer in a plain brown suit. By his side was a sample case full of bottles of colored water that bore the label Wilson's Nervous Tonic and Spine Restorative. He'd come up with the name himself as a bitter joke directed at the president. The case of fake samples gave him instant legitimacy as a traveling salesman. It also made him all but invisible, since drummers were too common to attract notice, from the police or anyone else.

Battle's late dinner consisted of roast pork and baked potatoes, but the food was not nearly as interesting as the news of the day. Special editions of the newspapers had been coming out every few hours, and he enjoyed reading their accounts of Artemus Dodge's murder. He considered St. Paul's newspapers, like most others, to be servants of the oligarchs who ran the country, and he had no illusions about their truthfulness. Still, the rags could be entertaining, especially when they fawned over a dead tyrant like Artemus Dodge.

"More coffee, sir?" asked the waitress who'd brought him his meal. She looked down at the newspapers with their ominously oversized headlines and said, "A real mystery, isn't it?"

"No more coffee," he said, "but you are right about the murder. It's a most shocking thing. Who do you suppose is behind it?"

"Oh, I'd have no idea, sir. The newspaper says radicals and anarchists and people of that sort are probably responsible."

"Well, you can't always believe everything you read in the papers," Battle said with a smile as he looked into the girl's pretty brown eyes. She was perhaps sixteen, slender and fresh, and he knew he could have her if he wished. There was a telltale hunger in her eyes, a yearning to experience the mysterious pleasure that polite society fought so hard to deny her. Showing her what she was missing would be an exquisite experience, but he couldn't risk it. There was too much else to do and too many eyes looking for him.

He put down a silver dollar as a tip and said, "Thank you for your fine service, my dear. Perhaps when I'm back in town, I'll see you here again."

"Yes, that would be nice, I'm sure, sir," she said, blushing slightly.

Battle walked out into the surprisingly warm night and headed up to Sixth Street, where he turned east. When he reached Dodge Tower, he noticed that lights still burned in many of the office windows, but he couldn't see the recessed penthouse where Artemus Dodge had met his well-deserved fate. Battle smiled as he imagined the moment when the old criminal caught the bullet, aware for an agonizing instant that his life of greed and violation had been terminated. The look on his face would have been a beautiful thing to see.

A handful of people remained around the tower's entrance, where newsboys hawked their special editions. Two burly cops guarded the doors. Battle strolled past the policemen, then glanced across the street at the Ryan Hotel. A blazing sign announced "SHAD'S PLACE," the words spelled out in bold Roman letters. Battle was tempted to go in for a drink and take the measure of the saloon's owner, who'd been prominently featured in the newspapers. He decided there wasn't enough time, so he kept walking until he reached the U.S. Hotel at Fourth and Robert streets.

The tottering brick flophouse, long past its heyday, had accommodated Jesse James one night in 1876 before his gang's disastrous attempt to rob a bank in the small town of Northfield, Minnesota. Battle greatly admired James, but he had no intention of duplicating his failure. The outlaw had lacked good intelligence and a good plan. Battle was sure he had both.

He'd arrived in St. Paul a few days earlier, eager for the fight that lay ahead. Only twenty-eight, he was already a legend in the radical underground, a figure who inspired admiration and fear in equal measure. "Walter Battle" was one of his many aliases. He also knew a hundred tricks of disguise (and could even pass for a woman if need be), mixed as easily with members of the Harvard Club as with a crew of West Virginia coal miners, and was expert with explosives and guns. He was known as a man who would not shudder in even the most desperate of circumstances, and the *Chicago Tribune* had dubbed him the "cool Napoleon of terrorists," a description he rather liked. The Pinkertons had been after him ever since the Wall Street bombing four years earlier, as had U.S. marshals and police in a score of jurisdictions. He'd eluded them every time, slipping away "like a ghost in fog," as one frustrated agent put it.

Such was his reputation that only a month earlier a secret order had been issued to marshals to shoot him down on sight as an enemy of the nation. Some said the order had come from President Wilson himself. Battle, whose real identity was known only to a handful of close associates, found it darkly amusing that in the land of the free and the home of the brave a man could be executed just for arguing that the land was, in truth, neither free nor brave.

Still, the shoot-to-kill order had caused him to be more cautious, and in recent weeks he'd been constantly on the move, traveling mostly by rail as a hobo. He wouldn't be going anywhere for a while, however. Artemus Dodge had only been the beginning of his business in the city. There was much more work to do.

After a brief nap, Battle began writing the ransom note he planned to send off in a few days. It took half an hour to get the wording just right. He folded up the note and put it in an empty bottle in his sample case, next to ten sticks of dynamite. He took out one stick and slipped it into a special pocket inside his raincoat. Then he checked his .45 caliber Colt automatic pistol and reholstered it. Everything was perfect.

Battle went back downstairs to wait for his ride. His two companions for the night showed up right on time at half past ten. He slipped into the back seat of their sedan and said, "I assume you know where we're going."

"Dietsch's Hall," the driver said. "We'll be there in ten minutes."

. . . . .

The hall was a well-worn brick building in the Frogtown neighborhood, not far from the sprawling Jackson Street Shops, where the Great Northern Railway serviced its vast fleet of locomotives and cars. Long a favorite gathering place for the shops' legion of workers, the hall consisted of a saloon on the first floor and a meeting room upstairs. Illegal prizefighting had prospered for years in the upper room, but those days were over, and now it was mostly used for wedding receptions and union meetings.

Harlow Secrest arrived outside the hall just after eleven o'clock. Two other agents from the safety commission were supposed to meet him, but he couldn't find them amid what looked to be the beginnings of a riot. A surly crowd of several hundred streetcar motormen, many wearing hats and other insignia from the Twin City Rapid Transit Company, milled around in front of the hall as a dozen or so wary policemen looked on. The union meeting, which Secrest had been told would be a clandestine strategy session to make final plans for a strike, had obviously been no secret to the police. Still, Secrest had no idea why the crowd was outside rather than in the hall, so he asked a nearby idler what was going on.

"Not sure," the man said before spitting out a choice glob of tobacco. "From what I hear, somebody up there shouted something about company spies being in the crowd, even before the meeting began. Then a fight broke out, I guess. Me, I'm just here for the entertainment. How about you?"

"Business," Secrest said, watching as three young men beneath a corner streetlight pried a chunk of concrete from the sidewalk and heaved it toward one of the policemen. It sailed just past his head.

"Oh, there'll be trouble for sure now," said the man. "The coppers, they don't like it when stuff gets thrown at them."

"No kidding," said Secrest, who'd been on both sides of riots in his day and didn't care for either.

The policeman who'd dodged the concrete missile went charging after the troublemakers. Other cops followed, ready to apply a little hickory to the first body that got in their way. Secrest watched with a wary eye as the confrontation exploded into a tangled chaos of roundhouse punches, flailing nightsticks, and shouted curses.

"Damn," said Secrest's fellow observer, "this is going to be good."

Secrest didn't see it that way. He'd come to gather intelligence and look for the mysterious man named Walter Battle. A riot could make either job all but impossible, especially if Secrest got swept up in the mayhem.

At first the cops appeared to be losing the fight, but reinforcements quickly arrived by foot and in cars, and the tide began to turn. The police formed a solid blue line and advanced on the taunting crowd, swinging their nightsticks with gusto. The mob responded with a shower of rocks, bottles, and more chunks of concrete, along with a steady stream of obscenities. One small group detached themselves from the mob and raced over to a police Model T parked near the hall. The men overturned the car, tossed a match in the gas tank, and ran away as it burst into flames.

Secrest knew that riots took on their own life, like a chemical reaction gone out of control. Anything could happen. He was about to walk away from the madness when he caught a glimpse of a compact, dark-haired man in denim work clothes and a snap-brim hat emerging from the hall's lighted entryway. Secrest felt his heart skip a beat, then speed up like a train pulling away from the station.

Flush with adrenaline, he fought his way through the crowd in hopes of spotting the man again. If the man was who Secrest thought he was, caution would be in order. The man would be well armed, possibly with sticks of dynamite or grenades in addition to at least one pistol, and he would not hesitate to kill. Secrest wished more than ever that he had backup. Taking down such a vicious and practiced killer was not a job for one man.

Secrest managed to weave his way over to the far side of the hall, on Western Avenue, where he finally got another glimpse at the man, who had two big bruisers with him, just as they all climbed into a black sedan. Ignoring his own advice about playing hero, Secrest drew his revolver and ran toward the car, hoping he could shoot out a tire and then hold the men at bay until help arrived.

He got down on one knee and took aim, but before he could fire he was knocked to the pavement by a blow from behind. His revolver went clattering away toward the curb. His back and shoulders stinging with pain, he rolled over and found himself staring at a big bull of a policeman.

"Go for that gun and I'll blow your goddamn brains out," the copper said, then whacked Secrest on the back of the neck with his nightstick. After that, Secrest had no more memories of his adventure at Dietsch's Hall.

Shadwell Rafferty had his own method of "figurin' a case," as he called it. Sherlock Holmes was a thinking machine, clues and events lined up in his mind like a company of soldiers in the service of truth. Rafferty's way was much less organized. He liked to let a problem "percolate" in his head, free to wander where it might, and only rarely did he sit down and consciously try to work out a solution. The answers he needed came when they were ready to, and no sooner. So did the questions.

As he tried to fall asleep that night, one thought kept intruding itself like a persistent knock on the door. Why had only one shell casing been found in the old capitol's tower? The obvious answer was that the sniper had needed only one shot to bring down Artemus Dodge. Rafferty believed that such a bravura display of marksmanship was possible, but it was a long shot in every sense of the term.

At least two other explanations presented themselves. The sniper could in fact have fired several rounds before hitting his target, then inadvertently left a single casing behind in the tower. But in a crime as carefully calculated as Dodge's murder, would the sniper have been that careless? Rafferty doubted it. A shooter either picked up all of his shells or he didn't bother with any of them. Another possibility was that the shell casing had been left as a souvenir to taunt authorities. This idea made more sense to Rafferty. There was, after all, a kind of adolescent showiness to Dodge's murder, a delight in mystifying all who came upon it.

The shell casing wasn't the only issue that preoccupied Rafferty. How, he wondered, had the sniper gotten into the tower of a well-secured building in broad daylight, fired a shot from a high-powered rifle that no one apparently could hear, and then left without being spotted? It was almost,

Rafferty realized, another locked room mystery. He was still considering this unpleasant possibility when sleep finally came.

Like every jail Harlow Secrest had ever been in, the Ramsey County version smelled of sweat, urine, and desperation. He woke up in a cramped cell with two other men who'd been hauled away from Dietsch's Hall by the cops. Although his head felt like it'd just been removed from a vise, he managed to get to his feet and look around.

"So you're not dead after all," said one of his cell mates, who was obviously a clever fellow.

"What time is it?" Secrest asked, still trying to clear his head.

"Why, you got someplace to go?"

Secrest stared at the man, wondering if he could take him. Probably not. The guy was all muscle and attitude. "I just need to know the time," Secrest repeated.

The other man in the cell said, "One o'clock in the morning. What difference does it make what time it is in a crap hole like this?"

Secrest had no answer to such a profound question, so he sat back down on his bunk and began rubbing his head. Then a guard came by and said, "Well, ace, I see that you're awake and just in time. Got somebody who wants to talk to you."

"I don't know. The talk in here is about as fascinating as it gets."

"You're a smart one, aren't you?" the guard said, unlocking the cell door. "Just don't get smart with me. Understand?"

"Perfectly."

The guard led Secrest out of the cell block and into an office with a sign on the door that read "Chief Deputy Sheriff." Secrest had no idea who held that exalted position, but it didn't matter. The man sitting at the chief deputy's desk was John McGruder, who told the guard he could leave, then motioned Secrest to take a chair.

Although Secrest had been a safety commission operative for five months, he'd met McGruder only once before, on the day he was hired. It had been an unpleasant experience—McGruder was about as warm and welcoming as a tombstone—and Secrest didn't look forward to another meeting.

"As I understand it, you managed to get yourself arrested at Dietsch's Hall after causing a commotion. You'd better have a good explanation."

Secrest felt an involuntary chill skitter down his spine as McGruder's bleak eyes locked in on him. "All I can do is tell you what happened," he said before launching into the story of his meeting with Alan Dubois and the man he'd later seen leaving Dietsch's Hall. When Secrest mentioned the man's name, McGruder froze.

"My God, are you certain of this?"

"Yes. I've seen him before, and there are not many operatives who can make that claim. It was in Michigan, during the copper mine troubles in 1913. He spoke to some of the miners at a secret meeting when I was working undercover for the Pinkertons."

"I see. So what you are really telling me is that you had this vile terrorist in your grasp and you let him escape. Explain to me why he is not now in custody or, better yet, shot dead."

Secrest was surprised by this attack but held his ground. "I have stated the facts to you, sir. There were no other operatives at Dietsch's Hall, and I have been told not to rely on the police. If I hadn't been blindsided by that copper—"

"Don't waste my time," McGruder snapped. "I have already had a very long day. The fact is, you lost him. It's that simple."

"I did the best I could under the circumstances."

"And it wasn't good enough, was it? You are all excuses, Mr. Secrest."

"No, I—"

"Quiet," McGruder shouted, drumming his fingers on the desk. "I am tired of failures."

Secrest said, "With all due respect, sir, the biggest failure was in not having more agents on the scene. I asked for at least two additional operatives, but they never arrived."

"Don't worry," McGruder said sarcastically, "you have plenty of company in your incompetence. I will deal with the other failures just as I deal with you. But first, you will tell me why it is that your source, Mr. Dubois, came to you with his information instead of coming directly to me, as he should have."

"I believe it is because he trusts me, sir. Ever since he first went undercover, we have met regularly. Unfortunately, when he called me to arrange our meeting by the river, he gave no clue that he intended to pass on information regarding a specific terrorist. Had he done so, I would have notified you at once."

McGruder wasn't appeased. "You should have contacted me anyway, but of course you didn't. As for Mr. Dubois, I will have a talk with him. He has done signal service for our commission, but that does not excuse his oversight, particularly in view of what happened to his employer today."

Secrest said nothing, but he could tell by the storm clouds gathering on McGruder's face that he was about to be fired. McGruder said, "You are through here, Mr. Secrest. I will not tolerate incompetence. You had a chance to apprehend or kill the most dangerous man in the country, and you let him escape. And do you think for a moment that his presence here and the assassination of Mr. Dodge this morning are a coincidence? I would stake my life that he and his henchmen are behind the murder."

Secrest was a quiet man but not a fearful one, even before the likes of McGruder. He'd worked for many powerful men, tycoons of industry or rich lawyers like McGruder, and they were all alike, intoxicated by their own righteousness. Too bad they had all the money. Secrest said, "I must respectfully disagree with you, sir. I did not have him 'in my grasp,' as you put it. I merely caught a glimpse of the man. After that, I did my duty to the best of my ability. I believe I can continue to render valuable service to the commission."

"I don't," McGruder said. "You will never work for the commission again. I have nothing else to say. Although you hardly deserve the favor, I have persuaded the police to let you go."

Secrest was seething but didn't show it. How could McGruder be so stupid and so ungrateful after Secrest had given him the tip of a lifetime? How else would he have learned that Samuel Berthelson, son of the late Sidney Berthelson, and the most savage terrorist in the land, was on the loose in St. Paul? There was going to be no end of trouble now—Secrest could feel it coming on like a deep ache in his bones—and McGruder had reacted in exactly the wrong way.

"Well then, it's your funeral," Secrest said. "I wish you good luck finding Samuel Berthelson now that you've fired the only man in your employ who knows what he looks like."

Book Two

THE TERRORIST

*C*rouched behind the ravaged hulk of a streetcar, his ears ringing from the latest explosion, Shadwell Rafferty watched and waited. Up ahead, in the smoky depths of the tunnel, he heard a quick volley of gunshots. A bullet thwacked into the concrete wall behind him, sending out a spray of sand and aggregate. Rafferty had been at First Bull Run, Antietam, and Gettysburg, among other sanguinary battlefields, but he'd never heard anything quite like this violent collision of lead and concrete. He wasn't sure where the bullet had come from but guessed it was a stray round from the shooting inside the tunnel.

Behind Rafferty, a stalled line of streetcars along Third Street had become wagons in a Wild West show, marauders circling all around them. Men armed with bats, broom handles, bricks, and rocks were smashing the cars' windows even as other rioters battled a handful of policemen trying to rein in the mayhem. Shouts and screams—some from fleeing passengers—added to the pandemonium.

The night was not supposed to have ended in such chaos. John McGruder and Michael Nelligan had forecast a triumph over terrorism that would catapult them to national renown. Instead, it was beginning to look as though they'd be regarded as laughingstocks before the night was done. For all Rafferty knew, he would be, too. If Samuel Berthelson got away, there'd be no end of blame and recrimination. There might also be no solution to the murder of Artemus Dodge.

Rafferty kept his eyes on the tunnel's portal, which was illuminated by a pair of ornate lamps. The tunnel itself was a black mystery, its lights shattered by the explosions. Wash Thomas was somewhere near the other end, a quarter of a mile away. Rafferty could only pray that his partner was all right. The whole night had gone cockeyed from the start.

The .44 caliber Colt revolver in Rafferty's hand was a stout weapon, deadly at close range. Trouble was, Rafferty—a crack shot in his prime— could no longer rely on hitting what he aimed at. If the situation got too hot, Rafferty knew, he'd have little chance of beating a safe retreat. With his size and lumbering gait, he'd be the biggest, slowest duck in the shooting gallery.

As Rafferty took a deep breath, a man came running out of the tunnel. A satchel dangled from his left shoulder. In his right hand was a carbine. Rafferty leaned out from behind the streetcar and took aim, hoping luck might be on his side.

10

"I'M SURE HE'LL HAVE MUCH TO TELL US"

"Can you keep another secret, love?" Steven Dodge asked, stroking Isabel Diamond's long, light brown hair. They were at his apartment early Tuesday morning, eating a breakfast of poached eggs, toast, flapjacks, and bacon he'd prepared himself. There was nothing, Diamond thought, like a man who cooked.

"You know I can," Diamond lied, marveling as she often did at Dodge's naïveté. Did he really think that a newspaper reporter was the best person with whom to share a secret? He probably did, she thought. Steven could be such a little boy sometimes, distracted and feckless. He must have driven his father crazy. "Is it a big secret?"

"Big enough," he said. "You see, the police know who killed my father."

"Do they now?" Diamond said, trying not to sound excited, even though Dodge's "secret" could be the biggest scoop of her career. "That's certainly fast work. So who are they looking for?"

"A very bad man," Dodge said. "I talked with Mr. McGruder this morning, and he told me that Samuel Berthelson is in St. Paul. Hard to believe, isn't it?"

John McGruder was having second thoughts as he woke up from another night of short, fitful sleep. Secrest had been right. McGruder needed him, despite his incompetence, because he alone in St. Paul could identify Samuel Berthelson on sight. Grumbling to himself, McGruder found Secrest's telephone number and had the operator connect him. Secrest sounded groggy when he answered. Probably out drinking, McGruder thought.

"I have changed my mind," McGruder said without preamble. "You may report back to my office at eleven."

"Why would I want to do that?"

"Because it is your duty."

"Good-bye, Mr. McGruder."

"Wait. There's a bonus in it for you," McGruder said, knowing that money above all else would appeal to a man like Secrest.

"How much?"

"Fifty dollars."

"Make it a hundred and I'll see you at eleven."

"All right," McGruder said, slamming down the phone and wondering, not for the first time, what had happened to good old American patriotism.

The gentlemen and one lady of the local press assembled at ten o'clock Tuesday morning in the mayor's office at St. Paul City Hall, a blustery stone pile on Fourth Street occupied by all the usual species of municipal officialdom. Mayor Vivian Irvin, whose unmanly first name had proved no impediment to electoral success, greeted the reporters one by one as they trudged into his office, assuring each that he'd have "real news" to offer.

Isabel Diamond, who was among the last to arrive, reacted to the mayor's promise with skepticism. "Viv, honey, you've been mayor for a year, and you haven't made any news yet," she said, giving him a playful pinch on the cheek, "but I guess there's a first time for everything."

The reporters all knew that Irvin intended to talk about the murder of Artemus Dodge barely twenty-four hours earlier. Under normal circumstances, the riot at Dietsch's Hall would have preoccupied the press, but there was only modest interest in that event. Dodge's murder remained the talk of the city, and both the *Dispatch* and *Daily News* had already put out early morning extra editions. These proved to be long on speculation but short on fact, which meant the press was ravenously hungry for "real news." The mayor intended to provide it.

Like most people, Irvin had been stunned by Dodge's murder. Only days before, the mayor had basked in the glory of Theodore Roosevelt's presence at the city's grand patriotic parade. Dodge's violent death had instantly extinguished the warm glow left by the ex-president's visit and turned it into cold fury. The radicals who Irvin was convinced had committed the outrage would be dealt with mercilessly, and the mayor intended to apply his sharpest spurs to the police department until the job was done.

He'd already pressed Chief Nelligan to solve the crime "yesterday, if not sooner." The big men of the city, most notably Louis Hill, were not pleased that one of their own had been killed, and Irvin had heard from all of them. He knew that a quick resolution of the case would so please the city's elite that they might be moved to contribute with unprecedented generosity to his reelection campaign.

The mayor's office—a Victorian carnival of turned woodwork, dark-hued art glass, and decorative plaster swirled into gaudy patterns—was jammed with reporters and the usual assortment of city hall hangers-on by the time Irvin rose to speak. Nelligan, resplendent in full dress uniform, stood behind the mayor as did Inspector Mordecai Jones. John McGruder was there, too, making a rare public appearance. Shadwell Rafferty, who had not been invited to the podium, sat at the back of the room, curious as to how the press would react to the mayor's announcement.

"I have called you here today," Irvin said, "to announce a breakthrough in the investigation into the brutal murder of Artemus Dodge, who as you all know was one of the leading men of this city and, indeed, of this nation. Chief Nelligan has informed me that he now has good reason to believe that the murder was, as many of us suspected, the work of the radical elements who pose such a dire threat to all of us in this time of war. The chief also knows how the crime was committed, a matter that has occasioned much speculation."

The mayor paused, giving the assembled reporters a chance to jot down his every word in their notebooks. He continued, "All that remains to be done now is to hunt down those responsible for this awful crime. The chief and his men, led by Inspector Jones, a detective who needs no introduction to you, will devote their full attention to this task. I have also been assured that Mr. McGruder's agents will render all possible assistance. The bottom line is that we will leave no stone unturned in our search for the evil men who committed this evil deed. I fully expect that arrests will be made shortly or that justice will be meted out by other means. Now, are there any questions?"

Isabel Diamond, as usual, got in the first query. "So, Viv, how did these so-called radicals manage to shoot Dodge? I hear the theory is that it was a sniper. Is that right?"

"I cannot discuss the details of what the police have learned," the mayor said, adding, "and please refrain from calling me 'Viv.' As I was saying, I do not wish in any way to jeopardize the work of the police, who have been most—"

"Oh, come on," Diamond interrupted. "Everybody in this room knows that the coppers were up in the tower of the old capitol last night." She looked at Nelligan and said, "You wouldn't deny that, would you, Chief?"

Nelligan, who normally could be counted on to speak at great length to the press, replied, "The mayor has answered your questions, I believe."

"No, he hasn't, and neither have you. If you want to be the great sphinx, be my guest. I know what's going on. So what about these radicals you mentioned, Mayor? Any names you'd care to share with us?"

Irvin said, "I am sorry, Miss Diamond, but even you must understand that we cannot compromise our investigation by alerting potential suspects that we are looking for them."

Diamond turned her attention toward McGruder, who did not look eager to speak. "What about you, McGruder? I understand there's one prime suspect your operatives are looking for. A very elusive fellow, supposedly."

McGruder's face reddened slightly as he stepped forward and said, "That is not correct. There are in fact quite a number of suspects. Beyond that, I cannot go into any specifics."

"Nor can I," the mayor hastily added.

The Diamond woman was a first-class nuisance, Irvin thought, even if he did entertain certain fantasies concerning how he might spend an evening with her. He asked, "Now, is there anyone besides Miss Diamond who has questions for me?"

As other reporters barked out their questions, Rafferty started making his way out of the room and into the wide hallway beyond. He wanted to be in a position to buttonhole Diamond once the press conference ended. Her question about "one suspect in particular" had clearly touched a nerve with the mayor, and Rafferty needed to know why. Diamond, he suspected, knew something he didn't.

"Ah, Miss Diamond, how nice to see you again," Rafferty said when he caught her eye outside the mayor's office. "May I take a minute or two of your time?"

"Sure," she said. "So, how come you weren't up there for that dog and pony show with Viv and big bad McGruder?"

"Why, 'tis a fact that I am too kindly to growl like a dog and not nearly frisky enough to prance like a pony."

Diamond laughed—a deep-throated bray that surprised Rafferty. Then again, she was by no means a proper Victorian lady, or so rumor held. "You are a funny man, Mr. Rafferty. I like funny men. There are never enough of them, I've found."

"Nor have I met many women who laugh as fearlessly as you do. 'Tis a rare virtue. I'm thinkin' that since we're so full of mutual admiration, we might be able to make a deal on a certain matter that concerns us both."

Diamond arched one of her carefully tended eyebrows and said, "I'm listening, Mr. Rafferty."

Rafferty extended an arm and said, "Why don't we take a little walk. This hallway is full of pryin' eyes and big ears. The council isn't meetin' today as far as I know. Perhaps we could talk in their chambers."

"That would be fine."

The city council chambers, not far down the hall from the mayor's office, was large and echoing. Its chief item of decor was a hideous chandelier that sprouted a wild profusion of lights at the end of long iron tentacles. The chandelier was ablaze even though the room was empty and sunlight streamed in through clerestory windows.

"Well, it looks as though the city has made sure the room is well lighted for our use," Rafferty said as they took seats in one of the back benches. "I used to come here all the time for council sessions in the old days. If you owned a saloon, you'd have to lay out a nice bribe or two if you expected to get your liquor license renewed. The whole city council was as crooked as Satan's elbow back then, but it was the best show in town, especially since the representatives of the people were rarely hampered by sobriety."

"They're all sober as judges now," Diamond said, "and about as much fun. So, Mr. Rafferty, let's talk about this deal you have in mind."

Rafferty nodded and said, "'Tis a simple proposition. I believe you know something about the Dodge case that I don't regardin' the radicals who may be behind it. In return for that information, I'll give you a big clue as to how the murder might have been accomplished, at least accordin' to the police theory. 'Twould be a real scoop for you. Of course, the information could never be attributed to me."

"All right," Diamond said with her customary decisiveness. "It's a deal. You first."

"Ah, I had a hunch you'd say that. I must rely on you to be as truthful with me as I am about to be with you."

"My word is good. Ask anyone and they will tell you so."

Rafferty then told Diamond about the shell casing that had been discovered in the old capitol's tower.

"So it was a sniper after all," she said. "How did he do it? All of the windows in Mr. Dodge's office were closed, and no bullet holes were found in the glass. It still sounds like a miracle to me."

"The police are workin' on a theory as to the supposed 'miracle,' but I fear I don't know the details," Rafferty said, neglecting to mention that he was considering the same theory. He also failed to mention that he thought the theory might well be wrong.

Diamond pressed for specifics, but Rafferty, pleading ignorance, wouldn't provide them. Diamond looked skeptical. She said, "Well, I for one don't believe in miracles, Mr. Rafferty. Assuming there was some trick to the bullet passing through the glass, the sniper would still have to have been quite a marksman, would he not?"

"He would, but the shot wouldn't be out of the question, either, and the shell casing certainly suggests that someone was up in the old capitol's tower with a rifle."

"I'm curious. Why are you telling me this? It will surely anger the police once the evidence of the casing becomes public knowledge."

"It will," Rafferty said, "but sometimes 'tis best for the public to know things the authorities wish to keep secret. I'm sure you would agree."

"Oh, you'll get no argument from me on that score. But I don't mind telling you I think you're up to something. You're a cannier man than you pretend to be, Mr. Rafferty. You may fool others, but you don't fool me."

"I doubt, Miss Diamond, that anyone fools you. Now then, please tell me what it is you know about the 'prime suspect' you mentioned to Mr. McGruder. He looked quite upset when you brought up the subject."

"So he did, and with good reason. You see, I have it on excellent authority that Samuel Berthelson is in St. Paul and has been here for at least two days."

Rafferty searched Diamond's face for evidence of deception. He saw none. "You are certain about this?"

She nodded.

"Why didn't you bring up his name at the news conference?"

"And give my scoop away to every other reporter in town before I get it in the paper? Not a chance."

"Who's the source of your information?"

"I can't say, as I'm sure you understand."

Rafferty thought for a moment, then said: "You directed your question about the suspect to Mr. McGruder and not to Chief Nelligan. Is it your belief that Mr. McGruder and his agents know about Berthelson but the police don't?"

"A good deduction, Mr. Rafferty, and worthy of your friend Sherlock Holmes. Yes, it my understanding that the police don't know about Berthelson because McGruder doesn't want them to know. He doesn't trust the police one bit."

"He's afraid a radical sympathizer in the department might tip off Berthelson, I imagine." Rafferty grabbed his cane and stood up. "Well, Miss Diamond, I'd say we've both profited. I look forward to readin' the *Pioneer Press* tomorrow. There will be quite a ruckus once your story appears."

"I love a ruckus," Diamond replied with a grin. "You won't have to wait until tomorrow to read the news. There will be a special edition this afternoon. If you have any more deals in mind, you know where to find me."

After Diamond left, Rafferty lingered in the council chambers, his mind preoccupied with one question. It was obvious Diamond hadn't learned about Berthelson from the police, yet Rafferty doubted her information had come from McGruder, either. So who was her source, and how did that person know so much?

When Gertrude Schmidt boarded the Selby Avenue streetcar late Tuesday morning for her ride to work, she was thinking about her future at the firm of Dodge & Son. With Artemus gone, his business—so dependent on his genius at manipulating money—might not survive for long. Young Steven, no genius, was more interested in chasing skirts than pursuing the almighty dollar. J. D. Carr was a fine second-in-command, but he had no great expertise in stocks and bonds. She also doubted whether Amanda Dodge had any desire to continue the business. Spending money, not making it, was her preoccupation. Perhaps an outsider—someone like Louis Hill—might consider taking over the business, but that seemed a long shot as well.

As she neared downtown, Mrs. Schmidt's thoughts turned to a more immediate concern. After Carr's visit the night before, she'd dug out her stenographer's notebook and read the letter regarding the Blue Sky Partnership that Artemus Dodge had dictated two days before his murder. Just as she remembered it, much of the letter dealt with complex financial calculations beyond her understanding. But it also contained a paragraph detailing "irregularities" in the handling of the partnership's accounts. It was no wonder, she thought, that Carr had asked her in effect to forget ever seeing the letter.

Carr had told the staff not to report until noon in view of the previous day's events, but Mrs. Schmidt, who was anxious to check her files at the office, reached Dodge Tower at quarter past eleven and boarded the elevator to the penthouse. She saw no police. Everything seemed back to normal, except of course for the fact that Artemus Dodge was dead. When she stepped out of the elevator, she was surprised to find Amanda and Steven Dodge sitting in the lobby, engaged in an intense conversation. They looked startled to see her.

"Good morning," she said. "Is something the matter?"

Amanda said, "No, everything is fine, or I should say as well as can be expected after yesterday's tragedy. I am reviewing some business matters with Steven. Don't worry about us. You may go about your work."

"Of course," Mrs. Schmidt said and went into her office. As she sat down at her desk, she overheard Amanda say, "Come along, Steven. There are some papers I need to look at in your office." Mrs. Schmidt listened as they walked down the hallway past her door, but heard no more conversation.

Quietly locking her office door, Mrs. Schmidt went to a bank of wooden file cabinets lining one wall. She opened the drawer where she'd filed a carbon copy of the Blue Sky letter. The copy and the folder in which it had been placed were gone. There could be only one explanation. J. D. Carr, she assumed, had taken it, and when he arrived, she would not be afraid to ask him for an explanation.

After the mayor's press conference, Rafferty returned to his tavern, where Wash Thomas and two bartenders were already setting up for the lunch crowd. Rafferty had owned "Shad's Place," as the tavern was called, since the opening of the Ryan Hotel in 1885. The tavern's longevity was more a testament to Rafferty's outsized personality than his business acumen. He'd made a good living from the place, but he would have made much more if he hadn't been so willing to dole out money to down-and-out customers or to pour a good brand of house liquor instead of the rotgut many other joints served. Rafferty had made Thomas a partner in the business years ago, and it had proved to be a wise move because Thomas was far better with the books than he was.

The tavern was still profitable, but Rafferty believed the end was near. He was forced now to close at ten o'clock at night, a requirement that was somehow supposed to enhance the war effort. There was also talk that the federal government, to conserve grain for feeding soldiers, would soon order a cut in the alcohol content of beer to under 3 percent. If that happened, Rafferty would have no choice but to offer his patrons the wretched liquid known as "near beer."

Worse, the "drys" and their fellow do-gooders were pushing prohibition with the zeal of evangelists, and it looked as though Congress would vote to approve the Eighteenth Amendment. If enough states ratified it, prohibition would become law, and Rafferty would have to close shop. Much of Minnesota had already gone dry, as had many states, but thankfully the good citizens of Ramsey County, numerous thirsty Irishmen and Germans among them, had shown no inclination to do so.

Rafferty had always believed prohibition to be a terrible idea, not just because it would put him out of business but because it went against human nature. In his view, there was no cure for living except the ultimate one, and anything that could bring a man some small measure of cheer was to be welcomed. But the "drys" saw only the scourge of alcoholism, not the sweet pleasures of a civilized drink and good companionship, and there seemed to be no stopping their misguided momentum.

"What did the mayor have to say?" Thomas asked as Rafferty came up to the long mahogany bar and perched himself on one of the stools.

"Viv was his usual excitin' self," Rafferty said, then provided a brief summary of the news conference.

"Sounds like a waste of time," Thomas said.

"Not entirely. I had a chance to chat with Isabel Diamond. You'll never guess who's supposedly in town—Samuel Berthelson."

"Jesus."

"Don't forget Mary and Joseph," Rafferty replied with a smile.

"Do you think he's behind the murder?"

"Could be, Wash. Word is he arrived in St. Paul a few days ago, so there's a good chance he was involved. He even could have been the shooter, for all we know."

"Are the police onto him?"

"That's the funny thing. Miss Diamond tells me that the coppers are in the dark about Berthelson because McGruder over at the safety commission doesn't trust them. I'm assumin' the commission's operatives are out lookin' for Berthelson as we speak. In any case, I doubt the two of us will find him, so we might as well do some snoopin' around elsewhere."

"Any particular place in mind?"

"Dodge Tower. I want to talk to Mr. Butler, the lawyer, while you quiz the guards in the lobby. I suspect you'll learn more from them than I could."

. . . . .

Mordecai Jones was suspicious. Something was going on behind his back, and he was sure Nelligan and that blowhard McGruder were at the root of it. After the news conference, during which he'd posed behind the mayor like a piece of cheap statuary, Jones had caught McGruder gesturing toward the chief. Then the two of them had disappeared into Irvin's private chamber, no doubt to further refine their conspiracy.

"Christ, I don't know what the hell is going on here," Jones told Carroll as they made their way out of the mayor's office. "We're being gamed. I can feel it in my bones. Did you hear that question from Isabel Diamond?"

"Which one was that?"

"The one about whether there's a particular suspect we're supposed to have in mind? Good lord, man, what question did you think I meant?"

My, aren't we irritable today, Carroll thought. He could tell that Jones was about to blow. The inspector's volcanic temper was legendary, although his eruptions of late were not as frequent as they'd once been. Even so, a wise man would try to be somewhere else when the blast occurred. Fortunately, Carroll had come into possession of an item of information that just might forestall a full-scale explosion.

They had just reached city hall's front entrance on Wabasha Street and felt the first cool rush of outside air when Carroll said, almost casually, "I think I know who Miss Diamond was asking about."

Jones came to a dead stop on the steps and stared hard at his longtime assistant. "Really?" he said. "And who might that person be?"

"Samuel Berthelson. He is in the city, according to my informant."

"Goddamn it," Jones said. It was the first time Carroll had ever heard the inspector blaspheme, and he liked him better for it. "I knew it. I knew we were being kept in the dark about something big. McGruder knows?"

"Yes. His men are looking for Berthelson as we speak, or will be soon enough. My informant tells me that McGruder intends to send out every agent he has. Their orders will be to shoot on sight. The fear is that Berthelson is plotting another murder or some other outrage if the transit workers go on strike."

"What about the chief?" Jones asked. "Is he in on the secret, too?"

"Don't know," Carroll admitted, "but he seems to be thick with McGruder."

"Then he must know, and yet he's not telling us. Can you imagine that? The chief of police is hiding vital information from his own investigators. It's dereliction of duty if I ever saw it."

"Not if the mayor knows too, it isn't," Carroll noted. "I don't think you'd get much support from him if you made a scene with the chief."

Jones was starting to cool down. He said, "You're right, sergeant. We need to be careful. But maybe we can trump the chief and McGruder and even the mayor if we play our cards right. Now, tell me this: Who's your informant?"

"If you don't mind, I'd rather not say, sir. I want to protect the man, and the fewer people who know he's been talking with me, the better."

Jones wouldn't have it. "I understand what you're saying, but I must know who he is. We may have to make use of him again. You can be sure that I will not give him up to Nelligan, McGruder, or anyone else. Tell me the name, sergeant."

Carroll knew an order when he heard it. "Of course, sir. His name is Harlow Secrest, and he's one of McGruder's operatives."

"How is it he came to confide in you?"

"I met him awhile back when I was investigating that big cargo theft at the FOK warehouse across the river. Secrest went undercover there for the Pinkertons. Damn near got found out and could easily have been beaten up or worse. He's a cool customer, but he doesn't like McGruder. Not one bit. Anyway, when I got off my streetcar this morning, there he was. We said 'hello,' and before I knew it, he'd slipped a note in my hand about the hunt for Berthelson. After he gave me the note, he walked away fast, like he didn't want to be seen with me any longer than necessary."

"This is a big break for us," Jones said. "Maybe Mr. Secrest will pass along other information when the time comes."

"Could be," Carroll agreed. "So where to now, sir?"

"The station. Nelligan wants to meet at eleven. I'm sure he'll have much to tell us and even more to hide."

11

"THIS IS A THING I DO NOT LIKE"

The offices of Butler & Quinn, attorneys-at-law, were just as Rafferty pictured them in his mind's eye. The walls were paneled in fine red oak, the chairs were hefty and plush, the artwork was expensive but quietly tasteful, and the dry aroma of law books hung in the air like the scent of something old and dead. Butler & Quinn was the city's most prestigious law firm, its client list including many of St. Paul's merchant princes. Rafferty arrived at quarter past eleven, after leaving Thomas down in the lobby to extract whatever information he could from the guards there. Rafferty had been around powerful men long enough to know that they always liked to keep visitors waiting, and he was not surprised that it took fifteen minutes before Patrick Butler, the firm's senior partner and chief litigator, came out to greet him.

"My apologies for the delay," he intoned, the words sounding well practiced, "but something came up at the last minute. Let's talk in my office."

Butler was a short, round man in his fifties with the fierce features of a pit bull and, it was widely known in legal circles, an attitude to match. The twin arches of thick eyebrows dominated his broad, pugnacious face. He'd recently been the subject of a long profile in the *Daily News* in which it was claimed that the "mere mention of Patrick Butler for the defense is sufficient to instill fear and doubt in anyone who opposes him." Rafferty knew Butler, though not well, because he occasionally imbibed at the tavern.

Once they reached Butler's private office, which offered more oak paneling and shelves bulging with statute books, Rafferty took a long look around. The office, it appeared, was directly below that of Artemus

Dodge and offered an identical set of windows—three facing west and three toward the north. Butler's large desk was in about the same place as Dodge's, though it didn't occupy a podium. Whereas Dodge's desktop had been tidy, Butler's was strewn with papers.

"You will have to excuse the mess," Butler said, motioning Rafferty to take a seat across from the desk. "I'm in the midst of a case involving the First National Bank and several trust accounts. It may last forever at the rate it's going."

"Well, a lawyer could do worse, I imagine, than collect an eternity's worth of fees," Rafferty noted.

Butler let out a hearty laugh. "Right you are, Mr. Rafferty. I should not be complaining, should I? Now then, you are here to talk about Artemus Dodge, as you told me on the phone. You should know that I spoke with Inspector Jones early this morning and told him all about the will. I thought the two of you were working together."

"We are, but the inspector, who is a busy fellow, sometimes neglects to tell me things, so I like to do my own sleuthin' just to be safe."

"Sounds more like a competition than a partnership," Butler said with a shrewd smile. "In any case, I must say I'm surprised that either of you would come to see me, since from what I hear, the police already have their man."

"I wouldn't go that far," Rafferty said. "I'm curious, though. What exactly have you heard?"

"Just that the police have identified a suspect and that they have also determined how Mr. Dodge was killed. Beyond that, I know only what I read in the newspapers. Who is the suspect, if I may ask?"

"I'm afraid the suspect's identity is not a matter the police or the safety commission wish to have publicly known at this point. If you read a special edition of the *Pioneer Press* later today, you may well be enlightened."

"Then I will be sure to do so. Now, as I understand it, you are interested in the terms of Mr. Dodge's last will and testament."

"I am indeed. Anything else you can tell me about Mr. Dodge that you believe could bear on his murder would also be most helpful."

"Well, let's begin with his will," Butler said, taking a document from the top of his desk and paging through it. "I reviewed it just this morning. The final version, executed last May, contains no great surprises. Mr. Dodge willed his mansion, his personal possessions, and the sum of one million dollars to his wife, Amanda. His business interests, which are complex and varied, go to his son, Steven. There are several other personal bequests, including one hundred thousand dollars to Mr. Carr, his assistant, and ten thousand to his secretary, Mrs. Schmidt, plus lesser amounts to several distant relatives. The rest of the estate goes to charity."

"And just how much is the entire estate worth?"

"Hard to say, given the kinds of investments in which Mr. Dodge was involved. But if everything were liquidated, I imagine the total would be in the range of thirty million, perhaps a bit more."

Rafferty leaned back in his chair and said, "Well, that all sounds quite normal, Mr. Butler, just as you indicated. However, 'twould be helpful if you'd tell me the real story."

Twisting his lips into a half smile, Butler said, "And just what might that be?"

"Why, I'm guessin' Mr. Dodge was preparin' to change his will so that Amanda, who'd apparently been visitin' beds other than his, wouldn't receive a dime. I'm also thinkin' that something funny was goin' on with his business—something that caused him to schedule a special meetin' yesterday. Of course it had to be canceled after someone put a bullet in his brain. Am I wrong about any of this, Mr. Butler?"

If the lawyer was taken aback, he didn't show it. Staring at Rafferty, he said, "Let me ask you a question. Is our conversation one that might someday end up as a report in the newspapers, where fairy tales are told, or will whatever I tell you be kept in the strictest confidence?"

"The latter," Rafferty said without hesitation. "And as you well know, I can keep a secret."

Butler nodded, thinking back to a night three years earlier when, after losing a big case in federal court, he'd gone on a terrible bender, ending up drunk and disorderly in Rafferty's tavern. He'd made some sort of awful scene—he remembered little of it—but when he awoke the next morning in his apartment, there was a note from Rafferty. The note assured him that everything had been "taken care of with the police" but also warned him not to repeat his behavior. He'd taken that warning to heart.

"Yes, I know you're reliable, Mr. Rafferty, so I will tell you in confidence that you are correct about Amanda. Mr. Dodge did indeed plan to cut her from his will."

"When did he tell you this?"

"Just last Friday. I told him I could have the revised will ready for his signature late Monday afternoon—yesterday, in other words. But it was too late by then."

"So the old will remains in force?"

"Yes, though it could be contested in probate court, as with any other will."

"Did Mr. Dodge tell you who Amanda had been dallyin' with?"

"No. He simply said he had 'good reason'—those were his exact words—to believe she had been unfaithful and that he wanted her cut from the will. It was a very brief conversation. Mr. Dodge was not one to explain things or to discuss personal matters in any detail. He told me what he wanted done and that was it."

"Do you know if Amanda was aware of her husband's intentions?"

"I don't believe so, but I could not say for certain."

"What about Mr. Dodge's business? Were there any big problems of the sort that might have caused him to schedule a special meeting with his staff?"

Butler rubbed his fleshy chin and said, "I'm not sure how to answer that question. I have no specific information as to any problems with the business. But when I talked to Mr. Dodge on the phone a week or so ago about a routine matter, he said he might have 'a big job' for me soon. He didn't say what it was, although he mentioned that he'd already talked to his auditors."

"Did a firm here in St. Paul audit his books?"

"No, he used accountants in New York. I've dealt with them, and I can tell you right now that they will not give you so much as the time of day without a subpoena ordering them to do so."

"Ah, I see. Can you tell me in a general sort of way how Mr. Dodge earned his money? I know he played the stock market, but did he have other interests as well?"

"Stocks and bonds were Mr. Dodge's lifeblood—he was a brilliant investor—but, yes, he had a variety of other interests. He was behind an array of partnerships, for example, that invested in new businesses and the like. He also did some commodities trading, mainly in gold and silver, and he owned a good deal of real estate here and elsewhere."

After a few more perfunctory questions relating to Dodge's finances, Rafferty turned to another topic. "Yesterday, at around eight thirty in the mornin', were you here in your office?"

"Yes, I believe I was."

"And were those windows to your right open?"

Butler looked at the three north-facing windows and said, "Yes. I opened them just a crack to get some fresh air. I wanted to open them more, but it was too windy."

"Now, at about that same time did you hear anything unusual? The sound of a window slamming shut, say, or even a gunshot?"

Butler shook his head. "One of the policemen who canvassed the building yesterday asked the same question. Unfortunately, I didn't hear anything unusual until the alarms went off in Mr. Dodge's office."

"What did you do then?"

"Nothing. There have been quite a few false alarms with Mr. Dodge's security system, so I didn't think anything of it."

"'Tis the problem with alarms, isn't it? They are always goin' off at the wrong time, and before long people pay them no heed. Let me ask you one other thing. Did you notice anyone unusual in the building yesterday? A stranger wanderin' the halls, say, or perhaps a person you'd never seen before, like a new delivery man?"

"Yes, I noticed someone, as I already told one of Inspector Jones's men. There was a repairman in the hall when I came to work yesterday morning."

"You mean in the hall outside your offices?"

"Yes."

"What time was this?"

"Seven thirty. That's always when I arrive at the office."

"Can you describe this fellow?"

"As I said, he was a repairman. At least, that is what I assumed, since he had a large tool box in one hand and the name of McQuillan Brothers Plumbing and Heating was stamped on the back of his overalls. I just caught a glimpse of him as he was going into the men's lavatory. I didn't see his face but got the impression he was quite young, perhaps in his twenties. He had a slender build and was not especially tall. Beyond that, I cannot tell you much."

"Well, what about the tool box he carried? Was it the open type with a handle, or did it have a cover of some kind?"

"I really don't know. I didn't really take a good look at it. Do you think this repairman was involved in Mr. Dodge's murder?"

"I have no idea," Rafferty said, truthfully. "'Tis simply one more matter to be checked. Now then, Mr. Butler, I know that your time is money, so I have just one more question: When and where will Mr. Dodge's will be read?"

"Right here at noon sharp next Monday. Mr. Dodge's funeral, as you may know, will be Thursday. Mrs. Dodge requested a reading of the will as soon as possible after a suitable period of mourning."

"The lady is not one to waste time," Rafferty remarked as he lifted himself from his chair. "You have been most helpful, Mr. Butler. Most helpful indeed."

George Marshall and Robert Hicks were the two regular day-shift guards stationed in Dodge Tower's lobby. Rafferty had wanted to talk to them on Monday afternoon after the murder, but they were already being grilled by the police, and so he'd had to put it off. It was just as well, Rafferty thought, to let Thomas question them on his own. Both guards were black, and Rafferty's long association with Thomas had taught him that black men were often wary souls, especially when it came to dealing with whites. The black community in St. Paul was small and tight-knit enough so that almost everyone knew one another, and Thomas was in fact casually acquainted with both men.

When Rafferty returned to the lobby, Thomas was still talking with the guards, but he quickly wrapped up the conversation and came over to join his partner.

Rafferty asked, "Did you find out anything from those fellows?"

"Maybe. There was at least one unusual visitor in the building yesterday. A plumber from—"

"McQuillan Brothers," Rafferty cut in. "Mr. Butler saw him briefly on the twenty-ninth floor. Did the fellow provide a name when he signed in?"

"He did, and you won't believe it. He signed in as Lon Schott." Thomas spelled out the name for Rafferty. "It can't be a coincidence that it sounds like 'long shot.'"

"No, I don't suppose it is. 'Twould appear we have a criminal who possesses a dark sense of humor. What time did he sign in?"

"At seven twenty. He showed the guards a work assignment from the building manager that said he was to fix a broken faucet in a lavatory on the twenty-fifth floor. The assignment sheet looked authentic, so the guards let him in."

"Was he carryin' a tool box?"

"Yes."

"Open or closed?"

"Closed."

Rafferty nodded and said, "Instead of the twenty-fifth floor, he ends up on the twenty-ninth. I'm bettin' the building manager didn't issue that work order and that McQuillan Brothers has no one by the name of Lon Schott in their employ. By the way, did the guards tell the police about the mysterious Mr. Schott?"

"They did. Both of them talked to Sergeant Carroll. I assume he'll check the plumber's story, if he hasn't already."

"And we'll do the same. What did this supposed plumber look like, accordin' to the guards?"

"Midtwenties, medium height, wiry build, regular features, dark brown eyes, pencil mustache, short brown hair. The guards said he was friendly and chatted with them about the nice weather."

"What time did he sign out?"

"Eight thirty-eight on the dot."

"Ah, the timing works out nicely. The rear door alarm in Mr. Dodge's offices sounded at eight thirty-two and that must have been when he was shot. When did word of Mr. Dodge's murder reach the guards here?"

"They were notified by Kretch as to what had happened at eight forty-one. He told them to lock down the building, which they did. The police, including Chief Nelligan, arrived five minutes later."

"'Tis perfect then. Our plumber arrives in plenty of time for the murder but leaves before the building was shut tight. As you said, Wash, 'twas not a coincidence."

"The question is, what was he doing on the twenty-ninth floor? He can't have been the shooter. So why was he up there?"

"Well, we know he wasn't fixin' the pipes. We also know he wasn't in the law offices. So he must have gone into one of those vacant offices we looked at."

"I understand. But I still don't see what he could have done up there that would tie him to the murder."

"Nor do I," Rafferty admitted. "'Tis a point I'll have to ponder."

Sergeant Carroll had in fact contacted McQuillan Brothers but didn't hear back from the firm's owner until late in the morning. The company had no plumber named Schott and had not sent out anyone Monday morning to make repairs at Dodge Tower.

"The pieces are beginning to come together," Jones said when Carroll passed on the news. "There was someone on the inside—this phony plumber—and he was on the twenty-ninth floor before the murder, according to Mr. Butler, the lawyer. There was also a shooter up in the old capitol, and the two of them found a way to kill the old man in his office. Did you get a description of the so-called plumber?"

Carroll nodded and gave Jones the same description Thomas had obtained from the guards. Then he asked, "Any idea who this fellow might be?"

"I'm not sure. I doubt it was Berthelson, since he must have been the shooter up in the old capitol's tower. I'm guessing the fake plumber was one of Berthelson's men, probably from out of town. By the way, sergeant, I just received a report back from the laboratory. There was human blood on that squirt gun we found in the alley."

"Do you suppose it could be Mr. Dodge's blood?"

"Could be, but if it is, I'm having a hard time figuring out how—and why—it got there."

Among the out-of-the-way places in downtown St. Paul was a crooked little alley known as Bench Street. It angled down the bluff tops from Wabasha Street to an old steamboat landing, and it was so steep, narrow, and rutted that only pedestrians—and not many of those—used it. Milwaukee Road trains, sometimes fifty or more a day, rumbled nearby along the riverfront, their giant Mikado and Pacific locomotives sending up choking clouds of coal soot, which had long since darkened the street's collection of tumbledown stone and brick warehouses.

In the days when riverboats by the hundreds churned upriver to St. Paul, Bench had offered a convenient way from the landing to the main portion of downtown. But when steamboats vanished before the surge of iron rail, the street became largely forgotten, its aged warehouses abandoned to hobos, rats, spiders, and other living things viewed with distaste by polite society.

The squat limestone building at No. 5 Bench was typical of the street's uninspiring architectural ensemble. Built to store goods bound for St. Louis and other points south along the river, the warehouse had for a brief time in the 1860s been the province of an ambitious young clerk named James J. Hill, who helped manhandle merchandise into and out of its dim interior. By 1917, however, it was a ruin, much of its roof caved in and its walls slowly coming undone under the assault of water, wind, and time.

Early Tuesday morning, well before dawn, Samuel Berthelson left his room at the U.S. Hotel and walked two blocks to the old warehouse, which had been set up as a safe house by friends in the movement. It was provisioned with a mattress, a lantern, and tins of food. Berthelson slept a few hours, then reviewed plans for the night ahead. Just before noon he heard footsteps coming around the back of the building toward an old doorway bent out of shape by the sagging walls. The footsteps stopped, and a soft voice said, "The tyrant is dead."

"And may he rot in hell," Berthelson replied, opening the door to reveal two men. One was tall and lanky and wore a blindfold. The other, who was short and swarthy, said: "Here he is, just as you wanted him."

"Good. Bring him in and wait outside," Berthelson told the short man. Then he said, "Welcome, Mr. Dubois. We have much to talk about."

After locking the door, Berthelson led Dubois to a room in the rear of the warehouse. Rusted tools, three beer kegs, and the remains of several hobo encampments littered the dirt floor. Berthelson lit a kerosene lantern and helped Dubois to a seat on one of the beer kegs.

"Is this blindfold really necessary?" Dubois asked.

"No, I suppose not, but if you take it off, I'll have to shoot you."

"Are you joking?"

"What do you think, Mr. Dubois? Am I?"

"No, I would guess not."

"Then you are a wise man. I'm glad you could stop by my humble abode. Not quite the penthouse of Dodge Tower, I'm afraid."

"Not quite," Dubois agreed. "May I ask why you had that lout bring me here at gunpoint? It really wasn't necessary, you know."

"A man can never be too careful, Mr. Dubois. I am alive because I refuse to be stupid or sentimental. Now, do you have what I want?"

Dubois reached into the breast pocket of his suit coat and withdrew a long manila envelope. He handed it toward where he imagined Berthelson was sitting. Inside was $5,000 in currency.

Berthelson methodically counted the bills, then said, "Operations money is always welcome."

"So what happens next?"

"Better that you don't know," Berthelson said, giving his unlikely coconspirator a good looking over. The details of Dubois's recruitment were well known to Berthelson. Only six months earlier, Dubois had gone to a meeting of the local socialist's club out of "pure curiosity," as he'd put it. Gradually, he'd been radicalized. Berthelson had seen it happen before— a young man becoming aware for the first time in his privileged life of the vast injustices upon which the capitalistic system was built. The big break-through had come in late August when Dubois agreed to work "under-ground" in support of the movement. He'd already done a great deal, but more would be expected of him in the near future.

"Tell me about the investigation," Berthelson said. "Is it any threat to us?"

"Only if you get caught."

"That won't happen. I made up my mind a long time ago that I'd never go to prison."

"So you'll die with your boots on, I suppose."

"Something like that. Now, what of the investigation?"

"Well, as you know, McGruder and his men have identified you as the prime suspect after finding the bullet up at the old capitol. He's briefing the men as we speak. McGruder is trying to keep the police out of it, but that won't last for long. Rumors are starting to fly, so I think you can safely assume the police will join the hunt before long. There's also one other potential problem—a fellow named Rafferty."

"Yes, I read about him in the newspapers. I even went by his saloon. Claims to be a friend of Sherlock Holmes. He sounds like an old blowhard to me."

"Maybe, but I've heard he's smart. He could be a problem down the line."

"Well, we'll worry about that when the time comes. For now, I suggest you get back to work. I need to know what's going on at Dodge's offices and at the safety commission."

"How will I get in touch again?"

"Leave that to me. Good luck, Mr. Dubois."

"Thank you. Great days are ahead, I believe."

"Yes, they are," Berthelson said. "Great days for all of us."

J. D. Carr sat in his office with the door locked and reread the letter Arte-mus Dodge had sent to his lawyer, Patrick Butler. It was more revealing than Carr had anticipated. The letter showed that Dodge had found out the secret of the Blue Sky Partnership. Although the letter's wording was quite matter-of-fact, Dodge must have been outraged by the gross violation of his trust. But what must have angered the old man even more, Carr knew, was the amount of money that had been consumed, as completely as if it had been set upon a pyre and burned to ashes. In the letter Dodge demonstrated, with his usual financial acumen, where the dollars had gone and how they had been lost. The letter, however, didn't identify the culprit behind the fraud, and now that Dodge was dead the truth would never have to come out. That was a good thing, Carr thought. A very good thing.

Mrs. Schmidt, of course, knew about the letter, but Carr was certain she'd keep quiet. Besides, he'd filched the carbon copy from her files. As Carr pored over the letter one last time, there was a knock at the door, followed by Mrs. Schmidt's familiar voice.

"Mr. Carr, it is important that I talk to you," she said.

"What about?" he asked, slipping the letter into his desk drawer. He went over to the door and looked through the peephole. The stony look on Mrs. Schmidt's face told him that she'd found the letter missing from her files. He would have some explaining to do.

"I think you know why I wish to talk. Now, will you let me in?"

Carr took a deep breath and opened the door. "By all means, come in, Mrs. Schmidt," he said, trying to sound as pleasant as possible. He closed the door behind her and locked it again. "I suppose it is about the letter. Why don't you have a seat?"

"I will stand," she said. "So you admit that you took the letter. You must tell me why you would do such a thing."

Carr smiled and said, "As I explained to you last night, Mrs. Schmidt, the letter contains information that might embarrass the firm. It is that simple."

"Yes, but then why did you steal it when I told you I would 'forget' about it, as you asked me?"

"Very well, I will be absolutely honest with you, Mrs. Schmidt. I simply had to take it. There is information in it that could destroy this company. If it came to light, you would be out of a job, I would be out of a job, and so would young Steven and everyone else. There would be much embarrassing publicity as well. That is why I took the letter. And if you have any additional copies, I must insist that you give them to me immediately."

Mrs. Schmidt paused, then said, "There are no more copies."

"You're sure?"

Another pause. "Yes, but I must say to you right now, Mr. Carr, that it is a very suspicious thing you have done. Tell me, please, about these matters that are such a threat to the company that you would take the letter out of my files."

Carr chose his words carefully. "As you know, the letter concerned certain financial irregularities involving the Blue Sky Partnership. These irregularities do not amount to anything illegal or dishonest, I assure you, but are merely a matter of mistakes being made. However, in the type of work we do, trust is essential. It is particularly important that our partners have full faith and confidence in our integrity, as well as our competence. Fortunately, the mistakes made in the Blue Sky matter can be easily rectified, which is what I intend to do."

"So it is what is called a cover-up. Is that it?"

"No, not at all. It merely comes down to resolving a problem the easy way rather than the hard way. One of the Blue Sky partners, for example, might decide to file a civil lawsuit, which would be long and costly. By dealing with the matter in-house, we can easily avoid that situation."

"I see. Then tell me, please, if that is the way it should be done, why was Mr. Dodge writing to his lawyer?"

Good question, Carr thought. "I think Mr. Dodge was simply laying out his concerns to see if any legal action would be required. But as I said, it isn't."

"I would like to read the letter again," Mrs. Schmidt announced.

"I'm afraid that would be impossible," Carr lied. "I have already disposed of it."

"You are a man of quick action in this matter. You are not always so quick otherwise. So, you are assuring me that no wrong has been committed with this letter?"

"You have my word, Mrs. Schmidt."

"Very well," she said, turning to leave. "Then I will say no more, except that this is a thing I do not like."

Carr jumped up and went over to open the door for her. "Believe me, I understand your concerns. But you will be doing the right thing for all of us if you banish the letter from your mind."

"So you say," she said, and left without another word.

Watching her walk off down the hall, Carr wondered if she'd told him the truth about other possible copies of the letter. He also wondered who else might know the sorry details of the Blue Sky Partnership.

12

"WE'LL TALK AGAIN SOON"

John McGruder's greatest regret was that he had not become a general. As a young man, he desperately wanted to attend West Point, but his father, like him a lawyer, wouldn't hear of it. The military would never yield more than a modest living, his father said, and besides the nation was at peace. What good was it being in the army if there was no war to fight? So young McGruder had dutifully studied law, only to see the Spanish-American War break out not long after he had gone to work for his father's firm. The glorious charge of Teddy Roosevelt's Rough Riders at San Juan Hill had left McGruder brimming with envy, but by then it was too late to think of a life in the military. The opportunity to serve on the safety commission, with its intoxicating power, at least gave McGruder the chance to act like a general, albeit of a very small army.

His "troops"—twenty agents, mostly ex-Pinkerton, police, or military men—waited for him now in the old capitol's senate chambers. McGruder was eager to address his operatives. He was also worried. He had hoped to keep Samuel Berthelson's presence in St. Paul a secret, but Isabel Diamond's persistent questioning had suggested she knew something was up. McGruder had once proposed censoring all of the state's newspapers as long as the war lasted, but his fellow commission members, including the governor himself, had vetoed the idea. So it was, he thought bitterly, that sedition was allowed to run rampant for the sake of constitutional niceties.

At half past noon McGruder strode to the podium. He wore his usual dark gray suit, starched white shirt, and black tie. His wire-frame bifocals rested near the tip of his nose so that he could look down to read his speech, and he might easily have been mistaken for a middle-aged accountant instead of the general he fancied himself to be. The men assembled before him were hardly military in their bearing or attire, either. Most were in their thirties or forties and wore cheap serge suits. But they were the only army McGruder had, and they would have to do. Their mission would be to hunt down Berthelson—"the most dangerous, cruel, and elusive terrorist in America," as McGruder called him.

McGruder believed the search for Berthelson would be the defining event of his life. If the commission's agents could track down the terrorist and excise him from the body politic like the cancer he was, McGruder knew it would be a great service to the nation. Even President Wilson might take note of such an achievement. McGruder envisioned himself shaking the president's hand at the White House as photographers recorded the moment for posterity.

The problem was how to catch Berthelson, and McGruder thought he had figured out a way. He'd spent the past hour talking with Harlow Secrest. The agent was a thug and blackmailer in McGruder's eyes, but he couldn't do without him. No good photographs of Berthelson were known to exist, making Secrest's firsthand knowledge essential.

"Men, I called you here today because you are about to embark on a mission of vital importance to this country," McGruder began. "You are going to capture—or better yet, kill—Samuel Berthelson, a vicious character if there ever was one. I will tell you now how you're going to do it."

McGruder then laid out his two-pronged plan. Agents would begin by staking out six supposed "safe houses" in St. Paul whose occupants were known to harbor fugitives like Berthelson. With luck, Berthelson would appear at one of the houses and be caught in an ambush.

If the stakeouts proved barren, a new "strategy of infiltration," focusing on the union representing streetcar motormen and conductors, would be adopted. McGruder believed Berthelson had come to St. Paul for two reasons. The first was to kill Artemus Dodge, which he'd already done. The second was to incite riotous bloodshed or commit some other act of terrorism when the streetcar workers went on strike—an event set to occur on Saturday unless the Twin City Rapid Transit Company agreed to a settlement. McGruder, who'd been in close contact with company officials, knew that was not about to happen.

"If we do not kill or capture Berthelson tonight, then we will so completely infiltrate the unions that Berthelson will inevitably be drawn into our net," McGruder said.

Secrest spoke up, much to McGruder's displeasure. "You've all received the description of Berthelson I've provided, but don't be deceived by his ordinary appearance. You must be very careful if you spot him. Berthelson will assuredly be armed. He is known to carry several pistols, sticks of dynamite, and grenades. He is almost always accompanied by one or more bodyguards, men as ruthless as he is. He will not be taken without a fight."

McGruder broke in, his voice booming, "Shoot first, men, shoot first. If you see him, kill him, for he will surely kill you if he can. I am also authorized to tell you that the agent who brings him down will receive a bonus of five thousand dollars." A low murmur went through the crowd.

"One more thing. You are not under any circumstances to work with the police of this city, unless you have express permission from me. There are good men in the St. Paul Police Department, but there are also men who sympathize with the unionists and might tip them off regarding our plans. I will make life miserable for any man who shares intelligence with the police. You will all receive special orders after this meeting. Good luck to you all, and Godspeed."

After most of the agents had left, Secrest stayed behind to talk with the four other operatives—all ex-Pinkertons like himself—who had been assigned the task of infiltrating the transit union. Two of the men had already insinuated themselves into the union's ranks, and Secrest hoped that he and the others could get inside with their help. Normally, it took weeks or even months to infiltrate, but now it would have to be done in a matter of days.

"So what do you really think about this business?" one of the agents asked Secrest.

"Dicey," he replied, lighting a cigarette. "Very dicey. There will be blood spilled, I'm sure, before it's all done. Don't count on that five thousand just yet. It won't do you any good if you aren't alive to spend it."

. . . . .

Amanda Dodge had never paid much attention to her husband's business—she couldn't analyze a stock deal or follow the intricacies of double-entry accounting—but she could read his moods with remarkably accuracy. At their last meeting Sunday night in his apartment, she'd known at once that something was amiss. Pain was evident in his eyes and the droop of his chin and in the slight wobble of his voice, which was usually strong and clear.

She'd asked him what was wrong, but he'd denied anything was bothering him. He was always like that. He had feelings, she supposed, but he'd never expressed them, even in bed, where he seemed to find more embarrassment than pleasure in the act of making love. Still, as they sat on the overstuffed divan in the apartment, she'd pressed him until he finally admitted that "a personal business matter"—those were his exact words—was weighing on him. Beyond that, he'd refused to go into detail, but Amanda had now concluded that the "business matter" gnawing at Artemus must have been the Blue Sky Partnership.

As she drank her late morning tea at River's Edge, she considered what to do with the incriminating documents she'd found in the basement safe. She didn't trust Carr, who was a winding road with no straightaways. Steven was, for all of his charms, rather simpleminded. Butler, the lawyer, would probably cause her all manner of trouble if she gave him the documents. As for the police, Amanda had no idea what they might make of "irregularities" in the company's books. For all she knew, her inheritance could be greatly reduced if the fraud was discovered.

Once she'd finished her tea, Amanda's thoughts turned to her other big problem—Peter Kretch. She had to find a permanent solution to his blackmailing, or he would slowly bleed her dry. Kretch didn't know it, but Amanda could be a devil in velvet if need be.

The phone rang, and Amanda got up to answer it. She recognized the caller's voice. "You won't believe what that bastard Kretch is up to," the man said.

"I know all about it," she replied calmly. "We need to talk. I'll stop by your place this afternoon."

. . . . .

Shadwell Rafferty had known Allen Stem for at least fifteen years, going back to the days when the architect and his partner, Charles Reed, maintained one of the largest practices in St. Paul and designed buildings, especially railroad stations, all across the country. Their biggest plum had been Grand Central Terminal in New York City. A bitter fight with other architects who wanted the work, as well as the stress of supervising so vast an undertaking, had sent Reed to an early grave in 1911. After that, Stem ran the firm on his own. He'd overseen every detail of Dodge Tower, from the crockets and pinnacles decorating its roof to the lobby's mosaic ceiling, which required the work of twenty Italian artisans to fabricate and install.

Stem's offices were on the tower's second floor, and it was there that Rafferty found the architect early Tuesday afternoon. "By God, and if it isn't the biggest Irishman in St. Paul," Stem said when Rafferty appeared at the door.

"'Tis true, I fear, and further expansion may well occur," Rafferty said, patting his stomach.

"Have a seat," Stem said after shaking Rafferty's hand. "Did you get the set of plans I sent over last night?"

"I did, and I thank you. They've been most helpful. 'Twas also helpful to learn that you sent a set to that safe company in London. I'm hoping Sherlock Holmes will be able to take a look at them."

"Well, I hope the great detective finds no flaw in them. Now, is there something else I can do for you? I must tell you I am still shocked by the murder. I was returning from Chicago yesterday afternoon when I heard the news. Is what I read in the papers true?"

"Mostly, though the tale has been dramatized a bit. As I told you, I've been asked to help out with the investigation. Since you designed this building, and know it as well as anyone, I thought you might be able to tell me more about Mr. Dodge's well-fortified office."

"Well, I'll tell you what I can. Fact is, I was just up there. I was curious to see if anything had been tampered with, given the big mystery over how Mr. Dodge was killed."

"Ah, and did you find anything amiss?"

"I did. One of the windows in Mr. Dodge's office has two severed sash cords. But I suppose you and the police already know that."

"We do. Anything else look suspicious to you?"

Stem shook his head. "I examined the floors, the walls, the ceiling, the windows, and doors—everything. That penthouse was just as it was supposed to be. I do not see how anyone could have gotten inside under the circumstances described in the newspapers."

"Well, you'll be interested to know that the theory of the moment holds that Mr. Dodge was killed by a sniper's bullet."

"Then it must have had the ability to pass through glass without breaking it," Stem noted.

"Perhaps," Rafferty said, "but I'll not trouble you with any speculation on that matter. If you don't mind, I would like to trouble you for some facts regardin' the construction of Mr. Dodge's office and apartment."

"What would you like to know?"

"I'm curious about how the design was worked out. Was Mr. Dodge himself involved?"

"Intimately. He insisted on reviewing and approving every detail, no matter how small."

"Were others also involved in this process?"

"I know that Peter Kretch, Mr. Dodge's security man, reviewed some of the specifications. As I recall, Mr. Carr and Steven Dodge were also consulted on occasion."

"What about Mrs. Dodge?"

Stem allowed himself a small, unprofessional grin and said, "I would describe her architecture as being quite magnificent. In fact, if I were a much younger man and unmarried, I might have designs on her myself."

"You and just about every other healthy male in St. Paul," Rafferty agreed.

"Be that as it may," Stem continued, "I'm not aware that she had any say in the design of Mr. Dodge's offices. The mansion, of course, was a different matter entirely. She had plenty to say about that."

"Women always do when it comes to a home. Now, gettin' back to this building, I assume you have complete working drawings for the thirtieth floor."

"Of course."

"Tell me, if you would, what the drawings include? For example, did you actually design all the windows and those two big security doors for Mr. Dodge's office and apartment, or was that work left up to the manufacturers?"

"Well, the windows are of a standard type, except that their locks are larger and stronger than usual. In the case of the doors, however, I simply designed a frame for them. Mr. Dodge himself specified the features they were to have, and Mosler in Ohio built them. They are very expensive custom items."

"What about those extra-thick walls, floors, and ceilings?"

"They are of reinforced concrete, eighteen inches thick, very similar to what you would find in a bank vault. There is nothing unusual about their construction, except of course that most offices are not built in such a massive way. The window bars are also standard items that came from highly reputable manufacturers. I must say, Mr. Rafferty, I am a bit surprised by your questions. Do you think the construction was somehow flawed?"

"No, I am just tryin' to cover all my bases. The fact that Mr. Dodge was shot tells us that his office was, in one way or another, not the impregnable fortress he believed it to be."

"I suppose you're right," Stem admitted, "but for the life of me I can't explain how such a crime was possible."

"At the moment, neither can I," Rafferty said, "but I'm workin' on it."

At precisely eleven o'clock, Inspector Mordecai Jones and Sergeant Francis Carroll appeared at the door of Chief Michael Nelligan's office. Like the police station itself, the office was scarred and dingy, though Nelligan had tried to liven it up with a new coat of pale blue paint and a colony of potted plants by the windows. The one improvement Nelligan had insisted on when taking over the job was a large new desk. He sat behind it now, like an admiral on the bridge of a battleship. His old desk, a massive Victorian affair as ornate as a cathedral, hadn't conveyed the proper image of modernity to Nelligan's way of thinking. The chief viewed himself as a thoroughly modern man, and he saw his mission as one of updating and streamlining a police department that hadn't changed with the times.

Jones held a far different opinion of the chief. The improvements he constantly boasted of—adding patrol cars, better communications, more use of fingerprinting—were real, but their purpose, as Jones viewed it, was simply to make Nelligan look better in the eyes of the press, the public, and the politicians he so assiduously courted. Nelligan had no real instincts as a policeman, no core of righteousness to guide him. He was just an ambitious politician who happened to wear a blue uniform. In a hard place, Jones believed, the chief couldn't be relied upon. There was also the fact that he was a goddamned liar.

Nelligan greeted Jones and Carroll curtly but didn't offer them a seat, an indication that the meeting would be short.

"I asked you here," he began, "to pass on some important information."

Jones was ready to enjoy the moment. "I presume it has to do with Samuel Berthelson, sir. I must say I am surprised that you waited until now to tell us about his presence here in St. Paul, but I am sure you had a good reason."

Nelligan didn't like Jones's tone. "Yes, Inspector, I did have a good reason, and you would do well to keep that in mind."

"I certainly will," Jones said, thinking that something must have forced Nelligan to come clean about Berthelson. He could think of at least one possibility. "Am I correct in fearing that the press has gotten wind of the situation?"

"Yes. That Diamond woman has somehow found out. It will be in the *Pioneer Press* this afternoon. Which brings me to why you and Sergeant Carroll are here. I have discussed the situation with Mr. McGruder at the safety commission, and we have agreed that from this point forward the two of you are to work with him and his men in tracking down Berthelson. It will be your one and only priority."

Before Jones could register an objection, Nelligan continued, "Mr. McGruder seems to think that our department cannot be trusted, but I have assured him that it can and that you in particular, Inspector, are an outstanding detective. I told him that if anyone can locate Berthelson, you are that man. I am sure you will not disappoint me. Therefore, you are ordered to liaison duty with Mr. McGruder at his office. You will report directly to him and to me. If, as I fully expect, you find Berthelson, I need not tell you what a feather in your cap it would be. Any questions?"

Good God, Jones thought, now I have two incompetent bosses instead of one. He said, "I am a bit uncertain, sir, as to how the chain of command will work. When you say that I am to report to Mr. McGruder, does that mean I am to follow his orders, or yours?"

"Mr. McGruder and I will be in constant communication. You are to follow both of our orders. For the time being, so as to facilitate your work, you and Sergeant Carroll will work out of Mr. McGruder's offices. You are to report there as soon as possible."

Jones said, "I must tell you, sir, that this is a highly irregular arrangement. I am a sworn police officer of the city of St. Paul, not an employee of the state."

"Well, you are now," Nelligan said, standing up. "There is nothing more to say. I will expect your first report this evening."

Jones erupted as soon as he and Carroll left the office. "It is the damnedest thing I have ever heard of, and I am sure it is illegal as well. We are pawns, sergeant, pawns in a power struggle between McGruder and Nelligan. Don't you see what's happening here? Nelligan wants us in McGruder's office so we can be his eyes and ears there. McGruder wants us so he can do the same thing when it comes to Nelligan. What both of them want is credit for nabbing Berthelson. We're nothing to either of them."

"So what do we do?" Carroll asked. He was an excellent police officer but lacked political instincts. That part of the job he left to his boss.

"We do as we're told, but we also protect ourselves."

"How?"

"We find a guardian angel," Jones said, "and I know just who it might be."

The telegram from Sherlock Holmes was delivered to Rafferty at the tavern after he returned from his talk with Allen Stem. The message was concise: "CASE FASCINATING. IN *TIMES* AND *TELEGRAPH*. WILL EXAMINE PLANS. HOLMES."

"Well, it looks like the game is afoot," Thomas said after reading the telegram. "The papers in London have picked up the story, just as you thought they would."

"Mr. Dodge was an international figure in financial circles, and a dead rich man is always news," Rafferty said. "Let's hope Fleet Street gets the story right so that Holmes will have good information to go on. Speakin' of papers, I'll be curious what Miss Diamond has to say in the *Pioneer Press*. She'll stir the pot, I'm sure."

"That seems to be her specialty. So what do we do next? Do you want to talk to Mr. Dubois about that dress receipt?"

"I do, but first I want to read the afternoon papers. Then I'm thinkin' I might run over to Kennedy Brothers for a bit." The firm of Kennedy Brothers was the largest gun shop in St. Paul.

"I don't imagine you're planning on buying anything," Thomas said.

"You're right, Wash. 'Tis information I'm after, and I know who can provide it."

The headline atop the Tuesday afternoon extra published by the *Pioneer Press* could not be accused of understatement: "TERRORIST IN ST. PAUL, KILLED ART. DODGE." An array of subheads lined up below like the tail of a gaudy kite. "SAM. BERTHELSON HUNTED. 'MOST DANGEROUS MAN IN AMERICA,' POLICE SAY. SHELL FOUND IN OLD CAPITOL. SNIPER SHOT DODGE. MORE VIOLENCE FEARED."

The story that accompanied these provocations showed that Isabel Diamond had lost none of her talent for drama and sensationalism. It painted a dire picture of a city at the mercy of a ruthless killer and called on the police, the safety commission, and just about anyone else who could form an armed posse to track down and kill Samuel Berthelson.

There was another interesting story on the front page, one that in normal times might have dominated the headlines. Union carmen and conductors had met after the wild scene at Dietsch's Hall and voted to go on strike against the Twin City Rapid Transit Company at midnight Saturday.

They wanted higher wages, better working conditions, and the rehiring of fifty-seven fired union workers. Their anger was palpable, as the account in the *Pioneer Press* made clear. "More violent riots are greatly feared," the newspaper reported, "and the police and sheriff are already adding special deputies to deal with any disorder."

Rafferty felt a sense of regret and deep rumbles of foreboding after he read the stories. He realized that he shouldn't have talked to Diamond. He'd wanted information from her, and he'd gotten it. In turn he'd fed her what he regarded as a crumb about the shell casing found in the old capitol. It hadn't occurred to him—it should have, he now realized—that Diamond would leap to the conclusion that Berthelson was the man who pulled the trigger. Rafferty certainly regarded the young anarchist as a prime suspect, but he still had many questions about the circumstances behind Dodge's murder. The crime, in his mind, remained an open case. Now Diamond had struck a match to the situation at a time when the city was already primed to explode in a violent strike.

"I have been a fool," Rafferty said to Thomas as they drank coffee in his office.

"Wouldn't be the first time," Thomas remarked. "But given your advanced age, it might be the last."

"There's a cheery thought, Wash. I guess there really is no fool like an old fool. But if Berthelson is as smart as he's supposed to be, maybe he's already left town."

Thomas said, "Wouldn't bet on it."

"Neither would I," Rafferty said. "'Tis a bad situation all the way around, and I fear it will only get worse."

Peter Kretch was called into J. D. Carr's office at two o'clock in the afternoon. He expected to hear bad news. After all, he'd failed to perform his most fundamental duty, which was to keep Artemus Dodge alive, so it was unlikely he'd remain on the payroll for long. Still, he felt entitled to a decent amount of respect. He got none.

"Your services will no longer be required here," Carr said with no attempt to soften the blow. "I think you understand why. You may collect your final paycheck from Mr. Dubois along with any personal items from your room. I will expect you to be cleared out within the hour."

So this is how it's going to be, Kretch thought. Tossed out like a piece of trash. "I believe I am entitled to two weeks' notice, especially in view of my loyal service."

"Your loyalty did not keep Mr. Dodge from being murdered," Carr replied acidly. "There is nothing more to say."

"I'm not so sure about that," Kretch said, quickly weighing his options. "In fact, I might have a number of things to say."

"Really? I'm not interested. Now, please leave at once."

"Very well. But I wonder what I should do with all the information I've collected regarding the Blue Sky Partnership. I wonder if Miss Diamond at the *Pioneer Press* would find anything of interest in it. I'll have to give her a call. Oh, and there's also that article on locked room mysteries I found on your bookshelf. I know Inspector Jones will enjoy reading it as much as I did. Good day, Mr. Carr." Kretch turned to go but didn't get far.

"Wait," Carr said, doing some fast thinking of his own. "Perhaps I have been too hasty, Mr. Kretch. Perhaps you should stay on the payroll, at least until the police have completed their investigation. Would that suit you?"

"It might. But I will need a raise. You may not know it, but before his most unfortunate death Mr. Dodge promised me an extra one hundred dollars a month out of appreciation for my service."

Now it's blackmail, plain and simple, Carr thought. If the old man were alive, he'd have booted Kretch out on his fat rear end. But Artemus Dodge was dead, and there were complications. Carr said, "Then it will have to be a posthumous award, won't it? I'll see to it. Now get out of my sight before I change my mind."

"Of course, sir. You know where to find me if you need me. We'll talk again soon, I'm sure."

Perhaps sooner than you think, Carr thought, wondering whether anyone would actually miss Kretch if, by some terrible mishap, he fell out a thirtieth-floor window and plunged, no doubt scheming all the way down, to his richly deserved demise.

13

"SOMETHING ABOUT IT LOOKS FAMILIAR"

When George Armstrong Custer went through St. Paul on his way to the western plains, he often stopped at M. E. Kennedy & Brothers Company on Sixth Street to look at their excellent assortment of weaponry. Local legend held that the final shots Custer fired at Little Bighorn came from a revolver purchased from the firm.

Rafferty doubted the Custer story, but he did agree that Kennedy Brothers, as everyone called it, was the best place in St. Paul to buy a high-quality firearm. He'd been collecting guns since his days as a Civil War infantryman, and he owned fifty or so rifles, shotguns, and pistols, most of which were stored in a gun cabinet in his apartment. Rafferty seldom ventured forth in public without at least one handgun on his person, on the theory that a man well armed was a man well prepared for whatever life might bring.

The staff at Kennedy Brothers included Tom Masterson, known simply as "the colonel," the rank he'd held in the U.S. Army, where he'd served for twenty years before retiring. A distant relative of the famous Kansas lawman, Masterson was a lanky man in his fifties with piercing gray eyes, a long hawk-nosed face, and a few strands of hair clinging like drought-stricken plants to the barren dome of his head. He had been trained as a sniper in the military and possessed the calm, unhurried demeanor of men who kill at a distance. Rafferty knew him well and had the utmost respect for his skills as a marksman.

On Tuesday afternoon, Rafferty walked over to Kennedy Brothers and found Masterson in the firm's back room, examining a vintage rifle. "I see you have a new toy, Tom," he said, going up to shake Masterson's hand before taking a closer look at the rifle. "By God, is that a long-range Creedmoor?"

"It is. Just bought it at an estate sale in Minneapolis. Haven't seen one like this in years. Vernier sight, custom grained stock, almost perfect condition. I could take out a squirrel's eye at a thousand yards with this beauty. But I imagine you're not here to talk about squirrels, Shad."

"'Tis bigger game I have in mind," Rafferty admitted. "I assume you've been readin' the papers."

"With great interest. If what they say is true, it sounds like a sniper took out Dodge, even though—"

"I know, there were no bullet holes in the glass. 'Tis a problem bafflin' me and everyone else. Let's just say for purposes of discussion that this apparent conundrum can be dealt with by one means or another. Here's what I'd like to know, Tom. If it'd been you up in that tower with a rifle, could you have hit Dodge square in the head with a single shot? The shell we found was in the .50 caliber range."

"A big bullet for this day and age. Small and fast is the ideal now. No matter. What's the distance? A thousand yards or so?"

"A bit less. I looked at a downtown map and made a rough estimate. As best I can figure, the shot would have been somewhere between seven hundred and fifty and eight hundred yards. Of course you have to take into account that it was a very windy day and you'd be shootin' uphill. The old capitol's observation platform, I'm guessin', is a good hundred feet lower than the penthouse of Dodge Tower."

Masterson said, "Well, it certainly could be done with a good scoped sniper rifle. Even this old Creedmoor might do the trick. But at that range and under those conditions I wouldn't want to bet my life on hitting a man in the head, or even hitting him at all, with the first shot. The wind would be a real problem, especially the way it swirls and gusts between the buildings downtown. Shooting uphill also makes it trickier to calculate the trajectory. If you gave me four or five shots, I'd be able to dial in, though even then it wouldn't be easy. But just one shot . . . well, it'd be a feat of marksmanship, that's all I can tell you. Either that, or the shooter got very lucky."

"My thinkin' exactly," Rafferty said.

"Then again, has it occurred to you that the sniper might have picked up his other shells and left one there by accident?"

"It has. Trouble is, I don't know if any other bullets struck the outside of the tower near Mr. Dodge's office, but I'm checkin' on it. If the shooter had to dial in, as you say, then there should be some evidence of missed shots. Still, this was about as carefully planned a murder as you'll ever see. Nothin' was left to chance. I just don't think the shooter would be careless enough to leave one shell behind by accident."

Masterson said, "Maybe Dodge was shot from inside the building."

"Ah, there's the rub, Tom. An inside job looks impossible."

"Looks can be deceiving."

"True enough. In fact, I'm beginnin' to think that almost everything about the case is a lie in one way or another."

"Then you've got your work cut out for you," Masterson noted.

"That I do," Rafferty said with a rueful smile. "Thanks for your help, Tom."

"I'm told you are the best man for this business," John McGruder said, staring across his desk at Inspector Mordecai Jones, who sat stiffly in a straight-backed chair. Sergeant Carroll sat beside him, looking equally uncomfortable. "We will see about that, won't we?"

"I'm sure we will," Jones replied, trying not to sound as angry as he felt. He and Carroll had gone to the commission's offices, as ordered, early in the afternoon. A little snip of a clerk had already pointed them to their desks, pathetic wooden wrecks crammed into a dusty nook beneath a stairway. It was all going to be just wonderful, Jones thought, and to top it off McGruder, with his bellowing voice and crazed eyes, appeared to be every bit the obnoxious tyrant everyone said he was.

"You may begin by telling me how you propose to look for Berthelson," McGruder said, displaying no taste for small talk.

Maybe we'll start by looking up your big fat ass, Jones thought, but kept the notion to himself. Truth was, he intended to keep most of his thoughts to himself, including how he would go about tracking down Berthelson. He said, "To find a man, Mr. McGruder, I must first know him. I must know his haunts and habits. Know his family and friends, if any. Know his history. Above all, I must know how he thinks. Therefore, my first course of action will be to find out as much as I can about Samuel Berthelson. I assume the commission has a file on him. I would like to see it."

This was not the answer McGruder had hoped to hear. "We have no file on Berthelson to speak of," he said, "since he has never before been in Minnesota to our knowledge. In any case, I do not think that we have time for the sort of leisurely inquiry you seem to have in mind. This is a crisis, Inspector, and decisive action is required."

"Decisive action without a strategy is of no use," Jones said. "I have no particular ideas as to where Berthelson might be, since I know little about him other than what I have read in the newspapers. I do not even know for a fact that he is in St. Paul."

"He has been seen," McGruder said, "as recently as this noon."

Nice of you to tell me, Jones thought. "Where and by whom?"

"At an old warehouse on Bench Street. He was holed up there apparently. I sent a team of agents to the scene at once, but he was already gone by the time my men arrived."

"And who did you say saw him there?"

"I did not say. It is unimportant."

"To me it isn't. I take it you have an informant."

"Perhaps, but for reasons of security I cannot reveal his name."

"And if you passed on the informant's name to me, you apparently believe that I would immediately blab it about or perhaps even pass it on to Berthelson, assuming I could find him. Is that your line of thinking, Mr. McGruder?"

"Enough!" McGruder said, slamming his fist on the desk. His jowly cheeks went red, and a bulging vein in his forehead began to throb. "You are not here to question authority! Now, by God sir, I expect you to live up to your lofty reputation. You are the greatest detective in the Northwest, or so Chief Nelligan assures me. Very well, get to it. Find Berthelson. How you do it is your business. That is all."

"Nice fellow," Carroll said as he and Jones went back to their desks.

"A charmer," Jones agreed. "He gives us not one whit of information, offers no assistance or resources of any kind, and tells us that we are supposed to deliver the most elusive terrorist in the country to his doorstop, and to do so immediately, if we would be so kind. If it were possible, Sergeant, I would like to deliver McGruder to the tender mercies of Samuel Berthelson."

"That would be a sight worth seeing, but I don't think we'd ever be so lucky. So what's our next step?"

"We have one clue, which was that Berthelson was supposedly hiding in a warehouse this morning. I'm sure one of McGruder's men can provide us with the address. We'll go have a look and see if his team of geniuses missed anything."

On his way back from Kennedy Brothers, Rafferty stopped to see Alan Dubois in his office at Dodge Tower. The young accountant didn't look especially happy to see Rafferty but agreed to answer a few questions.

"I am curious about something," Rafferty began, "and I'm hopin' you'll be able to help me out. I found a receipt in Mr. Dodge's pocket for a dress purchased at a shop in Chicago. The dress, I've been informed, was for Mrs. Dodge. And yet the shop's owner informs me that you, Mr. Dubois, picked it up. Is it possible you and Mrs. Dodge were, perhaps, intimate friends?"

"Don't be ridiculous," Dubois said, remembering how Carr had coached him to answer questions about the dress. "I was in Chicago on business, and Mr. Dodge asked me to pick up the dress for him. He was afraid it might be damaged in the mail."

"Was he now? I was not aware that dresses are so fragile. So you simply folded it up and put it in your suitcase, is that it?"

"Yes."

The phone on Dubois's desk rang. He answered it, listened for a moment, and said, "I'm sorry, Mr. Rafferty, but I must take this call."

"I understand," Rafferty said, lifting himself out of his chair. "I'll leave you to your business, Mr. Dubois. I just hope you've told me the truth."

Dubois watched Rafferty lumber out the door, then resumed his phone conversation with John McGruder.

"So you say you missed Berthelson. How can that be? I told you exactly where he was."

"Well, he was gone when we got there."

"I'm sorry to hear that," Dubois said, neglecting to mention that he'd waited a half hour after leaving the warehouse to contact McGruder. It was all part of the plan. Berthelson actually *wanted* the authorities and the public to know he was in St. Paul, just to increase their sense of terror. Dubois wasn't so sure that was a good idea, but no one told Berthelson what to do. If the terrorist lived to be thirty, Dubois thought, it would be a miracle.

McGruder said, "Berthelson is a cautious man, always on the move. If you had called before you went to the warehouse to see him, it would have been a different matter."

"But I couldn't. I explained to you that a man simply came to my door and told me to come along with him. I had no chance to call you."

"Well, you might have found a way to alert someone," McGruder said, not sounding at all sympathetic, "but it is past arguing over now. Any idea where Berthelson might have gone?"

"No, he's too clever to tell me his plans."

"All right. Keep in touch. I may have more work for you soon."

After Dubois hung up, he went over to the windows and stared out idly at the downtown skyline. He felt as though he'd begun a potentially fatal descent, falling ever deeper into a hole with no bottom in sight. The idea of leaving St. Paul for good looked more appealing than ever. Once Berthelson left town, Dubois decided, he would, too.

Not long after noon, Amanda Dodge's chauffeur let her off in front of the Golden Rule Department Store. She normally preferred to do her shopping in Chicago, where stores were much larger and more up-to-date than those in provincial St. Paul, but it was not unheard of for her to stop at the Golden Rule, the Emporium, or Schuneman's to look for household items. After instructing the chauffeur to pick her up at two o'clock, she went into the Golden Rule, stopped briefly in linens, then walked back out to Seventh Street, where she found a taxi. It took her to a brownstone townhouse on Farrington Street, a few blocks from the cathedral.

Amanda knew the home and its occupant well. Taking a deep breath in anticipation of possible unpleasantries to come, she told the driver to wait for her, saying she'd be "no more than ten minutes." She stepped out of the cab and walked briskly up to the home's massive oak door, set deep within the shadows of an elaborately carved stone arch. It was like going into a cave, she'd often thought, with her very own caveman inside. Before she could ring the bell, the door swung open.

"Right on time," Steven Dodge said, ushering her into the front parlor with an exaggerated bow. "Do you know how unusual it is for a woman to be punctual? By the way, you look lovely today, if I may say so."

"Spare me," she said, stepping past him and seating herself on an over-stuffed couch. The room was, as usual, a mess. Although Steven Dodge was fastidious about his personal appearance and always wore the latest fashions, he took no interest in housekeeping, and even the weekly efforts of a cleaning woman had done little to reduce the chaotic condition of his residence. Amanda took in the scene—plates of half-eaten food piled on tables and chairs, a colorful array of clothes strewn about like wilted flowers, a mosaic of urine stains from Steven's beloved cats defacing the rug—and said, "I see you are still living the life of a pig, Steven."

"Pigs are actually quite tidy. I believe I read that somewhere," he replied, sitting down beside her and giving her a peck on the cheek. "I wish I could say the same for cats. Mmm, is that a new perfume?"

"Stop it," she said, sliding away. "You've had your fun, Steven. Now it's time to act like an adult. We have important matters to discuss. We didn't get a chance to go over the matter completely this morning at the office, I'm afraid."

"That old hag, Mrs. Schmidt, does have a way of interrupting things, doesn't she?" Dodge said. "Still, my dear, I do so hate discussing important things. They're always, well, so boring."

She'd heard this complaint before. The trouble with Steven, she knew, was that he never felt the need to grow up. And why should he, with so much money to play with?

At first, Amanda had been enchanted by Steven's juvenile insouciance, which she found refreshing compared to Artemus's grim and stingy pursuit of the dollar. Steven was also young and handsome and loved a good time—all qualities notably lacking in his father. So it was that she'd bedded Steven only four months after her marriage, and to her delight he'd proved to be an athletic and highly capable lover. Boys at heart like Steven were always grateful for sex, she'd found, and were easily trained. She'd enjoyed giving him lessons, and they'd had a fine fling, even spending a summer weekend in Chicago while Artemus went off to New York to close a stock deal.

After a while, however, Amanda realized that she'd made a mistake with Steven, who'd actually fallen in love with her and had even brought up the ridiculous idea of marriage. She'd tried to let him down gently and ease out of the affair, but spoiled lad that he was, he'd thrown a fit. Then he'd flown into the arms of Isabel Diamond, which was also a problem, simply because Steven didn't know how to keep his mouth shut. God only knew what he might be telling the Diamond woman, who was undoubtedly using him for her own devious purposes.

"Let's not waste time," Amanda said, as though admonishing a troublesome schoolchild. "You know why I'm here. I do not like being blackmailed."

"Nor do I," Steven said. "Not one bit. Kretch always seemed like a nice enough fellow, but this, well, I never expected it. What do you suppose we should do? Perhaps if we gave him more money, he would just go away."

"Don't be an idiot. The man is a serpent. Giving him more money will not solve anything, Steven, as even you must realize. Once he's tapped the keg, he will keep on drinking. He's already asked for five thousand dollars from each of us, and when he's spent that money, he'll be back for more."

"Well then, as I said, what are we to do?"

"We must stop him. It's that simple. Tell me, Steven, is it true you frequent the local gambling halls?"

"Yes, I've been in some of them, but—"

"And is it also true that many rough, dangerous men can be found in such places?"

"I guess so."

"Well then, I think I know of a way to deal with Mr. Kretch."

"What do you mean?"

"I will tell you what I mean," Amanda said. "Just listen now, and before long our troubles will be over."

J. D. Carr had always thought of himself as a fixer, not in any illegal sense, but simply as someone who knew how to analyze a problem at its root and repair it, much the way a good workman might trace a leak in the walls to some distant source on the roof. After his talk with the insolent Peter Kretch, Carr realized that his skills as a fixer were about to be put to the ultimate test. If he failed, the very foundations of the house of Dodge might well be swept away in a tide of disaster.

Alan Dubois would have to be on board if Carr had any hope of resolving the Blue Sky problem. When Dubois appeared at the door to his office, Carr invited him in with a friendly wave of his arm. "Have a seat, Alan," he said. "I trust you are feeling better than you did last night. By the way, what did that Rafferty fellow want? I saw him in the hallway."

Dubois recounted his conversation with Rafferty, then said, "I'm not sure he believed me."

"What he believes is irrelevant. All that matters is what he knows. And unless you tell him, Alan, Mr. Rafferty will never be able to prove that Steven ordered the dress. It was very careless of him to leave the receipt where Mr. Dodge could find it, but then, that is just Steven being Steven. There is, however, a matter that does concern me. As you know, Mr. Dodge always maintained the highest standards in his business dealings. He was a speculator, to be sure, but he was not a cheat. Unfortunately, it appears that some things were done in recent months in his name that were not entirely legitimate. Do you know what I'm talking about?"

"I'm afraid I don't," Dubois lied, thinking Carr must have figured out what was going on with the Blue Sky Partnership.

His fears were quickly confirmed. "I'm concerned about the Blue Sky Partnership, Alan."

"How so?" Dubois asked, his voice betraying no concern. "I believe the partnership is doing quite well."

Was Dubois telling the truth or just covering himself? Carr couldn't be sure. In recent months the Blue Sky operation had acquired a score of new investors—there were more than thirty in all—each lured by the promise of quick profits. Some of them had put in as much as fifty thousand dollars. So far, their dreams of easy money remained intact, but Carr knew it wouldn't be for long. A rude surprise lay just around the corner unless Carr could find a way to handle the situation.

"The accounts are all right for the moment," Carr said carefully, "but I am concerned about the long-term consequences of some of the investments. Therefore, I would like to see all of the most recent account statements for the partnership. Once I've examined them, I may be able to make some adjustments. Get them to me by the end of the day if you would. Oh, and don't bother Steven about any of this. He has more than enough to worry about at the moment."

"I understand, sir," Dubois said, feeling deeply worried. He didn't need more trouble at the moment. The partnership was nothing but trouble, and Dubois knew he could end up right in the middle of it unless he was very careful.

"I would also appreciate it if you made no mention of the partnership to outside parties, including the police," Carr added. "It would only complicate our situation."

"You may rely upon my discretion," Dubois said, wondering at once what he should—or shouldn't—tell McGruder. He'd have to think about it.

"Good. By the way, how is Steven doing? I've not been able to talk with him much since his father's murder."

"I believe he is doing as well as can be expected under the circumstances."

"That is good to hear. I will keep you no longer, Alan."

Once Dubois left, Carr loosened his tie and got out a bottle of single-malt Scotch from the sideboard next to his desk. Artemus Dodge had always taken a dim view of alcohol, and Carr claimed to be an abstainer. But there were times when a man simply needed a drink. Carr poured a shot, downed it in a single gulp, and began to think that he'd finally encountered a problem he couldn't fix.

. . . . .

"Quite the dump," Sergeant Francis Carroll said to Mordecai Jones as they rummaged through the abandoned warehouse on Bench Street where Samuel Berthelson had last been seen. "I doubt we'll find much here."

"Maybe so. Then again, maybe we'll catch a break."

Jones knew they'd need a break to find Berthelson, who seemed to roam the nation with impunity despite being its most wanted fugitive. He'd gone completely underground after being linked to the bombing of a post office in Chicago in early 1916, and since then there'd been only periodic sightings even though authorities continued to attribute all manner of violent crimes to him and members of his "anarchist gang."

Before going to the warehouse, Jones and Carroll had stopped at the new public library on Fourth Street and spent an hour reading periodicals in hopes of learning more about Berthelson. An article in *Collier's Weekly* had proved especially revealing. It detailed how Berthelson kept constantly on the move during daylight hours to avoid detection and slept in a different place every night. He had shadowy associates, the article reported, who set up "safe houses" around the country. The owners of these houses rarely, if ever, knew Berthelson by sight and were simply told, sometimes at the point of a gun, that a "visitor" needed to spend the night.

As he poked through the debris scattered around the warehouse's rotting plank floor, Jones wondered where Berthelson would be sleeping come nightfall. If he had a "safe house" in St. Paul, Jones didn't know about it. He thought McGruder might, not that it mattered. The old bastard, Jones knew, would never share that sort of information with him or anyone else in the police department.

"Finding anything, Sergeant?" Jones asked, looking over at Carroll, who was walking slowly behind the beam of his flashlight, methodically inspecting the floor. Jones was doing the same thing at the other end of the warehouse, which consisted of two rooms divided by a flimsy wooden wall.

"I'm looking," Carroll said. So far he'd found three bottles of Mrs. Pinkham's Miracle Oil, bedsprings, an old whiskey flask, two empty cans of beans, and a *Saturday Evening Post* from the past February.

As Carroll riffled through the magazine, Jones said, "Don't dally, Sergeant. I want to make sure we have a thorough look at this place before it gets dark."

"Just checking to see if there's anything . . . hey, what's this?"

Jones hurried over. Carroll was crouched over the magazine, which he'd opened to page thirteen. The entire page was devoted to an advertisement for Chesterfield cigarettes, with a smiling young man touting the brand's "smoothness." In the upper right-hand corner, however, someone had drawn a crude map. It showed the lines of what seemed to be a street and railroad tracks meeting at a right angle. The street was labeled STC, the tracks RR. Another line led from the tracks across what looked to be a bridge and then up to a rectangle that presumably represented a building. There was nothing to indicate the drawing's orientation.

"What do you make of it?" Carroll asked. "Could be just some idle doodling."

"Could be," Jones said, "but I have to tell you, something about it looks familiar. I just can't say what it is."

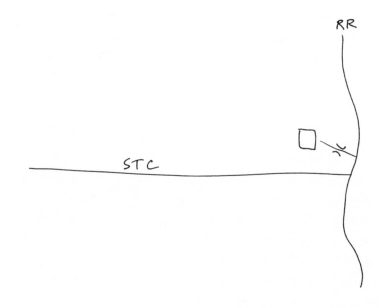

14

"NOT EXACTLY"

After talking with Dubois, Rafferty returned to his office, which was not the sort of boozy hideaway that might be expected of a tavern keeper. A wall lined with books was perhaps the greatest surprise. Rafferty had been an especially voracious reader in his younger days. Edgar Allan Poe had hooked him long ago on detective fiction. Then he'd moved on to Jacques Futrelle, Gaston Leroux, E. C. Bentley, Melville Davisson Post, and others. Rafferty collected so many books that every year he donated a pile to the public library to keep his shelves from overflowing.

Although Rafferty loved detective fiction, he never mistook it for reality. In stories the detective was always uncanny and godlike, a thinking machine—as Futrelle called his detective—who gathered small pieces of evidence and fit them together in the manner of a jigsaw puzzle. Rafferty never found the jigsaw image convincing. A jigsaw puzzle consisted of a known quantity of pieces, and in the end there could be only one solution. In the real world, where humans moved like burrowing animals through secret realms of thought and desire, perfect solutions were impossible. Doubt always lingered.

The newspapers, however, seemed to think that the puzzle had already been solved and that when the last piece finally fell into place, it would reveal the face of Samuel Berthelson. Rafferty had to admit that Berthelson was a logical suspect. By all accounts he was smart, ruthless, and driven—a killer ready to sow terror in the name of a sacred cause. But did he possess the kind of patient, inventive, and brilliantly devious mind that had plotted Artemus Dodge's murder? Rafferty wasn't sure. While it was possible that Berthelson orchestrated the crime, Rafferty thought it more likely that the terrorist was an accomplice rather than an instigator. Who, then, was pulling the strings?

A knock on the door interrupted Rafferty's reveries. It was Wash Thomas.

"You look tired," Thomas said, taking his usual seat at the desk while Rafferty lounged on the couch.

"'Tis one of the mysteries of my life, Wash. The older I get, the less I sleep, and the less I sleep, the older I feel. Nature, I believe, is preparin' me for a mighty letdown."

"I'm not so sure. You just might live to be a hundred."

"Ah, there's a comfortin' thought. I trust you'll visit me as I drool away the hours at the county home."

"Every day," Thomas said with a grin. "In the meantime I've got some interesting news. A copper I know told me there was blood on that water pistol in the alley. Trouble is, nobody really knows what to make of it."

"I'm not sure I do either, though I'm beginnin' to get an idea."

"A crazy one, I imagine."

"Of course. This whole business is nothin' if not an incubator of strange and outlandish notions. I tell you, Wash, the mind behind Mr. Dodge's murder is as deep and twisted as they come. Any other news to report?"

"Plenty of it. The copper I talked to also told me that Samuel Berthelson was supposedly seen around noon at an old warehouse down on Bench Street. McGruder sent a big squad of agents to go after him but he got away. The copper believes he might have left town by now."

Rafferty shook his head. "Not a chance. The carmen's strike is set for midnight Saturday. Berthelson will stay around at least until then to foment trouble."

"Any idea where he might be?"

"Not a clue, Wash. I've always said that if you want to be a good detective, don't take cases that you can't solve. Findin' a clever man who doesn't want to be found isn't a job for old warhorses like you and me. 'Tis best we leave the job to the police or McGruder's hired army. Besides, I'm thinkin' Berthelson might just be a sideshow."

"What makes you say that?"

"I don't know. Let's just call it an intuition."

"Uh, oh. Now we're in trouble. The last big intuition you had was that President Wilson would never win a second term and we'd never go off to fight a war in Europe."

Rafferty let out a gale of laughter. "By God, Wash, you've got me there. But the logic of the Jesuits teaches us that just because a man is wrong once doesn't mean he'll be wrong twice."

"I'll give you that. I can recall at least a few occasions when you were right. Even so, if you really think Berthelson's a sideshow, you're the only one in St. Paul who believes it. I was out visiting our suppliers this morning, and Berthelson was all they could talk about. They're afraid he's going to blow up the town before he's done. He's the very devil in their eyes."

"Well, maybe that's a good thing. While everybody else is out scourin' the woods for him, we'll have the main highway to ourselves. Speakin' of hittin' the road, I've got a couple of jobs for you, Wash. Do you still have that small telescope you use for stargazin'?"

"I can find it. I think I know what you have in mind." He then described exactly what Rafferty wanted him to do.

"Ah, you're far too smart for me," Rafferty said. "All right, once you're through telescopin', I'd like you to pay a call on Gus Klemmer. I have an idea or two I want you to check out for me, and you know Gus better than I do."

Gustave Klemmer owned St. Paul's largest locksmithing shop, on East Seventh Street. Thomas once worked for him as an apprentice and might have made a career of locksmithing if he hadn't gone into the saloon business with Rafferty.

"I'm assuming you have some questions about the locks in Dodge's office," Thomas said.

"I do. The locks, doors, and everything and anything else related to them. I've even got a list of questions I drew up for you. They're in the top desk drawer."

Thomas got out the list and read through it. He said, "I'm not so sure Gus will be able to answer most of these, Shad. Mosler out in Ohio would probably be the only ones who'd know."

"I know, but go have a talk with Gus anyway. If he doesn't have the answers, maybe he can tell us who does."

Thomas nodded. "I'll go see him as soon as I can. What'll you be doing in the meantime?"

"Thinkin' as hard as I can, which is always an arduous and painful process," Rafferty said as he lay back down on the couch.

Rafferty had barely settled in before Thomas was back. "This just came," he said. "It's another telegram from Holmes."

"Ah, perhaps he's figured out something," Rafferty said as he opened the telegram. It read: "SOLVERS' CLUB PAPERS, 1915–16, P 47. HOLMES."

"Do you know what Holmes means?" Thomas asked.

"I think I do. Hold down the fort, Wash. I need to visit the library."

The new St. Paul Public Library was a handsome building of pink Tennessee marble that overlooked Rice Park on the western side of downtown. In the main reading room, beneath a graceful row of arched windows, Rafferty found a librarian who knew all about the *Collected Papers of the Solvers' Club, 1915–16,* and retrieved the volume from the stacks. Rafferty went to page forty-seven, where he found what Holmes wanted him to read. It was a long essay titled "The Locked Room Mystery: Its Seven Common Types and How to Solve Them." The author was Dr. Gideon Fell, identified as a "connoisseur of mystery who lives in St. Paul, Minnesota." Rafferty assumed the name was a pseudonym.

Rafferty knew of the Solvers' Club. Holmes—who else?—had founded it some years earlier and had even written its inaugural paper, a brilliantly reasoned essay titled "A Comparison of English and Continental Shoe Treads." Holmes had invited Rafferty to join, but he'd politely declined. His investigative style wasn't especially scientific, and in any event, he knew he'd never have time to read the papers.

Now, he wished he'd taken Holmes up on his offer because the essay on locked room mysteries was dazzling. It broke them down into distinctive types, each with its own colorful name. "Out of Time" concerned cases in which the murder occurred much earlier than appearances suggested. "Down and Dazed" covered crimes in which the victim was somehow incapacitated before being killed. "Revenge by Suicide" told how acts of self-destruction could be staged as homicides. "Gas, Guns, and Goonies" dealt with killing agents—chemical, mechanical, or animal—secretly introduced into the locked room, as in Holmes's celebrated case of "The Speckled Band." "Disguised for Death" centered on all manner of masquerades used to confuse the locked room investigator. "Last Wrongs" focused on murders committed during or after the supposed discovery of the body.

But it was the seventh and longest chapter—"Tricks and Tampering"—that Rafferty found most instructive. It offered an exhaustive analysis of how a room, even one as seemingly impregnable as Dodge's office, could be penetrated by means that ranged from the surprisingly simple to the amazingly complex. None of the tricks fit the exact circumstances of Dodge's murder. Even so, the chapter opened Rafferty's mind to new possibilities.

When he got back to the tavern, he told Thomas, "I'm beginnin' to see how the thing could have been done. 'Tis possible we've been lookin' in the wrong direction all along."

"So what will you do with all the money you're inheriting?" Isabel Diamond asked when Steven Dodge answered the phone.

"Why, marry you, my love," Dodge replied with his usual nonchalance. "A big white gown, the cathedral, the cream of high society gathered all around. It'll be the event of the season. What do you say?"

"I say you're full of you-know-what. By the way, anything new on Berthelson? I've got two men in green eyeshades breathing down my neck."

"That sounds exciting."

"I'm serious, Steven. You know how the news business is. All editors care about is the next story."

"No resting on your laurels, is that it? Too bad, I've always found your laurels quite attractive."

"Oh, stop it. Come on, tell me what you've heard."

"Are you coming over tonight?"

"Maybe."

"Is that a definite maybe?"

"Yes."

"All right. Well, I hear that they almost caught Berthelson this noon, down on Bench Street. Missed him by a matter of minutes."

"Give me the details."

Dodge did so, then said, "There's something else."

"I'm listening."

"Well, I've heard that Inspector Jones is off the case."

"What do you mean?"

"I mean he's not heading the police investigation anymore."

"You're joking."

"No, not at all. I called his office not ten minutes ago to find out how he was doing, and the person who answered the phone told me he was away on special assignment. Said I could leave my number, and he'd get in touch with me. Isn't that the craziest thing you ever heard? I have half a mind to call Nelligan right now and ask him what the devil is going on."

Diamond said, "Steven, darling, why don't you let me call the chief. I'll get to the bottom of this."

"Yes, that's a good idea. What time will I see you tonight?"

"Late. Probably not until midnight or so. I have lots of work to do. Now if you hear anything else, Steven, let me know at once." Then she said good-bye.

Samuel Berthelson had taken refuge in the damp, cold basement of a vacant building on Rosabel Street in St. Paul's gritty wholesaling district. He'd heard about the raid at the warehouse where he'd been hiding earlier in the day. The city, it appeared, was in an uproar about him, and that was just what he wanted.

Before settling into his basement hideaway, Berthelson had been in contact with several local anarchists, and they'd agreed on a plan. Although the city's union streetcar workers weren't supposed to go on strike until Saturday, Berthelson knew that a group of militant union members planned to anticipate the walkout by staging "protests," beginning in a day or two.

Berthelson thought the protests would be perfect for his needs. The militants were angry not only because the company had fired union members but also because motormen and conductors aligned with a company-controlled union intended to ignore the strike and keep on working. In this toxic atmosphere of anger and recrimination, Berthelson believed he could achieve a triumph of provocation that would rock the city and perhaps even the entire nation.

The militants planned to protest at two places. One group would gather downtown at Seventh and Wabasha streets, the city's main streetcar transfer point, where six lines intersected. Another group intended to mass around the Selby Avenue tunnel, near the cathedral. The tunnel, Berthelson had decided, was where he would strike.

For the next few hours, Berthelson refined his plans by the light of a kerosene lantern. Then he changed clothes and left the building, heading east. He was dressed as a tramp, and he attracted little notice as he crossed the long iron bridge at Sixth Street and made his way down a steep embankment into the hobo jungle of Swede Hollow.

Harlow Secrest didn't like the setup. He had only two men with him—hardly a posse when it came to facing the likes of Berthelson. Still, McGruder wanted an ambush team at every "safe house" in St. Paul thought to be used by radicals on the run. There were six in all, and Secrest had picked one at random to stake out.

Waiting now in a back room, Secrest hoped that he wouldn't run across the terrorist. Let someone else have the glory, he thought. Better to be alive than a posthumous hero. How many men had Berthelson supposedly killed? Eight? Ten? Secrest wasn't sure, but the number didn't really matter. Berthelson had killed before, and he'd kill again in the blink of an eye. Secrest lit a cigarette and looked at his pocket watch. It was half past six, and deep autumnal darkness had clamped down like a vise. Secrest had the feeling it was going to be a long night.

Peter Kretch had agreed to the meeting, at seven o'clock at night and in a rather inconvenient place, only because he knew there would be money in it. The High Bridge, which climbed up toward the West Side bluffs, was a half-mile-long iron span that angled across the river valley, and it had always felt as cockeyed to Kretch as a door with a crooked hinge. Its old plank sidewalks inspired even less confidence, creaking underfoot and buckling like loose piano keys every time a heavy wagon or truck passed by. Still, the bridge offered a fine view of downtown's lighted buildings, and Kretch, who was standing at a point midway over the river channel ninety feet below, took in the scenery while waiting for his contact to arrive. Although he anticipated no trouble, he'd brought along his revolver just in case.

Kretch was pleased with his overall situation. Under most circumstances, the murder of Artemus Dodge would have done grievous harm to Kretch's prospects in the security business. But his after-hours snooping had provided him with insurance that promised to pay benefits for years to come. Why work when people would pay him for doing nothing?

Amanda Dodge's infidelity—and with her stepson, no less—had been Kretch's greatest discovery, and the $5,000 she'd already agreed to pay him was only the beginning of what he expected would be a long and lucrative relationship. Young Steven had promised to pony up an equal amount.

There was also the intriguing matter of the Blue Sky Partnership. Kretch had found out about it a week earlier during a meeting with Artemus Dodge in his office. The old man had gone into his apartment to use the bathroom, and Kretch had taken the opportunity to scan a page of scrawled notes on Dodge's desk. The notes suggested that a very large sum of money—at least $1 million—had vanished from the partnership.

When Kretch mentioned the partnership to J. D. Carr, the reaction had been quick and forceful. On the verge of being fired, Kretch had gotten his job back and a pay raise to boot. Carr clearly had something to hide, and Kretch suspected that Steven Dodge and Alan Dubois might be in on the secret as well. The Blue Sky Partnership, Kretch foresaw, would have to be covered up with large shovelfuls of hush money, and he intended to collect his share before the burial was complete.

Striking a match, he looked at his watch and saw that it was five past seven. He would wait until quarter past—no later—since he didn't believe in rewarding tardiness. Moments later, he caught sight of a man in a dark raincoat striding up from the lower end of the bridge. As the man drew near, passing through intersecting pools of light cast by the bridge's lamp-posts, Kretch saw the briefcase in his hand.

"Do you have what I want?" Kretch asked.

"Not exactly," the man said in a strangely accented voice, then dropped the briefcase.

Before Kretch could say anything more, he received the shock of his life.

15

"IT IS A MATTER OF LIFE AND DEATH"

Shadwell Rafferty sat in his tavern, thinking. Mounted on the wall above him was the biggest fish he'd ever caught—a twenty-pound northern pike pulled one fine May morning from the depths of Lake Osakis. The fish, one of many mementos strewn about the tavern, was known to one and all as Ossie the Pike. It always brought back memories for Rafferty of the rune stone murders of 1899, which had occurred not far from Osakis on the western Minnesota prairies. He, Sherlock Holmes, and Dr. Watson had worked together to solve that troublesome business, and what a great adventure it had been.

Artemus Dodge's killer, unlike the plump pike on Rafferty's wall, was proving very hard to catch, in waters that grew murkier by the day. Rafferty had even begun to wonder if he was trying to hook the wrong fish. Was Berthelson the real trophy? Or was it someone else?

Rafferty looked up and saw Wash Thomas striding into the tavern with a three-foot-long telescope slung over one shoulder and a satisfied look on his face. "Ah, come and join me and we'll have some supper," he said. "Any luck with that telescope of yours?"

"I think so," Thomas said. He put down the telescope and slid into the booth. "You know that new hotel up on St. Peter Street? The doorman's a friend, and he let me in. Went up to the roof and got everything set up just right. You wanted me to look for any signs of bullet holes in the walls around Mr. Dodge's penthouse. Well, I looked back and forth and up and down, but I didn't see anything that looked like a hole or any other kind of damage to the stone. The walls looked clean as could be. If the shooter did fire off some shots before hitting the bull's-eye, they must have gone awfully wild."

Rafferty said, "I'm not surprised. We are left to believe Mr. Dodge was killed by the sniper's first and only shot. We'll just see about that. By the way, did you get a chance to talk to our locksmithing friend yet?"

"No, but I'll stop by Gus's shop tonight. He always works late."

Danny Grimes, one of the bartenders, came up to the table with a copy of the *Pioneer Press*. "Looks like another special edition. Just came in. Big news, I guess."

Under a massive headline that simply said, "ALMOST," Isabel Diamond recounted, in prose more breathless than accurate, the near-capture of Samuel Berthelson on Bench Street. "Had they arrived but a minute earlier," she wrote, "the safety commission agents who swooped down on the old warehouse like an avenging horde would surely have caught or killed the man all of America is searching for. Instead, he remains at large, alone in the night, plotting some great evil."

Rafferty, who read the story out loud, found its last paragraph to be particularly interesting. "The *Pioneer Press* has learned," Diamond wrote, "that Inspector Mordecai Jones is no longer leading the St. Paul Police Department's investigation into the murder of Artemus Dodge and has in fact been assigned to 'special duty.' What this duty may be is unknown, and Chief Nelligan refuses to speak of the matter."

"'Tis a regular nest of intrigue," Rafferty observed. "Our friend Inspector Jones must have stepped on the wrong toes."

"Makes you wonder what he's doing if he isn't investigating the murder," Thomas said. "Maybe you should talk to the chief."

"No, Nelligan would just tell me a tale. I have a better idea. I'm thinkin' Louis Hill will have the inside story."

After a quick supper of roast pork, boiled potatoes, and coleslaw, Thomas left to pay a call on Gus Klemmer while Rafferty telephoned Hill. As Rafferty had suspected, Hill knew all about what had happened to Mordecai Jones.

Hill described the inspector's new assignment with the public safety commission, then said, "I'm surprised you weren't informed of all this, Mr. Rafferty."

"A mere oversight, I'm sure. Has Inspector Jones made any progress on the case?"

"Not that I have heard. But the pressure is on to find Berthelson. At least we know now who committed the crime."

"So it would appear."

"Well, I must go," Hill said. "Keep me informed if anything develops."

"I will," Rafferty promised.

Peter Kretch felt lucky to be alive. The bullet had passed right through the thick layer of fat on the left side of his stomach. There was plenty of blood but no serious injury. Still shaken, he was nursing his wound and a beer at Dandy Jim's Tavern on West Seventh Street. The place was dark, smoky, and full of men from the Schmidt Brewery drinking their dinners, but at least it was safe.

Although the encounter on the High Bridge had lasted only seconds, it was already lodged forever in Kretch's memory. As the man approached, Kretch got a good look at him. His face—youthful, stubbled with a new beard, and definitely Slavic—was unfamiliar. After the man spoke and dropped his briefcase, he slipped his right hand into the pocket of his raincoat. Only then did Kretch realize what was about to happen. It was too late to pull out his own revolver, holstered under his left arm, and also too late to turn and run.

With death an instant away, Kretch charged, head down, and heard the crack of a gunshot just as he slammed into the man. After that, there was a chaos of flailing fists and the glaring headlights of a car and then more lights and then the man was suddenly gone, running back down the bridge and shouting, in his thick accent, "You are dead! You are dead!"

When Kretch got back to his feet, he refused help, telling motorists who had stopped to help that he was fine and that he'd report the assault to the police. Of course he couldn't do that. The police would ask questions, and it would not take them long to discover that he was a blackmailer.

There would be newspaper publicity, perhaps even criminal charges, and his life would be in ruins.

Yet Kretch also knew that he could not just go on as though nothing had happened. The man in the raincoat had obviously been hired to kill him, and there was no reason to think he might not try again. You'd better think, Peter boy, he said to himself, and think hard, or you'll be fertilizing the flowers at Oakland Cemetery before long. Kretch soon decided what he had to do. When he left Dandy Jim's at eight o'clock, he went out the back door, just in case.

Klemmer Lock Company occupied a small brick building on East Seventh Street, two blocks from the Golden Rule and Emporium department stores. When Wash Thomas stopped by, he found Gus Klemmer in the rear of the shop, installing a new lock in a small commercial safe.

"*Ach, mein Gott,*" he said, stepping forward to shake Thomas's hand. "Not for a long time have I seen you." Klemmer was a short, wide man with jolly eyes, plump red cheeks, and a nose big enough "to hang a sausage from," as Rafferty once put it.

"It's been a while," Thomas acknowledged. "Looks like you're busy as usual."

"Oh *ja*," Klemmer said in his heavily accented English. Born in Germany, he'd emigrated to the United States when he was twenty years old. "Always there is plenty to do. How is that big friend of yours?"

"Shad's fine. He's slowed down a bit with arthritis and whatnot, but he's still as sharp as they come."

"Well, that is *sehr gut*. So, is it a job you are looking for, Herr Thomas? Remember what I told you long ago?"

"I do," Thomas said with a smile. "You said I had the hands and mind of a locksmith."

"*Ja*. And what happened? You became a saloonkeeper. What a waste, I say, of your talent."

"If it's any consolation, I've found good use over the years for what I learned from you. In fact, it's locks I've come to talk about."

Klemmer nodded, wiping his hands on his work apron. "I see. Come with me then. We talk in my office."

The office was small and cramped. File cabinets and bookshelves filled with manuals from lock companies took up much of the space, leaving room only for a desk and a couple of slat-backed chairs.

"You are wondering about this murder of Herr Dodge, are you not?" said Klemmer. "I have been reading the papers like everyone else."

"Yes. Mostly, I want to know if you or any other locksmith in town worked on the doors and locks in Mr. Dodge's office. I know Mosler made the doors, which are of the bank vault type, but I am curious if any modifications were made locally before or after the doors were installed."

"I did not do such work. That I can tell you at once. But I have heard that work was done, by a locksmith in Chicago."

"Do you know his name?"

"*Nein.* Our trade, it is a very secretive one, and jobs are not discussed. Still, there are little birdies who sing. One of them told me that a large sum of money was paid for the work. It was all very hush-hush, I think."

"Can you tell me what kind of work a locksmith might do to modify a vault door?"

Klemmer shrugged. "*Ach,* it is hard to say. You see, if there is work to be done, it does not usually happen until after the vault has been used for many years. And then it will be the manufacturer who is called in. For a locksmith to do such work, well, that would be rare because it is very expensive. Do you see what I am saying?"

"I see. Modifying a vault door is not something you'd normally expect a locksmith to do."

"You have said it exactly. I have never done such a thing myself, and I have been here thirty-five years now."

Thomas consulted the list of questions Rafferty had prepared and saw that most of them could be answered only by the locksmith who'd actually worked on the door. He found one more worth asking, however. "How difficult would it be to, say, modify a vault door's locking mechanism?"

"It would be a job of many hours, requiring torches, special cutting tools, and the like. The men who make vaults, they are not stupid, and they build in many things designed to keep away the thieves. The Mosler men are especially good at this."

"Not good enough, perhaps," Thomas said as he thanked Klemmer and left.

As night fell, Samuel Berthelson was holed up in a hobo camp below the tracks of the Chicago, St. Paul, Minneapolis & Omaha Railroad in Swede Hollow. The hollow was a deep trench cut by Phalen Creek through the blufflands east of downtown. Theodore Hamm's Brewery, a stone castle presided over by a dome the color of dark ale, rose above the north end of the hollow, as did the brewer's grand Victorian mansion. Down in the hollow itself only the poor made their homes, in shacks cobbled together from waste lumber and wooden boxes. The shacks followed the line of the fast-flowing creek, which conveniently bore away the sewage dropped from outhouses built above it.

Berthelson had reached the encampment late in the afternoon. The hobos, he found, were good enough fellows, happy to share a meal, but there were always a few who liked to throw their weight around. Berthelson had been forced to put his .45 caliber Colt revolver to one oaf's chin to convince him to back down. After that, no one had bothered him.

Berthelson thought the encampment, where most of the men got along well, was just as society itself should be, and in fact would be once the new order was in place. Although he'd had to preserve his own well-being at the point of a gun, Berthelson was convinced that people in their natural state were kind and decent. But the ruling classes, with their wars and money and patriotic folly, had corrupted all that was beautiful in the human soul. Justice was Berthelson's avowed goal, but he knew it could not come without the copious spilling of blood. There was no other way the revolution could be achieved.

During his years as an agitator, Berthelson had worked with Wobblies, anarchists, farm radicals, and not a few men who simply liked trouble for its own sake. He'd even spent an evening debating the fine points of philosophy with the Italian socialist Carlo Tresca, who'd only recently been arrested in Chicago. Yet none of these men was a true revolutionary in his eyes. The Wobblies were mostly interested in striking back at the rich men who'd abused them for so long. The anarchists, not surprisingly, were disorganized and lacked strategic vision. The farm radicals just wanted more money for their crops, while socialists like Tresca thought that by reforming government they could turn the United States into a paradise of equality.

Berthelson knew better. The nation didn't need a new government; it needed purification, a white-hot fire that would burn away all that was rotten and corrupt. The fire had to begin somewhere, and Berthelson believed St. Paul was as good a place as any to strike the match.

Still, there were problems. The streetcar motormen and conductors preparing to go on strike were not men of vision. They did not see that their only real hope lay in the utter undoing of the system that held them in chains. Instead, the poor fools simply wanted more money, not realizing that money itself—the filth and unfairness of it—was at the root of their problem.

Berthelson's father had died for the dream of a better world. Berthelson expected the dream would claim him, too, but not before a great movement toward freedom began sweeping across the globe, as irresistible as the ocean tides. The armies of Europe and the United States, he was sure, would exhaust themselves in the trenches, along with the rotten system that sustained them. Then a new order would rise from the ashes.

After dining on a stew of mysterious contents, Berthelson set off in the darkness along the Omaha tracks, which passed under twin arches beneath Seventh Street before curling west toward the downtown riverfront. The night was cool and still, and stars twinkled through the haze of locomotive smoke hovering over the tracks. Berthelson had a knapsack full of dynamite slung across one shoulder, and he moved cautiously, keeping an eye out for the railroad bulls who liked to harass tramps.

At Sibley Street he passed near the tracks of St. Paul's temporary railroad station, which had been pressed into service after fire destroyed the Union Depot. The temporary station was grossly overcrowded, especially now that servicemen had begun to fill the trains. Berthelson ignored the crowds and kept walking west, following the tracks as they joined up with those of the Milwaukee Road at river's edge.

In a short while he saw a cluster of wood-frame houses beneath the High Bridge. The hand-built houses were set in tidy fenced yards with vegetable gardens and outbuildings for chickens and goats. The settlement, inundated almost every spring by the Mississippi, had originally been called the Upper Levee Flats or simply Bohemian Flats. Since the turn of the century, however, its population had come to consist largely of Italian immigrants, and so the neighborhood inevitably became known as Little Italy.

Berthelson had been given an address on Mill Street, the settlement's main thoroughfare. Little Italy had no electricity or other utilities, so it took Berthelson several minutes to find the address. He walked past the house, looking for any sign of trouble. He found a hideaway behind a shed and waited for a half hour. He saw nothing suspicious. He doubled back to the house, took one more look around, and knocked four times on the front door. A small man in overalls, a briar pipe stuck in his mouth, opened it. He was Italian by the look of him.

"I am the one," Berthelson said.

The man looked at Berthelson but said nothing. His eyes were wide with fear.

Berthelson dropped his knapsack, lowered his left shoulder, and with a sudden burst drove the startled man backwards into the house. In the same instant Berthelson drew the Colt from his waistband and shot the man in the gut. Another man, armed with a pistol, came out from a doorway straight to the rear. The man fired a wild shot before Berthelson shoved the dying Italian aside and squeezed off two rounds. With a startled cry, the man at the doorway staggered back as Berthelson veered to his left, toward a ragtag sofa set beneath a flimsy window.

"I've been shot," the man shouted, but Berthelson hardly heard him. He jumped up on the sofa and crashed through the window, which gave way in an explosion of glass and wood. Berthelson hit the ground hard, shards of glass lodged like random jewels in his heavy wool jacket. One shard had penetrated into his left shoulder, but he ignored the pain as he rolled up to his feet and sprinted toward a shed behind a neighboring house. Shots rang out, and a bullet buzzed past his head as he zigzagged toward the shed. Another round kicked up dust at his feet. He heard footsteps—from at least two men—and more gunfire. Still running at full speed, he circled around the shed and did something his pursuers could not have anticipated. He headed back toward the Italian's house.

"Where'd he go?" he heard a voice shout, and then came another shout, "He went back! Get him!"

Berthelson was young and fleet afoot—qualities both his pursuers lacked—and before long he'd opened a wide lead over them. Cutting through yards and gardens and vaulting over chicken-wire fences, he made his way north, back toward the railroad tracks. He saw the light of a locomotive bearing down from the east and ran toward it. The locomotive was moving slowly, and as he drew close Berthelson saw that there were no cars other than a tender behind it. He grabbed the handrail at the rear of the locomotive and swung himself up into the cab, much to the amazement of the engineer and fireman.

"What the hell do you think you're doing?" the fireman said, picking up a heavy wrench. "Get off, you son of a bitch, or—"

Berthelson leveled his revolver and said, "Take it easy, fellows, and you'll both have a fine story to tell when the day is done." He cocked the revolver and told the engineer, a wiry man with a soot-blackened face, "Speed up. Now!"

Glancing out the far side of the cab, Berthelson spotted his pursuers. There were two of them, and they'd come to a stop. They obviously knew they couldn't catch the locomotive, but they weren't ready to give up either. One of the men was down on one knee, aiming what looked to be a carbine.

"Faster," Berthelson commanded, putting the revolver to the back of the engineer's head, "or you're a dead man."

The locomotive surged ahead as a bullet pinged off the side of the cab.

"Christ, they're shooting at us," the fireman said, crouching down to take cover.

"Don't worry," Berthelson said. "They've already proven that they can't hit anybody. Just keep moving, the faster the better."

Two more rounds struck the locomotive before the shooting stopped. A mile down the line, with his pursuers out of sight, Berthelson ordered the engineer to stop.

"Quite an adventure, wasn't it?" he said, climbing down from the cab.

"You fellows can go on to the yard now, but don't look back, if you know what's good for you."

The engineer nodded, and the locomotive lurched forward. Berthelson watched it for a while, then walked off into the night.

River's Edge had been Artemus Dodge's dream, Eden on forty acres. Its luxuriant forest of oaks, elms, and sugar maples harbored a burbling creek that flowed into a man-made pond named Lake Amanda in honor of the estate's mistress. Every spring it was stocked with bass and bluegills, which guests could catch from a small dock or from one of the rowboats Dodge always kept on hand. The pond was directly north of the main house, a vast Georgian affair in red brick that sported three porticos, the largest overlooking a grand mall, or allée as Dodge called it, that extended due west to the river road. To the south of the house was a sunken garden set behind low walls decorated with statuary. Amanda Dodge had given many summer parties in the garden, flitting about like a golden butterfly while Artemus, who disliked most forms of amusement, wandered off to smoke cigars in solitude.

Although Amanda had decorated and furnished every one of the mansion's twenty-two rooms in the latest fashions, she felt no attachment to the house, and now as she sat on the front terrace smoking a cigarette in the still night air, she considered her next move. River's Edge was too remote and isolated to suit her purposes. The only entrance to the grounds was from Mississippi River Boulevard, which was not much more than a dirt path. The boulevard attracted little traffic after dark, and once the sun went down, Amanda felt marooned. The encounter with Kretch the night before had only increased her feeling of vulnerability.

Her plan was to subdivide the estate and sell off the lots at a nice profit. The mansion itself could stay or go—she didn't really care. Once she'd dealt with the estate, she intended to move to New York, where she'd make a grand impression. A Park Avenue apartment would suit her perfectly. And then perhaps she'd meet some rich young man of impeccable breeding who'd sweep her off her feet and introduce her to an exciting new world of wealth and luxury.

Amanda stubbed out her cigarette and went inside. One of her nightly rituals was to consult a deck of tarot cards she kept in the library. She didn't really believe that the tarot could divine her future. Then again, there'd been times when the cards proved remarkably prescient. She sat down and turned over the top card. It was the Eight of Swords, which showed a bound and blindfolded woman penned in by a fence of long swords stuck in the ground. The card, Amanda knew, represented feelings of entrapment and persecution. Yet Amanda didn't feel hemmed in. She'd soon be free and rich, and the life she'd always dreamed of was about to be hers.

She slid the card back into the deck and tried to read for a while, but she couldn't concentrate, so she went upstairs to her bedroom. She opened the balcony doors to catch the breeze. She heard the rhythmic chirping of crickets and the calls of night hunters circling above the trees. Almost as soon as she lay down, she fell asleep.

The sound that awakened her was at first indistinct, a soft shuffling in the shrubs below the balcony. She sat upright, listening. She thought she heard whispering but couldn't be sure. Maybe it was just the wind rustling through the trees. She got up, threw on a robe, and tried to turn on a bedside lamp. It wasn't working for some reason. She grabbed Artemus's pistol from the top drawer of the bed stand. The house servants were sleeping in their quarters at the rear, while the chauffeur and groundskeeper had their own apartment above the garage. Both were drunks and heavy sleepers. There were no guard dogs, either, since Amanda hated the idea of animals in the house.

She walked out onto the balcony, which overlooked the sunken garden. She noticed that none of the yard lamps were on. There had obviously been a power outage. A pale intermittent moon provided the only light. Something's not right, she thought, just before she heard a gunshot.

By the time Jones and Carroll returned to the safety commission's offices after grabbing a quick meal, it was already dark. Jones was eager to study the drawing they'd found in the ruined warehouse, but a call from the chief intervened. Nelligan accused him of leaking news of his reassignment to Isabel Diamond at the *Pioneer Press*. Jones replied that the very idea was preposterous, and he convinced the chief that someone else in McGruder's office must have been the culprit.

It was a whopping lie. Jones had in fact called Diamond to offer himself as a confidential source. It was, from his point of view, a matter of self-preservation. Jones believed that the chief and McGruder would ultimately try to hog all the credit for solving Dodge's murder and capturing, or killing, Berthelson. Even worse, they'd work tirelessly to pin the blame on him if the investigation failed. Jones couldn't let that happen, so he'd cut a deal with Diamond. He'd feed her information now and then; she in turn would be sure to keep McGruder and Nelligan honest. Diamond was a pain, Jones knew, but she was also absolutely fearless in the presence of authority. She was the guardian angel he needed.

Outside, it was turning colder, and Jones wouldn't have minded a long night's sleep in his own bed, but he knew it wasn't to be. Time had become a bully, threatening him with every tick of the clock. He needed a breakthrough in the hunt for Samuel Berthelson, and he needed it soon. The drawing from the warehouse, he hoped, might provide just such a clue.

Jones pestered one of the commission's agents for a good city map and pored over it, looking for any spot in St. Paul that the drawing could conceivably represent. He assumed that STC stood for St. Clair Avenue, a main thoroughfare in the western part of the city. Stickney, a far shorter and less prominent street on the West Side, was also a possibility. St. Clair did pass over the Milwaukee Road's short line at one point. But what did the other line and the small bridge in the drawing indicate?

He was still puzzling over the drawing at nine o'clock, when McGruder came up to his desk, looking even grimmer than usual.

"There's been a shooting in Little Italy," he announced. "Berthelson was there, and we missed him again."

"Anyone hurt?" Jones asked.

"There's a dead wop, and an agent was wounded. That's all I know. Get over there right away. Berthelson escaped on a train. He's probably somewhere near the Omaha yards. I'm sending men out to search now."

When McGruder left, Carroll said, "Looks like we're chasing the ghost again."

"And we won't find him, not the way McGruder is doing it."

Jones let out an involuntary yawn, rubbed his tired eyes, and took one last look at the city map on his desk, following the line of St. Clair Avenue from Seventh Street to its termination at Mississippi River Boulevard, commonly known as River Road.

"My God," he said, standing straight up and feeling a tingle run down his spine. The initials RR on the map didn't stand for railroad tracks, Jones realized. They stood for River Road.

"What's up, boss?" Carroll asked.

"I'll explain later," Jones said. "I know where Samuel Berthelson has gone. Get us a car or a cab as fast as you can. I'll meet you out front." He told one of the agents in the office to contact McGruder immediately and have him send out as many men as possible. The agent looked dubious.

"Do it!" Jones shouted, so loudly that the man nearly fell off his chair. "It is a matter of life and death."

16

"WE'LL FIND HER"

Jones received no answer to his phone call—the line apparently was out of order—and felt a sense of dread as he went out onto the front steps of the old capitol. Carroll, with his usual efficiency, had managed to round up a taxi, and Jones made it clear to the driver that he should feel free to break any and all speed laws on the way to their destination. The driver, a young fellow wearing a cap set at a jaunty angle, was more than pleased to comply.

"Are more men coming?" Carroll asked as they sat back in their seats.

"I've got the word out to McGruder, so let's hope so. It's likely we'll be first on the scene, so we'll have to be careful. Berthelson is a cold-blooded killer."

They reached River's Edge at quarter to ten. The wrought-iron front gate, which displayed the estate's name atop elaborate swirls of ornament, was closed as usual, but the lamps mounted atop the two massive gate-posts were dark. High brick walls marched off into the darkness to either side of the gate. Add some archers and a few pots of boiling oil, Jones thought, and the estate could pass for a medieval fortress.

"Something's wrong," Jones said as the cabbie pulled up next to the gate. "The old man always kept the lights on at night."

Jones and Carroll got out to look around. "We've got trouble all right," Jones said, shining his flashlight on the gate. "There's been a break-in. Somebody smashed the lock. The power must be out, too. The lights along the driveway aren't on."

"Should we drive up to the house?" Carroll asked.

Jones peered through the gate, trying to catch a glimpse of the mansion, but it was screened by a row of trees, their shadows etching long lines in the moonlight. "Too risky," he said. "We'd just be announcing ourselves. Best we go in on foot."

After instructing the cabbie to wait, Jones pulled open the gate just enough to make his way through, with Carroll right behind. Rather than follow the winding drive, they headed toward the grassy mall leading up to the mansion. A line of elms, laid out as precisely as the columns of a Greek temple, bordered the mall. Jones and Carroll used the trees as cover as they approached the house. They saw no signs of life, and no lights inside.

A tall portico faced the mall. Jones had been to the mansion once before—to offer Artemus Dodge some advice on security arrangements—and he knew that the porch sheltered the front door. But he couldn't make out the door in the deep shadows, and he feared Berthelson could be lying somewhere in wait, ready to ambush them.

"That porch should be lit," Jones said. "If Berthelson is here, we'll have a devil of a time finding him. It's best we wait for reinforcements. Otherwise—"

The gunshot startled them both.

"Around back," Carroll said, a sharp urgency in his usually calm manner.

Jones drew his revolver. "We can't wait any longer. You go left and I'll go right. Be careful."

When Samuel Berthelson broke through her bedroom door, a flashlight in his hand, Amanda Dodge took aim with her pistol and pulled the trigger. All she heard was the dull click of the hammer. Before she could try another shot, he grabbed her.

"Give me that," he hissed, pulling the gun from her hand and pushing her to the floor. He was on her at once, straddling her torso with his legs. She felt the barrel of a pistol against her head. "Don't move or I'll kill you."

Amanda could tell by the tone of his voice that he meant it. Her first thought was that he intended to rape her. Instead, he tied her hands behind her back with a heavy cord and pulled her up to her feet.

She had never been so frightened in her life. "What do you want? If it's money, I can—"

"Shut up. It is you I want. Do exactly as you are told and you will be all right. Scream, and I will shoot you. Resist in any way, and I will shoot you. Understand?"

"Yes," Amanda said, her mind working furiously. It wasn't long before she concluded that her captor must be Samuel Berthelson. The afternoon papers had been full of stories about him, and Amanda realized that she was being kidnapped for ransom.

Berthelson shoved her out the door and into the upstairs hallway. He hurried her down the grand staircase and then through the kitchen to a service hall leading to the back door. Amanda was surprised that Berthelson appeared to know exactly where he was going, as though he'd been in the house before.

They were just stepping outside, onto a small porch, when she heard the sharp crack of a gunshot. She instinctively recoiled, but Berthelson grasped her so tightly by the arm that she winced in pain.

"Come on, Amanda darling," he said. "There's nothing to be afraid of. Just the usual death and destruction under the light of the moon."

She looked up and saw a figure running toward the back of the estate's garage, where six cars were kept. She saw something else—a man sprawled on the driveway in front of the garage doors. He wasn't moving.

"We'll catch our ride here," Berthelson said, pushing her up toward the garage. She looked down at the body, which lay faceup, and saw that it was her chauffeur, Michael O'Brien. One of his eyes was gone, turned to red mush by a bullet.

"My God, he's dead," she said and felt a great urge to scream. She knew she couldn't.

"Yes, he is," Berthelson said matter-of-factly, "and you will be too if you don't hurry it up."

· · · · ·

Jones ran out from the cover of the trees and across the mall toward the south side of the house. He turned the corner and saw another porch, with a balcony above it, facing out toward the sunken garden. He carried a flashlight but didn't use it, fearing he'd be too obvious a target. The garden was only dimly visible, its ring of statuary evoking the lost splendors of Pompeii. Jones saw a man running through the garden at full tilt toward the perimeter wall beyond.

"Halt!" he shouted and blew his whistle. Where, he wondered, were his reinforcements? The man kept going and soon reached the wall. He pulled himself to the top and then dropped down into a thick stand of trees on the other side. Jones gave chase and was panting by the time he got to the wall. After a pause to catch his breath, he muscled his way up and over it. A narrow path led off through the woods.

Jones did his best to follow the path but tumbled over a tree root and went crashing to the ground. Cursing, he got back up and switched on his flashlight. He followed the trail for fifty yards or so, then emerged onto a street with houses along one side and lampposts illuminating the grassy boulevard in front of them. The street itself ended just to his right at the river road.

There appeared to be no one on the street. Perhaps, Jones thought, the man had cut through one of the yards. Or maybe he'd sprinted across the river road and gone clambering down into the steep Mississippi River gorge. Jones heard an automobile engine sputtering to life. He glanced up the street and saw a Model T parked a half block away. A man scurried out from behind the car, opened the door, and got behind the wheel.

"You there! Hold it!" Jones yelled and blew his whistle again. The driver ignored the order. Running without lights, he sped up the street and turned right at the first intersection. That was the last Jones saw of the car.

Sergeant Carroll crept along the north side of the house, past a semicircular porch that overlooked the estate's small lake, which was ringed by a dark wall of trees. There was a mere breath of wind, and two rowboats tied up at a dock bobbed in the light chop. Nothing else appeared to be moving. Carroll continued toward the back of the house, where there was an attached garage with an apartment above. He saw no one until he walked past a hedge of yews bordering the garage's driveway and nearly stepped on a body.

The man was lying faceup in the grass. Carroll shined his flashlight on the victim's bloody, disfigured face. He didn't recognize the man, who was wearing long woolen underwear and nothing else. Probably a servant, he thought, brought out into the lethal night by some disturbance. Carroll got down on his haunches to feel the man's carotid artery for a pulse. There was none. Carroll stood up and slowly looked around, wondering if Berthelson might be hiding nearby. It was not a pleasant thought.

Amanda Dodge was crouched down in the front seat of a black Cadillac sedan that had been one of her husband's most treasured possessions. Berthelson stood in front of the car, next to the garage's entrance door, peering through a small window at Carroll and feeling ever so slightly anxious. If the copper didn't clear out soon, Berthelson would have to shoot him, and that might bring even more police to the scene. But he couldn't wait much longer. He had to clear out with his prize before the place swarmed with lawmen.

Cocking his pistol, Berthelson watched as Carroll stood up and turned toward the garage. Time to act. He put his hand on the doorknob, intending to step out and shoot Carroll dead, when he heard the distant shriek of Jones's whistle. Carroll ran off toward the back of the garage.

"Now's our chance," Berthelson said. He pulled open the garage's overhead door, then swung into the Cadillac beside Amanda. The car had an electric starter, and the keys were in the ignition. Before he started the engine, Berthelson pressed the barrel of his revolver to Amanda's forehead. "I always mean what I say," he told her as she felt a wave of terror and nausea course through her body, "and if you give me even the slightest trouble, you will be dead. You know that, don't you?"

"I know it," she said, barely able to speak.

"Good. Now stay down. It would be a pity if you got shot trying to leave your own house." Berthelson turned the ignition key, put the roadster in gear, and stomped on the accelerator.

When Carroll heard Jones's whistle, he knew it meant that the inspector had either found something or was in serious trouble. He raced around the garage to the south side of the house just in time to see Jones pursuing the man in the garden. Carroll's instincts told him to follow, but then something flashed in a corner of his eye. He looked over his shoulder and saw, to his astonishment, a sedan speeding down the estate's asphalt drive toward the entrance gate.

Carroll did some quick thinking. The entry gate was almost completely closed, which meant the car's driver would have to stop to open it. That delay, Carroll thought, might give him a chance to catch up on foot. He wheeled around and sprinted toward the drive. He saw the sedan's taillights disappear around a bend but kept running. By the time Carroll finally saw the gate, his lungs were on fire. The car had stopped, and the driver was opening the gate. Carroll kept going, but he couldn't maintain his pace. He slowed down, his heart about to burst out of his chest.

The driver, his face obscured in shadow, pushed the gate open. He ran back to the car but seemed to have trouble getting it into gear. Carroll drew up close, shined his flashlight through the rear window, and managed to blurt out, "Police, stop," just as the Cadillac took off through the open gate. Out of breath, Carroll went down to his knees, chest heaving. He looked past the gate and saw the taxi driver coming up toward him.

"What was that all about?" the cabbie asked.

"I'm not sure. Did you see who the driver was?"

"No, but there was somebody crouched down next to him. It could have been a woman."

"Oh Christ," Carroll said, his stomach suddenly gone to knots. "All right, come along. We've got to find my boss."

Harlow Secrest lay in a bed at the gloomy old City Hospital on Colborne Street, almost within eyeshot of the house in Little Italy where he'd been shot. He was one of a dozen or so patients in a barracks-like ward that smelled of bleach and decay. Although he was hurting, Secrest knew he'd been lucky. The shots from Samuel Berthelson hadn't hit anything vital. One slug had torn through his upper arm and made a clean exit; the other had trimmed some hair just above his right ear.

He was fortunate, too, that the two agents posted outside the house had come to his aid at the sound of gunfire instead of fleeing in the opposite direction, as some men were wont to do. If they hadn't come running, Berthelson—known to be a "finisher" when it came to spies and undercover men—would undoubtedly have paused to put a final round in Secrest's head.

The arm wound, which had missed the bone, hurt like crazy, but Secrest had refused morphine. He wanted to be in full possession of his faculties when the inevitable confrontation came with John McGruder, who would not be pleased that Berthelson had gotten away. Secrest expected no sympathy. Nor would McGruder care that an innocent man had been killed. Secrest had hardly talked to the Italian, whose name was Giovanni Marzitelli, but suspected he was a dupe who knew nothing about Berthelson or his activities.

Marzitelli himself had had no say in the stakeout. Secrest and the other two agents had barged into the house at gunpoint, evicted Marzitelli's wife and children, and told him to cooperate or else. But the Italian had frozen when Berthelson came to the door, and now he was dead, for no good reason. Although Berthelson had pulled the trigger, Secrest felt that he and his men, and beyond them John McGruder, had put Marzitelli in the line of fire. There were bloodstained hands all around, and a widow keening in the night. Secrest knew that he couldn't go on doing McGruder's business any longer. He'd dig ditches if he had to, but it was time to find a new line of work.

Secrest was still waiting for the pain in his arm to subside when McGruder and one of his jut-jawed assistants arrived. McGruder didn't bother with small talk.

"What happened?" he demanded, pulling up a chair beside the bed but showing no interest in Secrest's condition.

"I'm doing well," Secrest said, giving McGruder an insolent stare. "Did I tell you I was hit twice? One bullet came within an inch of killing me, and the other took a nice chunk out of my arm. But I just want to say how much I appreciate your concern."

McGruder ignored the provocation and said, "You do not look all that bad to me, Secrest. Now, I repeat, what happened? You had perfectly good intelligence, you set the trap, and yet you let Berthelson escape once again. How could that be?"

"You had to be there," Secrest said. "Berthelson is a vicious killer, and he proved it tonight. That Italian fellow who died with a hole in his gut had a wife and four children. I wonder what will become of them. Do you wonder about that, Mr. McGruder?"

"What are you talking about? It's unfortunate that the man died, but Berthelson must remain the focus of our efforts. Now, I want your report, and I want it now."

"Very well, here it is. You, Mr. McGruder, are the biggest ass I've ever met. Report complete. Any questions?"

"How dare you!" McGruder yelled, his cheeks flushing as though the blood might burst through his skin. "You will never work in this city again. I will see to it. Do you hear? You are finished."

"Yes, I am," Secrest said calmly. "I'll pick up my last paycheck in the morning. Make sure you don't short me."

"Oh, you will be short, and it will be for the rest of your miserable life," McGruder said, then rose from his chair and stomped out. His young aide, who'd sat in stunned silence through the confrontation, followed him out but not before looking back at Secrest with a smile.

Rafferty was oblivious to the excitement occurring in Little Italy and later at River's Edge. After his chat with Hill, he'd written out a brief message to Holmes, asking if he knew the identity of Dr. Gideon Fell, author of the locked room monograph. If the mysterious Dr. Fell was still in St. Paul, Rafferty wanted to talk to him.

Once the message had been delivered to a nearby Western Union office, Rafferty went up to his apartment one floor above the tavern. The five-room suite had been his home for nearly thirty years, and he'd transformed it into a comfortable retreat. So comfortable that, even though he had much on his mind, Rafferty fell asleep moments after slumping into the leather easy chair in his front parlor.

He woke up at half past eleven, feeling like an idiot. "'Tis only the biggest crime in decades, and here I am sleepin' through it," he mumbled to himself.

Rafferty brewed a pot of strong coffee. He drank two cups, feeling a jolt from the caffeine, and went into his library. Paneled in quarter-sawn red oak and outfitted with built-in bookshelves and display cases, the library was Rafferty's favorite room. It not only held his huge collection of detective novels—"the seamier the better," he liked to say—but also two glass display cases filled with "souvenirs" from his investigations. His collection, easily a match for that of Mordecai Jones, included such grisly relics as the short-handled ax used to kill the butcher Arbogast in 1905, the scissors that took the life of Mrs. O'Reilly, the Mt. Airy abortionist, and the air rifle with which young George Lucey had shot out his father's eye and then bludgeoned him to death.

Surveying his little museum of crime, Rafferty wondered if he'd ever be able to add a souvenir from Artemus Dodge's murder to his display of solved cases. The problem was that, for all the hoopla over Berthelson, Rafferty still didn't understand how Dodge had been shot. Jones obviously thought he did, and Rafferty had a pretty good idea as to what the inspector was thinking. But what if Jones was wrong? What if there were more layers of deception in the case than Jones realized? A great injustice might be done, and a cunning murderer might go free. Rafferty had to be sure.

He was returning to the front parlor when he heard Wash Thomas's distinctive triple knock. "Got some news," Thomas said through the door. "Big news."

Rafferty consulted his pocket watch. It was close to midnight. He let Thomas in and learned that his partner had not been exaggerating.

"I just got a tip from a copper I know," Thomas said. "You won't believe what's happened."

Thomas's account of the shoot-out in Little Italy and Amanda Dodge's abduction took Rafferty by surprise.

"Well, 'twould appear I slept through it all, like the old man I am," Rafferty said, "but there will be no more sleep for us this night."

"We are in for it now, I'm sure," Carroll remarked when a police car bearing Chief Michael Nelligan shot up the drive and stopped near the Dodge mansion's front porch.

"I'm sure we'll be getting medals," Jones said. He was exhausted and deeply angry. They had been close enough to Berthelson to have him in their grasp, but like all the other lawmen before them they'd just missed him. Worse, Amanda Dodge had been spirited away, presumably for ransom, unless she was already dead.

Nelligan, dressed in a tuxedo, came bounding out of the car like a man afire. His lean, pinched face had a horribly pained look, as though all the blood had been drained from it and replaced with corrosive acid.

"Well, do you know what an awful mess we have now?" he said, striding up to Jones. "Do you have any idea what fools we look like? How did this happen?" He smelled of alcohol and cigars. Must have been at a party, Jones thought.

If the chief expected a cowering response, he was about to be disappointed. Jones's legendary dander was up, and he was in no mood for tact or compromise. "That is a good question, Chief," he said. "Perhaps you should ask Mr. McGruder the same thing."

"What do you mean?"

"I mean this: Sergeant Carroll and I drove here all the way from downtown as soon as I became aware that Mrs. Dodge might be in danger. I instructed one of McGruder's men to contact him and tell him to send out as many agents as he could to back us up. No help arrived—not a single man—which meant that the sergeant and I were faced with the task of trying to find Berthelson and his accomplice on an estate forty acres in size, heavily wooded, and without so much as a single light to guide us. It was a job that required manpower, a lot of it, and there was none, thanks to your friend McGruder, who in my considered judgment is incompetent and a disgrace."

"I must—"

"Don't interrupt," Jones said, glaring at the chief. "Had this been a police matter, as it always should have been, I could have had two dozen officers here in a matter of minutes, and I assure you Berthelson would not have escaped. I will not be hung for this matter."

"You are insubordinate," Nelligan said.

"No, I am merely being truthful. Now, sir, I propose to go about my business, if you have no objections. Every minute we stand is a minute we aren't hunting for Mrs. Dodge."

Nelligan backed off. "Very well, but I expect results—quick results. We cannot allow Mrs. Dodge to die."

"We'll find her," Jones said, though in truth he had no idea where she might be.

17

"I HAVE BAD NEWS"

Amanda Dodge wasn't sure how far they drove after leaving River's Edge. She was crunched down in the front seat, her hands bound behind her, and Berthelson had made it clear what he would do if she tried to raise an alarm. When Berthelson pulled the Cadillac to a stop, he ordered her out. She tumbled to her feet, her arms and shoulders aching. She saw a low brick building set in front of a dense grove of silvery cottonwoods. Farther back were high, chalky cliffs. A floodlight illuminated the building, which bore a sign too faint to read. At first, Amanda didn't know where she was, but she soon caught a glimpse of rails gleaming in the moonlight, water rushing past, and the silhouette of distant bluffs. She was somewhere along the riverfront.

"Hold it," Berthelson said. He untied her, grabbed her by the shoulders, and pulled her around until she was looking right into his eyes. He was handsome, even boyish, and she could feel his anxious breath. "How about a kiss, my darling?" he whispered.

She tried to push him away, but he was too strong.

"Ah, I thought not. You prefer whoring with older men. Well, have it your way."

Stepping back, Berthelson yanked a small locket and chain from Amanda's neck. Inside was a picture of her father, who'd raised her and her three siblings after their mother's death.

"Give it to me," Amanda screamed, trying to pull the locket from Berthelson's clenched hand.

"Not a chance," Berthelson said, grabbing her by the wrists and forcing a kiss. "It's mine now, just like you are."

Amanda was terrified but continued to struggle. "Stop it!" she yelled. "Stop it!" She began to feel faint but refused to give in to the sensation. She had to try to keep a clear mind. She had to stay strong. Otherwise, she would have no chance of surviving.

"All right, we'll have our fun later," Berthelson said. "Now get moving."

Holding her by one hand, he pulled her along a winding path bordered by low scraggly bushes. "We're not far now."

They reached a narrow ravine cut through walls of fine-grained white sandstone. A tiny, foul-smelling creek flowed through it, tumbling over small rocks and piles of trash.

Berthelson shined his flashlight along the stone walls, which were covered with graffiti. "Used to be quite a popular place. Now, as you can plainly see, it's deserted."

"Where are you taking me?" Amanda asked. "If it's money you want—"

"Oh, it's money I want, all right, and I will get it. Until then, I don't want you going anywhere, so I've picked out a nice new home for you."

"I don't know what you mean," Amanda said. A bat darted past her face, and she screamed. Berthelson was amused.

"One of your new neighbors," he said. "Ah, here we are." He shined his flashlight up ahead, and Amanda saw the wide, low entrance to a cavern. Part of it was filled in by sand and debris, and a cold, musty breath poured out from inside.

"Welcome to Fountain Cave," he said. "I'm told it's very historic. Now, you'll be the one making history here."

Rafferty wanted to talk with Jones, but when he telephoned the offices of the public safety commission, the agent in charge of the night desk said he didn't know where the inspector was. Nor was John McGruder available.

"We're out of the loop," Rafferty said to Thomas. It was well after midnight, and they were still in Rafferty's apartment. "I suppose we should go out to River's Edge to see what we can find there, but I fear it'd be a waste of time. The forces of law and order will have trampled through the place by now, leavin' us to pick through the remains."

"Then I say we find some better use of our time," Thomas said. "If Berthelson can hide himself when the whole city is looking for him, then he can hide Mrs. Dodge, too, if she's not dead already."

"I think she's still alive. Berthelson is a clever man, and he'll always have a backup plan in the event of trouble. It behooves him to keep her alive until he's got the ransom."

"Maybe so, but he won't keep her for long, unless—"

There was a knock at the door.

"Are you expectin' visitors at this late hour?" Thomas asked.

"No, but I'm hopin' it's not the Grim Reaper come at last," Rafferty said.

Thomas went over to the door and looked through the peephole. "There's a fellow out there, and he doesn't look so good. Got a big bandage wrapped around one arm."

Opening the door a crack, Thomas said, "Is there something I can do for you, sir?"

"Yes, I'd like to speak to Mr. Shadwell Rafferty. My name is Harlow Secrest, and I have some information I believe he'll find interesting."

In the earliest days of St. Paul, Fountain Cave was considered a natural wonder. Located a mile upriver from downtown, the cavern took its name from a creek that issued from its mouth and riffled through a twisting sandstone chasm before joining the Mississippi. Pig's Eye Parrant, the city's ne'er-do-well founder, sold whiskey from the cave. When he was booted out, the cave became a tourist attraction, its thousand-foot-long passageway an ideal place for boyish adventures, secret spooning, and the telling of ghostly tales. As railroads, breweries, and other businesses filled in along the riverfront, the cave lost its charm. By the turn of the century, its once crystalline creek had become a sewer, part of its entrance had caved in, and its polluted depths sheltered only the most desperate of men.

Among the cave's little-known features was that it connected, via a narrow and all but hidden passage, to a far larger man-made system of caverns beneath the Joseph Schmidt Brewery. Berthelson had learned of the caves from his chief associate in St. Paul and thought they would be an ideal place to stash Amanda Dodge while he attended to the final details of obtaining the $100,000 ransom. He'd shied away from kidnapping in the past, not out of any moral scruples, but simply because it was a difficult crime to complete.

Killing was easy and neat—a bullet fired from a gun, a living being turned into a corpse—but kidnapping was full of complications. The biggest one was how to collect the ransom without getting caught. His associate, who was quite brilliant, had figured out a way to do it. Even so, Berthelson had decided to keep Amanda alive as insurance in the event that something went wrong. Once he got the ransom, he would have to kill her, a regretful but necessary step. Alive, she would simply be too much trouble, a millstone—albeit a beautiful one—around his neck.

It had taken them fifteen minutes, mostly walking but in two places crawling through low tunnels, to reach the room that would become Amanda's prison. Eight feet square and about as high, the room was directly off the cave's main passageway, close to where it connected to the brewery's underground complex. A barred steel door guarded the only entrance.

"Well, isn't this nice," Berthelson said, pushing her into the room and securing a heavy padlock on the door. "You've got a new place of your own, Amanda. I'm sure you'll enjoy your stay."

He shined his flashlight around the room, which Amanda thought must have been used originally to store something of value. Otherwise, what need would there have been for a barred door? Whatever the valuables had been, they were gone. Berthelson's light revealed the remains of a wooden keg, its staves scattered like kindling, and a collection of broken beer bottles. Closer to the door was a small wooden tub filled with water.

"As you can see, all of your needs are provided for," Berthelson told her. "Shelter, water, and plenty of peace and quiet."

His taunting finally caused her to snap. "I suppose you're going to leave me here to die," she said, "just like the scum you are."

"Do not accuse me of being scum," he said with quiet fury. "It is you and the people like you who are the real scum, the bloodsuckers who bleed men dry. Well, your money will do you no good now. Judgment day is coming for you and all of your kind, and it is coming sooner than you think." Without another word, he walked away, his light disappearing with him.

Amanda called out after him, begging him to leave her a light, but there was no reply. The darkness consumed her. She had always been resourceful—it had been no easy thing to lift herself out of the shantytown where she'd been born—and she tried to think through her situation. Screaming in the dark was useless. No one would ever hear her. Still, she had to at least try something. Hope was panic's best antidote, and she needed to give herself a dose. Think, think, she said to herself, and then, struck dumb by her own stupidity, she remembered what she usually kept in the pocket of her robe.

Raspberry Island was a narrow spit of land, a city block long, that divided the Mississippi River beneath the Wabasha Street bridge. The Minnesota Boat Club maintained a clubhouse on the western side of the island, while the eastern end was a small wilderness of trees and vines in which a few squatters had built rude cabins. There had been a time when the island provided a convenient spot for fishermen, but now only channel catfish, scuffling along the filthy bottom, flourished in the rank waters.

On Tuesday night members of the boat club were holding a banquet on the upper floor of their spacious building, which provided a good view of the river. The view was not quite good enough, however, for two young club members, a seventeen-year-old boy and his sixteen-year-old girlfriend. Just before midnight they wandered downstairs and out onto a patio near the island's western tip. The moon was out, and the island's old cottonwoods, survivors of many a flood, swayed in the breeze. The boy led the girl past the patio and down a steep wooded embankment, where they would be out of sight of anyone in the clubhouse. He was about to try his luck with a kiss when the girl screamed.

"God, you scared me," he said. "What's the matter?"

The girl pointed down to a man's body, which had washed up to shore in a tangle of driftwood and tree roots. The man had a long white face, and his eyes were open, staring at the incomprehensible moon.

John McGruder had a sour stomach and a team of tiny men pounding hammers inside his forehead. He sat in his office, staring out through a tall window at the darkness beyond. One o'clock in the morning and all was definitely not well. Berthelson's escape from the trap in Little Italy and then his brazen kidnapping of Amanda Dodge had left McGruder and his men looking like fools. The police had fared no better. Worse, there was surely bigger trouble to come, as evidenced by the contents of the gunnysack Berthelson had abandoned at the Italian's house.

McGruder's agents had found fifteen sticks of dynamite in the sack, along with blasting caps, two hand grenades, a pistol, and a bowie knife. Berthelson was preparing for war, and McGruder had no doubt it would begin with the upcoming carmen's strike. That left only three days to find Berthelson and kill him. Capture, McGruder had come to believe, was out of the question. His agents had already begun a manhunt, but now the police would have to join in, much to McGruder's displeasure. He was convinced Berthelson had a source in the department and that the added police manpower would be of little use in tracking him down.

Amanda Dodge's kidnapping only served to complicate matters. McGruder's first instinct had been to rush to River's Edge the moment he learned of the crime, but he soon thought better of it. News reporters, he realized, would descend on the estate, and they'd be looking for someone to blame for the night's distressing events. McGruder would gain nothing by letting the press tear at his flesh.

But how to catch Berthelson? If anyone might know, McGruder thought, it would be Alan Dubois. His work as an undercover agent had been stalwart, and even though the young man seemed to have lost his nerve of late, he still knew as much as anyone about the violent radicals who inhabited St. Paul's underground. And, of course, he'd actually talked with Berthelson at the warehouse on Bench Street. McGruder had been trying for several hours to reach Dubois at his apartment, but there was no answer, and he wondered where the young man could be at so late an hour.

Harlow Secrest required only a few minutes to tell his story to Rafferty and Thomas, aided by a double shot of Irish whiskey.

"'Tis quite the tale," Rafferty said when Secrest finished. "But I'm wonderin' why you decided to share it with us, since I'm assumin' by the lateness of the hour that this is not a social call."

Secrest let out a small chuckle. "Well, your whiskey is most sociable, but you are right, Mr. Rafferty, I am not here to tell stories. I am here to offer you my help. When I left City Hospital tonight, I made a vow of sorts. I said to myself that I would do something forthright and honest for once in my life, instead of slinking around in the dark as I have for so many years. It probably sounds silly to you, but I want to be on the right side for a change. I've heard from many people that you are an honorable and decent man and that you have a thirst for justice. Well, so do I. I have been parched for too long."

Rafferty thought it a remarkable speech. "You are an eloquent man, Mr. Secrest, and that is a rare gift. I can also tell that you are a man who knows how to handle himself in a tight spot. We will officially designate you from this moment forward as one of the Robert Street Irregulars."

"That will be an honor," Secrest said with a broad smile. "So where do I begin?"

"Perhaps you can start by tellin' us what you heard about Mrs. Dodge's abduction before you left the hospital tonight."

"I overheard a copper saying that Berthelson had left a note in the house. It said he wanted one hundred thousand dollars for Mrs. Dodge's return and that he'd provide instructions later about collecting the ransom."

Thomas let out a low whistle. "That could buy a lot of dynamite."

"But will it buy Mrs. Dodge's release? That's the real question, and I fear we all know the answer," Rafferty said. "She will die unless we find her first."

· · · · ·

Isabel Diamond was among the reporters who rushed out to River's Edge to cover the story of Amanda Dodge's kidnapping. She was used to demanding—and receiving—cooperation from the police. Coppers, in fact, were usually easy. Just spell their names right, offer a paean or two to their bravery, and they'd be happy to be quoted in the newspaper.

To her surprise, Diamond received little cooperation from the police at the estate. Under Chief Nelligan's direct supervision, the men in blue had done an unusually thorough job of sealing off the mansion, and Diamond was unable to get inside despite cajoling, threatening, and even offering a substantial bribe to officers stationed at the doors. Still, she had numerous contacts in the department and was able to obtain useful information. When Nelligan finally came out to talk to the press, Diamond was ready for him.

"Is it true, Chief," she began, "that a ransom of one hundred thousand dollars is being asked for Mrs. Dodge's return?"

"I cannot comment on that."

"So you don't deny it?"

"As I said, I cannot comment."

"Is Inspector Jones still leading the investigation, or have you turned that duty over to John McGruder?"

Nelligan glared at her and said, "Inspector Jones is in charge. Mr. McGruder and his men are providing us with welcome assistance."

"A likely story. Is it correct that at least one other man was involved with Berthelson in the kidnapping and the murder of the unfortunate chauffeur?"

"We are still investigating in that regard."

"So you don't know the identity of Berthelson's accomplice?"

"I didn't say he had an accomplice."

"All right, he didn't have one, is that what you're telling me?"

"I am not saying one way or the other."

"So I must assume there was an accomplice?"

"You may assume whatever you please, Miss Diamond."

"You've got that right, Chief. Since we're all busy making assumptions, can we assume that Mrs. Dodge is still alive?"

"I see no reason to think otherwise."

"Do you have any idea where she might be at present?"

"If we knew where she was, Miss Diamond, we would go get her," Nelligan said with exasperation. "I assure you, we will find her, and we will make sure that Samuel Berthelson pays for his crime."

"How nice," Diamond said, closing her notebook. "I'm sure Mrs. Dodge will be greatly comforted to know that you're guaranteeing her safe return. If she's alive, that is."

As a girl, Amanda Dodge and her schoolmates had toured a mushroom cave cut into the bluffs on the city's West Side. Her mind retained three distinct memories of the tour. The first was the smell of the cave—an unpleasant blend of straw, manure, and mustiness. She also remembered how pitch black it was when their guide extinguished his lamp. Her classmates at first giggled, and a boy had tried to grope her, but then everybody grew silent and nervous. The lack of light was quietly terrifying, just as it was now in the depths of Fountain Cave. Her final memory was of something the guide had said as he led them out. He told them that the cave wasn't natural but had been excavated by men using picks and other hand tools. Their work, he said, had been quite easy because the fine-grained sandstone was "like a hard lump of sugar." The guide then gave a demonstration, using a small pick to gouge out a chunk of the stone.

The memory of that tour gave Amanda an idea. First, she needed light, and she said a silent prayer as she reached into the pockets of her robe. If she was lucky—

"Thank God," she said out loud, her words echoing in the darkness. There was a small box of matches in the left front pocket. Amanda liked to smoke at night on her bedroom balcony and so usually kept matches on her. She opened the box, hoping it would be full. She was disappointed to discover, by fingering each match, that only five remained. She knew from her long walk into the cave that five matches would not be nearly enough to illuminate the way back. But they would certainly be of help as she began to grow a plan out of the rich soil of desperation. It would be a long shot, of course, but it was the only chance she had.

Berthelson thought her to be stupid and feckless. He was mistaken.

Amanda had lived on the hard side of the world for much of her life, and she'd met her share of wild, violent men. Berthelson, she believed, would kill her—and probably rape her first if he could—once he had the ransom. Or he simply might leave her to die of starvation. In either case, unless she could escape from her underground cell, she was a dead woman.

She took a deep breath, then lit the first match. The light seemed brilliantly sweet and intense, like a starving man's first taste of food. She used the light to examine the barrel staves on the sandy floor. One of them had a sharp pointed end where it had been broken off. She grabbed it. As the match flared out, she crawled over to the steel door that imprisoned her and set to work.

After leaving the cave, Berthelson enjoyed a few more minutes behind the wheel of Artemus Dodge's Cadillac before abandoning it in a parking lot behind the city morgue—among the last places, he thought, that the police might look for it. Then he set off on foot for the warehouse basement in Lowertown where he'd hidden out earlier.

For all of his daring, Berthelson was not a spontaneous man. He always had a backup plan, which is why he'd been willing to abandon his gunnysack full of dynamite when the trouble started in Little Italy. He had another fifteen sticks of dynamite, along with an extra pistol and a rifle, stashed away in the warehouse, and he found everything in order when he returned around two in the morning.

Berthelson should have been bone tired, but he felt invigorated. He regarded sleep as a waste of time and was used to functioning on very little of it. Still, he allowed himself a brief nap before laying his final plans for the day ahead. His associate, who'd helped plot the kidnapping of Mrs. Dodge, had devised an ingenious scheme to escape with the ransom money. What his associate didn't know was that Berthelson intended to alter the plan. Why settle for half of $100,000 when he could have it all? Great surprises were in store, and Berthelson could hardly wait to spring them.

. . . . .

Dr. James Dahlberg, the Ramsey County coroner, had already had a busy night by the time he arrived at the morgue to look over the body pulled from the river at Raspberry Island. Earlier in the evening, he'd examined the corpse of the poor Italian shot by Berthelson. Then came the hullabaloo at River's Edge, and another dead man, the chauffeur. Dahlberg couldn't remember the last time he'd been called to two separate murder scenes in one night. He hadn't gone out to inspect the body in the river because he'd assumed it was an accidental drowning or, more likely, a suicide. Regardless, there'd be at least three coffins before the night was done.

When Dahlberg lifted the sheet from the body, he was stunned to see who lay on his autopsy table. The man's picture had been in the *Pioneer Press* just the day before. His death would come as another shock to the city. It didn't take long to determine that the man had not died in an accident or by his own hand. There was no water in his lungs, but there was a bloody wound at the back of his skull, which had been split open by a blow from a blunt object. It was clearly a case of murder.

As a matter of routine, Dahlberg went through the dead man's clothes. He found a wallet with $50 in cash, loose change, a fountain pen, and a water-soaked robusto cigar with its name band—Ramon Allones—still wrapped around it. Although it was three o'clock in the morning, Dahlberg got on the telephone and eventually managed to make contact with Michael Nelligan, who'd just arrived home.

"I have bad news for you, Chief," he said. "Somebody has murdered Alan Dubois. You'll be interested to know what kind of cigar he had in his coat pocket."

18

"THIS IS WAR"

On Wednesday morning St. Paul awoke to a frenzy of screaming head-lines. From the old Swedish enclave on Williams Hill to the boggy flatlands of Frogtown to the blufftops of Summit Avenue, readers sat uneasily at their breakfast tables, appalled by the news of Amanda Dodge's kidnap-ping and the cold-blooded murders that preceded it. The name of Sam-uel Berthelson now summoned up the most sinister associations, and the citizenry could not be faulted for feeling as though Old Nick himself had come to torment them.

As though to underscore the city's mood, a pall of dark smoke soiled the air. A cold front had swept in overnight from the Canadian prairies, evicting the last remains of Indian summer and plunging the temperature below freezing. No one could remember such a deep chill so early in the year, and coal furnaces went to work in thousands of basements, sending out clouds of black smoke that settled beneath a low deck of clouds once the winds died away.

In normal times the weather would have been much discussed, but it went all but unremarked amid the uproar over Berthelson. As usual, Isabel Diamond provided the most thorough account of the night's events in a special edition of the *Pioneer Press*. She had the whole story of Berthelson's daring escape from the trap set for him in Little Italy. She interviewed the wife and children of Giovanni Marzitelli, and also reported that an uniden-tified agent of the safety commission shot during the incident was expected to recover from a bullet wound to the arm.

Diamond devoted another, even longer story to the kidnapping of Amanda Dodge, and offered details, such as a lengthy description of her bedroom, that could only have come from an inside source. The story went on to say that Berthelson was "planning some vast act of terror" and that "no one in St. Paul will be safe until he is captured or killed."

Among the most interested readers of Diamond's story were Rafferty, Thomas, and Secrest, who had gathered at the saloon to eat breakfast and "cogitate," as Rafferty put it. Although Dubois's murder had occurred too late to make the morning newspapers, Rafferty had been tipped off by Dr. Dahlberg. It was yet one more mystery for the trio to chew over with their bacon, eggs, and hash browns.

Secrest was full of surprising information about Dubois's undercover work as a double agent for the safety commission. "I don't know exactly when or how he was recruited—McGruder always kept such matters to himself—but it must have occurred months ago. The anarchist groups are notoriously difficult to infiltrate. Oddly enough, the fact that Dubois worked for a hated tycoon like Dodge may have made him especially appealing to Berthelson and his ilk."

"How did you find out that he was working for the commission? I don't suppose Mr. McGruder broadcast that fact," Rafferty said.

"You're right. As it so happened, I was assigned to be his contact man. I don't think anyone else at the commission, except for McGruder of course, knew that Dubois was an agent. It was all supposed to be top secret."

"How could Berthelson or anyone else in the radical crowd ever have trusted a man like Mr. Dubois?" Thomas asked. "It seems very strange."

"I'm sure Berthelson didn't trust him—at least not completely. Berthelson always takes great precautions when he meets anyone outside his small inner circle to avoid being set up. I can guarantee you that Dubois would have been required to perform some violent or even murderous act to prove his commitment to the cause."

"Like murdering Mr. Dodge?" Rafferty suggested.

"That would be possible."

Thomas asked, "Could it be that Mr. Dubois was not merely a double agent but a triple one? Maybe he was loyal all along to the anarchists, who instructed him to offer his services to McGruder as a spy."

"Ah, you're givin' me a mighty headache," Rafferty said. "For now, let us just assume that the young man was playin' both sides of the street, to one effect or another. As little as I think of Mr. McGruder and his witch-hunters, I do not believe they would resort to out-and-out murder, though I may yet be proved wrong. We know, on the other hand, that Berthelson is capable of it, and I'm assumin' it was he or one of his men who killed Mr. Dubois, for reasons unknown to us."

"I agree," Secrest said, touching the bullet wound to his arm, which still caused him considerable pain. "As I learned firsthand, Berthelson is a very violent man."

Thomas had another question. "So are we or are we not thinking that Mr. Dubois had a hand in Mr. Dodge's murder, as well as the kidnapping of Mrs. Dodge? The newspapers say Berthelson had at least one accomplice in the kidnapping."

"Mr. Dubois is a likely enough suspect," Rafferty replied, "and I do not doubt that Mr. Dodge's murder was an inside job to one degree or another. But our first duty now is to help find the missin' lady. The police and Mr. McGruder's agents are presumably scourin' the city as we speak, but I have no great confidence they'll find her. Mr. Secrest, you know more about Berthelson than Wash and I do. Where do you think he's stashed the poor woman?"

Secrest shrugged and said, "I'm at a loss to say. It will be a place where he can keep control of her while he goes about his business. Maybe the basement of an old building or an abandoned house. Or he may have taken her from the city, to Minneapolis or somewhere out into the countryside. But without clues pointing to her whereabouts or some great piece of luck, I do not see how we will find her."

The work was slow and exhausting. The sandstone was soft, but it was stone nonetheless, and as Amanda Dodge gouged at it with her wooden tool, she realized it would take many hours to carve out a hole big enough for her to escape through. Her hands were raw and bloody, and her wrists, arms, and shoulders ached. Worst of all were the dark and the silence. Amanda desperately wanted to strike a match, just to experience the wonder of light, but she had only four left, and she knew she needed to save them if she hoped to make her way out of the tunnels. Hour by hour she worked in the inky blackness, completely by feel. What drove her was her certain belief that once Berthelson returned, he would violate her and then kill her. Escape was her only hope.

At precisely nine o'clock on Wednesday morning, a towheaded boy whose ragged clothing and bold manner identified him as a street urchin, walked into the lobby of Dodge Tower and went straight to the guards' desk. Without a word, he dropped off a plain white letter-sized envelope with the name of Steven Dodge printed on it. Before a guard could stop him, the boy raced back out the door and disappeared into the crowds along Sixth Street.

The guard promptly telephoned the penthouse, where Steven Dodge had just arrived after performing the task of formally identifying the body of his friend and coworker Alan Dubois. Because of Amanda Dodge's kidnapping, two police guards were stationed in the offices as a security measure. When the letter was sent up, Steven immediately notified the policemen that it might be a ransom note.

Chief Nelligan reached the offices ten minutes later. Donning a pair of white cotton gloves, he opened the envelope and found a handwritten message inside: "To Steven Dodge, $100,000 in cash, no bills over $100, for Mrs. Dodge's safe return. Bring money tonight, 11 p.m., upper end of Selby Ave. tunnel. Come alone. No police, no commission agents, no press. Once money has been paid, you will be told where to find her. This is your only chance or she dies." Enclosed with the note was the locket Berthelson had ripped from Amanda's neck.

"We will get him now," Nelligan said. "The tunnel will be his trap, and death will finally turn the tables on him."

A deep sense of unease marked the rest of the day.

In the penthouse of Dodge Tower, J. D. Carr spent many hours on the telephone, making it clear to his underlings that he did not wish to be disturbed. He left early, just after three o'clock, telling Mrs. Schmidt only that he had some "private matters" to attend to.

Steven Dodge, who'd looked wan and shaken after returning from the morgue, huddled with Nelligan and Jones for much of the morning. They discussed strategy for the ransom exchange. The chief reminded Dodge several times that there could be no advance publicity about the drop or Amanda would be killed. Dodge said he understood and would follow the chief's instructions to the letter. Early in the afternoon he went home, supposedly to "get some rest" but in truth to meet with Isabel Diamond, who stayed for over an hour before rushing off to write her next story.

Gertrude Schmidt worked in her office almost all day, searching the company's voluminous files. She had suddenly recalled a very early memo she'd received from Artemus Dodge regarding the Blue Sky Partnership, but she couldn't remember where she'd filed it. If she could locate the memo, she knew, it could prove very useful.

No one in the office seemed to notice that Peter Kretch did not show up for work.

At the public safety commission, John McGruder, who hadn't slept for thirty-six hours, directed the hunt for Berthelson and Amanda Dodge. Although he'd been notified of the ransom note, McGruder was not inclined to wait for Berthelson to show himself. Instead, he sent out his agents, along with members of the Home Guard and scores of police reassigned by Nelligan, to track down every known anarchist, socialist, union agitator, and miscellaneous radical in the city.

Jones thought it all a waste of time, and told Nelligan so. Berthelson was too smart to tell anyone his whereabouts. The chief refused to listen. Nor did he see fit to protest the brutal methods used by McGruder's men, who beat suspects with rubber hoses, assaulted them with fists, and put guns to their heads.

"Show no mercy," McGruder had commanded. "A good beating is hardly too harsh a penalty for treason."

These cruel tactics produced no useful information. Disappointed by the failure to flush out Berthelson, McGruder met later with Nelligan and Jones to make plans for the ransom drop, knowing it might well be his last chance to bring the terrorist to justice.

Rafferty, Thomas, and Secrest were equally unsuccessful. Thomas in particular had many sources in St. Paul's underworld, but none of them had any idea as to where Amanda Dodge might be. Early in the afternoon, Rafferty contacted an old friend in the police department, who passed on word of the ransom note and the planned drop at the Selby Avenue tunnel. "We are headed for trouble," Rafferty told Thomas. "I can feel it closin' in on us like the smoke in the air."

Amanda Dodge kept digging in the darkness, fueled by fear and hope.

Samuel Berthelson, after collecting his stash of dynamite and other weapons, spent his day at a "safe house" off West Seventh Street. His chief associate, who had many contacts, had already furnished him with several sheets of paper bearing the official logo of the Twin City Rapid Transit Company. Berthelson used a typewriter to write a "memo" of his own. Once it got in the hands of the right people, there would be more trouble than anyone could imagine.

Agents of the public safety commission began staking out the upper and lower portals of the Selby Avenue tunnel shortly after dark. At the upper end, next to the St. Paul Cathedral, two agents stationed themselves on the roof of the church's south transept. Four more were inside the rectory, just to the west, where they had a clear view of the drop site, which was well illuminated by streetlamps. Police officers were also hiding behind hedges, inside homes, and even perched in the limbs of tall trees. Inspector Jones and Sergeant Carroll were secreted inside the tunnel. Still more policemen and agents surrounded the tunnel's lower portal. Once Berthelson showed himself, McGruder and Nelligan believed, he had no hope of escape.

Rafferty had plotted a different strategy. He knew Berthelson would never be so stupid as to think he could approach Steven Dodge, take the ransom money, and then stroll away without the police pouncing on him.

"There are two possibilities," Rafferty explained during a late-afternoon strategy session. "One is that Berthelson will send a surrogate to fetch the money. It would be the logical thing to do in his situation, and yet I do not think he will do it. He thrives on danger. 'Tis an urge deep in his blood, and he must satisfy it. So, he'll come to the tunnel, probably in a disguise of some kind. I believe he'll arrive by streetcar. So must we, if we are to have any chance of stopping him and finding Mrs. Dodge."

"What exactly do you propose?" Secrest asked.

"'Tis simple," Rafferty replied, unfolding a schedule of the Selby–Lake streetcar line. "Most of us will be ridin' the rails tonight."

Amanda Dodge, who had lost all track of time, wanted to shout with joy when she finally punched a fist-sized hole all the way through the wall imprisoning her. She resisted the urge, fearing that Berthelson might be somewhere in the tunnels where he could hear her. Still, her success energized her. If she just kept at it, digging and clawing and kicking at the smooth, grainy stone, she could escape. There was no doubt of it now. She would never really know how long it took to enlarge the opening. All she knew was that after what seemed like an eternity of digging, she got her head and shoulders through the hole, pushed as hard as she could against the stone that circled her hips and finally popped out, like a newborn, into the world beyond.

She lay quietly for a few moments on the main tunnel's moist, sandy floor, catching her breath and collecting her thoughts. She had what could be a life-or-death decision to make. Should she try to return along the tunnel the way she had come in, risking a possible encounter with Berthelson, or should she go in the opposite direction, deeper into the cave? She remembered Berthelson's comment that the tunnel extended all the way to the basement of the Schmidt Brewery. Did he really know that, or was he just spinning a tale? She figured he was probably telling the truth if only because he gained nothing by lying, since he obviously believed that she would never escape from her cell.

Amanda decided to go farther into the cave, toward the brewery. She got back on her feet and felt in the pocket of her nightgown for her matches. She cautiously removed the small box, knowing that it held the keys to her survival, and clenched it in her hands. Then she slid the box open, took out a match, and struck it forcefully.

The flame that flared to life was blinding in its intensity, and Amanda had to force herself to keep her eyes open. As her eyes adjusted, she scouted out the tunnel ahead, looking for any side tunnels or obstructions. None was evident. The tunnel appeared to go in a level, straight line through the rock. Once the flame died out, Amanda crept forward, feeling her way along the tunnel's arching walls. Somewhere up ahead, she prayed, there would be an end to her ordeals.

"Are you ready for this?" Nelligan asked Steven Dodge. "You know it could be dangerous."

"I know, but it is the least I can do to avenge Alan's murder. I will try to be brave."

"You'll be fine," Nelligan assured him, looking at his pocket watch. It was quarter to eleven.

They were sitting in Dodge's apartment. A valise rested on the low table in front of them. Inside was $100,000 in cash. Dodge had at first not known how to obtain so much cash on short notice, but some of the big men of the city, including Louis Hill, had stepped in to help, and the necessary cash quickly materialized.

"It's time to go," Nelligan announced. "Now, remember what we talked about. Just do what you're told when Berthelson or whomever he sends approaches you. Once you've handed over the money, walk away as fast as you can. That's all there is to it."

Dodge downed a last shot of Scotch, nodded at the chief, and grabbed the valise. "I guess I'm as ready as I'll ever be. Let's just get this over with."

The Selby–Lake streetcar line, which extended from downtown St. Paul to south Minneapolis, was one of the busiest in the Twin Cities. Even late at night, cars ran every seven minutes. At ten o'clock, Thomas boarded an eastbound trolley at Mackubin Street, two blocks west of the tunnel. He rode it through the tunnel to the stop at Seven Corners. By this time, Rafferty had boarded a westbound trolley with the intention of riding up to Mackubin. There, he'd have time to catch the eastbound trolley following the one ridden by Thomas. Thomas in turn would ride the next westbound streetcar. The idea behind this endless loop was simple: if Berthelson rode a trolley to the site of the ransom exchange, either Rafferty or Thomas would be close enough to take swift action once he got off and tried to collect the money.

Secrest, meanwhile, was in a second-floor apartment on the south side of Selby Avenue directly across from the cathedral rectory. Rafferty knew someone who knew someone else who was a friend of the apartment's occupant, a salesman away on business. Armed with this information, Rafferty had sent Wash Thomas to pick the lock so that Secrest could station himself inside the apartment, which offered an excellent view of the tunnel's upper portal. If Berthelson arrived on foot, the odds were strong that Secrest would spot him.

The meeting of St. Paul local No. 22 of the Amalgamated Street Railway and Electrical Men's Union began promptly at eight o'clock in the downtown Labor Temple, a new brick building on Franklin Street that served as home for the city's powerful Trades and Labor Assembly. The 250 or so carmen had gathered to take a final vote on authorizing a strike, set to begin in three days, against the Twin City Rapid Transit Company. T. F. Shine, a union vice president from New York, presided over the meeting, which was long and contentious. Shine spent two hours reviewing the situation and answering questions. Transit company officials still refused to negotiate with the union, he reported, and a strike appeared to be the only way left to force them to the bargaining table.

Once Shine had finished, each carman received a paper ballot. It took only ten minutes to complete the voting and not much longer to tally the results. At quarter to eleven Shine announced: "By a vote of two hundred and forty-six to one, a strike is authorized."

The crowd broke out into cheers. Deeply angered by the company's refusal to negotiate, the carmen were itching for a fight. Some men talked openly of staging an immediate wildcat strike or even of attacking streetcars operated by nonunion carmen. Shine did his best to suppress such talk, but the mood in the room was tense and volatile.

As the meeting was about to break up, a slender young man dressed in a cheap brown suit and sporting a neatly trimmed beard beneath his wire-rim spectacles, stood up and asked to address the crowd. Samuel Berth-elson was about to set his plan in motion. Identifying himself as Richard Smith, he said that until the day before he had been employed as a clerk for the transit company at its headquarters in Minneapolis. He'd been fired, he claimed, because he "raised a stink" about a memorandum written by the company's president, Horace Lowry.

"I have come here to tell you," Berthelson proclaimed, "that you are all fools if you think that the company will either negotiate with you or even permit you to hold your jobs, and I have the proof right in my hand."

Waving the sheet of paper like a bloody battle flag, Berthelson strode up to the podium and handed the document to Shine. "You must read this," he declared. "It is a terrible thing the company plans to do."

Shine scanned the note, which bore the company's official logo, then said in a shaky voice: "I think this is a matter best left for the union executive committee to consider."

The crowd would have none of it. "Read it!" a man shouted, and he was soon joined by a chorus. "Read it! Read it! Read it!"

Shine saw that he had no choice. "All right, I will read it, gentlemen, but I do not wish you to get overly excited. It is a memorandum that could be of great value to us, but we must not lose our heads. We do not even know if it is legitimate, since we have only the word of—"

"Read it! Read it! Read it!" the crowd chanted.

"Very well, but I implore you to remain calm. The document reads as follows: 'To all division superintendents: In the event of a strike, all carmen taking part in this illegal action will be immediately and irrevocably fired, and a note will be placed in their files that will make them all but unemployable in this city again. This is our chance to destroy the union once and for all, and we must take it. Once we are rid of it, we will be able to adjust all carmen's salaries downward to a more reasonable level and thereby increase our profits. I expect your complete support in this effort, and I am authorizing a bonus of one thousand dollars to every executive of this company as a reward for devoted service. Signed, Horace Lowry.'"

The hall erupted into tumult. For all of its vaunted efficiency, the company had never shown a decent respect for its men, paying them miserable wages and firing them at will, often for the most petty and obscure of rea-

sons. The last straw had come more recently, when the company began docking the pay of employees required to report during working hours to the local draft board for their preinduction physicals. Not even patriotism, it seemed, could loosen Horace Lowry's purse strings. In this regime of harsh parsimony, grievance grew like a worm in the heart, and when the memorandum was read, the crowd's anger exploded, just as Berthelson had thought it would.

Shine again urged calm, but he could barely be heard above the din. Then a voice boomed out, "To the streets, men, to the streets! This is war and we must fight!"

Pounding his gavel like an angry judge, Shine called for order, but the crowd paid no attention to him. He yelled, "Gentlemen, gentlemen, please do not do anything foolish. We will defeat the company in the end, but not if we resort to violence. Now go home, please, go home."

His words had no effect. One man rushed up past the podium to a closet used for storing brushes, brooms, and buckets. "These will work," he said, and began distributing them to the crowd. Two wooden flagpoles were also commandeered. Other men armed themselves with folding chairs.

With a handful of agitators leading the way, the crowd poured out of the hall like burning liquid. The largest part of the tide flowed east toward Seventh and Wabasha streets, where numerous streetcar lines converged. Another fifty or more men moved northwest, toward the Selby Avenue tunnel. Samuel Berthelson, his fake beard itching terribly, was not among them. He'd left a few minutes earlier to catch a streetcar.

19

"EVERYTHING HAS GONE TO HELL"

Rafferty boarded a Selby–Lake trolley at Seven Corners at twenty minutes to eleven. No one else was waiting at the stop. It would be Rafferty's fifth trip of the night through the tunnel. He took a side-facing seat behind the motorman and surveyed his fellow passengers. There were seven, all men, and none appeared to fit Berthelson's description. Rafferty suspected he might be on another dry run or that Berthelson had decided to send a surrogate.

As the motorman was about to close the front doors, a bearded man carrying a satchel rushed up and stepped aboard. The man, dressed in a long wool coat, walked past Rafferty and sat down, facing forward, near the rear. Rafferty stole occasional glances at the man and thought he could be Berthelson. The man was the right size and had an air of coiled energy, fidgeting in his seat and swiveling his head, as though on the lookout for trouble. There was also something odd about how he sat, leaning back with his right leg extended forward. It was just how a man hiding a rifle under his coat might sit.

Although Rafferty had been a match for any man in his day, he was old now, and getting the drop on an agile young killer like Berthelson would be asking too much. He decided to sit quietly until the trolley reached the top of the tunnel, where the man, if he was indeed Berthelson, would presumably try to claim the ransom. Plenty of police would be there to help. Surrounded by lawmen, even a magician like Berthelson would be hard pressed to escape. Or so Rafferty thought.

. . . . .

From his vantage point in the cathedral's rectory, John McGruder waited impatiently for the ransom pickup. He'd decided to take personal charge of his men at the scene, and his orders were simple. Whoever tried to claim the ransom from Steven Dodge was to be shot, no questions asked. "This is war," he had told his men, "and we will take no prisoners."

McGruder was certain the night would end triumphantly. More than forty men were stationed around the tunnel, ready to trap and kill Berthelson. Chief Michael Nelligan, who stood next to McGruder, was less certain of success, nor did he like the shoot-to-kill order. With Berthelson dead, what would become of Amanda Dodge? How could she be found? McGruder argued that she was already dead and that killing Berthelson had to be their top priority. As usual, McGruder had prevailed.

Nelligan was not given to premonitions, but the knot twisting in his stomach reminded him to be wary. Berthelson was a man of great daring and also, as his long history of narrow escapes suggested, a man who always seemed to have luck on his side. Nelligan could only hope that the terrorist's luck was about to run out.

At the top of the tunnel, Steven Dodge waited beneath a streetlamp. He held a satchel containing the ransom money in his right hand. Dodge had never lugged $100,000 around before, and the bag felt as heavy as if it was full of stones. He glanced at his watch and saw that it was five to eleven. Nearby, two men and a woman stood waiting for a trolley. They didn't know it, but they had put themselves in harm's way, since the police didn't want to reveal their presence in the event Berthelson had agents of his own watching the area.

Dodge lit a cigarette and inhaled a soothing dose of nicotine. He felt quite calm despite his perilous situation. The policemen hiding all around probably thought he'd get cold feet, but they were wrong. He would do what needed to be done. He finished his cigarette, stomped out the butt, and looked again at his watch. One minute before the hour. Selby Avenue was quiet. Most of St. Paul had gone to bed.

As Dodge scanned the darkness, a distant sound caught his ears. Before

long, it grew louder, like an approaching locomotive, and then it turned into a tumultuous roar. It was coming from the east, where the tunnel descended into the depths of Cathedral Hill. Dodge looked that way and saw a band of men, and a few rough women, running up the public stairway next to the tunnel.

"What do you want?" Dodge asked when the leader of the group, a barrel-chested man dressed in overalls and carrying a baseball bat, approached.

"Why, we want justice," the man said, raising the bat like a scepter. "Justice for the carmen of this city. Now step aside, or there will be trouble."

Dodge moved back, not wanting a confrontation, just as he spotted a trolley coming along from the west on Selby. Its motorman, no doubt shocked by the sight of a mob in the middle of the street, stopped a hundred yards or so from the tunnel's entrance. The crowd rushed forward and swarmed the trolley. One man began knocking out windows—every trolley had more than thirty—with a broomstick. Another climbed up on the roof and ripped the car's power pole from its base. With no connection to the wires overhead, the streetcar was stranded.

A dozen or so passengers, along with the motorman and conductor, made a hasty exit and ran toward the tunnel, perhaps thinking it offered protection. Dodge recognized one of the passengers as he went past. It was Rafferty's black friend, whose name Dodge couldn't remember. His presence couldn't have been a coincidence. What had he been doing aboard the streetcar? Dodge wasn't sure. He tightened his grip on the satchel.

Rafferty had encountered the swarm of rioters a few minutes earlier at the bottom of the tunnel, where a hundred or more men stopped his streetcar and ordered everyone off. It didn't take Rafferty long to realize that the mob must be part of Berthelson's plan. Chaos was always a good cover for bold action. Rafferty saw no hope of calming the rioters, so he left the streetcar with the other passengers. The bearded man quickly slipped into the crowd. It had to be Berthelson.

Rafferty followed, manhandling his way through the rioters, who were in a frenzy of destruction. They attacked the car's windows with bats, used box cutters to slash the rattan seats, hacked at the side panels with hatchets, and pried away the fare box. Others in the mob climbed to the roof to rip away the power pole. In a matter of minutes, the sixty-ton trolley was an immobilized ruin.

"Fire it up," a man carrying a can of gasoline shouted. The rioters surrounded the trolley and watched it burst into flames, cheering like students at a bonfire. Rafferty had never seen anything like it.

Berthelson by this time had joined a group of men who'd broken off from the main mob and were racing up the steps beside the tunnel. Rafferty suspected their intent was to disable or destroy the first streetcar they came across. With trolleys marooned at both ends of the tunnel, the Selby–Lake line would grind to a halt.

The staircase leading up the hill was long and steep, and Rafferty couldn't keep up with Berthelson and his fellow rioters. Falling far behind, he paused to rest halfway up the steps as Berthelson disappeared over the crest of the hill. Moments later, Rafferty heard the first explosion.

Inspector Mordecai Jones and Sergeant Francis Carroll were secreted in a small utility room just inside the tunnel's upper portal. Their orders were simple. Once Berthelson approached Dodge, police whistles would sound. Jones and Carroll would then close off the tunnel as a means of escape in the event Berthelson managed to flee in that direction. The tunnel would be his "door to doom," or so Nelligan had proclaimed in a moment of hyperbole.

The chief, as usual, was soon proved wrong. As Jones and Carroll waited in tense silence, they began to hear shouts, screams, and pounding footsteps outside the tunnel. The din grew so loud that Jones decided to step out for a look.

"I don't believe it," he said. "There's a riot going on up there."

Carroll came up beside him. "Jesus, now what?"

Jones wanted to run out and try to restore order, at gunpoint if necessary, but he couldn't risk it. Like Rafferty, he suspected that Berthelson had fomented the riot as a diversion and intended to snatch the ransom amid the chaos. For all he knew, Berthelson might even be one of the rioters. What a goddamn mess, Jones thought. What a complete goddamn mess.

"Come on, Sergeant," he finally said. "We're of no earthly use here. Let's see if we can find Berthelson."

Harlow Secrest saw the mob coming and knew that events were spinning out of control. He left the apartment and went out to Selby, where rioters were attacking the trolley Thomas had left only minutes earlier. Across the avenue, the vast granite walls of the new cathedral had become a stage set for the night's violent entertainment. Secrest saw a couple of coppers peeking out from one of the cathedral's side doors, but they showed no interest in taking on the mob.

Secrest headed for the tunnel because he didn't know what else to do. Spotting Berthelson amid the bedlam would be all but impossible, but Secrest was determined to try. He was fifty yards or so from the upper portal when he saw a man crouched in the front yard of an old house directly across from the cathedral. A match flared in the darkness, and Secrest smelled gunpowder. He was running for cover when the dynamite exploded.

After escaping the streetcar mob, Wash Thomas ran with his fellow passengers down to the tunnel's portal. Some of the passengers wanted to go inside for cover, but Thomas told them not to. "Just get away from here as fast as you can," he said, "but don't panic."

Thomas didn't join in the great escape. Instead, he went into the tunnel, where he encountered Jones and Carroll coming up toward him.

"I might have known," Jones said with an air of disgust. "I suppose that old faker Rafferty is hanging around here somewhere."

"He is," Thomas admitted, "but he wasn't expecting a riot."

"Who the hell was? Go on and get out of here before—"

The electric lights that illuminated the tunnel went off, as did all the streetlamps along Selby.

"Now we're in for it," Jones said.

· · · · ·

The man with a carbine slung over his shoulder and a gas mask obscuring his face seemed to materialize out of thin air. Without a word, Samuel Berthelson yanked the satchel from Dodge's hand. Dodge made no attempt to resist but soon found himself choking and gasping for air. Berthelson had dropped a smoke grenade. Dodge's eyes began to smart and burn, and he lost sight of the terrorist.

A thunderous blast knocked Dodge to the ground. Shaken but unhurt, he struggled back to his feet. When the smoke dissipated, he saw a small army of policemen emerging from the cathedral, from yards and houses along Selby, and from parked cars. Two more explosions, smaller than the first one, boomed out. One came from somewhere behind Dodge, and the other from the direction of the cathedral. Dodge dove to the ground, his arms covering his head, and stayed there until someone touched him on the shoulder.

"Are you all right, Mr. Dodge?" Chief Nelligan asked.

"Yes, I think so. What happened?"

"He got the damn money, that's what happened," Nelligan said. "You should leave right now. We don't know if there'll be more explosions."

"So you haven't gotten him yet?"

"No, but we will," Nelligan promised, trying not to think of what would happen if Berthelson got away. "He can't have gone far."

Inside the tunnel, the smoke was almost unbearable. Thomas had drawn his revolver, but how could he shoot at a target he couldn't see? And where were Jones and Carroll? As he went down on one knee, fighting for air, he heard footsteps and saw a glowing light move past like a ship in fog before it vanished into the smoke. Coughing and wheezing, his eyes afire, Thomas stumbled up to his feet to follow the light. He managed only a few steps before a deafening explosion knocked him down. Thomas tried to get up but couldn't. He felt dizzy. He rolled over on his side, waiting to catch his breath. Then two more distant explosions echoed through the tunnel.

When the smoke began to clear, Thomas saw that Jones and Carroll were close by and had also been sent sprawling by the explosion. Thomas crawled over to them. Jones appeared to be unconscious, blood oozing from a wound at the back of his head. Carroll was conscious but dazed.

"I'll go for help," Thomas said, his ears ringing like Christmas chimes. Even with the pandemonium inside his head, he could hear the sharp, persistent sound of gunfire coming from somewhere down in the depths of the tunnel.

When Rafferty heard the first explosion, he did something that only the coolest of men can do in the roar of battle. He paused to think. Berthelson, he assumed, had set off the explosions to sow confusion while he grabbed the ransom money. But how would he get away? Coppers and McGruder's agents surrounded the upper end of the tunnel. On the other hand, Rafferty had seen only a handful of lawmen at the lower end, and they were preoccupied with the rioting. Berthelson's escape route would probably take him back down the tunnel. Rafferty would have to try to stop him.

He made his way back down toward the tunnel's lower portal, which was set between high concrete walls that followed the curve of the tracks toward Third Street. The streetcar he'd left only minutes earlier was a burnt-out carcass, like a big dead animal left on the tracks. The rioters by this time had spotted another trolley approaching on Third and were running down the tracks to intercept it. Not a single copper was in sight. Whatever plan had been devised to catch Berthelson appeared to be in tatters. Rafferty heard two more explosions boom out from somewhere up the hill.

The wrecked streetcar, which Rafferty hoped would provide some cover, was still smoldering when he reached it. He went down on one knee and drew his revolver, keeping an eye on the tunnel's portal. Two street-lamps still glowed beside the portal, but the tunnel itself was pitch black. Something—probably the explosions—had caused the tunnel's lights to fail.

Rafferty had barely settled into his position before a man came out of the tunnel, running at full stride. A satchel hung from his shoulder, and he was carrying a carbine. Although a mask covered the man's face, his long coat identified him. Samuel Berthelson was making his escape. Rafferty saw no reason to announce his presence. He leaned out past the streetcar's rear platform and took aim. Berthelson was a moving target, and it would be no easy shot in the poor light.

Just before Rafferty squeezed the trigger, Berthelson caught sight of him, darted to his left, and hurled a grenade. It hit the ground with a metallic clunk a few feet in front of Rafferty, and for an instant he thought he'd be blown to bits. Instead, a cloud of acrid smoke engulfed him. Rafferty fired three more shots before the smoke blinded him. He wasn't sure if he'd hit Berthelson.

Rafferty's uncertainty didn't last for long. Hidden inside the cloud of smoke, Berthelson opened fire, raking the streetcar with a burst of bullets. Rafferty heard the slugs slamming into the trolley's charred remains. He felt a stab of pain in his left shin, as though he'd been run through with a small but very sharp lance. He ducked around the back of the trolley to take cover behind its heavy wheels. Not for the first time it occurred to him that he was an old man trying to do a young man's job.

Rafferty heard footsteps but saw nothing as he peered out into the smoke. The footsteps rapidly grew faint. Rafferty struggled to his feet despite the searing pain in his leg. He assumed he'd been shot, but when he felt the wound, he discovered that a wooden splinter, propelled by one of Berthelson's bullets, had been driven like a small missile into his shin.

As the smoke dissipated, Rafferty looked down toward Third, where the mob had set another streetcar on fire, flames shooting up through its roof. Rafferty made out Berthelson running past the crowd. There was more gunfire—a furious drumbeat of sharp cracks—and the mob scattered like a flock of birds surprised by a cat. Rafferty heard a woman's piercing scream. He limped down toward Third just as a black sedan pulled up. Berthelson slipped inside. The car made a U-turn and sped away.

"Well, it looks like everything has gone to hell," Rafferty said to no one in particular. Berthelson had escaped with $100,000, Amanda Dodge was probably dead, and the city was being torn apart by riots. Worst of all, Rafferty didn't know if Wash Thomas was dead or alive.

· · · · ·

The basement of the Joseph Schmidt Brewery spread out into a vast cavern, honeycombed with tunnels and vaulted chambers, where the company had once aged its choice lager in long ranks of wooden barrels. The sandstone cavern had been excavated by the Stahlmanns, the first family of brewers on the site, and they might still have owned the brewery had it not been for tuberculosis, which killed Christopher Stahlmann and all three of his sons in the span of a decade. The cavern's musty air, redolent of grain and malt and gas from a nearby sewer, was often blamed for this catastrophe, and some brewery workers refused to go into "Stahlmann's Hell," as they called it, fearing they would meet the same grim fate as Christopher and his sons.

Now, however, the age-old process of "cellaring" beer had been replaced by mechanical refrigeration, and the cavern was all but abandoned except for a boiler room and a small storage space. Among the brewery workers who occasionally entered this subterranean realm was a nightshift building engineer named Otto Meyer. He was in charge of maintaining and operating the large coal boilers that heated the brewery complex in cold weather. Early Thursday morning, only hours after the mayhem at the streetcar tunnel, Meyer went down to inspect the boilers, which would require cleaning and repair before being fired up.

He was examining the heating chamber of the No. 2 boiler with a flashlight when he was startled by the sound of a heavy steel door swinging open behind him. He spun around and caught, in the beam of his light, a mirage. The mirage had long blond hair, wore a white robe, and held a stick in her right hand. Meyer was speechless, but the mirage was not.

"I am Amanda Dodge," said a quavering voice, "and I have been kidnapped. Please help me."

Book Three

THE DODGE FRAGMENT

uthor's note: This manuscript fragment, about four thousand words in its unabridged form, appears to have been written by Dr. John Watson in the early part of October 1917, at about the same time that Shadwell Rafferty was bringing the Dodge murder case to its conclusion. The composition date can be inferred from the fact that while the manuscript refers to a telegram from Rafferty and to accounts of the case in London's newspapers, it makes no mention of Samuel Berthelson, the kidnapping of Amanda Dodge, Alan Dubois's death, or the streetcar rioting. Presumably, Rafferty conveyed these developments in a later letter to Holmes that has never been found. Watson no doubt intended to complete his tale, which was tentatively titled "The Curious Case of the Magic Bullet," upon receiving additional information from Rafferty. It's not known whether the full story was indeed written, only to be lost, or whether Watson simply never got around to finishing it.

As the world's foremost consulting detective, Sherlock Holmes was often called upon for assistance in solving especially puzzling cases. In general, Holmes would offer his services only if he could take a direct part in the investigation, since he disliked "the dreary business of advising from a distance," as he described it. In certain exceptional instances, however, Holmes found a case so intriguing that even from afar he felt compelled to turn his incomparable mind to it, often with astonishing results.

So it was with the affair of the magic bullet, as Fleet Street came to call it, which preoccupied Holmes for several days during one of the darkest periods of the Great War in October 1917. The case, which Holmes pronounced "a most fascinating and instructive example of the so-called locked room murder," is but little known to English readers, having occurred in distant Minnesota. A voyage across the North Atlantic to America was out of the question at the time, and Holmes was therefore unable to investigate the case in person. Even so, his insights proved to be of enormous value to our American friend Shadwell Rafferty, who first informed us of the crime in a brief telegram.

The murder victim was the financier Artemus Dodge, who maintained his offices in St. Paul, Minnesota's capital city. Having spent a memorable fortnight in St. Paul during the winter of 1896, Holmes and I were familiar with the "terrain," as it were, although neither of us knew anything of Mr. Dodge or his far-flung business empire. The crime quickly became a sensation, even in the London newspapers, which trumpeted it as one of the most baffling murders of the century.

News of this singular case came at a propitious time. Holmes was restless and in bad humor. The strange affair of the corpse in the waxworks had recently come to an unsatisfactory conclusion, while the hunt for the German saboteur Walter Kleinschmitt, whose depredations are too well known to bear repeating, seemed to be making little progress. The Kleinschmitt case would soon take a dramatic turn, but in the interim Holmes welcomed the opportunity to consider Rafferty's "intricate little puzzle," as he described it. Dodge, a man of vast wealth, was shot dead in his supposedly impregnable office under the most curious and seemingly inexplicable of circumstances.

Author's note: I have omitted Dr. Watson's summation of the crime, since it repeats information already provided to readers.

Rafferty's message naturally piqued Holmes's interest, which was further stimulated by an account of the murder in the *Daily Telegraph*. Holmes read the article aloud as we sat by the hearth in our flat at 221B Baker

Street. I could tell at once that the case fascinated him because his reading was punctuated by numerous asides. "How peculiar this is," he commented at one point. "Most remarkable. I do not think I have ever seen the likes of it before," he said at another.

In his message Rafferty noted that a set of floor plans for the office where Dodge was murdered could be found, by a happy coincidence, at the Chubb Company in London. Holmes rang up the firm and quickly secured the blueprints. He then retreated to his room, plans in hand, and I heard nothing from him for many hours. Even an offer of supper from Mrs. Hudson could not lure him from his lair, and a lamp was still burning in his room when I retired for the evening.

At noon the next day Holmes finally emerged and favored me with his presence over a light lunch of cucumber sandwiches, biscuits, and tea. His festering unhappiness over the Kleinschmitt case had for many days taken the sparkle out of Holmes, like a bright piece of silver left to tarnish, but now the gleam was back in his eye.

"I see you have come to some understanding of the Dodge affair," I said.

"Ah, Watson, you know me too well. There is nothing like a day of hard thinking to lift me out of the doldrums. I do indeed have an idea as to how the murder of Mr. Dodge was accomplished. If my theory is correct, then his murder must certainly rank among the most ingenious cases of its kind in the annals of crime."

"I am eager to hear it, Holmes."

"And you shall. First, however, I would remind you that I do not believe in miracles. I believe in evidence. The bullet that killed Mr. Dodge did not pass in magical fashion through window glass or brick walls or steel doors. Therefore, its presence must be accounted for in some other way. Mr. Dodge's murder, I believe, was a supreme feat of deception, as elaborately staged as a grand Italian opera."

I took out my notebook, ready to record Holmes's words for posterity.

"Is this to be one of your stories, Watson?" Holmes asked.

"It could be," I said, adding with a smile, "but only if you display your usual brilliance."

Holmes offered a slight smile of his own. "My dear Watson, you grow ever more puckish in your old age. Well, I shall try not to disappoint you. I would note, however, that I am ignorant as to many features of the case. I know nothing of Mr. Dodge himself or of the people who worked in his office. Nor do I have any firsthand knowledge of the radicals who are suspected of killing him. Mr. Rafferty will no doubt provide much of this information in the letter he is sure to send. In the meantime, I have only newspaper accounts to go by, along with one illuminating piece of evidence, which is the plan of the late Mr. Dodge's offices."

Holmes paused to take a sip of tea and continued, "Let me begin by noting that, according to the *Telegraph,* all five members of Mr. Dodge's staff found his body after using an emergency door to enter his office. I would be interested to know *precisely* where each of the individuals was at the moment of discovery and during the few minutes before the police arrived."

"Why is that so important?"

"For the simple reason that every good magician's trick is, at bottom, an exercise in misdirection. So it was with this crime. The murderer wishes us to believe that the crime could not possibly have been committed, and yet voilà! there is the corpse before our very eyes, as mysterious as a rabbit pulled out of a top hat. At some point, for this trick to be accomplished, there had to have been some sleight of hand. And what better time to misdirect than at the moment the corpse is discovered? It must have been a shocking sight for those present, and their attention would certainly have been fixed on the corpse."

"You are certain then that it was an 'inside job,' as the Americans call it?"

"Yes, although I am not prepared to say that the murder was actually committed by one of Mr. Dodge's employees. It is possible an outsider was engaged to fire the fatal bullet. There is already a theory, advanced by the authorities in St. Paul, that Mr. Dodge might have been killed by a sniper hidden in the tower of a nearby building, if the *Telegraph* is to be believed."

"But how could that be," I protested, "when all the windows were found to be closed and undamaged?"

"I cannot say, Watson, which is why I am inclined to think that the fatal bullet did not come from outside Dodge Tower, or at the least did not come from a sniper hundreds of yards away. Indeed, I talked on the telephone this morning with Col. J. R. Camp, the rifle instructor at Sandhurst. He agrees that a sniper shot would have been most difficult, though by no means impossible, under the circumstances described in news accounts of the murder."

"Well, I still don't understand how the killer could have fired the fatal bullet from inside Mr. Dodge's office and then escaped detection."

Holmes offered one of his sly smiles and said, "Ah, that is the preeminent question, is it not? The answer, I believe, can be found in the plans of Dodge Tower's penthouse."

Holmes unfolded a blueprint and spread it on the table between us. He pointed to a small room identified as the "guard's station" and said, "The problem begins right there, Watson. It is all wrong."

"You mean because of something the guard did?"

"No, Watson, the problem is that the guard's station, as it is shown, is not of much use for guarding."

"Why?"

"It is a simple matter of what the guard can and cannot see from his station. As the plan reveals, he has a view of the elevator, the main staircase, the lobby, and the secretary's office. He can also see down the main hallway until it branches to either side. But you will note that he cannot see the entrances to Mr. Dodge's private office, Mr. Carr's office, or the office of young Mr. Dodge and Mr. Dubois. Equally important, he has no direct line of sight to the rear stairway. All of which leads me to wonder why Artemus Dodge, who we are informed was obsessive about his own security, would have approved such an unsatisfactory plan."

"Perhaps Mr. Dodge believed he was so safe within his inner sanctum that he overlooked these deficiencies," I offered.

"Perhaps," Holmes replied, reaching in his pocket for a pencil. "But as you can see here"—he drew several quick lines on the plan—"it would have been a simple matter to make all of the offices and even the back stairway visible to the guard."

"You are right, but I don't see that it makes any great difference."

"Perhaps not. I would call your attention to another point, which concerns a conspicuous example of alignment in the plan. Do you see it?"

I studied the blueprint for a few moments, then said, "I'm not sure what you mean. Why would 'alignment,' as you call it, be so important?"

"It is important, my dear Watson, because it suggests the means by which Mr. Dodge was murdered. A straight line, after all, is the shortest path between two points."

"That seems to me to be a rather obvious statement."

"True, but the biggest mistake a detective can make is to disregard the obvious. I would be curious to know whether Artemus Dodge himself reviewed and approved these plans, or if someone else was in charge of that work."

"I presume you mean someone like that supposed security expert who worked for Mr. Dodge. He was mentioned in the *Telegraph* article."

"Peter Kretch is his name. Yes, he certainly comes to mind. Or perhaps the responsibility was delegated to Mr. Dodge's chief assistant. Do you remember reading about him?"

"I believe so. What was his name?"

"Carr. J. D. Carr. There is also Mr. Dodge's son, Steven, who seems to have taken a large hand in the business, not to mention the young accountant, Mr. Dubois. As it so happens, I know one of these gentlemen."

I was mystified by Holmes's statement. I thought back to our trips to Minnesota, beginning more than twenty years earlier, and tried to dredge up an image of Carr or of the two younger men, who would have been mere boys at the time. Nothing came to mind. "Come now, Holmes, you are pulling my leg," I said.

Holmes set down his pipe, leaned back in his chair, and clasped his hands behind his head while resting one foot on the tabletop. It was, I must say, one of his most annoying habits, although this "thinking position," as he liked to call it, often led to revelations. Such was the case now. "My dear Watson, I assure you that your leg is quite safe. I don't know the man in person. I know him only by his work. You see he is a member of the Solvers' Club."

The club, which Holmes had founded in the early years of the century, was an elite group of one hundred or so men, and at least two women, from around the world. Its ranks included police officials from as far away as Hong Kong, coroners and police surgeons, fingerprint and ballistics experts, chemists, scholars, and, of course, a certain well-known consulting detective from London. The club's purpose was to advance the work of criminal detection by exchanging information and ideas. As far as I knew, the group held no meetings or other formal deliberations, and membership was by invitation only.

"How did the man come to be admitted to such exclusive company?" I asked.

"Ah, that is a most interesting story. About two years ago, I received an unsolicited manuscript from a certain Dr. Gideon Fell—I believe you were out of town when it arrived—titled 'The Locked Room Mystery.' I read it, of course, and found it to be a trenchant analysis of the various types of so-called impossible crimes. To my knowledge, it is the only monograph of its kind in existence. Conveniently, the author provided a postal box number in St. Paul if I wished to contact him.

"I did so, since I suspected the name of Gideon Fell was a pseudonym. Indeed, I thought at first that our friend Mr. Rafferty might be up to one of his tricks. However, when I received a reply to my letter, it was signed by none other than Mr. J. D. Carr, who proclaimed himself the author of the monograph."

"My God, Holmes, then it must be this Carr fellow who planned the murder."

"Why do you say that?"

"Isn't it obvious?"

"No. Remember, Watson, we are dealing here with a crime of great deliberation and subtlety. It is possible the killer knew of Mr. Carr's monograph and used it as a primer to plan the murder. It is also possible that someone pretending to be Mr. Carr responded to my letter. Keep in mind that I have never met the man. I only have a letter purported to be in his hand. There is yet another possibility, which is that the monograph is a mere coincidence with no connection whatsoever to Mr. Dodge's murder."

"How many times, Holmes, have you told me that you are always suspicious of coincidence?"

"Simply because coincidences are rare does not mean that they never occur," Holmes remarked with some asperity.

"Has it occurred to you that Mr. Carr might in fact want you to believe that the connection between his monograph and the murder is too obvious a clue to implicate him in the crime?"

"Watson, you are beginning to think like a real detective. Mr. Carr may indeed be 'playing' us, as Mr. Rafferty might put it."

"Speaking of our friend, have you told him about Carr and the monograph?"

"I pointed it out to him in my last telegram, but I didn't mention that Mr. Carr was the author. I wanted to see first if Mr. Rafferty had any inkling as to the real identity of Dr. Gideon Fell. It appears he does not. I will inform him of Mr. Carr's avocation in my next telegram."

"Well, I am sure he will find all of your insights of tremendous value to his investigation," I said.

Holmes suddenly appeared lost in thought, his head tilted back like a dreamy boy gazing up at the clouds. When he came out of his trance, he said, "I nearly forget something, Watson. It has to do with a certain type of weapon Colonel Camp told me about. I must ask Mr. Rafferty as soon as possible whether anyone in Mr. Dodge's office, or for that matter Mrs. Dodge, recently visited Austria."

Book Four

SECRETS OF THE LOCKED ROOM

s rain pummeled the windows of her late husband's office, Amanda Dodge felt desperation growing like a tumor in her gut. Was it really possible that the fortune she'd sold her body and soul for could turn to dust because of a few words scrawled on a piece of paper? A codicil, that slimy lawyer Patrick Butler had called it. If Artemus had indeed written her out of his will, she needed to find and destroy the codicil before Butler or anyone else got their hands on it. Otherwise, a dismal life of want awaited her. Butler had suggested in his usual roundabout way that the codicil might be secreted in Artemus's office. But where could that sly old bird have hidden it?

Amanda told herself to calm down. It was unlikely anyone else would be in Dodge Tower's penthouse on a Sunday night, and there was no reason to rush. Yet as soon as she'd stepped into Artemus's office and closed the security door behind her, she began to feel ill at ease. A faint whiff of death lingered like flowers gone to rot, and traces of blood still stained the rug where Artemus had taken his last breath. Amanda was not a dewy-eyed or timid woman, but the blood disturbed her. The sooner she left, the better.

The police had combed through the office and adjoining apartment several times, but Amanda wouldn't be surprised if they'd missed something. Her kidnapping and Berthelson's incredible escape had left her with a low opinion of the force. The police were simply not to be relied on.

Amanda went through Artemus's desk, peeked behind the curtains, looked under the sofas, pulled up corners of the rug. She examined the innards of the stock ticker, went through cigar boxes, and opened the back of the grandfather clock. Nothing.

She moved on to the apartment, which offered more hiding places than the office. Her first stop was the wall safe in the closet. The police had already opened the safe and found nothing of value to their investigation. Amanda, who'd wheedled the combination from Artemus long ago, decided to check the safe one last time. The codicil wasn't inside. She wondered if Carr, who probably knew the combination despite claiming otherwise to the police, had removed the codicil for his own devious purposes immediately after Artemus's murder. She wouldn't put such deceit past him.

Amanda closed the safe and continued her search. She inspected every book on the shelves, but the only item of interest she found was a secret stash of lewd pictures in a volume titled *Great Poems of New England*. Apparently old Artemus liked a little pornography with his poetry. She sifted through the bathroom and medicine cabinet, examined every article of clothing and every box in the closet. She removed wall paintings to look for another hidden safe. She flipped over the mattress of Artemus's bed. She ran her fingers around every piece of paneling in hopes of finding a latch that might cause a door to spring open. Still nothing.

She began to wonder if there really was a codicil. Was Butler or some-one else—Carr perhaps, or Steven Dodge, or that prying old biddy Ger-trude Schmidt—playing tricks on her? Even if the codicil did turn up, Amanda planned to contest its authenticity in court. It had to be a fake, she would argue, since if Artemus really intended to make a last-minute change to his will, he would have made sure to give the document to his lawyer. Yet Butler claimed he had never actually seen the codicil. He'd only heard of its possible existence, or so he claimed.

Amanda returned to the office and sat down on the sofa to think. She wished she could hire a crew to tear the office apart piece by piece, but she knew she couldn't. She lit a cigarette to calm her nerves, only to be startled by a familiar voice coming out of the intercom on Artemus's desk.

"Amanda, is that you in the office? We need to talk at once."

20

"I FEAR WE ARE NOT DONE WITH THIS BUSINESS YET"

A ten o'clock on Thursday morning, Mordecai Jones met with the "unholy trinity," as he called Vivian Irvin, Michael Nelligan, and John McGruder. Jones had made a rapid recovery after being knocked unconscious in the tunnel. At first it was feared he'd been shot, but doctors at City Hospital found that his head wound was from flying debris propelled by one of the explosions. Although the wound wasn't serious, Jones had been kept in the hospital overnight. Two dozen people had been injured during the night of riots, explosions, and gunfire, but by some miracle there were no deaths. Nelligan, Steven Dodge, Sergeant Carroll, Wash Thomas, and Rafferty were among the injured who had not required hospitalization.

Jones's head still hurt, and he was in his usual dyspeptic mood when he arrived at the mayor's office. He was pretty sure why he'd been summoned, and he had a surprise in store for his three inquisitors.

"We are in a difficult situation," Irvin began. "I need not tell you that the public is very unhappy about what transpired last night. As for the press, well, it was a crucifixion. Amanda Dodge is a heroine, while we are idiots who allowed Samuel Berthelson to escape and the streetcar men to run wild."

Jones, who had brought along a copy of the *Pioneer Press,* said, "I'm not sure 'crucifixion' is the right word, Mr. Mayor. I would say Miss Diamond's story was more like a flaying. I assume you've all read it. She's quite a prose artist, don't you think?"

The story began as follows:

In a most remarkable display of courage and coolness of mind, Mrs. Amanda Dodge, kidnapped Tuesday night by the terrorist Samuel Berthelson and facing almost certain death—or worse—clawed her way to freedom from an underground dungeon as scores of police officers and public safety commission agents allowed Berthelson to slip from their grasp with $100,000 in ransom money. Meanwhile, rioting by hundreds of carmen and their sympathizers convulsed the city, and authorities appeared as helpless as babies against the raging mob.

Wrapped in a blanket, Mrs. Dodge was taken at once to City Hospital, where she was pronounced well despite her ordeal. Chief Nelligan arrived shortly thereafter and undertook the unpleasant task of telling Mrs. Dodge that her kidnapper had eluded the law.

"Samuel Berthelson is a thoroughly vile and despicable man," Mrs. Dodge later told this reporter. "How could the police let him get away?"

It is a question all of St. Paul is asking this morning.

Indeed, given the abject failure of the authorities to capture Berthelson, to rescue Mrs. Dodge, to control rioting, or to solve the murder of Artemus Dodge, the people of St. Paul have every right to wonder whether their mayor, their police, and their public safety commission can be regarded as even minimally competent to protect them.

How many more depredations and outrages must the city endure before law and order prevail?

McGruder took the newspaper from Jones and tossed it in the wastebasket. "This Diamond woman should be arrested," he said. "How dare she question authority at a time like this?"

Jones made a show of retrieving the paper, then said, "Challenging authority is what the press does for a living, Mr. McGruder. I believe there may even be something in the Constitution about it."

"Do not talk to me of the Constitution. We are at war. Am I the only one here who understands that?"

Irvin said, "All right, let's calm down. The question is what we should do now. I have scheduled a press conference at noon, and I need to offer some positive news, or it will be another flaying, to use Inspector Jones's word. As it so happens, the chief has an idea in this regard."

"I do," Nelligan said. "I think there is a way to turn things to our advantage. It is my understanding that Inspector Jones has discovered how Mr. Dodge was murdered. I am correct, am I not, Inspector?"

Jones nodded, adding, "I also know which member of Mr. Dodge's staff conspired with Berthelson to commit the murder."

"Why have I not been told of this development?" McGruder demanded.

"For the very simple reason that I did not wish to compromise my investigation. You see, the coconspirator was none other than Mr. Alan Dubois, who unless I am mistaken was supposedly working as one of your spies."

"Why that is simply ridiculous," McGruder said.

"Is it? Let me show you something."

Jones opened a satchel he'd brought along and produced two items—a box of Ramon Allones robustos and a leather-bound volume. "I found these items earlier this morning in Mr. Dubois's apartment. The cigars speak for themselves. As you may recall, a robusto of this brand was found in Mr. Dodge's office. The volume is far more interesting. It's Alan Dubois's journal, and it clearly reveals that he was actually working for Mr. Berthelson and his friends while pretending to be a spy for the commission. Imagine how embarrassing it would be if this unfortunate fact become known to the public."

McGruder grabbed the notebook and began reading. He scanned several pages before closing the volume in disgust. He didn't return it to Jones, however.

"This journal is undoubtedly a fraud, and under no circumstances will its scurrilous contents be revealed to the public. Am I correct, Chief?"

Nelligan, who'd been blindsided by Jones, was seething. "I'll see to that. Inspector Jones, I fear, is not always as forthcoming with his superiors as he should be. Now, however, he will tell us at once what he knows. Then we will announce that we have solved the mystery of how Samuel Berthelson killed Mr. Dodge, after which the unfortunate business of last night will no longer preoccupy the press. As for the journal, it will not see the light of day until it's been thoroughly vetted."

Jones stared at Nelligan and said, "Why, sir, I fear I cannot do as you ask. You see, I have decided to quit the force. Indeed, I have my letter of resignation with me right now, if you would care to see it."

"I don't give a goddamn about any letter," Nelligan said. "I have given you a direct order, Inspector, and you must obey it."

Jones responded by removing an envelope from his breast pocket and setting it on the mayor's desk. "As I said, I am resigning. There is no law I am aware of that requires me to serve any of you until death do us part. It has been a privilege working with you, Chief, and with you, Mr. McGruder, and with Your Honor the mayor. A rare privilege. I am sure the three of you will have plenty to tell the newspeople, though I fear the press will be in a surly mood, given all that's happened. Incidentally, I am reliably informed that Alan Dubois's journal includes a second, and even more revealing, volume. I can only hope it doesn't turn up someday on the desk of Miss Diamond at the *Pioneer Press*. Good day, gentlemen."

McGruder looked ready to kill, the mayor seemed stunned, and Nelligan's cheeks turned a deep shade of red. Jones was halfway out the door when McGruder said, "All right, tell us what you want."

A deal was quickly cut. Jones would be released from further service to McGruder and would be given complete control of the murder investigation. He would also be allowed to explain to the press how he'd solved the mystery of Dodge's death. In exchange, Jones promised to make no mention of Dubois's journal or of his work for the commission. Jones also assured the mayor, Nelligan, and McGruder that he would hail them for their "magnificent leadership" in cracking the case.

"You better have some good answers, Viv," Isabel Diamond told the mayor as he entered the city council chambers for the press conference. Nelligan, McGruder, and Jones were right behind.

"I think you'll find them to be quite good, my dear," Irvin said with his best politician's smile.

The room was packed with reporters, municipal functionaries, and members of the public, including Shadwell Rafferty and Wash Thomas, who sat at the rear beneath the portrait of some long forgotten civic notable.

"This ought to be good," Thomas said.

"Could be a regular barbecue," Rafferty agreed. "I wonder who'll be first up on the spit."

Nelligan had the honors, and what he said caught Rafferty and everyone else in the room by surprise: "I am pleased to announce that the murder of Artemus Dodge, one of this city's most distinguished citizens, whose funeral will be this afternoon, has been solved. Inspector Mordecai Jones, who led the investigation with his usual brilliance and tenacity, will now describe exactly how this awful crime was committed and who was behind it."

A clamorous buzz broke out as Jones stepped forward, looking natty in a coal black suit, white ruffled shirt, and red silk tie. He stood silently for a moment, his eyes sweeping the audience.

"Well now, isn't this a surprise," Thomas said. "I think you're about to be upstaged, Shad."

"'Twouldn't be the first time, but I'm mighty curious what the inspector will have to offer as evidence."

Jones caught Rafferty's eye, smiled, and then began his presentation: "The murder of Mr. Artemus Dodge on the morning of October 1, 1917, in his offices atop Dodge Tower has occasioned much interest from the press and the people of this city, as well as much fear. I can now tell you that the person responsible for this awful deed has been identified and that the modus operandi of the crime—that is, the manner of its commission—has been discovered as well.

"The identity of the murderer will come as no surprise. Samuel Berthelson, whose entire life has been devoted to criminality of the most cruel and heinous kind, murdered Mr. Dodge and did so out of hatred for the system of government that is the very foundation of our great nation. I regret to report that Berthelson is not yet in custody, but I am certain that he will be found very shortly and dealt with in the most severe fashion."

The inspector paused to take a drink of water, well aware that he had every member of the audience—Rafferty included—in his spell. Jones savored his moment and felt a deep sense of pride. He'd outfoxed the unholy trinity and would soon become a hero to the public at large. Before long, he fully expected, he would be chief of police.

"While it is no great mystery that Samuel Berthelson was behind Mr.

Dodge's murder, the means of carrying it out have proved baffling to many people," Jones continued. "However, I was able to determine in short order how this seemingly impossible crime was committed by means of a trick that relied on nothing more complicated than a small piece of wood."

A murmur flowed through the crowd as Jones held up the broken one-by-two board found beneath Dodge's desk. "It was in fact this very piece of wood that did the trick."

Jones paused once more to let anticipation build before he launched into the explanation everyone was waiting to hear: "At some point on the morning of October 1, Samuel Berthelson, by all accounts an excellent marksman and a clever burglar, made his way sight unseen into the old state capitol. Once inside, he picked a door lock to gain access to the lookout tower's staircase. The tower, as most of you know, has an open-air observatory.

"Berthelson was armed with a high-powered rifle undoubtedly equipped with a scope. The exact model has yet to be determined, but it was a large caliber weapon and probably quite old. Once in the tower, Berthelson positioned himself to take a shot at the penthouse of Dodge Tower, some eight hundred yards away. Although this would seem a daunting distance, I can assure you that a well-trained sniper is entirely capable of hitting a very small target at that range. Berthelson is known to possess such marksmanship skills, and he may even have taken practice shots in the days before the assassination. So it was that this most evil of men, motivated by his hatred for America and a desire to avenge his father's death, carefully took aim and shot poor Artemus Dodge dead."

"Wait a minute," said Isabel Diamond, popping up from her chair. "Just how did this magic bullet pass through the window in the old man's office without shattering the glass?"

"Ah, Miss Diamond, that is indeed the question, is it not, and for a time, I will confess, even I was stumped. However, I have made it a practice in all of my investigations to most thoroughly and rationally consider every possibility, even if at first blush it would appear to be utterly impossible, and that is where this piece of wood comes into play. Now, as most of you recall, Monday was an unseasonably warm day. Mr. Dodge undoubtedly wanted some fresh air and decided to open a window."

"Not true," Rafferty whispered to Thomas. "All of his staff told us the old man never opened a window up there, no matter how hot it was."

Jones continued, "When he went that fateful morning to open the window closest to his desk, he made, I believe, a curious discovery, which was that both of the window's sash cords were broken. I cannot tell you what he made of this fact, but I can assure you that the broken cords were no accident. Someone severed them. Since no one other than his office staff and wife were usually allowed to enter his inner sanctum, we must assume that the mysterious cord cutter was in fact someone in the office."

There were gasps from the audience, followed by shouts of "who was it?"

"Quiet, quiet please," Irvin said. "Let the inspector continue. All of your questions will be answered, I assure you."

"Thank you," Jones said. "As I was saying, the sash cords were deliberately cut by a member of Mr. Dodge's staff. Whoever did so was clearly part of the murder conspiracy with Berthelson. I believe that person was Alan Dubois, who of course is dead."

"But why would he do such a thing?" Diamond asked. "Was he paid off?"

"Miss Diamond, I must ask you not to interrupt again. As the mayor indicated, your questions will be answered in due time. I will tell you this, however. Thanks to splendid work by Mr. McGruder and his agents, it is now known that Alan Dubois had contact with Samuel Berthelson in the days before the murder and may even have helped him plot the crime. His motives may never be fully known, but it appears that Mr. Dubois, despite his excellent position with Mr. Dodge, harbored sympathy for Berthelson and his ilk. How such perfidy could occur is best left to those more capable than I am of probing the darkest depths of the human heart.

"Now then, let us return to the circumstances of Mr. Dodge's murder. I believe I can say without fear of contradiction that Alan Dubois cut the sash cords to prepare for the assassination. This was probably done on the Saturday before Mr. Dodge's death, since that is the last time staff members are known to have been in his private office. So it was that the following sequence of events occurred on the morning of Monday, October 1:

"As Artemus Dodge begins his usual day of work, he finds that his office is quite stuffy. He goes to the nearest window and notices the broken sash cords. He is irritated and surprised. Still, he wishes some relief from the heat, so he does what all of us have done at one time or another; that is, he uses the stick I've shown you, which was probably left in his office by one of the conspirators, to prop open the window."

"Well, I'll be damned," Diamond said.

"Ah, I see now that you are beginning to perceive how the deed was done," said Jones, sounding very satisfied with himself. "Mr. Dodge, as I've said, uses the stick to keep the lower sash open. He then turns to his business. Moments later, peering through the scope of his rifle, Samuel Berthelson sees his target through the open window. He fires. Traveling in excess of a thousand feet per second, the deadly bullet severs the stick into two pieces. Part of the stick is blown into the office; another part flies away outside the window.

"The bullet, meanwhile, continues on its course and smashes into Mr. Dodge's skull just as the lower window pane, with no prop or sash cords to support it, slams shut. And there, ladies and gentlemen, is the simple solution to what at first glance appeared to be an insoluble mystery. Are there any questions?"

There were many, and Jones handled them deftly, patiently explaining how he had reached his conclusion and also taking time to praise the fine work done by Nelligan, McGruder, and the mayor in overseeing his investigation.

Thomas said, "By God, Shad, that's the same theory we've talked about."

"Yes, and it gets no better simply because Inspector Jones is the one proclaimin' it. 'Tis like watchin' a man spread butter on a gob of cow manure. No matter how the inspector tries to disguise it, crap is still crap. 'Tis also interestin' that he made no mention of Mr. Dubois's activities with the safety commission. I imagine Mr. McGruder saw to that little cover-up, since it would be mighty embarrassin' if the public knew that his supposed secret agent was in fact workin' for the other side."

"Well then, maybe you should let the public know," Thomas suggested.

"Not yet, Wash. 'Tis always good to save some ammunition for a rainy day."

When the press had finally sated itself with questions, Jones said, "I think we are done here—"

"Not quite," said Rafferty, rising slowly to his feet. "You see, Inspector, I don't believe your version of events for one minute, and I can prove you are wrong."

Rafferty instantly had the attention of everyone in the room. Jones appeared unruffled, and his reply was contemptuous: "I think you are out of your element here, Mr. Rafferty. I would suggest you confine yourself to serving beer to idlers and drunkards and leave criminal investigating to professionals."

Rafferty ignored the provocation and said, "I will not deny that I've served much good beer in my time, even to Mayor Irvin himself, who is no idler in my estimation. 'Tis also true I've met my share of drunkards, which is why I know a cock-and-bull story when I hear one."

McGruder cut Jones off before he could respond. "You say you have proof, Mr. Rafferty. What is it?"

"Why it is the simplest proof of all," Rafferty said. "I contend that not one marksman in a hundred, at best, could make the shot the inspector has described. In fact, I am willin' to wager the sum of one thousand dollars that the inspector himself, who is reputed to be the best marksman in the police department, could not duplicate the shot, and I will even give him ten chances to do it."

"A ridiculous idea," Jones scoffed.

"Oh no, I'd say it's a wonderful idea," said Diamond. "Quite wonderful. All Mr. Rafferty is asking you to do is to show that the thing is possible. Come now, Inspector, are you up to the challenge?"

"Well, it will not happen," Irvin said, stepping up beside Jones. "I will not turn this city into a shooting gallery to test Mr. Rafferty's crackpot theories. I personally think that Inspector Jones's explanation of this terrible crime is perfectly plausible, and as far as the city of St. Paul is concerned, the case is closed except for the apprehension of Samuel Berthelson, which I have no doubt will occur shortly."

. . . . .

Diamond rushed over to talk with Rafferty after the news conference broke up. He continued to press for a "a shootin' match," as he called it, and also advised her to talk with Thomas Masterson at Kennedy Brothers. She promised that she would.

"That was quite a scene you made," Thomas said after he and Rafferty left city hall. "Did you really think Jones would go for your idea?"

"No, but I think Miss Diamond did."

"You have a newspaper campaign in mind, I take it."

"I do," Rafferty admitted. "I am sowin' the seeds of doubt to buy us some time. If the press and public accept the inspector's cockamamie theory, then the case will close shut like the lid of a coffin, buryin' any hope of gettin' at the real truth."

"Which is?"

"I'm still workin' on that, Wash, but I know we're missin' something. Mr. Dodge's murder was a parlor trick, a very fancy one, but a trick nonetheless. Where there is a parlor trick, there is usually a hidden device known only to the magician himself. The answer is in the old man's office. Something isn't right there. The theory that he was shot through a propped-up window can only hold true if phenomenal luck was involved."

"I see your point," Thomas agreed. "For one thing, how could the sniper be sure that Mr. Dodge would open the window in the first place?"

"He couldn't. Nor could he be at all sure about makin' such a perfect shot on the first try."

"Well, as you said, he could have gotten lucky."

"True, but whoever killed Mr. Dodge, and no doubt young Dubois as well, was not the kind of person to rely on luck. Too much planning went into this business to leave anything to chance. The killer had to be absolutely certain that the bullet would find its target. There could be no such certainty with a shot fired from a distance of eight hundred yards, uphill, on a day with winds swirling every which way."

"Fair enough," Thomas said, "but that still leaves the problem of how the thing was actually done. As you said, unless somebody comes up with a better theory, the press and everybody else are likely to accept Jones's explanation. You'll need to prove that he's wrong."

"Exactly. I'm thinkin' that our friend Colonel Masterson at Kennedy Brothers could be of use in that regard, especially if he were to have a nice little chat with Miss Diamond. In the meantime, I intend to have another talk with Mr. Stem. I want to go over the plans of Dodge's office one more time."

Later that afternoon, John McGruder sat in his cold gray office, thinking about Samuel Berthelson. Law enforcement agents everywhere were searching for the terrorist, and there'd already been a reported sighting in Chicago and another in Fargo. But what if Berthelson had defied all expectations by *not* fleeing St. Paul? What if he was still close at hand, hiding in a basement in Frogtown or at some confederate's house on the Upper Levee or camped out in the wooded bottomlands below the West Side bluffs? And what if he intended to thumb his nose at authorities by staging some outrageous new act of terrorism right in St. Paul? Such brazenness, McGruder believed, would be entirely in character.

The thought that Berthelson might still be in the city gave McGruder an idea. Instead of trying to flush the terrorist from his hiding place, why not lure him out into the open? But how? Before long, McGruder realized that the answer lay right before his eyes, in the afternoon edition of the *Dispatch,* where a front-page article promoted a patriotic rally on Friday. McGruder was sure Berthelson would be there to stir up trouble.

Pleased by his own brilliance, McGruder rewarded himself by downing a shot of well-aged Kentucky bourbon from a bottle he kept in his desk drawer. He felt he was finally making progress, despite all the naysayers, weaklings, and politicians who lacked the spine to do what had to be done. St. Paul needed an iron hand, and McGruder was more certain than ever that only he could provide it. The high and mighty men of the city— the Hills, the Weyerhaeusers, the Ordways, and all their ilk—were behind him, McGruder believed, and they'd been appalled by the streetcar strike and Berthelson's reign of terror. Order had to be restored and patriotism enforced, and once McGruder consolidated his power, there would be no tolerance for treasonous dissent.

McGruder had other plans as well. St. Paul was awash in liquor and gambling and every other low human vice, and McGruder intended to purge the city of its sins. He'd already imposed strict limits on taverns' operating hours, but his goal was to shut them down entirely. One saloon in St. Paul was famous above all others, as was its meddling owner, and closing the place for good by order of the public safety commission struck McGruder as an excellent idea.

Back in his office, Mordecai Jones was fuming. He'd expected praise as the man who'd solved the most baffling crime in St. Paul's history. Instead, reporters badgered him about what that fool Rafferty had said.

Once Jones cooled down, he realized that Rafferty might have a point. It would have required an amazing shot to kill Dodge. Jones was also bothered by a loose end. Just what had that fake plumber been doing in Dodge Tower on the morning of the murder? Maybe Rafferty knew. Worse yet, maybe the old barman was planning to blow James's carefully crafted solution to shreds. Deciding he couldn't take that chance, Jones called Sergeant Carroll into his office.

"I have a little job for you," he said. "It will be tricky, but I have confidence that you are the man to do it."

After Jones described what he wanted done, Carroll said, "I will do my best, sir, but it will take several men."

"I will see to that. I will expect regular reports."

"Of course, sir. May I ask why you want to do such a thing? It is a bit irregular, and, well, I'm just not sure—"

Jones had no interest in hearing doubts. "Leave the thinking to me, Sergeant. If there's any trouble afterward, I will take full responsibility. You and whatever men you pick can start immediately. That is all."

"Very well, sir," Carroll said, although he found himself wishing that the inspector's orders had been in writing.

Rafferty had always possessed a sixth sense, which more than once had saved his life, or so he believed. At Gettysburg, where he'd fought with the First Minnesota Volunteers and helped repulse Pickett's charge up Cemetery Ridge, Rafferty had moved among the crazed scrum of soldiers with the instincts of a born survivor. Men to his immediate left and right had died that day, pierced by bayonets or cut down in screaming swarms of projectiles, and yet he'd somehow left the battlefield without a scratch.

As he walked out of his tavern and headed across Sixth Street to Dodge Tower, he sensed that he was being watched. He stopped outside a jeweler's shop and casually inspected a display of diamond necklaces and rings, hoping to catch a suspicious reflection in the window. He saw no one who looked out of the ordinary. Deciding to take no chances, he walked east past the entrance to Dodge Tower and went as far as Jackson Street. There, he stepped into Freeman's Penny Arcade.

The proprietor, Saul Freeman, was ensconced behind the front desk and greeted Rafferty with a broad smile.

"Well, well, if it isn't my favorite Irish saloonkeeper," he said. "Long time no see, Shad. Here to do a little shooting?"

Back in the day, Rafferty had been known to drop by the arcade every so often and show off his marksmanship with one of the house air rifles. It had been years, however, since he'd done any shooting at the arcade.

"Ah, I'm too old for that," Rafferty said, glimpsing at the rear shooting gallery, where a half dozen or so young bloods armed with Daisy rifles were plinking away at fast-moving rows of metallic rabbits, squirrels, and foxes. "Looks like business is good."

"Never better," Freeman said. "Every boy in St. Paul is dreaming of going off to war and killing Krauts. If only they knew."

Rafferty nodded. "Boys never do, Saul, and that is why we have armies."

Glancing out toward the sidewalk, Rafferty caught the eye of a stocky man in a gray wool topcoat passing by. The man looked away and kept walking.

Freeman saw the man, too, and said, "Somebody you know?"

"Not yet, but I expect I will. Take care, Saul."

By the time Rafferty stepped outside, the man in gray had vanished, presumably around the corner on Jackson. There was no sense in trying to follow him, so Rafferty backtracked to Dodge Tower. When he arrived at

Allen Stem's second-floor office, he found the architect hunched over his drafting table.

"'Tis some new masterpiece you're workin' on, I imagine," Rafferty said.

Stem stood up to greet him. "It's a small staircase detail for a railway station in Tacoma," Stem said with a weary smile, "and it's driving the whole office crazy, myself included. You're a welcome break. What do you need?"

"I have a bit of curiosity that needs slakin'. I'd like to know more about that security door in Mr. Dodge's office."

"Well, there's not much more I can tell you other than what we've already talked about. Mosler made the door—and the emergency door in the lobby—as a custom order to the precise specifications of Mr. Dodge himself and shipped them here from their plant in Hamilton, Ohio. The emergency door came right on time, but there was a problem with the one for the office."

"What kind of problem?"

"It arrived late, which caused quite a headache for us."

"How late?"

"Close to two weeks."

"Was the door late comin' out of the factory?"

"No, there was a holdup of some sort in the rail yards in Chicago, which is hardly uncommon. It's a wonder anything ever gets through that city."

"Do you know what caused the delay?"

"Not exactly, but I believe it was something about a freight car being shunted off to the wrong yard. I do know that Mr. Dodge himself or someone in his office finally had to raise a stink."

"Ah, I see. Did you personally supervise the installation of the door?"

"No. Mosler provided its own man, though there was a bit of delay with that, too."

"How so?"

"Well, Mosler was supposed to send out its installation manager, but something happened to him. I believe he met with foul play in Chicago. So the company had to find another man for the job."

Rafferty's ears perked up about as much as they were capable of doing at his age. "Just what sort of foul play did this poor fellow from Mosler meet?"

"I'm not sure. I think I heard he was assaulted, or perhaps even killed. It was during a robbery, as I recall. But you'd have to check with the people at Mosler to be sure. I can give you the phone number at Mosler's head-quarters, if that would help."

"I'd be much obliged," Rafferty said. "Much obliged indeed."

As he went back across the street to his saloon, Rafferty looked again for the man in gray but didn't see him. If he was being followed, he figured there must be at least two men on the job. Once he'd settled in his office, Rafferty placed a long-distance call to the Mosler Company's headquarters in Ohio. What he learned came as a shock. Rafferty immediately placed another call, to a police captain he knew in Chicago. After a bit of thought, Rafferty made a third call, to Louis Hill.

"I must ask a favor, Mr. Hill. I'm lookin' for a railroad car that may have something to do with Mr. Dodge's murder. I think you're just the man who could help."

"Why is this car so important?"

Rafferty described the security door and its mysterious two-week hiatus in Chicago. He also passed on shipping details he'd received from Stem. "I am no railroad man," Rafferty said, "so I don't know how on earth you'd track down one car amid the thousands that must go through Chicago every day. I figure if anyone could find the answer quickly, it would be you."

Hill, who prided himself on his knowledge of operational details, was pleased by the flattery. "You are correct in that regard, Mr. Rafferty. In point of fact, it is quite easy to track down a car in Chicago if you know where to ask."

"Ah, I thought so. Where might that be?"

"The Belt Railway of Chicago. The vault door would have gone via the Baltimore and Ohio Railroad from Hamilton to Chicago. There, it would have required transfer to the Burlington and Quincy yards in order to continue its journey to St. Paul. That is where the Belt Railway comes in. It provides the means to transfer freight cars from one railroad to another. I will call the Belt Railway's yardmaster to get the specifics."

"You know him, I take it."

"No, but he will know of me. I will get back to you shortly."

Rafferty thanked Hill and rang off. Then he called in Thomas for a strategy session. Rafferty recounted his conversations with Stem and Hill. He also mentioned his suspicion that he'd been followed on his visit to Stem's office.

"Who do you think's on your tail?" Thomas asked.

"I wish I knew. Could be McGruder, could be the coppers, could even be someone from Dodge's office."

Thomas nodded and said, "In the meantime, I suppose I'll be going to Chicago. How soon do you want me to leave?"

"As soon as I hear from Mr. Hill," Rafferty said. "We have no time to waste."

Artemus Dodge's funeral, at the House of Hope Church on Summit Avenue, drew only a modest crowd. J. D. Carr wasn't surprised. Artemus had been a cold, solitary man, and there were few friends to mourn his passing. Carr was in a front pew with the other members of the office staff, while Amanda sat in lonely splendor across the aisle, managing to produce a small sob every so often. Carr had to give her credit. She knew how to put on a good show.

Amanda squeezed out a few more tears at Oakland Cemetery, where Artemus was buried beneath a seventy-foot-tall granite obelisk inscribed with his name and the number 33051. Amanda had never been to the grave site before, and as everyone walked back to their cars, she asked Carr in an innocent way what the number stood for.

"I believe it's how much Mr. Dodge paid for the obelisk and his mausoleum," Carr said. "He was amused by the idea of leaving something mysterious behind. He told me once that a hundred years from now people would wonder what the number stood for."

"How very strange," Amanda said, knowing full well that the number had another meaning. She wondered if Carr knew the truth as well.

Steven Dodge, who was walking behind them, overheard the conversation and said, "Strange but not surprising. Dollars meant everything to dear old dad. Speaking of money, you'll never believe what I just heard."

"What is that?" Amanda asked.

"The police found some of the bills used to pay the ransom at the Union Depot. They apparently had some sort of special marking."

"Where did you hear of this?" Carr asked.

"Let's just say I have my sources," Dodge said, thinking back to the phone tip he'd received from Isabel Diamond just before the funeral. "Anyway, it was quite the find. Seems like it's been one surprise after another, doesn't it?"

"And I have no doubt there will be more to come," Carr said with a shake of his head. "I fear we are not done with this business yet."

21

"INSIDE JOB"

The discovery of the $100 bills, in a toilet stall at the depot, inspired special editions of both the *Dispatch* and *Globe*, which speculated that Berthelson had lost the money just before taking a train out of the city. The police, however, were suspicious, with Mordecai Jones stating in one article that the bills might well be a "plant designed to mislead investigators." A reporter had also contacted Rafferty, who voiced similar doubts even while admitting that, for all he knew, "Berthelson might be halfway to Timbuktu by now."

J. D. Carr was among those who read the special editions with intense interest. He'd returned to his office after the funeral and had Dodge Tower's penthouse to himself, staring out his windows as the day's last light flowed like paint across the Mississippi's wooded bluffs. Then the light was gone, and the bluffs turned to dark shadows above the black ribbon of the river. Carr turned away and suddenly sensed the cold presence of dread, like a hawk beating toward him in the darkness. Something was terribly wrong.

Carr tried to salve his anxiety with a liberal application of reason. As far as he could tell, he'd done everything right. He'd begun covering up the dirty tracks left by the Blue Sky Partnership. He'd made sure young Steven Dodge stayed strong. He'd given Amanda Dodge exactly what she deserved, and he'd made an ally of Mrs. Schmidt. Peter Kretch was missing in action and seemed to pose no threat. Alan Dubois would be silent for all eternity. Why then, Carr wondered, did he feel so uneasy?

He went down to the building's lobby and picked up the regular afternoon edition of the *Dispatch*, where there was an account of the press conference at which the mayor and police had claimed success in solving Dodge's murder. Their announcement came as good news. With Berthelson firmly established as the killer, Carr believed, the police would have no reason to investigate Dodge's business affairs, including the Blue Sky Partnership.

Back in his office, Carr read the entire story and found that it contained one dark cloud in the form of Rafferty's challenge to the police's sniper theory. Carr was not fooled by Rafferty's comic, shambling routine. The saloonkeeper, like Artemus Dodge, was a sharp customer, and if he kept on digging into the case, who knew what incriminating information he might uncover? Carr thought there was a way to shut down Rafferty's investigation, and he immediately placed a call to the chief of police.

"I'm very pleased with the work you and your men have done in discovering who murdered Mr. Dodge," Carr began, knowing the value of flattering a man like Nelligan. "You have done yourself proud. By the way, any news of Berthelson?"

"Not really. There've been many supposed sightings, but nothing has panned out. I remain confident we will find him soon."

"As do I. Still, one small matter troubles me. It concerns Mr. Rafferty. I must tell you that I do not understand why the police continue to permit him to meddle in the investigation. The man is a charlatan. Now that you have so brilliantly solved Mr. Dodge's murder, it is time for someone to tell Mr. Rafferty to mind his own damn business, if you will pardon my language. I have much to attend to if I am to set Mr. Dodge's affairs in order, and I cannot afford to waste my time with some nosy old barkeep who fancies himself a detective. I would greatly appreciate it, Chief, if you could help me in this regard."

"I will see what I can do," Nelligan promised, "but you must understand that Mr. Rafferty is something of a gilded man. He has support in high places, and that makes it hard to deal with him. Believe me, I would like nothing better than to be rid of his meddling, but that may not be possible."

Carr was disappointed but didn't say so. "Well, I know you will do the best you can."

After he hung up, Carr contemplated other means by which he might rid himself of Rafferty. Several ideas came to mind.

Gertrude Schmidt had taken Artemus Dodge's dictation, written his letters, and filed his documents for two years, and in that time she'd learned much about how his business worked. She was no accountant, but she'd learned enough to realize that the Blue Sky Partnership was a fraud. Money came in from the partners, who included some of St. Paul's leading business-men, but there was no evidence it had ever been invested in stocks, bonds, or anything else. Instead, the money had vanished into a dark hole with no apparent bottom. What she didn't know was who had masterminded the scheme.

The most obvious suspect was Carr. He'd tried to hide the facts from her by confiscating Artemus's letter to Patrick Butler and then secretly removing documents from her files. Even so, Carr hadn't managed to wipe out all records of the partnership. Mrs. Schmidt still had every word of the letter in her stenographer's notebook. She'd also managed to find incrimi-nating documents tucked away in odd corners of her filing system.

Other suspects couldn't be ruled out, however. Perhaps Carr was sim-ply trying to cover up someone else's misdeeds. Alan Dubois, who'd been very good with numbers, could have engineered the scheme. Or maybe Steven Dodge, or even Amanda, had put him up to it.

Mrs. Schmidt believed the police should investigate the fraudulent partnership, but they'd shown no interest in doing so, especially now that they were obsessed with finding Samuel Berthelson. Even if the police did start asking questions, Mrs. Schmidt feared that Carr would deflect their inquiries in his usual devious way. Mrs. Schmidt knew she had to do some-thing. The very idea of fraud offended her.

But who would investigate, if not the police? Mrs. Schmidt thought she knew just the right man for the job. She'd read how Rafferty had chal-lenged the police at the press conference. He clearly wasn't afraid to stir up trouble. Mrs. Schmidt had already prepared copies of all the Blue Sky doc-uments she'd collected. She put them into a manila envelope and sealed it.

Then she left her apartment to catch a streetcar. There were always plenty of boys idling about the downtown streets. One of them would be happy to earn a dollar by delivering the envelope to Rafferty.

"I'm glad this business is over," Steven Dodge said as he and Isabel Diamond enjoyed early evening drinks in his apartment. "It's been a terrible week for me. First Father, then Alan, and then Amanda's kidnapping. I still can't believe that Alan was somehow involved in Father's murder."

"It's difficult to comprehend," Diamond agreed. "Did you have any idea that he harbored radical sympathies?"

"No, not for a minute. Alan was always a secretive man. In all the time I knew him, I was never once invited to his apartment."

"So I take it you're satisfied with Inspector Jones's explanation as to how your father was murdered?"

"Shouldn't I be?"

"I don't know, but I sure wish Jones had taken up Rafferty on his bet."

They were seated on a tufted sofa that was all too familiar to Diamond. It was where Steven had first tried to seduce her. She'd resisted but had also let him touch her in a way that kept up his hopes, not to mention something else. Steven's favorite cat, the unruly Hades, occupied one of the sofa's armrests and stared at Diamond with a look that suggested he'd be pleased to eat her if he could.

Dodge, who'd already consumed three glasses of whiskey, was feeling frisky and put an arm around her shoulder. "Well, I guess it would have been fun to see bullets flying about, but I don't think it would have proved anything. Besides, it's all over and done with now. Father has been buried, and that crazy Berthelson fellow has left town."

"I'm not so sure the case is closed. I had a talk this afternoon with Thomas Masterson—he's an old military man who works for Kennedy Brothers—and he thinks the sniper theory is nonsense."

"Well, it sounds good enough to me," Dodge said, sliding his arm down Diamond's back. "But why talk of murder at a time like this?"

She gently removed his arm. "Not tonight, Steven, but I will say you are incorrigible."

"I know. Isn't that why you love me so?"

"I wouldn't go that far. You do need to be serious for a minute. Don't you see that you're in danger?"

"Danger? Why do you say that?"

Diamond fixed her eyes on Dodge and said, "Tell me this, my love: who gets the money?"

"What do you mean?"

"I mean your father's fortune, Steven. Isn't that lawyer, Mr. Butler, scheduled to read the will on Monday?"

"Yes, but there'll be no surprises. The house and a lump sum of money go to Amanda, and I get the business."

"I see. What do you suppose would happen if by some chance you die before the estate is settled?"

Dodge suddenly looked sober. "Why, I'm not sure."

"Then you'd better find out," Diamond said as she stood up and put on her coat. "Your life could depend on it."

Peter Kretch had taken refuge at the Hotel Vendome, a run-down establishment in the skid row district of Minneapolis. His room was small, well-worn, and cold, even though a steam radiator hissed vehemently in one corner. The furnishings consisted of a lumpy bed, a slat-back chair, and a desk whose drawers yielded two Gideon Bibles. Kretch didn't care for the Bibles, but he was reading every newspaper he could lay his hands on. Inspector Jones, that supposed genius, appeared to think that the case was over, except for finding Berthelson.

Kretch knew better, and he still shivered at the thought of how close he'd come to being killed on the High Bridge. The would-be assassin's broad Slavic face remained a vivid presence in Kretch's mind, as did the short-barreled pistol he'd pulled from his coat pocket. The man had clearly been hired help, and Kretch doubted that he'd ever see him again. But he had no doubt who had hired the assassin. Amanda Dodge would pay dearly—and soon—for what she'd done.

Amanda Dodge was thinking about Kretch as she idled over a bowl of lobster bisque that evening in the dining room of the St. Paul Hotel. She'd heard nothing from the blackmailing security guard since their meeting at River's Edge. The plan she'd concocted with Steven had apparently worked. Kretch was out of the picture. Once Artemus's will was read on Monday, she'd be rich, and then she'd move to New York. Who there would care about a small-time scandal in St. Paul, even if word of it did somehow come out?

Since escaping from the old brewery caves, Amanda had been staying in the hotel's penthouse suite. She felt much safer there, with people all around her, than in the isolation of River's Edge. Before leaving the mansion, she'd taken along a few prized personal possessions as well as documents relating to the Blue Sky Partnership and a copy of Artemus's last will and testament. She knew the provisions by heart. River's Edge was to be hers, as was a lump-sum payment of one million dollars.

Amanda had already talked to a real estate broker about selling River's Edge. The estate had never seemed like a real home to Amanda, who knew that to Artemus she was just another expensive piece of furniture, purchased in a vain attempt to fill the void of his life. He'd never been cruel to her, but he'd never been kind either, and she had no illusions that he'd ever loved her. Money—the getting of it mostly—had been his one true passion, and now that he had so conveniently exited the world, she intended to complete the equation of his long sour life by spending every last dime of his fortune.

After finishing her meal, Amanda bought a copy of the *Daily News* at the hotel's cigar stand, then took the elevator up to her twelfth-floor suite. She'd just stepped inside and locked the door when a man emerged from the bedroom.

"Come right in," Peter Kretch said. "We have a lot to talk about."

. . . . .

Wash Thomas reached St. Paul's train depot just after five o'clock. A few years earlier, the city's old Union Depot had burned down, and the railroads, displaying their usual distaste for cooperation, had been squabbling over a replacement ever since. What now passed for a depot was a makeshift affair occupying the ground floor of a brick warehouse on Sibley Street. Its dim and grimy waiting room was a noisy chaos of travelers who moved in great buzzing swarms, like bees smoked out of their hive.

Thomas had always been what Rafferty called "a last-second man," and he took quite literally the idea of "catching" a train. The Great Northern's Oriental Limited was due to depart at five past the hour. Thomas intended to be on it. He made his way through the jammed waiting room and out to the smoky twilight of the depot's iron train shed, which had survived the fire. He was just in time to see the Limited's line of green and black cars inch forward. Thomas sprinted toward the rear observation platform and pulled himself aboard.

As he stood panting on the platform, Thomas saw yet another latecomer running for the train. He held out his hand to the man, who wore a gray raincoat and matching felt hat. The man ignored Thomas's offer of help and pulled himself up on the platform. He looked at Thomas briefly, said nothing, then went into the observation car.

Thomas wondered if he was being followed. Hadn't Rafferty mentioned a suspicious man in a gray coat who'd tailed him that afternoon? Then again, it wasn't unusual for a white man to snub Thomas's hand, presumably for fear of being infected with black pigment. Thomas followed the man inside, where he took a seat in the observation car. Thomas went on to the next car. The man didn't follow.

Although Thomas loved to travel, trains were a trial. Officially, there was no segregation in the North, but Thomas knew his options were limited. The rules of the road for a black man were well known: stay out of the fancy club cars, dine alone, and don't even think about sitting next to a white woman. Thomas found a seat in one of the train's middle coach cars. The car was crowded, but no one sat next to him. He looked at his watch and calculated that he'd roll into Chicago just after one the next morning.

Thomas had brought along sandwiches, two apples, and a stash of oatmeal cookies. He nibbled at a cookie while he reviewed his instructions from Rafferty. He was to begin by contacting a Chicago police captain named Thomas McGuire, an old friend of Rafferty's. Then he was to proceed to the offices of Midwest Security and Locksmithing in the Chicago suburb of Cicero. Rafferty had learned from Louis Hill that the railcar carrying Artemus Dodge's security door had been shunted to the locksmithing company after arriving at the Belt Railway of Chicago's yards on the western edge of the city. The door had been picked up seven days later and returned to the yards, where it was shipped on a Burlington and Quincy freight bound for St. Paul.

Rafferty had instructed Thomas to work at "top speed" in Chicago and then return to St. Paul on the first available train. Thomas figured he wouldn't have much time for rest, so he settled into his seat and let the swaying train lull him to sleep. With any luck, he thought before he drifted off, he just might return to St. Paul carrying the secret of the magic bullet that had killed Artemus Dodge.

Danny Grimes, one of Rafferty's bartenders, knocked on his office door at half past five, bearing a manila envelope. "Some kid dropped this off for you," he said. "It's supposed to be important."

"Well, then, I guess I'd better have a look. Did you recognize the lad?"

"Never saw him before. He marched in, said the envelope was for you, and then went out the door lickety-split."

"All right, Danny, thanks."

Inside the envelope Rafferty found twelve carbon-copied pages of documents concerning the Blue Sky Partnership. By the time he'd finished reading them, he was pretty sure he'd found a motive for murder.

"So what's Rafferty up to?" Jones asked Sergeant Carroll, who'd been summoned to the inspector's office late in the afternoon. "I want a full report."

"Very well, sir," Carroll said, glancing down at the scribblings in his small notebook. Carroll described Rafferty's movements from the time he left the saloon to his return after visiting Allen Stem's office.

"Are you sure he went to see Mr. Stem and not someone else in Dodge Tower?" Jones asked.

"Yes. My man talked with the elevator operator and then kept watch outside the office until Rafferty left."

Jones wondered what Rafferty had wanted from the architect. "Anything else to tell me, Sergeant?"

"Yes. Thomas, that colored fellow Rafferty works with, left the saloon about quarter to five. As of the moment, he hasn't returned."

"All right, stay on it. Rafferty is up to something. Of that I'm certain."

When Carroll left, Jones picked up the phone and instructed the operator to place a call to Stem's office. The architect proved to be most accommodating. Jones thanked him and decided he'd have to take another look at the security door in Artemus Dodge's office.

"What are you doing in my room?" Amanda Dodge demanded, staring at Kretch, who sat nonchalantly on a plush armchair, his legs propped up on a leather ottoman. "You will leave at once or I will call hotel security."

"Don't worry," Kretch said, "I'll only be here a minute. I just wanted to tell you that the price of my services has just gone up—way up. I don't know who that thug you sent to kill me was, but as you can see, he didn't succeed."

"I have no idea what you're talking about."

"Oh, I doubt that is the case, my dear, I doubt that very much. So here's the new arrangement. I want another ten thousand, and I want it by Monday morning. Otherwise, the newspapers will have quite a feast, and you'll be the main dish. I'm sure all of St. Paul will enjoy reading of your little dalliance with your stepson."

"Get out," Amanda said.

Kretch smiled, rose from his chair, and ambled toward the door. Amanda tried to step aside, but Kretch grabbed her roughly by the wrist, squeezing so hard that she winced in pain. "Monday," he said, "or the world will know just what a little whore you are. I'll be in touch when the time comes and tell you where to bring the money. Don't even think of calling the police if you want to save your reputation from ruin."

"Take your hands off me," Amanda said, trying to pull free from Kretch's grip.

He let go of her wrist but only after he'd kissed her lips. "We'll be talking again soon," he promised, and left.

Amanda felt as though she'd just touched something filthy. She washed her hands and face in the bathroom, then called the front desk and reported that an intruder had somehow gotten into her room. The locks would have to be changed.

By order of the public safety commission, Rafferty and every other saloon-keeper in the state was forced to close at ten o'clock sharp for the duration of the war. It was beyond his ken how closing saloons so early contributed to killing Germans halfway around the world, and he'd bitterly opposed the order. But patriotic fever was burning, and few people seemed willing to challenge the commission, however pointless its actions might be.

When the last patrons had been shooed out the door, Rafferty retired to his office while Danny Grimes and a small crew of helpers went about the usual nightly cleanup. Rafferty had gotten into the habit of inspecting his books after closing, and it was not a happy task. The shortened hours hurt business, causing a drop in revenues even as wartime inflation sent costs soaring. His tavern was still in the black but not by much, and with prohibition looming, Rafferty knew his days as a saloonkeeper were numbered.

Shortly after eleven the first edition of Friday's *Pioneer Press* came out, and Rafferty was pleased to see that Isabel Diamond had taken up his suggestion to interview Thomas Masterson. Her story, under a headline that read "FAMED MARKSMAN DOUBTS POLICE VERSION OF DODGE MURDER," offered a lengthy interview with Masterson, who made no attempt to disguise his contempt for the theory that a sniper had managed to kill Artemus Dodge with a single shot from the tower of the old capitol. "It is all a lie," Masterson declared in the story's opening paragraph, "and if the police believe it, they are fools. The chances against a single shot killing Mr.

Dodge in the manner described by Inspector Jones would be a thousand to one in my estimation."

The inspector is going to be an unhappy man, Rafferty thought as he went back to his receipts. A very unhappy man.

Grimes soon poked his head in the door once again. "You're a popular man tonight, Mr. Rafferty. First that message and now a telegram. The Western Union boy just delivered it."

"Thanks," Rafferty said, feeling a surge of excitement. The message was brief but provocative: "HAVE INSPECTED PLANS. HALLWAYS KEY. NOTE ALIGNMENT. WHAT COULD GUARD SEE? ALARM NO COINCIDENCE. AUSTRIAN GUN? INSIDE JOB. CARR MONOGRAPH AUTHOR. LETTER TO FOLLOW. HOLMES."

Rafferty read the telegram several times, parsing each word. He was particularly interested in Holmes's mention of "alignment" and his reference to an "Austrian gun." The revelation that J. D. Carr authored the locked room monograph was equally intriguing but hardly proof that he'd murdered his boss. For the time being, Rafferty decided, he'd share the secret of Carr's authorship with Wash Thomas and no one else. If the right time came, they'd confront Carr and see how he reacted.

Later, before going to bed, Rafferty consulted a half-dozen books from his library having to do with old and unusual rifles.

22

"DO YOU SEE WHAT IT MUST BE?"

The crowd began forming at eleven o'clock Friday morning, egged on by provocateurs in the employ of John McGruder as well as a *Pioneer Press* story announcing a "grand patriotic rally" at the Germania Life Insurance Building. "Let all symbols of the Hun be expunged from our city," McGruder was quoted as saying. "There is no room for disloyalty, and there can be no comfort to the enemy in time of war."

Rafferty, who'd been awaiting a call from Thomas in Chicago, decided he'd have to see what the fuss was all about, so he walked over to the Germania Building, just three blocks from his saloon. He found a noisy throng of several thousand people gathered in front of the building at Fourth and Minnesota streets. A chant of "down with the Huns, down with the Huns" echoed across the intersection. Traffic was blocked, and streetcars were already backing up on Fourth.

As he made his way around the corner on Minnesota, Rafferty saw why the crowd was chanting. A twelve-foot-high bronze statue of the mythic female warrior Germania, which crowned the building's entrance, was being lowered from its perch by a crane. Using his cane as a prod, Rafferty pushed toward a landing area that had been carved out of the crowd like the eye of a hurricane. A cordon of policemen struggled to keep it open. McGruder, Mayor Irvin, Chief Nelligan, and other dignitaries stood nearby on a makeshift stage to oversee the officially sanctioned vandalism.

Once the statue settled on the ground, lying on its side like a fallen soldier, McGruder shouted: "It is done, men; it is done. This ugly symbol of the Hun will be melted down to make instruments of war. Let it also be known that terrorists, anarchists, radicals, shirkers, pacifists, and all their ilk will receive no sympathy in St. Paul. Let it be known that we will hunt down all such traitors. Let it be known that the only kind of Americanism St. Paul will tolerate is one hundred percent Americanism."

The crowd, its most enthusiastic members well fortified with alcohol, let out an enormous cheer. McGruder smiled. He was certain Samuel Berthelson lurked somewhere in the mass of people before him. At least fifty police officers and special agents were secreted in nearby buildings. Once the crowd quieted down, McGruder intended to announce Berthelson's presence. Then the police and McGruder's men would move in, like a tightening noose. The terrorist would have no means of escape.

"Do you really think Berthelson will show up?" asked Sergeant Carroll. He and Jones were watching the crowd from the window of a vacant office on the Germania Building's second floor.

Jones, who was peering through binoculars in hopes of spotting the terrorist, stubbed out his cigar and said, "Your guess is as good as mine. McGruder believes it, but you could just as well argue that Jesus Christ himself is out there turning water to wine. McGruder's got religion, but as for the facts . . . well, the facts be damned as far as he's concerned. All I can say is—"

Jones dropped his binoculars, stunned by what he saw. Carroll was equally nonplussed.

"Oh, Christ," Jones said. "That idiot McGruder has done it again."

The carefully orchestrated rally had accounted for everything except human nature. As McGruder was about to conclude his oration, a lanky man—much too tall to be Berthelson—produced a hatchet from inside his trench coat, waved it like a battle flag, and burst through the police lines to deliver a ringing blow to the statue's neck. Within seconds the police cordon gave way, and the crowd rushed in to attack the despised statue or, better yet, claim part of it as a patriotic souvenir. In the middle of the rush a man was knocked to the ground. He retaliated by attacking the man nearest to him, who in turn began to throw punches at anyone in the vicinity. A woman screamed, police whistles pierced the air, and the rally became a free-for-all.

Rafferty tried to escape—a riot was no place for an old man—but the crowd was so tightly packed that it was like wading through chest-deep molasses. Before long, a surge of humanity rolled past him and broke like a wave against the wooden stage, which gave way as easily as a twig snapped in two. McGruder, the mayor, and Nelligan went sprawling. Rafferty lost sight of them. Nelligan, blood streaming from a cut on his forehead, was the first to reappear. He helped the mayor and McGruder back to their feet just as Rafferty came up to join them.

"We need to get into the lobby," Rafferty shouted to the chief above the din.

Nelligan nodded. "All right, let's go. I'll help the mayor."

Rafferty turned to McGruder, who had the glazed look of a man undone by fear. "Come along," he said. "We can't stay here."

An egg flashed past Rafferty's right shoulder. Another soon followed. Both found their target. One struck McGruder square on the chin, and the other burst open on his chest like a yellow boutonniere. McGruder appeared paralyzed. Nelligan and Irvin were already moving toward the Germania Building's lobby. Rafferty grabbed McGruder by the arm and followed.

Once they were inside, McGruder regained his courage. "By God," he said, wiping the egg from his chin with a handkerchief, "that madman tried to kill me, didn't he?"

"Which madman would that be?" Rafferty asked.

"Why Berthelson of course. I knew he'd be here."

Rafferty glanced at Nelligan, who was rolling his eyes. Irvin looked equally skeptical. "Well, Mr. McGruder, you may be right," Rafferty said, "but I'm thinkin' that if Samuel Berthelson really wanted to kill you, he'd have used a gun."

Captain Thomas McGuire of the Chicago Police Department was a bluff and hardy man with a jowly pumpkin face, cauliflower ears, and a wild scramble of reddish gray hair. A bristly mustache erupted from his upper lips and spread across his cheeks like the pelt of some feral animal. He offered Thomas a firm handshake when they met Friday morning in his office at police headquarters just south of the Loop.

Knowing that no downtown hotel would have him, Thomas had spent the night at a friend's house on the South Side, but he hadn't gotten much sleep. It must have shown, because McGuire said, "You look like a man who's been up all night. Care for some coffee? There's a pot over there in the corner. Help yourself."

Thomas poured a cup, took a sip, and said, "Hot and strong enough to clear a man's sinuses, just like Shad said it would be. He told me I couldn't leave Chicago without having a taste of Tom McGuire's coffee. Said it would keep me awake for the rest of my life. I do believe he was right."

McGuire laughed and motioned Thomas to take a seat. "So how is the old dog?"

"Well, Shad's not as spry as he used to be, but he's still a man you'd want next to you in a hard place."

"Ah, truer words were never spoken. I still remember a night long ago when Shad was in town for something or other and we went drinking and carousing down in the Levee at a place called the Peacock Feather. Fanciest whorehouse you ever saw and full of gangsters, stickup men, hired guns, and just about every other kind of vermin in the city. Shad was young and wild then, and I was even younger and wilder. There was trouble that night and plenty of it, and we had the time of our lives. Ah, but I'm sure you're not here to listen to an old man reminisce. I've got the report Shad wanted. Not much to it, but take a look, and I'll tell you what I can."

The report consisted of two pages describing the discovery, on August 16, of a man's body in the dark, polluted waters of the Chicago Sanitary and Ship Canal near the suburb of Cicero. The body was later identified as that of Henry Merrivale, an employee of the Mosler Safe Company. A coroner's autopsy revealed that Merrivale had suffered a fatal wound to the back of the skull, from a heavy club or maul of some kind. His wallet and pockets were empty, and he was identified only after the Mosler Company filed a report about a missing employee last seen in Chicago.

"Looks like a strong-arm job that went too far," McGuire said after

Thomas finished reading. "Happens all the time. We did some checking. He was seen about Cicero a day before his body was found."

"Any idea what he was doing there?"

"The company told us he was looking for a door that had somehow been lost or misplaced during shipment. So he might have been nosing around the rail yards in Cicero. Or maybe he was just looking for a good time. Cicero ain't the sort of place that attracts tourists unless they're interested in visiting a whorehouse."

"I suppose there were no eyewitnesses to the crime."

"In Cicero there are never eyewitnesses."

Thomas smiled. "I see. So I take it you haven't developed any good leads as to who might have murdered Mr. Merrivale."

"No, but we're still looking into it. Say, why is Shad so interested in this fellow anyway? All he told me was that it might have something to do with that Dodge murder up in St. Paul."

"Then you know about as much as I do. Shad likes to keep his little secrets, even from me. I can tell you that Mr. Merrivale was supposed to install the security door in Dodge's office. Then he got killed. Could be a coincidence, but Shad doesn't think so."

"Well, ain't that interesting. Listen, make sure if Shad solves the case that he makes a point of mentioning the help he got from me and all the other fine coppers in Chicago. Understand?"

"Perfectly."

"Good. Now, what else can I do for you?"

"There's just one more thing. What can you tell me about an outfit called Midwest Security and Locksmithing out of Cicero?"

"Shad asked me about that, and I did some fast checking with the coppers out there. It's a small operation run by a fellow named Hank Bencolin. He was a yegg in his day, or so I was told, but now he's supposedly gone straight. Either that, or he's paying off the coppers to look the other way. You can never tell in Cicero."

Or Chicago, Thomas thought. He said, "I guess I'll have to go out there and have a talk with Mr. Bencolin."

McGuire's eyes narrowed. "I wouldn't advise that."

Thomas understood. "I've heard about Cicero."

"Then you know you'd be wise to be careful. Very, very careful. Negroes have never been welcome in Cicero, and they're even less welcome than usual right now. It's been crazy everywhere after what happened over in East St. Louis."

Thomas nodded. Race riots there in June and July had been heavily covered in the newspapers. Some said as many as two hundred black men, women, and children had been killed, along with a smaller number of whites. No one knew for sure.

"I thank you for your concern," Thomas said, "but I have a job to do. Don't worry, I can take care of myself."

"Not if a mob is breathing down your neck, you can't. Tell you what: if you want to go out there and look around, I can have one of my men drive you."

Normally, the idea of a police escort didn't appeal to Thomas, but then again, he didn't normally go to a place like Cicero, and he accepted the captain's offer.

By the time the streets were finally cleared in front of the Germania Life Building, two dozen rioters had been arrested and another ten had gone to City Hospital, along with several of Nelligan's men. One figure notably absent from the melee was Samuel Berthelson. No trace of him had been found.

A round of recriminations began as soon as McGruder, Nelligan, and Irvin returned to the mayor's offices. Nelligan was furious at McGruder for orchestrating the rally at a time when the city was already reeling from Dodge's murder and the streetcar riots. McGruder was equally angry at the police's failure to control the crowd and capture Berthelson. Irvin, who'd wrenched his knee when the stage collapsed, wasn't very happy either, but he tried to calm the argument.

"I don't think laying blame will do us any good," he said. "Sometimes things simply don't work out as planned."

"Nonsense," McGruder replied, scraping at the dried egg on his suit coat. "Your police failed miserably once again. I have half a mind to call in the National Guard right now and turn this whole rotten town inside out."

"I believe only the governor can call in the guard," Nelligan said, "and I see no need—"

McGruder cut him short. "The governor will do what I tell him to, and so will you, Chief, if you know what's good for you. You can begin by arresting that Rafferty fellow."

"On what grounds?" Nelligan asked.

"On the grounds that he threw two eggs at me," McGruder shouted, pounding a fist on the mayor's desk and glaring at Nelligan. "I saw him do it. The man has complete contempt for authority. He must be made an example of. I trust your men are capable of arresting the old rabble-rouser, or would that be asking for too much?"

"I didn't see Mr. Rafferty throw anything," Nelligan said, a sharp edge to his voice, "but I did see him drag you away from the mob. He may just have saved your life, and now you want me to arrest him. That's choice. If it was up to me, you'd be the one going to jail, McGruder. You have become a poison in this city. You are the man who put lives in jeopardy today and caused a riot for no reason other than some wild hunch about Berthelson."

"Do not question me," McGruder said. "Do not dare question me. I am sure Berthelson was there. You and your men simply couldn't find him. But that is an old story, isn't it?"

"You've got Berthelson on the brain," Nelligan said. "If you think he's here in St. Paul, show me the proof. Go on, prove it."

McGruder responded with a snort. "I do not answer to you, thank God, and if there is anything that needs to be proven, it's that you are not as incompetent as you seem. You would also be wise to remember, Chief, that you are working at my pleasure. I can remove you from office any time I see fit. Any time. Do not doubt that I will bring in the National Guard if you and your men fail to do their duty."

"We'll see about that," Nelligan said, turning away.

"Where are you going?" McGruder demanded.

"I am going to take back my department. This is insanity."

"I order you to stay right here."

"I report to the mayor, not you," Nelligan said. "Isn't that right, Mr. Mayor?"

Irvin was not famous for the stiffness of his spine, but even he'd had his fill of McGruder. St. Paul was being torn apart, turned into warring camps, and McGruder was the source of much of the trouble.

"By all means, go about your business, Chief," he said. "As for you, Mr. McGruder, I suggest you leave. There is nothing more for you to do here."

"Oh, I assure you there will be plenty to do soon enough," McGruder said, his voice dropping to an icy growl. "I know treason when I hear it. I will have the both of you put up on charges."

The Midwest Security and Locksmithing Company occupied a long, tall wooden shed set well back from Ogden Avenue in Cicero's industrial district. A rusty set of railroad tracks led up to the main door, which was large enough to admit a boxcar. Thomas's driver, a bored young police sergeant, swung his Model T touring car into the muddy, weed-choked driveway just before noon.

The sergeant, who'd relegated Thomas to the backseat, said, "I guess you came out here for nothing. The place looks deserted."

"I'll nose around anyway," Thomas said, stepping out into the weeds.

"Fine," said the sergeant. "Just don't do any breaking and entering. I got no jurisdiction here; plus I don't want to get caught up with no nigger."

Ignoring the slur, Thomas walked up to the shed. It bore no identification other than the crudely painted word "Midwest" on the door. Rickety board fences shielded the building from its neighbors. The sliding door was locked, so Thomas went around to the side, out of the sergeant's view, and found a smaller door, also locked. Using his picks, he sprang the lock and slipped inside.

The shed, lit by two small side windows and a row of sawtooth monitors above, was empty. Midwest Security and Locksmithing had obviously moved out. All that remained in the way of furnishings was a wooden table pushed up next to one of the windows. Thomas went over for a look. Yellowing copies of the *Chicago Tribune* were piled up on the table. The most recent edition was from August 18, two days after the death of Mosler's door installer, Henry Merrivale. It looked as though the company's departure had coincided with Merrivale's murder.

Thomas turned his attention to the dirt floor, which was bisected by a pair of rail tracks that ended in a concrete platform at the rear. A search of the floor turned up metal shavings, a scattering of nuts and screws, a rusted pair of pliers, and an empty bottle of George A. Dickel's Tennessee Whisky. Somebody at the company had excellent taste in liquor, Thomas thought, and the ability to pay for it.

Not optimistic that he'd find anything, Thomas made his way back to the platform and climbed up for a look. He found floor bolts that must have been used to anchor heavy machinery, small shards of glass, and a few tiny metal shavings. Otherwise, there was no hint as to what the company might have made—or modified—while it was in operation. Thomas jumped down from the platform and switched on his flashlight to examine the grooves around the tracks.

He was nearly back to the big sliding door when his beam caught a small bright object next to one of the rails. Thomas bent down for a closer inspection. The object was a cylindrical piece of glass, less than an inch in diameter, and cut so as to have a concave surface. It was, he thought, a curious thing to find in a metal shop. He slipped the cylinder into his pocket just as a voice startled him.

"What were you doing in there?" the sergeant demanded. He was standing by the side door. "Didn't I tell you not to go inside?"

"The door was open," Thomas lied, "so I just went in to take a peek. Didn't find a thing. The place is clean. Looks like the company is gone."

"Good, then we can get out of here," the sergeant said. "Like I said, I got no jurisdiction in Cicero."

Thomas called Rafferty as soon as his escort dropped him off at Chicago's Union Station. Danny Grimes answered the phone and said Rafferty was at McGruder's patriotic rally. "You just missed him. Do you want to leave a message? I don't think he'll be gone too long."

Thomas considered his options. A Milwaukee Road through train, due to depart in ten minutes, would be his fastest way back to St. Paul. Better to catch that train, Thomas decided, than to wait around to talk to Rafferty. "Tell Shad I'll try to call him when I get to Milwaukee. Oh, and tell him that I found something interesting at Midwest Security. He'll know what I mean."

"Will do," Grimes said.

When Rafferty returned to the tavern early in the afternoon, he learned that he'd missed two calls from Thomas.

"He just phoned from Milwaukee," Grimes reported. "Said he'd try again at the next stop."

"Did Wash leave any messages?"

Grimes nodded and told Rafferty about the first call. It was encouraging news. The pieces were finally coming together.

Rafferty looked up and noticed three men walking in from the Ryan Hotel's lobby. Only a few patrons were at the bar—afternoons were always slow—and Rafferty had plenty of time to take a good look at the trio. He didn't like what he saw. They were the kind of square-jawed, dead-eyed men that money hired to protect itself—Pinkertons, maybe, or just toughs rounded up from some dark corner of the city. All three wore black bowler hats, black suits, black ties, and white shirts. They might have been a small convention of undertakers except for the telltale bulges beneath their suit coats. Morticians weren't usually armed.

"Danny boy, why don't you move down to the end of the bar," Rafferty told Grimes in a soft voice. "I'll handle these fellows."

The leader of the trio, who had gunmetal gray eyes lodged above a wreck of a nose, came up to the bar, flashed a badge, and announced: "As a lawfully deputized agent of the Minnesota Public Safety Commission, I am hereby ordering you to close until further notice."

"Is that a fact?" Rafferty said, casually resting his forearms on the bar's well-worn mahogany counter. A man drinking at the bar got up from his stool and walked toward the door, sensing trouble. Rafferty didn't budge.

"You're damn right it's a fact," the agent said. "Now, clear the place out."

Rafferty stared into the gray void of the man's eyes. "And why exactly would you be tryin' to close us down?"

"Violation of the rule establishing hours of legal operation during time of war. You were open well past ten o'clock last night."

Rafferty knew this to be false. He was scrupulous about closing at ten o'clock, as the rule required. He said, "'Tis not true, and you know it. Now, if it's a drink you want, I suggest you and your two friends sit down, and we'll all have a nice little chat. Or you can leave. Which will it be?"

The agent broke out into a crooked smile matching his crooked nose. "This is what it will be," he said, and reached into his coat. He never got to his pistol. Rafferty grabbed the man's tie and yanked him forward until his chin struck the bar with a thud. A derringer appeared in Rafferty's right hand, and he nuzzled it up to the agent's head. The other two agents went for their pistols but changed their minds when Grimes produced a twelve-gauge shotgun from under the bar and chambered a round.

"Don't think that because I'm an old man I won't defend myself," Rafferty whispered into the agent's ear before letting go of his tie. "Now, I would suggest, very strongly, that you reach inside that coat of yours and very carefully produce whatever weapon you're carryin'. Your friends would be wise to do the same. Then, once we've collected all of the hardware, you and your friends will leave. If you decide to come back, bring an army. Have I made myself clear?"

The men did as they were told, dropping their revolvers to the floor.

Rafferty said, "I should report this incident to the police, but since I'm feelin' generous today, I'll let you fellows go. Of course, I'll take statements from everyone in the bar. I'm sure my faithful customers here would all agree that you fellows tried to pull off an armed robbery but were unsuccessful."

"You won't get away with this," the lead agent said, rubbing his bruised chin. "Not for a minute."

"Perhaps, but I have found through long experience that St. Paul is an amicable city where people get by with all sorts of things. 'Tis why I love it so. Now, pay my respects to Mr. McGruder and tell him I'll give back your guns when he calls to apologize for your felonious intrusion. Good day, gentlemen."

"Jesus, Shad, what was that all about?" Grimes asked when the men had left. The young bartender was shaking, and Rafferty poured him a shot of whiskey.

"Why, 'tis all about our friend Mr. McGruder thinkin' he's become God almighty," Rafferty said. "Just keep calm, Danny boy, but stay on your toes. There may be more trouble before the day is done."

Leaving Grimes to tend bar, Rafferty went back in his office and began making telephone calls. One went to the mayor, one to Nelligan, and another to Louis Hill. Rafferty needed help in high places to prevent McGruder's men from coming back in force. Rafferty had just finished speaking with Hill, who promised he'd "do what he could," when Thomas called.

"Ah, Wash, you missed some fun. I'll tell you about it when you return. Quickly now, what did you find out in Chicago?"

Thomas's report, delivered with his usual brevity, proved to be better news than Rafferty could have hoped for.

"By God, Wash, I think we're on to something," he said. "The trick of the magic bullet has been undone. What time will you be back?"

"Train's due in just before nine."

"I'll see you then. Unless I'm mistaken, we will soon get to the bottom of this whole nasty business."

John McGruder received a call later that afternoon from Louis Hill. Their conversation was brief. Hill suggested it was a poor time to close down Rafferty's tavern. McGruder disagreed. Hill mentioned the names of several prominent acquaintances in the Wilson administration. Among them was his "good friend" Colonel Edward House, the president's most trusted advisor. It would be a shame, Hill said, if he had to "to create a fuss in Washington." McGruder said that would indeed be a bad thing. "I knew I could count on your discretion," Hill said, and wished McGruder a pleasant day.

It had taken all of McGruder's self-control not to scold Hill for his meddling in the safety commission's business. Didn't he understand that the commission's orders were the law and could not be challenged? McGruder felt a wave of rage and disgust sweep over him. He was, he had come to see, a man alone, the last true patriot in St. Paul. Not only had the mayor and police chief turned against him, but even the governor was questioning his authority.

After the mayhem at the Germania Life Building and Rafferty's act of insurrection, McGruder had gone to Governor Burnquist and demanded a thousand National Guardsmen to restore law and order in St. Paul. Instead of offering help, the governor had been downright hostile.

"We do not need more troubles at the moment," Burnquist had said. "That is what President Wilson's people are telling me and other governors in no uncertain terms. They want peace on the home front, not riots and confrontations. I will not send out the National Guard to close a tavern simply because you dislike its owner. Moreover, from this point forward you must clear all of your agents' actions with me in advance. There is to be no exception to this rule."

Burnquist had always been a weak-willed fool in McGruder's estimation, and now he was turning out to be a coward as well. McGruder realized that he needed to whip up public support if he was to take on the governor and his cronies. Berthelson was the key. Put the terrorist and his diabolical intentions back on center stage, McGruder thought, and the public would demand harsh action. And if the sheer incompetence of the St. Paul police could also be demonstrated once and for all, so much the better.

An idea gradually formed in McGruder's mind. He got out a pen and paper and, after careful thought, began writing. It was nearly dark by the time he finished. In an hour or so, he'd call a trusted reporter at the *Daily News* with a story that was sure to make headlines in the morning.

After arriving back in St. Paul, Thomas went directly to Rafferty's apartment and showed him the small piece of glass he'd found in the shed. Rafferty was fascinated. He measured it carefully, rolled it around in the palm of his hand, and said, "I do believe we've found the holy grail, Wash. Do you see what it must be?"

Thomas grinned. "I do. As soon as I picked it up, I had an idea about where it might fit. Then I started putting two and two together, and pretty soon it all added up."

"'Twill not be easy, however, to connect this little item to the murderer, who is as clever as they come. As it so happens, I have some ideas in that regard."

"I thought you might," Thomas said, pouring himself another cup of Rafferty's coal black coffee. "So do I."

It was one o'clock on Saturday morning by the time Rafferty and Thomas finished working out their plan.

23

"THERE COULD BE BLOOD ON OUR HANDS"

Rafferty was as surprised as everyone else in St. Paul by a page one story that appeared Saturday in the *Daily News*. The newspaper reported that John McGruder, "at great personal risk," had met the night before with "a secret informant who provided irrefutable evidence that Samuel Berthelson is planning yet another attack in the city." A set of instructions "written in Berthelson's own hand and dated only yesterday are proof of his vile intentions," the story said. In response to this threat, McGruder promised that the public safety commission would "use every means at its disposal" to find the terrorist. McGruder also called on Governor Burnquist to mobilize the National Guard to keep St. Paul safe.

The tale of McGruder's late-night discovery appeared only in the *Daily News*. St. Paul's other dailies contented themselves with accounts of the riot in front of the Germania Life Building. Isabel Diamond's story in the *Pioneer Press* was especially thorough and by no means favorable to McGruder, who was forced to defend his ill-fated attempt to lure Berthelson out of hiding.

Rafferty, a faithful reader of all the city's newspapers, told Thomas that McGruder's story was "very odd." They were seated in a booth in the tavern, finishing up a hefty breakfast of eggs, bacon, and potatoes.

"I gather you think Berthelson has left town," Thomas said.

"In one way or another, yes, I do. A man like Berthelson doesn't hang around anywhere for long. That's how he's been able to elude the law. He's always on the move. I'll tell you something else. I'd like to see that 'set of instructions' McGruder so conveniently provided to the press."

"Good luck with that," Thomas said. "More eggs?"

Sergeant Francis Carroll sat in one of the fraying armchairs in the high-ceilinged lobby of the Ryan Hotel, trying to look interested in the newspaper he'd been reading for several hours. He thought the "tail" on Rafferty was ridiculous, but there was no arguing with Mordecai Jones. Carroll and another detective, who was stationed outside, were to keep an eye on Rafferty until further notice.

By half past eight, Carroll found himself nodding off, so he went into the hotel restaurant for a mug of coffee. On his way up to the front counter, he nearly bumped into J. D. Carr. Steven Dodge, a toothpick stuck in one corner of his mouth, was with him. For some reason, Carroll found it strange to see the two men together. Although they worked in the same office, it hardly seemed like they would be friends.

"Good morning, Sergeant," Carr said. "You're up early. On the job, are you?"

Carroll didn't consider eight-thirty on a Saturday morning to be "early." He said, "I'm just getting some coffee."

"Well, we won't detain you. By the way, will Inspector Jones be in the office today?"

"He's already there, I'm sure. Is there something you want me to tell him?"

"Perhaps," Carr said, his eyes shifting over to Steven and then back to Carroll. "I have certain concerns with the investigation into Mr. Dodge's murder."

"What kind of concerns?"

"Come to think of it, it might be better if I take that up with the inspector in person," Carr said, and wished Carroll a good day.

Shortly before noon, Rafferty made two phone calls. One went to a man who, Rafferty believed, could ignite the kind of fire that just might smoke out the murderer of Artemus Dodge. The other was to a woman not known for keeping secrets.

"Now we must bide our time," Rafferty told Thomas. "Tomorrow, I'm thinkin', will be a day to remember."

Sunday did indeed prove to be a day that Rafferty, and everyone else entangled in the affair of the magic bullet, would never forget. For Amanda Dodge, the day began with a piece of startling, and unwelcome, news. She was resting in her hotel suite when, just after ten o'clock, she received a telephone call from Patrick Butler.

"Good morning, Mrs. Dodge," the lawyer said, delivering each word as carefully as a bank teller counting out bills. "I must apologize for calling you on the Sabbath, but I fear a matter has come up that requires immediate attention. There is a problem, it seems, with your husband's will."

Amanda felt an ominous tingle run down her spine. "What kind of a problem?"

Butler cleared his throat and said, "I have just learned within the last hour that there may be a codicil to your husband's will relating to the disposition of his monetary assets. Therefore, I have decided to delay the official reading of the will until four o'clock tomorrow afternoon so that I can attempt to locate the codicil. I am sure you understand why this must be done."

"No, I do not," Amanda said. "I know of absolutely no reason why Artemus would have changed the terms of his will at the last moment."

"I understand," Butler replied smoothly, "but as a precaution—"

"I care nothing for your silly precautions," Amanda blurted out. "Where did you hear this ridiculous story of a codicil? I would certainly know if it existed, and I can assure you it does not."

"Unfortunately, I am not at liberty to reveal my source of information, Mrs. Dodge. All I can say is that I believe the information to be credible. As a result, I am obligated under the law to make a reasonable effort to locate the codicil, since it could contain significant changes in your late husband's wishes in disposing of his estate."

"This is simply absurd. You say there *may* be a codicil that *may* change the terms of the will, but you cannot say how you have come upon this information or, for that matter, where this supposed codicil can be found."

"I realize the situation is rather peculiar, but I have no choice in the matter. I would be negligent in my duties as the executor of Mr. Dodge's estate if I failed to do all in my power to ensure that his final wishes are honored."

God, Amanda thought, can there be anything worse than listening to a lawyer justify himself? She said, "You know Artemus's final wishes, Mr. Butler. The codicil is a fiction. Who put you up to this little trick? Was it Mr. Carr?"

"As I said, I cannot reveal my source, for reasons that will become clear in due time. What I can tell you is that the codicil is not at my office, nor was it in your late husband's safety deposit box. Therefore, I can only assume that if the document in question exists, it must either be at River's Edge or at Dodge Tower. You see—"

Amanda cut him short. "There is nothing to be found at River's Edge. Artemus rarely, if ever, brought business home with him."

"Did he have a safe there?"

"Of course, and I have already examined its contents, which consist solely of personal and family papers. There is no codicil."

"Well then, that leaves Dodge Tower, it would appear. I suggest we meet tomorrow morning, say at ten o'clock, in your late husband's offices. That will give us time to conduct a thorough search for the codicil. I know that the police already opened the large safe in Mr. Dodge's apartment and found nothing of note. Do you know of any other safe or hiding place your late husband might have used?"

Amanda paused. She was thinking, fast and hard. "No," she finally said.

"What about Mr. Carr or Steven? Would they perhaps have known about such a thing?"

"I cannot speak for them."

"I understand. I will be calling them next, and I will put the questions to them directly. Now then, I once again apologize for disturbing you with such unsettling news. I look forward to seeing you tomorrow morning. I am sure everything will be resolved then. Good day, Mrs. Dodge."

As soon as Butler hung up, Amanda let out a scream of frustration. Somebody—Carr most likely, but possibly Steven or even that schemer Kretch—was trying to cheat her out of her share of Artemus's estate. The codicil had to be a forgery and had probably been planted somewhere in Artemus's office so that it could be conveniently discovered in the morning. Amanda couldn't let that happen.

Feeling a rush of nervous energy, she looked out the window across Rice Park, its scattering of elms and maples afire with autumn color. Amanda knew she had to be patient. When darkness came, she would see to it that no one would ever find the codicil that threatened to ruin her life. She had plans as well for Peter Kretch. He thought he knew her, but he'd soon be in for a surprise.

When Butler called, J. D. Carr was in the front parlor of his apartment listening to *Eine kleine Nachtmusik* on his gramophone. He always found Mozart's balance and precision deeply soothing. The news from Butler regarding a possible codicil to Artemus Dodge's will was, by contrast, as jarring as a slap to the face. It could lead to unpleasant complications.

"I take it you have already contacted Mrs. Dodge," Carr said.

Butler said he had, adding, "Steven will be next. I also must ask if you have any idea as to where Mr. Dodge might have kept the codicil, if in fact he prepared one."

"I'm afraid I cannot say, since it is a matter he never discussed with me."

After Butler rang off, Carr shut off the gramophone and considered the new problem at hand. Someone was stirring up mischief, for reasons that were unclear. Once Carr figured out who that person was, he wouldn't hesitate to defend his interests.

Steven Dodge also reacted with dismay when he heard from the lawyer.

"I don't understand what's going on," he told Butler. "Why would my father change his will at the last minute? It was all cut and dried. I know nothing about this supposed codicil, and I certainly don't know where it could be found."

Butler sounded sympathetic. "I understand, Steven, and I must emphasize that the codicil is purely conjectural at this point. It may well be that it doesn't exist or that it simply can't be located. If either proves to be the case, then nothing will change."

"Well, it is a strange thing, Mr. Butler, a very strange thing. I don't know what else to say, except good day, sir."

A few minutes later, Steven picked up the phone again. When the operator came on, he said, "I'd like to speak to Miss Isabel Diamond. I have her number."

There was no answer at Diamond's apartment. "Connect me to the *Pioneer Press*," Steven instructed the operator. "Perhaps she'll be there."

Life, Shadwell Rafferty had been known to remark after a drink or two, was simply a spill God hadn't gotten around to cleaning up yet. This belief in the random workings of fate was wildly at odds with the tenets of the Catholic Church, in whose mysteries Rafferty had been raised by the good Jesuits of Boston. That was all history now.

Rafferty had drifted away from his old religious moorings long ago to take his chances on the rough seas of doubt. Still, he felt no need to deny others—or himself—the comforts of holy ritual, and Sunday afternoon he took the Selby Avenue streetcar up to the cathedral to light votive candles for his long-dead wife and son, as he had for many years. Rafferty held out no hope that they would all meet again in sweet fields of cloud and clover, but he was a soldier in memory's ancient rebellion against time, and as long as he was alive, Mary Rafferty and the infant boy they'd never had a chance to name would not be forgotten.

After his devotions, Rafferty went back out to Selby, where he ran into Gertrude Schmidt, who was walking up to the church. "Ah, Mrs. Schmidt," he said, bowing slightly, "how nice to see you again. I trust you're doin' well."

"As well as can be expected."

"That is good to hear. As it so happens, I've been meanin' to talk to you. The other day I received an envelope from an anonymous source. In it were many documents relatin' to a certain business enterprise called the Blue Sky Partnership. I am of a mind that you might have sent it."

Mrs. Schmidt looked Rafferty in the eye and said, "I know nothing of it. All I can tell you is that God works in mysterious ways. Do you agree, Mr. Rafferty?"

"I do, though I would note as a general proposition that people can be just as mysterious as the Almighty. For instance, I'm not sure who in Mr. Dodge's office was runnin' the partnership. Would you have any ideas about that?"

"No. Such matters are not revealed to me. I would say to you, however, that it is always a good thing when it comes to the business affairs of the office to talk to Mr. Carr. He is the man who is supposed to know everything. Now, I must go to church. Good day, Mr. Rafferty."

"And the same to you," said Rafferty, who had to admit that Gertrude Schmidt was a very convincing liar.

Next to Rafferty's tavern in the Ryan Hotel was a small cigar shop that overlooked the corner of Sixth and Robert streets. Harlow Secrest had stationed himself in the shop early in the afternoon. His assignment was to "see if anybody is lurkin' about," as Rafferty put it. Convinced that he was being shadowed, Rafferty hoped that Secrest would be able to spot the tail. He'd also instructed Secrest to keep an eye on Dodge Tower and let him know if anyone entered the building.

Secrest saw nothing of interest until just before three o'clock, when a streetcar and a large black sedan came within inches of colliding on Sixth just east of Dodge Tower. The near miss was followed by a shouting match between the automobile's driver and the streetcar motorman. Secrest couldn't help but watch the show. As he did so, a man whose face was all but hidden by a broad-brimmed hat slipped unseen into Dodge Tower's side entrance on Robert.

George Jacobson, the regular weekend guard at Dodge Tower, recognized the man despite his low-slung hat. Still, Jacobson was surprised to see the man on a Sunday afternoon. Old Artemus himself had usually been the only person to come in for work on Sundays. His gorgeous young wife had also been a frequent Sunday visitor—how Jacobson enjoyed seeing her!—but always in the evening. Jacobson, who was in his seventies and much tormented by arthritis, rose slowly out of his chair to greet his unexpected visitor.

"Good afternoon, sir," he said with as much enthusiasm as he could muster. "Fancy seeing you here on a Sunday. Must have some urgent business to attend to."

"Yes, I guess you could call it that," the man said with a tight smile. "Say, before I go upstairs, could you see if somebody left a package for me here? It'd probably be in that big drawer in your desk."

"Well, I don't recall seeing anything," Jacobson said, reaching down to slide open the drawer.

He never saw what hit him.

Outside the Ryan Hotel, Inspector Mordecai Jones maintained a lonely vigil. He'd been at his post since five in the afternoon and intended to keep watch all night if necessary until he found out what Rafferty was up to. He'd hoped to arrive earlier, but some dumb Swede had gotten himself murdered in a drunken brawl at Plague Court, a notorious old tenement in the Mt. Airy badlands. Jones had been ordered to the scene, and it had taken most of the afternoon to coax a confession out of the killer. Carroll was still at police headquarters doing all the required paperwork.

Before beginning his watch, Jones had called Rafferty to make sure he was in his apartment, hanging up as soon as the familiar Irish brogue came on the line. Jones was stationed on the ground floor of the Chamber of Commerce Building, a crumbling Victorian pile directly across Robert Street from Dodge Tower and catty-corner from the Ryan. From his vantage point he could see both entrances to the hotel. The inspector had brought along his own food and drink, and had even strapped on a "motorman's friend" so that he wouldn't have to take any bathroom breaks.

Jones was rarely inclined to play hunches, but he had a strong feeling that Rafferty had made, or was about to make, some important discovery—one that might just blow the official version of Dodge's murder to smithereens. Jones had known all along that his single-bullet sniper theory was deeply flawed. But the public, not to mention Chief Nelligan, had no interest in hearing nuances of doubt when it came to a big murder case. They wanted a tidy solution, and Jones had provided it.

If he was wrong, if Dodge had been killed in some other way, Jones knew he had to expose the error himself. He'd still face criticism, but he'd also earn plaudits for correcting his own mistake. On the other hand, if Rafferty offered a new and convincing solution to the crime, Jones's reputation would be in tatters. He couldn't let that happen.

Not long after Jones began his surveillance, Rafferty received a phone call from Harlow Secrest. "You were right," he said. "You're being watched. Jones himself is on the job. He's over in the Chamber of Commerce. Do you want me to distract him?"

"Are you still down in the cigar shop?"

"Yes."

"Have you seen anybody else lollin' about?" Rafferty asked.

"No, just the inspector."

"All right, stay where you are, and let me know if Jones goes anywhere."

"Sure thing."

"Let me guess. Jones has us staked out," Thomas said when Rafferty hung up. They were in Rafferty's apartment, eating an early supper. "What do you suppose he's up to?"

"I think the inspector is worried, Wash. He suspects we're on to somethin', and he doesn't want his bright star to be eclipsed."

"Well, we'll just have to shake him if tries to interfere tonight."

"Maybe," Rafferty said, digging into an outsized ham sandwich. "Then again, we might need all the help we can get."

"I have some strange news, my love," Steven Dodge said when he finally reached Isabel Diamond at the newspaper. "I'm told there may be a codicil to my father's will. Have you heard anything about such nonsense?"

There was a tone of astonishment in her reply. "My God, Steven, I have. A man called me this morning with a tip. He said your father had made big changes in the will at the last minute."

"What kind of changes?"

"The man didn't say, but he did mention something called the Blue Sky Partnership and claimed it could be a big fraud. Do you know anything about that?"

"Well, I was aware of the partnership, of course. I think Mr. Carr was in charge, with help from Alan. I can't believe any fraud was involved."

"My caller said otherwise."

"Did you recognize his voice?"

"No. So tell me, dear, do you have any idea as to what sort of changes may be specified in the codicil?"

"Hardly. I don't think Amanda or Mr. Carr knows either. Did the caller say where the codicil might be?"

"That's the funny part. He said it was 'hiding in plain sight.' When I asked him what he meant by that, all he said was that the police hadn't done a very good job of inspecting the crime scene. Then he hung up."

"Maybe he was just a crank."

"Maybe, but I can tell you this: When my story comes out in the morning, the police will swarm all over your father's office looking for anything they can find about that suspicious partnership. I imagine they'll look for the codicil, too. If it's there, they'll find it."

"Well, I guess we'll all just have to wait and see. By the by, are you coming over tonight?"

"No, I've got too much work. Maybe tomorrow."

"All right, I hope to see you then."

Dodge was soon on the phone again, talking with Carr, who assured him that everything would turn out all right. "You have nothing to fear," Carr said. "Nothing at all."

As the last afternoon shadows melted into darkness, Rafferty stood at the bay window of his apartment and looked across the street to Dodge Tower, where a pair of Gothic lanterns illuminated the main entrance.

Wash Thomas had just come in to join the vigil. Secrest remained in the cigar shop.

"So, you're certain it will happen tonight?" Thomas asked as he got a cigar going.

"No, I am not certain, but I do believe it will happen," Rafferty replied. "The stars are aligned, Wash, and I can smell mischief in the air."

"Can you now?" said Thomas, who liked nothing better than bantering with his partner. "What exactly does mischief smell like?"

Rafferty made a great production of sniffing, like a bloodhound closing in on a big hunk of sirloin, and said, "Why, 'tis an electrical sort of smell, like cracklin' wires. If you weren't wearin' that cheap cologne, you'd smell it, too."

"Ha, I doubt that, but I'll trust you, as I always do. Besides, tonight would be her best chance, all things considered, to sneak into the tower. Are you expecting she'll come right up to the main entrance?"

"Probably, but our friend Mr. Secrest will notify us if she decides to go around to the side doors on Robert."

Thomas blew a ring of blue smoke and said, "Let's just hope that we know what we're doing, Shad. What if Berthelson shows up out of the blue? There could be blood on our hands if things go wrong."

"Well, then, we must make sure that they do not," Rafferty said and kept staring out the window.

24

"COME MEET THE MURDERER OF ARTEMUS DODGE"

The man in the Packard Twin Six saw headlights coming down the winding drive of River's Edge and glanced at his watch. It was ten minutes past nine. A cold rain had started to fall, obscuring visibility, but he recognized the car as one of Artemus Dodge's Cadillac roadsters. The man had been parked along Mississippi River Boulevard for three hours, and he felt a surge of excitement when he spotted the car.

The dark green roadster, with Amanda presumably in the backseat and a chauffeur at the wheel, turned south on the boulevard, toward the man in the Packard. He ducked down as the Cadillac sped past, then made a U-turn, and tailed the roadster to West Seventh Street, where it turned northeast, toward downtown. The big Packard was a blue blood's car, richly appointed and throbbing with power, and the man had no problem keeping up with the Cadillac. He followed the roadster to Seven Corners, where there was a Pure Oil station with a pay phone inside. The man pulled in and made a call.

"She'll be there in five minutes or so," he said when his ally answered.

"Good. Call me from the lobby when you arrive."

"What about the guard?"

"He's been taken care of."

"All right, I'll be there soon."

The man had been contacted by his unlikely ally earlier in the day, with an offer that seemed too good to be true. All he had to do was assist in exposing Amanda's conniving and dishonesty. In exchange for his help, he'd tap into a river of gold beyond his wildest dreams. Or so his ally promised. But would the promise be kept? The man had his doubts, fearing that an elaborate double cross might be in the works. He would have to be very cautious and watch his back.

At nine thirty Mordecai Jones saw a Cadillac sweep by on Sixth Street and stop in front of Dodge Tower. The driver came out and went around to open the rear passenger-side door. Amanda Dodge, wearing a dark raincoat and a matching fedora hat, stepped out into the rain. She said something to the driver, who got back behind the wheel and drove off as Amanda went into the building. Jones was surprised by her appearance. What kind of business, he wondered, could the beautiful widow have at Dodge Tower on a Sunday night? Jones was tempted to go ask her but thought the better of it. Rafferty was his quarry, not Amanda.

"The lady has arrived," Rafferty announced, watching from his apartment window as Amanda went into Dodge Tower. "But where's the fellow we're lookin' for? I thought he'd be here by now."

"Maybe we missed him," Thomas said.

"I'm beginnin' to think the same thing," Rafferty said, worried that the event he'd so carefully orchestrated might be spinning out of control. "We'll wait a bit, I guess, but not for very long."

Ten minutes after Amanda Dodge made her appearance, a man in a yellow slicker came walking north on Robert, paused in front of the pitch-dark vestibule where Mordecai Jones stood, then crossed the street toward Dodge Tower. Jones couldn't make out the man's face, but there was something familiar about the way he carried himself. The man walked down to the tower's main entrance and disappeared into the lobby. Jones could hardly believe what he was seeing. First Amanda and now a mysterious man in yellow had turned up at Dodge Tower in the dead of night. What in blazes was going on?

The appearance of the man in the yellow slicker came as a relief to Rafferty. His plan, it appeared, was working. Thomas trained his binoculars on the man but couldn't get a good look at his face, which was shielded by a muffler and a tightly drawn stocking cap.

"Whoever he is, he's got a key to the building," Thomas said. "He just waltzed right into the lobby."

Rafferty said, "Then he's the man we've been waitin' for. Are you all set?"

Thomas grabbed his trench coat and said, "Everything's in my pockets. Two flashlights, a jimmy, lock picks, and a Colt Police Special in case there's trouble."

"And I will be assisted by Mr. Smith and Mr. Wesson," Rafferty said. "All right, let's go. We'll collect our friend Secrest on the way out."

Jones was debating what to do next when he saw the unmistakable profiles of Rafferty and Thomas emerging from the Ryan Hotel. A man Jones couldn't identify was with them. Jones now knew his suspicions had been vindicated. Something was about to happen, and Rafferty would be right in the middle of it. Jones planned to be right there with him, whether Rafferty liked it or not.

Amanda Dodge felt a flutter in her stomach when she entered Dodge Tower's dimly lit lobby, which was as hushed and mysterious as a Gothic cathedral. Overhead, amid leaping plaster vaults, the mosaics Artemus had so loved presented a saga of commerce in all of its glory. The Holy Church of Artemus, someone had once called the lobby, but Amanda was not in a religious mood. Commerce was a mere abstraction. It was $1 million in cold hard cash, the real stuff of dreams, that interested her.

The guard's desk was vacant, but a sign said he'd be back shortly. Amanda had chatted with George Jacobson many times and knew that the old man was forever taking bathroom breaks. Artemus himself had had the same trouble. Amanda went to the penthouse elevator and glanced up at the indicator needle. She was mildly surprised to see that the elevator was at the penthouse level. Normally, it was left on the ground floor after hours. Of course nothing had been normal of late, what with police and who knew how many other people coming and going from the penthouse. Still, she felt another faint stir of anxiety as she used her key to summon the elevator. What if someone was up in the penthouse? Be calm, she told herself, be calm.

When the elevator doors slid open, Amanda stepped inside and pressed the button for the penthouse. Everything is fine, just fine, she reassured herself. Go to the penthouse, search for the codicil, and destroy it if it's there. Otherwise, quit worrying and let the lawyers take over.

Amanda felt beads of sweat trickle down her face and neck as she rode up to the penthouse. Was the car steamily hot, or was it just her? She took a long, deep breath as the elevator came to a stop. The doors opened into darkness. Amanda was startled. The offices had always been brightly lit during her visits with Artemus. There was no reason for that now, she realized. She took a small flashlight from her purse and used it to guide her into the lobby, where she debated whether to turn on a lamp. Better not to, she decided. If Artemus had hidden the codicil, it would be in his office or apartment. She'd turn on lights there if need be.

Amanda crept down the hall toward Artemus's office, her shoes settling softly into the plush carpeting. The effect was unsettling, as though she was walking through clouds. The air was heavy and soundless, and she could almost feel the weight of it pressing against her. She was still perspiring, and she got out a handkerchief to wipe her forehead.

She turned right at the T in the hallway and passed J. D. Carr's office, wondering if he'd planted the notion of a codicil, or even forged such a document. It was just the kind of game he might play. Carr was smooth and oily, a machine with no heart, and now he might well be after her money. Just let him try, she thought.

Up ahead was the security door guarding Artemus's office. It was locked—Carr would have seen to that—but Amanda believed she could open it. Artemus had been the least sentimental of men, with one exception. He'd always spoken reverently of his younger brother, Emmanuel, who'd died at a young age in a gruesome mill accident in New Hampshire. Artemus had also made a point of celebrating Emmanuel's birthday, and he was often heard to remark, "My brother is my protector."

Amanda hadn't climbed out of the deep hole of the Connemara Patch by being stupid, and it occurred to her that Artemus might have memorial-ized Emmanuel by using his birth date—March 30, 1851—as the combina-tion to the security door. There was also the fact that the same number—33051—was carved on the obelisk above Artemus's grave. It couldn't be a coincidence. She'd stood behind Artemus on several occasions when he opened the door and had managed to see that the combination's first num-ber was three. Now she put her theory to the test. Holding the flashlight in her mouth, she dialed the combination of three, thirty, and fifty-one. Then she pushed down on the door handle.

The door clicked open, and she heard the buzzer sound at the guard's station. It didn't matter, since there was no one there to hear it. Thinking herself very clever, she went inside and shut the door, its security bar auto-matically dropping into place behind her. She should have felt safe but found that she didn't. There was blood in the room, and even though Artemus had been killed almost a week ago, she could still smell an aroma of death.

Feeling faint, Amanda turned on a lamp by the sofa and sat down. She desperately wanted a cigarette to steady her nerves and clear her mind, but she resisted the urge. The lingering odor of cigarette smoke might raise suspicions the next day. After a few minutes her nerves steadied, and she got up to begin her search.

She started in the apartment, but before long a disturbing thought elbowed its way into her mind. What if Carr or Steven or even Mrs. Schmidt already had the codicil, either because they'd found it or because Artemus had given it to one of them for safekeeping? Amanda tried to push the thought away as she surveyed the apartment's bedroom for pos-sible hiding places. The antique four-poster bed where Artemus had on several occasions made love to her in his repulsive and feeble way seemed a good place to begin. Amanda lifted up the mattress and looked under-neath. She found nothing.

Following instructions, the man who'd tailed Amanda stopped at the guard's desk in the lobby of Dodge Tower. The guard, as promised, was gone. The man used the desk phone to contact his ally, who picked up after the first ring.

"I take it you've had no problems," the ally said.

"No. I don't think anyone saw me coming in."

"Good. Do you have your elevator key?"

"Of course."

"Then come up at once. I'll meet you at the elevator, and we'll confront her with the truth. She'll have no choice but to give both of us what we want."

"All right, I'll see you shortly."

As he hung up the phone, the man noticed what looked like a small drop of blood on the desktop. Curious, he walked around the desk and found a few more dark splatters and streaks on the guard's chair and the floor. He bent down for a closer look. The blood was fresh, and it formed a trail leading to a narrow hall next to the elevator banks. The man followed the trail into the hall, but the light there grew so dim that he lost sight of it.

Standing in the darkness, his mind racing, the man debated what to do. Was he about to walk into an ambush? He wasn't sure, but he remembered what his ally had said about the guard being "taken care of." Those words took on an ominous ring in view of the blood on the floor. The man wondered if his turn to be "taken care of" would come next.

The man was returning to the guard's desk when he saw something that nearly caused his heart to stop. Back across the lobby three figures were outlined against the glass doors of the main entrance. It looked as though they were trying to get inside. The man slipped back into the shadows. He got out his revolver and waited.

Joined by Harlow Secrest, who was happy to be relieved of his dull duties as a sentinel, Rafferty and Thomas left the hotel and walked across to Dodge Tower in a driving rain. The downpour had driven pedestrians inside, and Sixth Street was deserted except for an occasional passing car. Secrest tried the main lobby doors, but they were all locked. Rafferty peered inside and could just make out the unattended guard's desk.

"I don't like this," he said. "'Tis best we go around the other way. There'll be less chance of being seen."

They walked around the corner and down Robert to the tower's side entrance—a pair of bronze doors sheltered beneath a deep arch. A sign above the doors said "DODGE ARCADE." With Rafferty and Secrest shielding him from any nosy passersby, Thomas went to work on one of the door locks.

After a short time, Rafferty said, "How's it look? I'd hate to have to break in like a common burglar."

"Don't worry, I'll get it," Thomas said without looking up. He'd already inserted a pair of picks into the lock and was manipulating them with his customary skill.

A good minute went by before Rafferty remarked, "As you know, Wash, I'm a patient man but not overly so."

Thomas gave a derisive snort and kept jiggling the picks. "Oh, you're patient all right, Shad, patient as can . . . ah, there it is!" The lock sprung open with a pleasing click. Thomas then used a long, slender tool to unlatch and lift the floor bolt.

Once they were all inside, Thomas closed and locked the door behind them. The arcade, lined by small shops catering to a wealthy clientele, led directly into Dodge Tower's lobby.

"We'll have some persuadin' to do if the night guard is at his desk," Rafferty said. "We'll need his elevator key, which he might not want to give us. His name is George Jacobson, and he's not a bad fellow, but he can be stubborn."

When they reached the lobby, Thomas said, "Well, it looks like old George is off on a break. Sign says he'll be back soon. Maybe he's doing his rounds."

"Not likely," Rafferty said. "George is the only one on duty—he's told me that several times—and he's supposed to stay close to his desk."

"Well then, he probably had to answer nature's call," Thomas offered, directing his flashlight beam around the desk. He spotted the blood drops at once and went down on his haunches for a better look.

"Looks like fresh blood," he said. "There's a regular trail of it on the floor."

"That can't be a good thing," Rafferty said, suddenly worried that he'd made a terrible miscalculation. "We'd best look for George."

They found him in a bathroom at the end of the hallway next to the elevator bank. Jacobson lay hog-tied on the white tile floor, a gag in his mouth and a nasty wound where he'd been hit on the back of the head. He was breathing but unconscious.

Rafferty said, "Mr. Secrest, see if you can remove that key ring attached to this poor fellow's belt. Then untie him and do what you can to stop the bleedin'."

Secrest yanked off the key ring and handed it to Thomas, who said, "I assume you want the key to the penthouse elevator."

"'Twould be most useful."

The ring was thick with keys, but Thomas knew what to look for. "Here it is," he said, sliding a square-headed silver key from the ring. "It's the type Otis uses."

"What if the man we're looking for comes back here to finish the job?" Secrest asked.

"You have a gun, Mr. Secrest, and you should feel free to use it."

Secrest nodded. "Are you and Mr. Thomas going up to the penthouse?"

"That's the plan."

Rafferty and Thomas returned to the lobby and used the guard's key to summon the elevator from the penthouse. Once inside the car, Rafferty took his .44 caliber Smith & Wesson revolver from his coat pocket. Thomas did the same with his Colt.

"I'm hopin' we're not too late," Rafferty said. "Just be careful up there, Wash, very careful. One man is already near death tonight, and I don't want us to join him."

Mordecai Jones watched as Rafferty, Thomas, and Secrest came around the corner on Robert and disappeared into the deep arch sheltering the entrance to the Dodge Arcade. Jones pulled up his coat collar and went out into the rain. Not wanting to raise suspicion, he walked at a normal pace down Robert on the side opposite Dodge Tower. He reached a point directly across from the arcade's entrance just in time to see one of the doors being pulled shut by an arm that quickly vanished inside.

Jones waited impatiently for a streetcar to lumber past and then crossed over to the arcade. Its doors were locked. He peered through the glass, hoping to catch a glimpse of Rafferty and his companions, but it was too dark to see anyone. Mumbling a curse, Jones was tempted to break the door glass with his flashlight. He decided instead to try the main doors. The guard in the lobby would let him in. Jones ran down to Sixth and turned the corner just in time to see the man in the yellow rain slicker leaving the tower.

"Hold it. Hold it right there," Jones shouted, drawing his pistol. The man started running, but Jones was much faster and overtook him within fifty yards. Jones knocked the man to the ground, straddled him, and put a gun to his head.

"Well, well," Jones said, his chest still heaving from his sudden sprint, "fancy meeting you here. Just what have you been up to?"

"I didn't do anything," the man replied. "You must believe me. I didn't do anything."

Amanda Dodge found it unsettling to be alone in Artemus's apartment, thick as it was with shadows and memories. She'd never really believed in ghosts, but she sensed that a residue of her late husband remained, like one of those childhood smells forever fixed in the brain. Artemus was dead, but somehow he wasn't quite gone. A bolt of lightning flashed outside followed by a menacing rumble. In spite of the thunder and her growing sense of uneasiness, Amanda kept searching. She found nothing. There was no codicil.

She went back into the office, convinced that she'd been made a fool of. The codicil was a fantasy or perhaps someone's idea of a bad joke. She'd just have to wait and see what happened tomorrow when the will was read in Butler's office. If the alleged codicil somehow oozed out of the woodwork and into the hands of Carr or Steven or anybody else, she'd denounce it as a fake. The courts, she believed, would never fall for such an obvious fraud.

Still, she wondered why anyone would go to the trouble of playing such a stupid trick, unless . . . A chill suddenly drove deep into her bones like the stab of an ice pick. What if, she thought, I'm not alone?

. . . . .

After Amanda slipped into her husband's office and closed the security door, the man who had been expecting her felt a deep sense of satisfaction. She'd taken the bait, propelled by her own bottomless greed. Everything was falling into place. A few minutes later, his supposed assistant called from the main lobby downstairs, and the man told him to come up to the penthouse. The unwitting assistant would of course be ambushed the minute he stepped from the elevator, since his real role was to serve as a scapegoat for murder.

But as the man watched the indicator above the penthouse elevator, it didn't move. After waiting for several minutes, the man concluded that something had gone wrong. Perhaps the scapegoat had somehow been detained in the lobby or had gotten cold feet and fled. In either case, the man had no intention of aborting his plan. He had confounded the world once, and now he had a heaven-sent chance to confound it again. He couldn't let the opportunity pass.

The man padded back down the nearly pitch-black hall to double-check his setup. Everything was perfect, just as it had been almost a week earlier when Artemus Dodge went to meet his maker. Only this time, it would be much easier. There would be no need to bother with alarms, misdirection, or other hocus-pocus. The killing would be clean and simple. The newspapers, the man knew, would love it, feasting on the bones of his clever mayhem for weeks to come.

As he reached toward the intercom on his desk, the man heard the elevator door open. It had to be the scapegoat, late as usual. The man now felt completely at ease, certain that the final flowering of the plan would be exquisite. There would be no loose ends to fret over, no explanations to offer, no danger of being caught. Everything would be perfect.

Smiling to himself, the man pressed an intercom key and said, "Amanda, is that you in the office? We need to talk at once." He eagerly awaited her reply.

The thought that someone might have lured her to the penthouse, might even be hiding somewhere in the shadows, deeply frightened Amanda. She tried to collect her thoughts as she sat on the sofa and lit a cigarette, no longer caring if she left the smell of it behind. She needed nicotine. Her panic, she hoped, would drift away with the smoke. Besides, was it really possible someone could be hiding in the office or apartment? She'd already searched the apartment and would have seen a person hiding there. As for the office, she could see with her own two eyes that she was alone.

She had an inspiration and got up to look at her portrait, which still hung on the wall beside Artemus's desk. Was it possible that Artemus, in a final ironic gesture, had hidden the codicil behind the portrait? She wouldn't have put it past him. She took down the picture and examined it but found nothing, so she rehung it and went back to the couch to finish her cigarette.

Still, she couldn't shake a sense of something closing in on her, as though she'd plunged underwater and was struggling for air. She became aware of the grandfather clock—Artemus's one nod to nostalgia—ticking away in the corner. She'd always thought the clock a hideous thing, its dark wood cabinet a maze of Victorian curlicues, but Artemus had refused to part with it. The ticking seemed to grow louder, and Amanda realized that it had probably been the last sound Artemus heard as he lay dying on the floor, his breath—and time itself—abandoning him. She shuddered to think of it, not because she missed him, but because she was reminded of her own mortality.

Amanda soon had another disturbing thought. What if someone was lurking elsewhere in the penthouse, beyond the protective walls of Artemus's inner sanctum? Perhaps she'd be foolish to leave. Then again, look what had happened to Artemus. He'd found no safety in his supposed fortress.

Something moved—Amanda saw it out of the corner of her eye— and she felt a slight rustle of air, cold as the night. Her heart accelerated. One of the drapes behind Artemus's desk was fluttering. A deep hole of fear opened inside Amanda, and her stomach seemed to drop out of her body. The window must be open, just as it apparently had been before Artemus was murdered. Was the killer out on the balcony, ready to take his shot?

"Amanda, is that you in the office? We need to talk at once." The voice from Artemus's intercom nearly caused her heart to stop. She knew the voice, but she didn't know if she should answer. How did he know she was in Artemus's office? Had he followed her? What did he want?

Then he spoke again, his voice filling the office. "Please, Amanda, I know it must be you. I think I've found what we're both looking for. Talk to me, Amanda, please talk to me."

Rafferty and Thomas cocked their revolvers just before the penthouse elevator doors opened. All they found was darkness. They cautiously stepped out into the office lobby, listening for any sounds. All was quiet. Thomas turned on his flashlight and sent the beam skittering around. The lobby appeared empty. Wary of an ambush, they went down the hall and slipped into Mrs. Schmidt's office.

"Mrs. Dodge must be in the old man's office," Thomas whispered.

"So it would seem," Rafferty agreed. He switched on his own flashlight and shined it across the top of Mrs. Schmidt's desk until he found her intercom. It was one of the latest Dictograph models, with neatly labeled keys for contacting every office in the penthouse.

Thomas swiveled his head around and whispered, "Did you hear that?"

"No."

"I could swear I just heard a door swinging open."

"Then she is in great danger," Rafferty said. He pressed the intercom key for Artemus Dodge's office and spoke in an urgent voice.

Amanda was stunned when she heard a new voice come over the intercom. "Mrs. Dodge, this is Shadwell Rafferty. You must do exactly as I tell you or you will surely die."

She couldn't say exactly why, but she took comfort in hearing Rafferty's voice. Something about the fat old Irishman made her trust him. Maybe it was the kindness in his bright blue eyes or the easy authority of his manner.

Amanda followed Rafferty's instructions. She dropped to her knees and crawled around Artemus's desk. It seemed silly to be on all fours like a baby, but she believed Rafferty must have good reason for his seemingly bizarre instructions. Artemus's intercom sat atop the corner of the desk. Still on her knees, Amanda got as close to it as she could, being careful not to lift her head above the desk. Her hands were trembling, her heart racing. She looked at the intercom's keys, saw the right one, then reached up to press it.

"Yes, I'm here," she said. "Do you really have the codicil?"

"I do," said the voice that wasn't Rafferty's. "Just stay where you are for a moment while I make sure we're alone. Then we can talk."

"All right," Amanda said. She kept her head low, as Rafferty had instructed her, and waited. She wasn't sure, but she thought she heard a very faint metallic sound, like a screw being turned, near the security door. Then she saw something she could scarcely believe.

Seconds later the voice returned over the intercom. "Amanda, darling, are you listening closely?"

"Yes."

"Good. I want you to look out the window behind you—the one that's open. Are you looking?"

"Yes," Amanda lied. She was still on her knees, between the desk and the windows.

Then it came—a sharp crack, loud as a lightning bolt—followed by a shower of splinters that stung her neck and shoulders. She covered her head with her arms and began to scream, afraid that she'd been shot. When she finally looked up, she saw a gaping hole in the middle of her portrait, right where her face had been.

"Now," Rafferty said when he heard the shot. Thomas bolted out the door and raced down the hallway toward Dodge's inner sanctum. Rafferty followed as fast as he could. When Thomas turned the corner, he found himself staring into the eyes of Steven Dodge, who stood just inside his office, behind a long rifle mounted on a tripod.

Cursing, Dodge swung the rifle around toward Thomas, who fired two shots from his Colt. One missed, but the other found Dodge's left shoulder, knocking him to the floor. He tried to get up but abandoned the idea when he felt the barrel of Thomas's revolver against his temple.

"It's over," Rafferty said, coming up and training his own weapon on Dodge.

"So it would seem," Dodge said with a crazy grin. "But wasn't it fun while it lasted?"

"No one move," said a familiar basso voice. "This is Inspector Mordecai Jones, and I will shoot anyone who gives me cause to."

"Sounds like the gendarmes have arrived," Thomas said.

"And, as usual, a minute too late," Rafferty said. Then he shouted, "In here, Inspector. Come meet the murderer of Artemus Dodge."

25

"I DO THE BEST I CAN"

When it came to murder, Shadwell Rafferty seldom found the usual explanations to be entirely satisfying. The smooth white walls of reason, he believed, were no match for the dark complexities of the human heart, and every murder left behind a residue of wonder and doubt. Still, the good people of St. Paul wanted assurances that Artemus Dodge's murder could be accounted for in a reasonable way, and Rafferty felt compelled to oblige them as best he could.

Normally, he would have been content to leave explanations to the police, but Inspector Jones had behaved badly after arriving at the penthouse with Peter Kretch. Jones, who'd arrested Kretch after running him down outside Dodge Tower, announced at once that he would "take complete command" of the situation, and the penthouse was soon swarming with coppers. Rafferty and Thomas were able to talk briefly with Kretch, who admitted to blackmailing but denied any part in murder.

Rafferty wanted to interrogate Steven Dodge as well, but Jones brushed him aside. The inspector, it was obvious, intended to hog the credit for solving Artemus Dodge's murder. Then Chief Nelligan arrived, fully prepared to seize his own outsized share of the glory. He and Jones decided to question Steven behind closed doors at City Hospital, where he'd receive treatment for his bullet wound. Rafferty wasn't invited to the party.

With nothing left for them to do, Rafferty and Thomas slipped away and took the elevator down to the lobby, where they found Secrest along with an unruly pack of news reporters. Isabel Diamond was among them.

"What's going on up there?" she asked Rafferty.

"Ah, 'tis hard to say in so many words, but you may be interested to learn that Steven Dodge has been arrested for the murder of his father."

"Holy mother of Mary," Diamond said.

"The police, I'm sure, will have a statement by morning. On the other hand, I might have a comment or two before then, if you'd care to come along to my apartment."

Diamond made a quick decision. "How could I turn down an invitation from a man as charming as you are, Mr. Rafferty? Lead the way."

So it was at half past midnight that Thomas, Secrest, and Diamond joined Rafferty for a "court of inquiry," as he jokingly called it, around a roaring fire in the front parlor of his apartment at the Ryan. The room was comfortable if not especially disciplined, its haphazard array of heavy oak furniture decorated with what Rafferty liked to call "debris"—old copies of magazines and newspapers, half-read books, cups and glasses, and not a few bottles of Yeorg's cave-aged lager. Dust and cigar smoke were the dominant odors.

After everyone had warmed themselves with a round of brandy, Diamond spoke up. "So when did you know it was Steven?" she asked, hoping that her own close relationship with the murderer would not come to light.

Rafferty said, "Before I can answer that question, I think it best to go back to first causes, as it were. Such was the manner of St. Thomas Aquinas, whose logical methods were drilled into me as a lad by the Jesuits."

"Just make sure you don't go all the way back to the creation," Thomas cautioned, "or we'll run out of liquor long before you're done."

Rafferty let out a whoop and said, "I promise brevity, Wash, insofar as any Irishman is capable of it. Let us begin then with what motivated young Steven to do his awful deeds. It was, I believe, a combination of greed and arrogance, two mighty engines in human affairs. Greed drove him to establish the Blue Sky Partnership, by which he hoped to make much more money than his father was inclined to pay him."

"What was the partnership?" Diamond asked, scribbling into a small notebook.

"I am no finance man, as Wash here will attest, but it appears that the partnership consisted of investors—there were ten or so to begin with and more later—who put fifty thousand dollars apiece into a fund for buyin' stock in up-and-comin' business ventures. Documents I received from an anonymous source state the partnership began in 1915 and that young Steven was in charge of its day-to-day operation. 'Tis possible Mr. Dodge thought the partnership would be a good experience for his son. It was, but not in the way Mr. Dodge assumed."

"How so?"

"To put it simply, Steven cooked the books, to the point, I'm sure, of sendin' out false statements to the investors. The partnership was a fraud. Instead of investin' the partners' money, Steven probably spent most of it at the local gamblin' dens he was known to frequent. He was a good sales-man, however, and he kept bringin' more investors into the scheme. This new money allowed him to pay dividends, as it were, to the original inves-tors. 'Twas a clever bit of business, but it couldn't last forever."

"I see where you're going," Diamond said. "The whole thing must have started falling apart this year."

"It did. As far as I can figure, once war began to loom, the men who'd invested in the partnership felt a patriotic duty to put more money into gov-ernment bonds. Maybe old Artemus himself urged them on, since he was in charge of the local bond campaign. Steven, I'm guessin', was asked to liq-uidate some of the stocks he'd supposedly bought for the partners. Trouble was, there were no stocks. Steven could see that his fraud was in grave dan-ger of bein' exposed. If that happened, he'd probably be disinherited by his father, and he might even go off to prison. He had to save himself."

"Did the old geezer know what Steven was up to?"

"I believe he did, which is why he intended to hold a special meetin' on the day he died. Its purpose would have been to confront Steven with his crime. The old man may have been ready to dress down Carr as well."

"So he was in on the scheme too?"

"Ah, Miss Diamond, you have a splendidly suspicious mind. I cannot say whether Mr. Carr had a hand in the fraud. My guess is that he did not. Still, I'm thinkin' he at least knew about it and was tryin' to cover it up—for the good of the company—when Artemus Dodge was murdered. Mr. Carr of course will never admit to such a thing, and it hardly matters now."

Rafferty sipped at his brandy and said, "Let us leave Mr. Carr for the moment and consider young Steven's situation. He knows his goose will be cooked unless he can find some way to raise a huge sum of money quickly. Bein' both clever and without a conscience, he hits upon an obvious solution to his problem. By doin' away with his father, he'll inherit the business and obtain enough money to pay off his debts and cover up his fraud. But how can he commit the murder without implicatin' himself in the crime?

"'Tis here that Steven's arrogance appears, big as a harvest moon on an October night. He could have hired someone to do the killin', much like Frank Dunn did with poor Alice McQuillan. Instead, Steven takes a far more devious course. He decides he'll commit the perfect crime by stagin' one of those locked room mysteries that have been the stuff of fiction ever since old Edgar Allan Poe unleashed his ape in the Rue Morgue. As it so happens, Steven found a handy guide for just the sort of crime he had in mind."

Rafferty held up a copy of the Solvers' Club collected papers. "In here you'll find a most insightful essay on locked room mysteries written by a certain Dr. Gideon Fell. The name, however, is a pseudonym. The real author is none other than J. D. Carr."

"Are you saying Mr. Carr helped plan the murder?" Diamond asked.

Rafferty shook his head. "I make no such accusations, but I do know, courtesy of a friend of mine, that Mr. Carr was the author of this monograph."

"And here I thought Carr was such a little weasel."

"Well, I'm pleased that your opinion of the gentleman has been reformed," Rafferty said. "I'm sure he'll be pleased as well."

"So how'd he become such an expert?"

"I cannot say. What's important is that Steven, by one means or another, learned about the monograph and used its principles to concoct a truly brilliant locked room murder."

Secrest joined in the conversation for the first time. "You're being a tease, Mr. Rafferty. How in blazes did Steven pull off the murder? That's really what we want to know."

Rafferty said, "We'll get to that soon enough. First, I must remind you that Steven almost surely saw his great fraud beginnin' to collapse many months before it was discovered. He therefore had plenty of time to prepare the perfect murder. The fact that he was involved in the plannin' of Dodge Tower proved crucial to his scheme."

"How was that?" Diamond asked. "Was there a secret passage or something like that?"

"In a way you could say so. I'm told by the architect, Mr. Stem, that the blueprints for Artemus Dodge's fortified office weren't finished until early this year, even though the buildin' itself was well under construction by then. Steven, it's a good bet, went over them with great care. At some point, he saw in them an opportunity to stage a most bafflin' murder. How long it took to work out all the details I can't say, but he left nothing to chance. The office's security door was the key. In August Steven arranged for the door to be detoured in Chicago so that it could be outfitted with a special feature."

"What sort of feature?" Secrest asked.

"I'll get to that. I believe Steven himself went to Chicago to examine the work. While there, he must have encountered Henry Merrivale, an employee of the Mosler Safe Company who was tryin' to find out why the door's delivery had been delayed. Mr. Merrivale was murdered in late August. I believe that Steven either killed him or, more likely, hired someone for the job. 'Tis not a difficult thing to find men in Chicago ready to take a life for a few dollars."

"Hold on a minute," Diamond said. "Why was this Merrivale fellow's death never reported in St. Paul if it was connected to Mr. Dodge's death?"

Wash Thomas provided the answer: "It's not hard to explain. When I went to Chicago to look into the matter, it was obvious the police there had no idea that Mr. Merrivale's case might be linked to events here. The coppers thought it was just another strong-arm robbery gone bad. The people at Mosler's headquarters in Ohio probably believed the same thing."

"All right, I guess that makes sense. So exactly what was done to the door in Chicago?"

"Shad will provide the details soon enough," Thomas replied. "Let's just say for now that the door was modified. I tracked down the shop where the work was done, by a man named Hank Bencolin. The Chicago coppers say he's a master machinist who makes special tools for safecrackers and their ilk. Unfortunately, he'd pulled up stakes by the time I found his place."

Rafferty said, "'Tis known in any case that the mysterious Mr. Bencolin completed his work on the vault door toward the end of August. It finally arrived here around the first of September and was installed as the last piece of Mr. Dodge's office. Steven, meanwhile, continued to refine his scheme and even performed at least one 'test run,' as it were. I think he intended to wait a few months before murderin' his father. He was forced to act more quickly when he saw that he was about to be exposed for the Blue Sky fraud. That's when he summoned Samuel Berthelson to St. Paul."

Diamond was nonplussed. "Are you joking, Mr. Rafferty? How could Steven 'summon' a man like Berthelson when the entire police force of this city has been unable to find him?"

Secrest jumped in. "I can answer that. He must have contacted him through Alan Dubois."

"So it would seem," Rafferty agreed. "Mr. Dubois was in his own way as strange a character as his office mate. I will not pretend to know Mr. Dubois's deepest thoughts, but over his short life he must have developed a profound hatred for men of wealth like Artemus Dodge. He was dreamin' of revolution, as young men do."

Diamond was skeptical. "Dubois was a silver spoon–fed blue blood if there ever was one. Why would he want to attack the very man who paid him a good salary?"

"'Tis a known fact, Miss Diamond, that revolutionaries are as often born with silver as pewter spoons in their mouths. Besides, Mr. Secrest can tell you that there was more to Mr. Dubois than met the eye. He was supposedly workin' as an agent for the public safety commission by posin' as a rich young fellow with radical ideas. The truth, which Mr. McGruder is hidin', is that Alan Dubois's ultimate loyalties were to Berthelson and his movement. So it was that when the time came to murder Artemus Dodge, Mr. Dubois not only abetted Steven but also enlisted the aid of Berthelson. And from Steven's point of view, what could be better than blamin' his father's murder on the nation's most feared terrorist?"

"This is getting juicier by the minute," Diamond said, writing furiously in her notebook. "So why was Dubois murdered if he was part of the scheme?"

"There can be little doubt that Steven murdered Mr. Dubois to eliminate a potential witness against him. 'Twas commendably thorough on his part, I suppose you could say."

"There seem to be plotters everywhere," Diamond said. "Who actually shot the old man? It must have been either Steven or Dubois."

"A fair assumption, though I'm thinkin' a third person was also involved."

"Now you're talking," Diamond said. "I love a good conspiracy. Who was it? Berthelson? Carr? Kretch? That old bat of a secretary? Or how about Mrs. Dodge? I'm sure she wouldn't have minded seeing the old coot dead."

Rafferty grinned and said, "Miss Diamond, you are not one for sugarcoatin', are you? Very well, let's look at the other suspects, beginnin' with Mr. Carr. He's a most interestin' fellow and slick as river ice. I don't believe he's a murderer, but I'm convinced he hasn't been entirely forthcomin' with me or the coppers. As I said before, Mr. Carr probably knew about Steven's fraud but wanted to hush it up for fear it would bring down the company to which he'd devoted his life. 'Tis even possible he intended to use this knowledge as leverage to keep Steven from tryin' to boot him out of the business. Of course I cannot prove it."

"And yet here you are raising your suspicions to a newspaper reporter," Diamond said. "Fancy that."

"Why, I'm sure you'll exercise the greatest discretion in writin' your story, though I will state right out that I do not like Mr. Carr. I think of him as 'he who whispers.' He's a conniver and a schemer in dark corners, and it would come as no surprise to me if he has dirty hands in this affair. He loves spinnin' webs, but I am of the opinion he's a reluctant spider when it comes to eatin' his prey. Nor do I have any reason to suspect Mrs. Schmidt. As for Amanda Dodge, I believe she was content to let nature take its course when it came to her husband's demise. Mr. Kretch, on the other hand, is something of a puzzle."

Diamond said, "I don't see it that way. I hear that he was arrested outside Dodge Tower tonight. He was probably in cahoots with Steven. Why, I'd bet a year's pay that Kretch was up to his neck in the murder."

"If I were a bettin' man," Rafferty said, "I might take you up on that. 'Tis clear that Mr. Kretch is an unsavory character. Even so, I'm not sure he was in on the murder plot. He's admitted that he tried to blackmail Amanda Dodge regardin' certain indiscretions with—"

"I knew it! I just knew it!" Diamond burst out. "Who was she sleeping with? Don't tell me it was Steven?"

"I have no knowledge of such things," Rafferty lied. "But Wash and I did talk with Mr. Kretch up in the penthouse. He claims that he himself was nearly murdered on the High Bridge and that Amanda was behind it. The real culprit, I'm sure, was Steven. It was this attempt on his life that caused Mr. Kretch to go into hidin', or so he says. Later, he contacted Steven, perhaps intendin' to blackmail him as well for one thing or another. Instead, Mr. Kretch became a patsy when Steven drew him into the plot to kill Amanda."

"And why would he do that?"

"I believe Steven intended to frame him for Amanda's murder, thereby eliminatin' yet another threat. Besides, Steven had to do some fast thinkin' because his original plan, I suspect, was to hire Berthelson to kidnap and then murder Amanda."

"My God, I never thought of that," Diamond admitted.

"Well, it makes sense if you follow the logic of it. In fact, Steven was in all likelihood the man Inspector Jones chased from River's Edge on the night of the kidnappin'. The abduction of Mrs. Dodge promised to give Berthelson somethin' he wanted, which was money to fund his terrorism, while Steven would be in for an extra payday of his own with Amanda gone. Under the terms of Artemus's will, River's Edge would go to Steven if Amanda died first."

"I suppose Steven figured he could sell off the estate to cover his debts," Secrest said.

"Probably," Rafferty agreed, "but Amanda blew his plan to smithereens by escapin' from the caves. That's why Steven brought Mr. Kretch into his scheme. He needed a scapegoat for Amanda's murder, and he also needed to put an end to Mr. Kretch's blackmailin' scheme. Had Mr. Kretch gone up to the penthouse, as Steven wanted him to, 'tis certain he would have been found dead there along with Amanda. I'm sure Steven would have staged the crime scene in a most convincin' fashion. What saved Mr. Kretch was that he got suspicious after seein' the guard's blood on the floor, and so he ended up fleein' into the tender arms of Inspector Jones."

Thomas said, "All right, Shad, you've set the scene. It's time to explain just how Mr. Dodge was murdered before our friends here consider a little mayhem of their own."

"Amen to that," said Diamond.

"Ah, the impatience of youth," Rafferty said, clearly enjoying himself. "Before I explain how the murder *was* committed, I must tell you how it *was not*. In fact, one of the most intriguin' features of this case is the length to which Steven Dodge went to convince us that the fatal shot had been fired from the old capitol's tower. The spent shell and streetcar button planted in the lookout were, of course, part of the deception.

"All that jiggerin' with the window in Mr. Dodge's office was even cleverer. I'm guessin' Steven himself cut the sash cords, most likely on the Saturday before the murder, when he had occasion to be in his father's office. He probably put that piece of wood under the old man's desk at the same time. Steven also pulled off another trick by spreadin' extra blood around the office to sow confusion."

"Why on earth would he go to all that trouble?" Secrest asked.

"Simple," Thomas said. "He knew that if blood from his father's head wound sprayed back toward the security door, it would suggest the shot had come from that direction. So he added blood to the scene to make it appear as though the fatal shot could have come through the supposedly open window."

"Added blood? How could he do that?" Diamond asked.

"'Twas one of Steven's true inspirations," Rafferty said. "Remember that toy squirt gun with traces of blood on it that was found in the alley outside Dodge Tower? I'm thinkin' Steven used it to stage his bloody deception. He probably drew some of his own blood shortly before the murder, then put it in the squirt gun and sprayed it around his father's desk while everyone else was distracted after discoverin' the body. Afterward, he tossed the gun out his office window and into the alley. As you know, one of Inspector Jones's men found the gun there. But nobody could figure out at first how it might connect to the murder."

"Why it's positively diabolical," Diamond said, sounding more thrilled than appalled. "I take it the reason for all of Steven's labors was to pin the murder on Berthelson or perhaps some labor radicals."

Rafferty said, "Exactly, and a brilliant idea it was. 'Tis the first locked room mystery of my acquaintance in which the murderer suggested a solution to the crime in order to conceal what really happened. If the police believed the fatal shot came from *outside* Dodge Tower, then they would naturally look to Berthelson as the prime suspect. On the other hand, a shot thought to have been fired from somewhere *inside* the penthouse would be much harder to attribute to him, given all of the security measures in place."

"You've whetted our appetites, Mr. Rafferty, but now it's time for the main course," Diamond said. "I want to know how the old buzzard was killed. Out with it, Mr. Rafferty, or I shall have to begin screaming at the top of my lungs."

"Ah, we can't have that. All right, Miss Diamond, since you are fairly burstin' with anticipation, I'll describe how the so-called miracle murder was accomplished. Keep in mind that I'll have to do a bit of speculatin' here and there, since I've had no chance to talk with Steven.

"Let's go back to the mornin' of October 1. Steven Dodge and Alan Dubois arrive for work at seven o'clock, a bit earlier than usual but no particular cause for notice. By then, Steven knows, or suspects, that his father intends to expose his fraudulent activities, and so he sets his murderous plan in motion. This plan relies on a secret weapon—an antique but very powerful air rifle."

"An air rifle?" Secrest repeated, sounding dubious. "You mean like one of those Daisy rifles in shooting galleries?"

"Oh no, 'tis a far more formidable weapon. Steven toured Europe earlier this year and spent considerable time in Vienna, as indicated by the large drawing of that city hangin' in his office. It was in Vienna that he must have acquired one of the famed air rifles made there in the late eighteenth century by Bartolomeo Girandoni, an Italian gunsmith. I collect antique weaponry myself, and I'd be most curious as to how Steven got his hands on the rifle. My friend Mr. Masterson at Kennedy Brothers tells me that well over a thousand Girandoni rifles were manufactured for the Austrian army but that only a few are still known to exist."

"What led you to suspect an air rifle was used?" Diamond asked.

"'Twas a process of elimination, more or less," Rafferty said. "Nothin' else made sense. I also happened to be in Saul Freeman's shootin' gallery a few days ago, and when I saw all the Daisy rifles there, it got me to thinkin'. And of course, I've got an air rifle—the one used by the killer George Lucey—in a little collection of criminal memorabilia I keep in my library. There's also the fact that a certain friend of mine, Mr. Sherlock Holmes, suggested that an Austrian rifle might be the murder weapon. I assumed at once that he must be referrin' to a Girandoni."

Diamond said, "My God, Sherlock Holmes was involved in this case?"

"We exchanged telegrams," Rafferty said matter-of-factly. "He found the case to be of considerable interest."

"Imagine that!" Diamond exclaimed. "Sherlock Holmes helped solve the murder of Artemus Dodge! What a scoop that will be. But I still don't see how an air rifle could be used to kill a man. It's a toy, isn't it?"

Rafferty shook his head. "Far from it, Miss Diamond. Why, legend holds that Napoleon ordered any enemy soldier carrying a Girandoni to be executed because they were so deadly. Mr. Masterson said they fire a round that could be lethal at a distance of several hundred yards or more, dependin' on where the victim is struck."

Turning to Thomas, Rafferty added, "If my partner hadn't been so quick with his pistol, he might have been another of Steven's victims. The Girandoni is no one-shot wonder. It can fire off twenty or more rounds once it's been properly pumped."

"Well, it's a pity Mr. Thomas didn't finish Steven off," Secrest noted. "He deserves to die for his crimes."

"The good state of Minnesota thinks differently, and so it will be a lifetime behind bars for him," Rafferty said. "Truth is, I've never much cared for executions, though I'd shed no tears if Steven went to the gallows. Now, where was I? Ah, the Girandoni rifle. As I said, 'tis as deadly as many powder rifles and can fire a ball close to .50 caliber in size at nearly a thousand feet per second."

Diamond said, "I like the air-rifle angle, but why did Steven use it?"

"No gunpowder," Thomas answered. "A regular rifle discharged inside the offices would have left behind the smell of powder and perhaps some visible smoke, even though the powder used these days is supposedly smokeless. In any case, there'd be no question where the shot had come from."

"By usin' the air rifle, Steven was able to create the impression that his father had been killed by a shot fired from outside Dodge Tower," Rafferty said. "'Twas very clever of him. I'd be curious to know if he obtained the rifle with the idea of usin' it to kill his father or if his murderous idea was in fact inspired by the peculiarities of the weapon. I'll ask him if I ever get the chance."

"When do you think Steven smuggled the rifle into his office?" Secrest asked.

"I'd guess he had it hidden away for quite a while. We can assume that when Steven got to his office that fateful mornin', he mounted the rifle on the tripod that he otherwise kept for his telescope. Mr. Dubois, of course, was in on the plan and was no doubt expectin' a handsome payment once the deed was done."

"Well, I still don't see how—" Diamond began.

"You will," Rafferty interrupted. "Now, the rifle had to be precisely aimed in order to deliver its lethal bullet. 'Tis likely that Steven and Mr. Dubois undertook at least one test shot, and perhaps even several, in the week or so before the murder. To do this, they had to disguise the considerable noise the air rifle makes when it discharges. I recall Mr. Kretch remarkin' on the day of the murder that there had recently been several false alarms in the office. They probably drowned out the noise from the test shots."

"Hold on," Secrest said. "If Steven and Dubois somehow managed to fire a test bullet from their office into the old man's office—and I still don't understand how they managed that—wouldn't it have left a big hole in the wall somewhere?"

"'Tis a good question, Mr. Secrest. The initial test shots, if there were any, would not have been designed to penetrate into Mr. Dodge's inner sanctum. Instead, they were probably testin' the bullet's trajectory. I'm sure Steven and Mr. Dubois, clever fellows that they were, could have found a way to make such shots without arousin' undue suspicion in the offices.

"Their final test shot, I believe, was a true rehearsal for the murder, and that brings me back to your question, Mr. Secrest. How did they avoid leavin' a hole in the wall? The answer is that they didn't. You see, Wash and I did find a hole behind the portrait of Amanda that hung near her late husband's desk. It was too small, however, to have been made by a bullet."

"So why does the hole matter?"

"I have a theory in that regard," Rafferty said, "which I'm hopin' Steven may eventually confirm. I think that when the test shot was fired, probably by Steven himself, Alan Dubois was stationed in Mr. Dodge's office, no doubt on the pretext of discussin' some business matter. Actin' on a signal from Steven, he took down the portrait and then hung a sheet of steel or some other piece of makeshift armor from a nail that had been inserted in the wall earlier and hidden behind the picture. The steel, or whatever was used, would have kept the test bullet from penetratin' into the paneled wall. Afterwards, Mr. Dubois slipped the piece of armor under his coat, pulled out the nail, and rehung the portrait, leavin' only a nail hole behind with no one the wiser."

Diamond asked, "What about old Artemus? Where was he when all this tomfoolery was going on?"

"Shad and I think that after admitting Dubois to the office, Mr. Dodge must have left him there alone for a few minutes," Thomas said. "I'm guessing the old man went to use the bathroom in his apartment. What's certain is that Steven would have arranged the test very carefully with Dubois to make sure no one else in the office, including Mr. Dodge, knew about it."

"There can be no doubt Steven was thorough and ingenious in everything he did," Rafferty said, rising from his chair. "Let me show you something."

Rafferty lumbered over to a side table, where he unrolled a blueprint and spread it out, fixing its corners with glass coasters. He invited the group to huddle around.

"'Tis time now to take a closer look at Steven's scheme," he began. "This blueprint, from my friend Mr. Stem, shows the plan of Dodge Tower's penthouse. When Sherlock Holmes examined it in London, he noticed at once that certain of the penthouse's office doors are in 'alignment,' to use his word. He also noticed that Mr. Kretch couldn't see any of the office doors, except for Mrs. Schmidt's, from his guard's station. Keep these facts in mind. Now, here's what I think happened in the minutes before and after Mr. Dodge's murder:

"Once the rifle was properly aimed, Steven called his father on the intercom. He knew from experience that the old man seldom sat at his desk in the mornin' when his back was stiff with arthritis. Instead, he preferred the sofa. This meant that to answer the call he had to go over to his desk, which as we know is set on a podium. Then he had to step up beside the intercom and bend over slightly to speak into it. In so doin', he unknowingly put himself in a perfect position to be murdered. In fact, I suspect Steven directed his father to look out the window on some pretext so that the fatal bullet would strike him in the back of his head.

"Once Steven heard his father answer on the intercom, Alan Dubois flung open their office door and stepped out into the cross hallway. Keep in mind that even if Mr. Kretch had been payin' diligent attention at his guard station, he couldn't have seen the open office door. 'Tis an important thing to know because Steven Dodge by this time was at the doorway, makin' final preparations to murder his father.

"Now then, Mr. Dubois continued along to the intersection with the main hallway, where he looked to see if Mr. Kretch was at his guard station. He wasn't. As Mr. Kretch stated after the murder, he was in fact in his room. With the coast clear, Mr. Dubois went to the security door guardin' Mr. Dodge's office and removed a small piece of it in a matter of seconds. He accomplished this task with the aid of a custom-made tool, which the police now have in their possession."

"What kind of tool?" Diamond asked.

"'Tis something like a tweezers, but with a spring in the middle and pins at the ends of its pincers. You will see soon enough what it was designed to do. Bear in mind that Steven was watchin' as Mr. Dubois went about his work. With the security door readied, Mr. Dubois came back down the hall and pushed open the back stairway door just enough to trigger the alarm. Steven then fired the lethal shot. Next, he closed his office door and got rid of the rifle by lowerin' it from one of his windows on a rope. In a vacant office on the floor below, a confederate—almost surely Samuel Berthelson—was waitin' to receive the rifle and remove it from Dodge Tower."

Secrest asked, "How do you know that?"

"I don't for certain. But descriptions from the guards downstairs and from Mr. Butler, whose offices are on the twenty-ninth floor, strongly suggest that it was Berthelson, disguised as a plumber."

"Let's get back to the murder," Diamond said. "I still haven't figured out how it was done."

Rafferty continued, "As you recall, we left Mr. Dubois out in the hallway as the fatal shot was fired. Pretendin' he'd been in the bathroom when the alarm rang, he knocked on Mr. Carr's office door to ask what the fuss was about. Here I should note that Mr. Dubois would have been careful to stand in front of the security door so that neither Mr. Carr nor anyone else could see what had been done to it. Moments later, after riddin' himself of the rifle, Steven emerged from his office.

"Events then proceeded as described to the police. There was a kind of scrum in the hallway followed by futile efforts to contact Artemus Dodge. 'Twas then decided to use the emergency entrance to gain access to his office. As everyone went back to the lobby, either Steven or Mr. Dubois lingered behind for a few seconds and returned the security door to its original condition. Later, when Mr. Dodge's body was discovered, I imagine Steven left the Ramon Allones cigar by the sofa as a clue pointin' toward Alan Dubois. The police, as you may recall, found cigars of that brand in Mr. Dubois's apartment after his murder."

"This is utterly fantastic," Diamond said. "Why would Steven want to implicate his own partner in the crime? If Dubois had been arrested, he surely would have told the police about Steven."

"True, but Steven didn't intend to let that happen. I have no doubt his plan all along was to kill Mr. Dubois and tie him into the murder plot with Berthelson."

"Speaking of Berthelson, are we to assume he's long gone?" Secrest asked. "I know the police found some of the ransom money at the train depot."

"So they did," Rafferty said, "but I wouldn't leap to any conclusions. The money may have been a plant designed to mislead us. Berthelson may still be here in St. Paul."

"Now that's a story," Diamond said. "Any idea where he might be hiding?"

"Perhaps, but I can't talk about it at the moment."

"All right, then let's talk about Steven. I must tell you that I have trouble believing he could be behind a scheme as devious as his father's murder. To be honest, I never took him to be all that smart."

Rafferty said, "You need to understand, Miss Diamond, that Steven is above all else a great fraud. He's one of those men—I've met others like him—who seem to glide through life without a care but who hide a corrupt and terrible intelligence behind their amiable manners. If you were to ask me why he decided on so elaborate a crime, I could only tell you that he takes pleasure in deceivin' the world. The right or wrong of a thing is of no importance to him, and I would not be surprised if he'd murdered before and gotten away with it."

"Well, he certainly fooled me and everybody else."

"So he did," Rafferty said, motioning everyone to return to their seats by the fire. "'Tis time now to explain the chief magic trick in our theater of murder."

Once everyone was seated and a log of white oak had been added to the fire, Rafferty mounted a search expedition through his numerous pockets before finally locating the small piece of glass cylinder Thomas had brought back from Chicago. "Here it is," he said, holding it up with two hands.

"What is it?" Diamond asked.

"'Tis a peephole, Miss Diamond, or at least a fragment left over from the one installed in the security door by Mr. Bencolin, the machinist in Chicago. Small openings of this kind are sometimes called a Judas window, and the term is apt, for it was the means by which young Steven betrayed and murdered his father.

"Vault-style doors, of course, don't normally come with peepholes. Even so, either Mr. Dodge himself or more likely Steven insisted on one being installed. So it was, at the Mosler factory in Ohio. Steven, however, hired Mr. Bencolin to fabricate and install a new peephole. This one came with a carefully threaded steel casing that, with the aid of the small tool I mentioned earlier, could easily be removed from its channel in the security door and just as easily be put back."

Thomas said, "Inspector Jones tried out the peephole after Shad showed him the trick with the special tool. It only took a few twists of the wrist to remove it or put it back in."

Rafferty nodded and said, "I think it will be clear now how the murder was accomplished. Mr. Dubois removed the peephole, and Steven fired a bullet directly through the opening on a line that he knew would kill his father as he hunched over the intercom. Then the peephole was restored to its place. Its threads and inner workings were cleverly hidden by the talented Mr. Bencolin, and no one—myself included—saw any reason to give the peephole anything other than a cursory inspection. Steven planned to murder Amanda in the same way tonight. Two seemingly impossible murders in the span of a week would surely have shocked the world."

"Amazing," said Diamond. "Just amazing. What a story it will make! By the way, just how did Mrs. Dodge and Steven end up here tonight? Did it have something to do with the will? I've heard rumors that old Artemus prepared a last-minute codicil."

Rafferty, who'd made up the story of a possible codicil and then persuaded Patrick Butler to spread the falsehood, thought it best not to claim authorship in the press for his "little fiction," as he called it. He said, "What I can tell you, Miss Diamond, is that someone apparently convinced Mr. Butler, the lawyer, that such a document existed and that it was probably hidden in Artemus Dodge's office. Naturally, he passed on this information to Amanda and Steven."

"Naturally," Diamond said, casting a shrewd glance at Rafferty. "How did you happen to hear about the codicil?"

"Ah, let's just say that in my line of work a man hears many things. In any event, it took no great genius to see that both Steven and Amanda might feel threatened by the supposed codicil. Nor was it hard to predict that Amanda, a very energetic woman, might go huntin' for the codicil in the dead of night. Steven came to the same conclusion and had Mr. Kretch follow her from River's Edge so that he'd know when she was comin' to Dodge Tower. When she arrived, he was ready for her, thinkin' he had another opportunity to commit a perfect murder. And he almost got away with it because I was careless."

"What do you mean?"

"I mean I should have anticipated that Steven would get to Dodge Tower many hours ahead of time to set himself up for another murder. He probably came in the mornin', with the rifle under his coat, and used the entrance on Robert Street."

Secrest said, "Mr. Rafferty may be unfairly blaming himself. I may be the one at fault. I was watching both entrances to Dodge Tower, starting at around noon, from the cigar shop downstairs. But there was a little scene out on the street—a trolley and a car almost collided—and it distracted me. It's just possible that was when Steven slipped into Dodge Tower."

"Well, it hardly matters now," Rafferty said. "Once Steven arrived, he knocked out Mr. Jacobson, the guard in the lobby, dragged him into the bathroom, tied him up, and then went upstairs to the penthouse."

"Why didn't Steven simply kill the guard, since he knew the poor fellow could identify him?" Secrest asked.

"Oh, I'm sure he intended to do just that once he'd taken care of murderin' Amanda up in the penthouse," Rafferty said. "The thing about Steven is that he always liked to have a backup plan. I'm assumin' he figured that if he somehow got trapped, he could always use Mr. Jacobson as a hostage. I'm told, incidentally, that Mr. Jacobson will be all right. He's a lucky man."

Diamond, who'd been writing all the while in her notebook, said, "I'm still curious about the supposed codicil, Mr. Rafferty. Was it one of your concoctions?"

Rafferty smiled and said, "I'm inclined to think it was the work of leprechauns. They can be very mischievous, or so I've heard."

"Ha!" Diamond said. "I suspect the leprechaun in chief was quite a bit larger than most of his kind."

"It could be," Rafferty said, "but I know you wouldn't print mere speculation in the *Pioneer Press*. 'Twould not be to your advantage. Some affairs, especially if they involve a man such as Steven Dodge, are best left private."

Diamond stared at Rafferty, trying to read his big wrinkled globe of a face. He knows, she thought, he knows about Steven and me. "You may rely on my discretion," she said, "just as I will rely on yours."

There was an awkward pause, then Secrest said, "I still wonder about Berthelson. How did he manage to escape, and with one hundred thousand dollars to boot? The whole city was looking for him, and yet he vanished as if he'd been swallowed up by the earth."

"Your metaphor may prove to be more apt than you think," Rafferty said. "As I told Miss Diamond, I have some ideas as to where the terrorist may be, and I believe he'll be found before long."

Diamond glanced at the grandfather clock ticking away at the far end of the parlor. "Good lord, it's two o'clock in the morning," she said, closing her notebook with a decisive snap and rising from her chair. "I have a deadline to meet if I'm to get all of this into a special edition. I warn you, Mr. Rafferty, Inspector Jones and Chief Nelligan won't be happy when they see my story. Neither will that ass McGruder when I reveal how Dubois double-crossed him. I imagine the three of them are planning a big how-do-you-do at city hall to tell us all how they cracked the case. My story will take the wind right out of their sails. I'd give a week's salary to see the look on that pill Nelligan's face when he finds out you've beat him to the punch."

"I'm sure it'll be a heartbreakin' sight," Rafferty said. "The chief is the sort of man who would take credit for daybreak if he thought he could get away with it. I imagine Inspector Jones will be equally crestfallen. 'Tis very sad to contemplate their misfortune."

Diamond startled Rafferty with a kiss on the cheek. "Thank you for all your help. Did anybody ever tell you that you're a sly old bird?"

"I fear I am more old than sly these days," Rafferty said, "but I do the best I can."

EPILOGUE: "THE BEST SALOONKEEPER AND FINEST DETECTIVE"

Isabel Diamond's account of Steven Dodge's dramatic arrest, as well as Rafferty's point-by-point explanation of the "miracle murder," appeared in a special noon edition of Monday's *Pioneer Press*. The article, which painted Rafferty as a hero, created a sensation, and he was toasted well into the night at his tavern, as were Thomas and Secrest. Even Louis Hill made an appearance, striding into the bar just before closing time. After ordering a pint of lager, he told the crowd that "Mr. Rafferty has done a signal service for the people of St. Paul and the nation. We are fortunate to have such a man in our midst."

While Rafferty enjoyed his "goddamn hallelujah chorus," as Jones put it, the official representatives of law and order in St. Paul held a news conference to proclaim their vital roles in bringing Steven Dodge to justice. McGruder, Nelligan, Jones, and Mayor Irvin all tried to take what credit they could, but their efforts met with little success. The press, which had hoped to hear fresh news, reacted with a collective yawn once it became apparent that the foursome could add little to what Rafferty had already told Diamond.

McGruder, however, came in for plenty of questioning about Alan Dubois's work as a spy for the safety commission even as he apparently participated in the murder of Artemus Dodge. Despite extensive evidence to the contrary, McGruder asserted that Dubois had remained "loyal to the cause of patriotism," and he scolded reporters for their "distrust of authority." McGruder also continued to insist that Samuel Berthelson was still in

St. Paul. "He will strike again," McGruder warned. "The document in his own hand that I revealed to the public on Saturday should leave no doubt that our war against terrorism is far from over."

Rafferty was skeptical of McGruder's claim, and that night he telephoned Sergeant Francis Carroll, with whom he'd remained on good terms, and made a suggestion. Carroll followed up on the tip, and the next morning a team of policemen entered the caves where Amanda Dodge had been held captive. There, in a side chamber not far from the Schmidt Brewery, they found Samuel Berthelson, buried beneath a loose pile of sand with a bullet in the back of the head. The coroner determined that he'd been dead for at least five days.

Inspector Jones theorized that Steven ambushed Berthelson when they rendezvoused in the caves, presumably to split the ransom money and dispose of Amanda Dodge. Steven claimed, however, that he never "saw a penny of the ransom" and that Berthelson had in fact intended to double-cross and kill him. The $100,000 was never found.

The discovery of Berthelson's body proved inconvenient for McGruder. How, the press and public wondered, had McGruder managed to obtain a document dated several days after its supposed author was dead? McGruder's answer was that he'd been misled by his informant, but his explanation didn't hold up for long.

Scenting scandal, Isabel Diamond hired an expert to compare a sample of McGruder's handwriting with that of the instructions supposedly authored by Berthelson. The expert found the handwriting samples to be "identical in every respect." A front-page story conveyed this astonishing news to the people of St. Paul. McGruder, citing fatigue and poor health, resigned the next day as chairman of the public safety commission. The truth, the press soon reported, was that the governor had kicked McGruder out the door.

Jones fared better. The inspector's sharp-elbowed political skills and his ability to keep himself in the headlines were rewarded when he was named St. Paul's new chief of police following Michael Nelligan's abrupt resignation in November. Nelligan told the newspapers that he was moving back to his home state of Massachusetts to "pursue business opportunities there." The real story, as everyone in city hall knew, was that the chief had become "entangled" with a secretary in the police department and resigned to avoid a public scandal.

Rafferty meanwhile kept a low profile, having no desire to "become a permanent spectacle," as he put it. He eventually received a long letter from Sherlock Holmes offering a rigorous analysis of the clues in Dodge's murder. The letter suggested that Steven Dodge and Alan Dubois "should be considered prime suspects" and also advised Rafferty to examine the security door's peephole "as a possible means by which the crime was committed."

As Rafferty ducked out of the public eye, other figures in the case continued to splash about in newspaper ink. J. D. Carr made headlines when it became apparent that the firm of Dodge & Son was in deep financial trouble. An audit revealed that Steven Dodge and Alan Dubois had systematically looted the company even before the Blue Sky venture collapsed into a sinkhole of debt and recrimination. Carr, with the faithful Mrs. Schmidt at his side, did all he could to keep the firm solvent, but it was not enough. Early in 1918, the company went bankrupt and abandoned the penthouse offices in Dodge Tower. Patrick Butler's firm moved up a floor to take over the luxurious offices, thereby confirming Rafferty's long-held suspicion that "the lawyers will get everything in the end." Carr moved back to New York City, while Mrs. Schmidt retired to her apartment.

Amanda Dodge also relocated to Manhattan, but not before more struggles. The $1 million bequest she was supposed to have received from her husband vanished into clouds of bankruptcy. But River's Edge was still hers, and she moved quickly to sell the mansion and its immediate grounds while subdividing the rest of the estate's forty acres. These transactions left her quite comfortable. A year or so after she left St. Paul, Rafferty spotted a small item in the *Pioneer Press* reporting that she had married a wealthy widower twice her age and was "residing in a large and elegant apartment on New York's famed Fifth Avenue."

Her nemesis, Peter Kretch, was never prosecuted for blackmail because Amanda refused to press charges against him, knowing how much embarrassing information would be aired at a trial. After spending a few nights in the county jail, Kretch was freed. Rafferty never saw him again but heard rumors that he'd gone to Chicago and wormed his way into a job as a security man for the Marshall Field family.

Harlow Secrest moved on as well. He took on a job with the AFL-CIO as a "security consultant" charged with rooting out company spies, Pinkertons, and other enemies of organized labor. Rafferty and Thomas gave him a farewell dinner at the Ryan Hotel before he left St. Paul in December. He later sent a letter to Rafferty saying he'd found "great satisfaction" in his new line of work.

Steven Dodge, confined to the Ramsey County Jail, amused himself by giving interviews to the press in which he cheerfully admitted his guilt. He was vague as to the details, however, and spun out conflicting stories to the police. "It all seems to be a game with him," Jones complained to Sergeant Carroll after one especially trying interrogation. "I do not believe he fears or values anything."

At his arraignment, Dodge startled the court, and his own attorney, with a plea of not guilty by reason of insanity. When asked to explain his plea, Dodge said, "What sane person would go through as much trouble as I did to kill my father?" His trial began in late November. The front benches in the courtroom were filled every day with admiring young women who seemed to find Dodge fascinating. One even offered to marry him, a proposal Dodge "reluctantly turned down," according to the newspapers.

The trial lasted a month and produced a number of revelations, including the fact that Dodge had managed to gamble away nearly $1 million in recent years. Dodge himself testified and offered a self-diagnosis of insanity. Remarkably, he never said a word about his brief affair with Amanda Dodge or his longer fling with Isabel Diamond. Rafferty, who sat in on the trial occasionally, remarked afterward that Dodge was "a perfect gentleman in his own strange way in that he did not think it proper to speak of his bedroom conquests."

The case went to the jury on December 23, and the eleven men and one woman required only four hours of deliberation to convict Dodge of first-degree murder. The judge then imposed a mandatory life sentence. On Christmas Eve, as guards arrived to transfer Dodge to the state prison in Stillwater, they found him dead in his cell. A note pinned to his shirt said, "Life and poison are best taken in jest. Please see to my cats." An autopsy revealed that Dodge had somehow managed to kill himself with a cyanide capsule smuggled into his cell—a final locked room mystery.

Six months after Dodge's suicide, Harper & Brothers of New York published *Secrets of the Miracle Murder*, Isabel Diamond's potboiling account of the case, and it became one of the most successful true-crime books of its time. D. W. Griffith later bought the movie rights but never filmed the story. Several newspapers began to court Diamond after the book appeared, and in August 1918 she went to work for the *Chicago Tribune*. Before leaving St. Paul, she sent Rafferty a small leprechaun doll with a note that said, "I talked with this little fellow, and he told me that you, Mr. Rafferty, spread that phony story of a codicil. Imagine that! Stop by for a visit next time you're in Chicago. Isabel."

Rafferty added the leprechaun to the collection of mismatched objects adorning the tavern's back wall. Some of them, like an autographed picture of Mark Twain, went all the way back to the 1880s. Yet Rafferty knew that his days of collecting souvenirs from good honest drinking men were all but over. Congress had already approved the Eighteenth Amendment, and the states were moving quickly to ratify it. The nation would soon go dry, and, as Rafferty liked to tell Thomas, "a saloon without liquor is unlikely to be a profitable operation."

Thomas agreed, and he and Rafferty began making plans to close the tavern and dissolve their long-standing business partnership. Rafferty worried how Thomas would support himself after the tavern was gone, since he was "the sort of man," as Rafferty put it, "who never saw the use in savin' money when it could be so pleasurably spent." Thomas, however, soon found work with Gustave Klemmer, the locksmith, and his talents were such that he took over the business a few years later when the old German, who had no sons, retired.

In the fall of 1918, Rafferty finally announced that Shad's Place would close for good and threw a party to mark the occasion. He received many homages that night, but the one that meant the most was a telegram from Sherlock Holmes. It said, "I TOAST THE BEST SALOONKEEPER AND FINEST DETECTIVE I HAVE EVER KNOWN."

Rafferty was in tears when he read it. As the party finally wound down, he made a second announcement, saying that he was also retiring as a detective, although he promised that he "just might write" his memoirs "one of these days." Rafferty never did get around to his memoirs, nor did his retirement from the "detectin' game" prove permanent. In 1928, he would rouse himself to investigate one last murder—a crime that would shake St. Paul to its very foundations and that would cost him his life.

AUTHOR'S NOTE

The Magic Bullet, like my previous adventures featuring Shadwell Rafferty and Sherlock Holmes, is a work of fiction built around an armature of historical fact. Most of the characters are fictional (Louis Hill, Allen Stem, and Vivian Irvin being the exceptions), while most of the settings are real. I've also mixed in real events, such as the 1917 strike by transit workers, but revised them to suit my storytelling needs.

I enjoy inviting historic figures into my tales because their presence adds a sense of authenticity to the proceedings. The decision to include Louis Hill in *The Magic Bullet* seemed a natural choice, since his father, James J. Hill, played a vital role in several of my earlier novels. James J. died in 1916, a year or so before the action begins in *The Magic Bullet*, so I thought it proper to assign his old duties as Rafferty's friend and protector to Louis, who'd succeeded his father as president of the Great Northern Railway.

Allen Stem, a prominent St. Paul architect whose most notable commission was Grand Central Terminal in New York City, wasn't as obvious a choice as Hill for a role in this book. I decided to make Stem the architect of Dodge Tower because the building lies at the center of the mystery and I thought it wise to bring in someone who really did know a crocket from a finial. Many of Stem's buildings, incidentally, still stand in St. Paul, and several are listed on the National Register of Historic Places.

The other real character is Vivian Irvin, who was indeed mayor of St. Paul in 1917. My excuse for including him is that I like the idea of a man named Vivian.

One other character, John McGruder, is based on an actual figure, John McGee, who led the Minnesota Public Safety Commission during its brief but tempestuous existence. McGee seems to have been just as fearsome a personality as his fictional counterpart. The commission itself was also alarming, since by most accounts it engaged in gross abuses of power during the World War I period. It was finally dismantled in 1920.

Most of the buildings and places described in *The Magic Bullet* are (or were) real. Dodge Tower, however, is my own invention (a four-story retail and office building actually occupied its site). Shad's Place, the Klemmer Lock Company building, and Dandy Jim's Tavern are also fictional.

Sadly, much of downtown St. Paul as it existed in 1917 is gone. The Ryan Hotel, where Rafferty operated his fictional saloon, fell to the wrecker in 1962, a great loss to the city. The old state capitol (officially known as the Second State Capitol) was demolished in 1938. Even so, a number of the buildings described in the book remain, including the Golden Rule and Emporium department stores (now office buildings), the Schmidt Brewery (no longer operating), the St. Paul Cathedral, House of Hope Church, the St. Paul Public Library, the St. Paul Hotel, the Minnesota Boat Club, and the splendidly restored Louis Hill House, still a private residence. The Selby Avenue streetcar tunnel was filled in long ago, but its lower portal, where Rafferty encountered so much trouble, remains visible below the cathedral.

Swede Hollow, Rice Park, and Raspberry Island are among places mentioned in the book that have survived to this day. Other locales are gone, including Bench Street (realigned and cleared of all its buildings in the 1930s), Little Italy (swept away after a severe flood in 1952), and Fountain Cave (destroyed by road building in the 1960s).

Although *The Magic Bullet* is a work of fiction, two major scenes—the riot by striking streetcar workers and the removal of the statue from the Germania Life Building—are loosely modeled on actual events. A 1917 transit strike in St. Paul included riotous behavior, but there was nothing like the mayhem at the streetcar tunnel depicted in my story. Nor was there a riot following removal of the statue. What is true is that the statue was taken down (in 1918) and that the Germania Life Insurance Company changed its name to Guardian in response to anti-German sentiment.

I'm often asked by readers how I set about creating a historic pastiche. The answer, in brief, is that it depends on where I start. Sometimes the idea for a story derives from a specific historical event, such as the Hinckley forest fire of 1894, which became the basis for *Sherlock Holmes and the Red Demon*. In other cases, I begin with an idea and then look for a suitable setting in which the story can play out. So it was with *The Magic Bullet*, which grew out of a simple question: How could a man be shot dead in a locked, vault-like office, when no one else was with him, no gun was found by his body, and there was no sign that the bullet had come from outside? I started, in other words, with the premise for a classic locked room mystery. Only later did I decide to set it in St. Paul in 1917, during a volatile time when patriotic fervor and labor unrest had combined to put the city on edge.

One final note: Readers well versed in the history of mystery fiction will recognize at once that this book is a homage to one of the grand old masters of the genre, John Dickson Carr, whose books I've always loved. It's no coincidence that a key character in *The Magic Bullet* is named J. D. Carr or that he is the author of a monograph on solving locked room mysteries.

Carr (1906–77) was a prolific writer best known for his atmospheric locked room mysteries, which by virtue of their intricacy, inventiveness, and variety have no equal in the literature. At the height of his powers in the 1930s and 1940s, Carr turned out as many as four mysteries a year, often of the highest quality. *It Walks by Night* (1930), *The Three Coffins* (1935), and my personal favorite, *The Arabian Nights Murder* (1936), are among his best books, as is *The Judas Window* (1938), which inspired certain features of my own humble attempt at a locked room mystery.

Many of Carr's novels feature a large, amusing, and very eccentric detective named Dr. Gideon Fell, who bears some resemblance to Shadwell Rafferty. Sir Henry Merrivale and Henri Bencolin are among Carr's other detectives, and I gave their names to minor characters in *The Magic Bullet*. Sharp-eyed readers will find other references to Carr's work scattered through my book.

—LARRY MILLETT, ST. PAUL, 2010

Larry Millett has written five previous Sherlock Holmes adventures (all but one featuring Shadwell Rafferty). He is an architectural historian and author of *Lost Twin Cities* and the *AIA Guide to the Twin Cities.* As a reporter for the *St. Paul Pioneer Press,* he covered many different beats and had the honor of writing clues for the newspaper's legendary Winter Carnival Medallion Hunt, which annually attracts thousands of treasure seekers. He lives in St. Paul.